Praise for Andrea G

'looks deep into the human heart and delivers an experience
that is moving and profound'
Sydney Morning Herald

'What may seem simple or trite feels revolutionary in
Goldsmith's hands ... With its richness of character,
challenging themes, exciting ideas and unsentimental sense
of place, *Reunion* deserves a prominent place in bookshops
and in conversation'
Weekend Australian

'A book, quite simply, to lose yourself in'
Canberra Times

'gloriously written ... Whole characters are born out of a
simple paragraph, deepening on the page to become fully
fledged figures sitting beside the reader, whispering their
story. It's a little bit spooky, little bit literary magic'
Courier-Mail

Andrea Goldsmith originally trained as a speech pathologist and was a pioneer in the development of communication aids for people unable to speak.

Her first novel, *Gracious Living*, was published in 1989. This was followed by *Modern Interiors, Facing the Music, Under the Knife, The Prosperous Thief*, shortlisted for the 2003 Miles Franklin Award, and, in 2009, *Reunion*.

Her literary essays have appeared in *Meanjin, Australian Book Review, Best Australian Essays, Heat* and numerous anthologies.

For further information visit andreagoldsmith.com.au.

ANDREA GOLDSMITH

the memory trap

FOURTH ESTATE

Fourth Estate
An imprint of HarperCollins*Publishers*

First published in Australia in 2013
by HarperCollins*Publishers* Australia Pty Limited
ABN 36 009 913 517
harpercollins.com.au

HarperCollins*Publishers*
Level 13, 201 Elizabeth Street, Sydney NSW 2000, Australia
Unit D1, 63 Apollo Drive, Rosedale, Auckland 0632, New Zealand
A 53, Sector 57, Noida, UP, India
1 London Bridge Street, London SE1 9GF, United Kingdom
2 Bloor Street East, 20th floor, Toronto, Ontario M4W 1A8, Canada
195 Broadway, New York NY 10007, USA

National Library of Australia Cataloguing-in-Publication data:

Goldsmith, Andrea, 1950–
   The memory trap / Andrea Goldsmith.
   ISBN 978 0 7322 9672 8 (pbk.)
   ISBN 978 1 7430 9898 1 (ebook.)
A823.3

Cover design by Christa Moffitt, Christabella Designs
Cover images: Woman © Ayal Ardon/Trevillion Images; Background image
© Andy & Michelle Kerry/Trevillion Images; Rainbow Lorikeet by Vanessa Mylett,
Dreamzone Photography
Author photograph by Celia Dann
Typeset in 11/16.5pt Berthold Baskerville by Kirby Jones
Printed and bound in Australia by Griffin Press
The papers used by HarperCollins in the manufacture of this book are a natural,
recyclable product made from wood grown in sustainable plantation forests. The fibre
source and manufacturing processes meet recognised international environmental
standards, and carry certification.

for
Jacqueline Eve Goldsmith

'Darkly rises each moment from the life
which has been lived and which does not die,
for each event lives in the heavy head forever,
waiting to renew itself.'
Delmore Schwartz

Chapter 1.

'Remember summer? Bubbles filled the
fountain, and we splashed. We drowned
in Eden ...'
Robert Lowell

1.

By the time she reached thirty, Nina Jameson had resigned
herself to a single life. A series of relationships each of which
had reduced her to a simpering, stress-filled sop had shown
that while she could be a loyal friend, a loving daughter, a
woman passionately engaged in her work, she was a failure at
romantic love. Within a short time of meeting an appealing
man, her well-oiled antennae would disintegrate and she'd be
brought to her knees. The last lover was a disaster of such
proportions that she was forced to accept the distressing truth:
she lacked the emotional backbone to withstand another
catastrophic relationship.

There was nothing in her past to explain it. She'd had
a happy childhood in suburban Melbourne, creative and
involved parents, a sister with whom she was close, success
at school, a wide circle of friends. And while she'd had to
contend with the spoiler next door, she rationalised that even
in the most contented of childhoods there's the pervert at the
playground, the bully in the schoolyard, the betrayal by a best
friend. So rather than being constrained by Ramsay Blake,

his living so close contributed to her early departure from home, the choice of an interstate university, overseas travel, work in New York. And when Ramsay himself turned up in New York, this became her catalyst for the move to London and her present career.

Nina is a consultant on memorial projects. She guides planning committees from their initial conception all the way to the unveiling ceremony. She advises on design competitions and fund-raising options; she draws up an estimate of costs; she divulges arcane processes for working with interest groups and not-so-arcane tax breaks to reduce costs. She is an expert in all aspects of monument creation aside from the actual chipping into the stone, or, given the current proclivity for water features, the design of the plumbing.

In the past several years she has worked on projects to commemorate people slaughtered by terrorism and others felled by natural disasters; she's consulted on monuments to honour famous people and others to mark significant sites. She relishes this career of hers, not simply that each job introduces her to a whole new fascinating area, but there is the excitement, the privilege too, of working with people when their passions are roused.

With work and family, friends and other interests, Nina believed she had more than enough to make a good life. So should she find herself lonely and longing for a partner, she would quickly summon up her track record: with such a mess of failures she'd be a fool not to banish romantic love.

Then Daniel Ryman appeared, divorced father of two, seventeen years her senior, a futurologist to her memory keeper, and her resolutions turned to dust. It shouldn't have happened, not simply her determination to be sensible and rational, but Daniel was not her type. He was too big for her taste, too muscular, and his jaw too square and the Hollywood-perfect hair not at all to her liking. He looked like a sportsman not a thinker.

'They're not mutually exclusive,' Daniel said later, when she revealed her first impressions.

And neither they were, but her usual type of man was tall on intellect and short on everything else: height, sight, hair, empathy, and consideration for her.

'Like a balding koala?' Daniel suggested, with a deliberate nudge at her being Australian.

She nodded. 'A Jewish balding koala with an excellent vocabulary.'

Daniel, like a number of her previous lovers, was Jewish, although with the exception of a devoted mother and a taste for pickled herring, in Nina's view he bore little resemblance to the usual stereotype.

'Now that we've left the shtetl and can enjoy all the new world has to offer, we've branched out,' Daniel said with a smile.

She liked his humour, within a short time she was drawn to almost everything about him, but at their first meeting, 1997 in Edinburgh, at the close of the first day of a three-day conference on Cultural Time, she was not impressed. A few of the delegates had adjourned to a nearby bar. The place was stuffy with cigarettes and end-of-week revellers. Jackets and ties were removed and Nina noticed Daniel's muscular physique. She dismissed him on the spot: time spent jogging and pushing weights had always suggested a mind predisposed to mindlessness.

And he was a futurologist, a breed of thinker who aroused her suspicions; some, she believed, were nothing more than articulate charlatans who shared more in common with fortune-tellers than scholars. And while his being a guest at this particular meeting suggested he was one of the more reputable practitioners, she avoided him at the bar, and again in the hotel restaurant the following morning when she came down for breakfast and found him already seated with food and newspaper.

Nina had trained herself to rise early in order to cope with her increasing workload, but constitutionally she was not a morning person. She woke to an alarm clock, showered and dressed in a semi-conscious state and then prepared herself for the day's demands over a slow breakfast, some serious reading and multiple cups of strong coffee. So when she entered the restaurant just after six and saw the muscle-bound futurologist she was furious. It seemed little enough to want to breakfast undisturbed, to set the day on its right course, and this man, this populariser-disguised-as-intellectual, had just wrecked it. She marched out of the dining-room – she'd find a solitary breakfast elsewhere – and might have continued across the lobby to the street, when one of those unpremeditated glimpses of the naked and, in this instance, unreasonable self stopped her. Such an extreme reaction to a man eating a bowl of cereal and reading a newspaper. When had she become such a slave to habit? It was a breakfast, she told herself, a single breakfast. And she wasn't presenting her paper that day, and tomorrow when she was to perform, she would not bother with the restaurant but use the reliably solitary room service instead. Thus she calmed herself and re-entered the room.

The futurologist glanced over the top of his paper and she steeled herself for pre-coffee civilities. But when he sank more deeply into his chair she realised he was as little interested in company as she was. She found a table on the far side of the room, sat with her back to him and selected from the à la carte menu so as to avoid meeting him at the buffet.

And soon he was forgotten as she ate her omelette, drank her way through a large flask of coffee and read her literary review. Coffee and interesting reading matter and she could block out anything – even in a public dining-room. She read an essay on Auden, followed by a long review of a book wanting to confine memory to biochemistry, an approach Nina believed sucked the human out of being a human. She should write her own response to the article, not a letter to the editor but an essay exploring her own approach to memory. She could shape it around some of her recent projects, use the essay to take stock of the rationale and moral stance of memorialising. And so engrossed was she, she did not notice that the futurologist had approached; only when he said her name was she pulled from her thoughts.

He was standing by her table, a questioning smile on his face. 'It's clear we both prefer solitude with our breakfast. But might we break the habit for a final coffee?'

A surprising surge of pleasure – the humour? his courtesy? the melodic accent? – and she invited him to join her. She noticed he drank his coffee black as did she, she noticed even though it should not have mattered. Her last lover, the one she counted as her most bruising disaster, took milk with his coffee. She made sure always to have fresh milk available never knowing when he might turn up. For the entire two years of the relationship there would be a line of cartons in the door of the fridge: fresh, nearly fresh, still usable, doubtful, definitely off, disgusting dollops. During those two years she had thrown out far more sour milk than he had ever consumed fresh.

The futurologist passed a few comments about the noisy bar the previous evening: impossible to talk, impossible to do anything but drink, and fortunate for him that the bar had specialised in single malts. He had found one of his favourites: Scapa 16-year-old, sherry cask, one of the Orkney Isle distilleries, he said, not that it, or indeed any Scotch, meant a thing to her.

Nina asked about his accent.

'French mother, Russian father, born in Argentina, raised in England, career mainly in America. And,' he added, 'I speak French, Russian, Spanish and English – all with an accent.'

'Like Daniel Barenboim,' she said. Then realising he mightn't share her knowledge of classical music, added, 'The conductor and pianist.'

The futurologist smiled. 'Barenboim speaks five languages, and yes, all with an accent. Five languages for him, four for me, and both of us at home in none.'

During the next hour while other delegates came and went, she and Daniel talked. It was odd how quickly the features she had found so unacceptably chiselled the previous night now relaxed into contours not simply inviting but homely in a familiar rather than unattractive sense. As for his being a charlatan, this man's grasp of the past, the present and the imagined future was breathtaking. And his memory! In that first hour, he spiked his conversation with quotes from Shakespeare, Heine, the Bible, Lorca, Dickinson and Martin Luther King – and probably a good many other luminaries she failed to recognise. Talking with him was to enter a brilliant piece of theatre in which history's best thinkers all had bit parts.

For most of the previous fifteen years Daniel had been based in Chicago to be near his former wife and their two sons. By the time he met Nina, both boys were in college, the wife long remarried and Daniel free to roam. A month after the Cultural Time conference he moved back to England, the country of his growing-up; within six months he and Nina were living together in Primrose Hill. On the anniversary of their first meeting they were married.

He was forty-eight and she was thirty-one. Seventeen years separated them, a prime number and therefore lucky, Nina thought. Although the sour-milk lover, three prime years her senior, had brought nothing in the way of luck – the primes had let her down there. And not just the three-year age difference: he was born on the twenty-third day of the eleventh month, Ramsay Blake's birthday, and not even the charm of primes could erase that uneasy coincidence.

From the very beginning with Daniel, theirs was such an easy fit, so much so that her past failures quickly slipped into the shadows. Even the issue of children was quickly resolved. Daniel, with two grown-up sons, preferred no more children, although he was prepared to change his mind should Nina want them. But his preference helped settle her own. While not entirely devoid of the biological urge to bear children and the maternal instinct to raise them, both drives were, Nina realised, so weak in her character as to make childlessness a viable option.

They both travelled for work, she more than Daniel, but when home together in London they lived closely. 'We're like the melodic lines of a fugue,' she once said to him. Of course there were differences. She would never come to appreciate whisky as he did, although she was drawn to the histories

7

of the distilling families, and the distilleries themselves with their proud and often quaint traditions. And the whisky locations, bleak, wild, chilly places in the far reaches of Scotland where for hours at a time she would tramp the peaty ground while Daniel talked and tasted with the whisky makers. The Orkneys in particular came to represent an idea of civilisation to her, a precarious balance between the natural world, traditional customs and selective borrowings from the twenty-first century. It was as if these islands monumentalised a specific type of existence too often shunted to the very edges of human progress. And, in fact, it was during one of their visits to the Orkneys that it first occurred to her that all landscapes were potential monuments, an idea that later played into an idiosyncratic book.

And Daniel would never share her attachment to music. He would accompany her to concerts, particularly if the orchestra was huge and the conductor a star from a BBC TV series. But he failed to understand how anyone could sit at home listening to a Mahler symphony or a Shostakovich quartet, just sit there without a book or email, no bill-paying, no browsing the web, just listening. And she would never understand Daniel's penchant for physical fitness. 'What sort of Jew are you?' Nina asked recently when he took a shine to yet another sport – a form of skateboarding that used an articulated device called a ripstick. He was aiming for an entry in that very slender volume *The Jewish Book of Sport*, he said with a laugh.

There was his tidiness and her mess; her flamboyance and his reserve; his chess and her Scrabble; his e-books and her real books; her work focused on the past, his on the future. And holding all the differences together was their love of reading and ideas, travel, food and cooking, their daily rituals and routines, and as the years passed, their common history.

2.

'There's not a single aspect of my life I'd change,' Nina said to Daniel, as she drove them down to Hampshire one stormy June evening. 'Besides having my family in the same country, and some Australian bush in easy reach of London.'

This was a celebratory weekend, their twelfth wedding anniversary and a lucky prime thirteen years together. They could have taken the Eurostar to Paris, they could have flown to Edinburgh, the place of their first meeting, but weather notwithstanding, they had chosen to stay at their cottage on the edge of the New Forest. A storm had been forecast all week and the skies were threatening when they left Primrose Hill. But early summer storms were quick boisterous affairs, and once this one had blown through, Hampshire would be green and tranquil. They could take their usual walks, perhaps even celebrate their anniversary with a picnic in the forest.

Nina's gift to Daniel was wedged safely in a corner of the car boot, its glitter wrapping concealed under an old blanket. After much thought in which she had considered and dismissed a pair of beautiful lapis lazuli cuff-links (he might find them showy), a jumper (too early in the season for good value), opera for the uninitiated (this was a perennial threat), she settled on a half yard of small whiskies, all single malts, each containing two shots and purchased from the Royal Mile in Bloomsbury, a shop Daniel described as whisky heaven.

9

She had packed a hamper containing cheeses, smoked fish, pepperonata, dolmades, olives – all their favourite foods, while Daniel had taken charge of the drinks, including, he said, a limited-edition cider. Cider was their summer drink, and this bottle would be the first of the season.

The clouds were massing dark and low, Turneresque, Daniel quipped, as they set off. Aesthetically pleasing they might be, but poor visibility was bringing out the dare-devil in a surprising number of drivers: it was chaos on the roads and the exit from the city maddeningly slow. But once they entered the M3, Nina felt, as she always did at this point, that their holiday had begun. Whoever was the least tired would drive, although Nina always chose the music – rhythm and blues, the only site in music's universe where their tastes were aligned.

It had been a busy week for them both. Nina was in the middle of a project designed to honour the third wave of feminism. The consultations had been strenuous and co-operative endeavour as taxing as apparently it had been in the 1970s. It was, in short, a job she would be happy to see finished. Daniel was hard at work on his new book, *The Future of Originality in an Age of Timelessness*. He was, he said, writing with a head of steam.

'I hope you left your laptop at home,' Nina now said.

He nodded. 'Although the work's quite portable,' and tapped his head.

The range and power of Daniel's memory had impressed her ever more forcefully over the years. He retained the essence of books and papers after a single reading, even technical ones outside his specialty; whole poems and paragraphs of prose were cemented into memory; and names – people, places, plants, birds – Daniel heard a name and it settled into his cortex forever.

'Don't worry,' he said. 'It's our anniversary weekend and I've no intention of working. I propose we make love till Monday.'

Daniel was a plain-speaking man. This quality had been evident with his very first words to her, and more emphatically a couple of days later when they were about to make love.

'You're my ideal woman,' he'd said when he saw her naked for the first time.

She was in a strange man's hotel room, she'd already cracked the foundations of her hard-made resolutions, she was breathlessly nervous, and, in her nakedness, precariously self-conscious. She believed herself to be so far from ideal she thought he was being polite. But she would soon learn that Daniel was hopeless at flattery, at any sort of dissembling. He truly liked hips to be full; her bottom, he said, was a wonder of nature; as for her heavy thighs, these were, if forced to choose, his favourite portion. 'What about my eyes?' she had protested, the large brown eyes that everyone remarked on. He had shrugged: large brown eyes were a dime a dozen among Jews, he said. And anticipating her next remark, he added that the same was true for smooth olive skin. He loved all of her, including the parts she liked least.

His appreciation had made a difference. Before meeting him she had tried to hide her full figure, but for a long time now she had lived comfortably inside her smooth olive skin – which Daniel with his Semitic background might not appreciate, but coming from a fair-skinned, pale-eyed family she certainly did.

'Yes. A weekend of sex and food, with an occasional walk to crank up our appetites.' He reached out, and with his forefinger lightly traced a line from her ear to her clavicle.

She picked up speed, but still the journey was frustratingly slow. The storm was powering in from the west and they were driving straight into it; she hoped the rain would hold off until they arrived. As she drove, Daniel passed her roasted almonds and they talked about her feminist project, then moved on to his book, and from there to a book by an old friend – a surprising disappointment that called into question their long-held belief in his talent. By the time they passed the Guildford turn-off they had shifted to politics, a conversational favourite.

'There's no leadership,' Nina was saying. 'And no vision.'

'It's the equality thing,' Daniel said, 'and we're all equal now. It doesn't sit well with any sort of leadership – political or moral,' and after a pause he added, 'or parental.' Daniel had struggled with his younger son for years. He rummaged in his bag for the fruit pastilles he was never without. 'Do you know that politicians now register lower than used-car salesmen on those "who-do-you-trust" scales?'

Nina was incredulous. 'Surely not.'

'That might be a slight exaggeration, but the fact remains that people don't think much of their politicians.'

'Courage and pragmatism are at the crux of it,' Nina said, bunkering into the topic. 'The two stances are naturally opposed, and politicians, being primarily motivated to keep their jobs, settle for pragmatism.' Her words streamed out, she was on a roll. 'The problem is their pragmatism is so transparent that to respect them is impossible, and the very fact of the transparency suggests they can't be all that bright, and why on earth would you trust your health, the education of your children, your nation's security to people whose actions condemn them as not as bright as you are?'

'I do like it when you're fired up.' Daniel was laughing. 'Of course our politicians would simply dismiss you as elitist.'

'Me and anyone else who values intellectual qualities. But they don't dismiss soccer players for being elitist, or tennis players, or racing-car drivers, or sprinters. No sportsperson is ever derided as elitist. But to refer to someone as an elite thinker is a back-breaking insult.'

'I count myself extremely fortunate in my sharp-tongued, elitist memory-keeper.' Daniel was laughing even louder now, and soon she joined in too. She didn't take herself quite so seriously these days.

Spikes of lightning flashed into the countryside and the first drops of rain spattered the windscreen; Nina concentrated on the road. Daniel slipped a CD into the deck and stared out the window. Just before the Winchester exit, Daniel jerked forward and shouted, 'Did you see that?' And then gripped her shoulder. 'No, don't look, watch the road. It's gone now anyway.'

It was a falcon, he said, with something in its mouth. 'I think it was a rabbit, or perhaps a squirrel.'

He was silent for a minute, then he turned to her. 'I never used to notice nature before you came into my life.' There was another pause and when he again spoke she heard wonder in his voice. 'In a very real sense you've given me nature.'

It was an extraordinary acknowledgment. Without taking her gaze from the road, she reached for his hand. He squeezed it briefly and then placed it back on the steering wheel.

A few minutes later lightning was all about them and the sound of thunder blasted into the car. Nina would be pleased when they were safe inside the cottage. And not far to go now, for they had entered Austen country. Our country, Daniel said, as he always did at this stage. He had proposed to her at Chawton Cottage, in the parlour right by the tiny circular table where Austen wrote her novels. Daniel had proposed and without a moment's hesitation she had accepted.

'We should pop across to Chawton some time this weekend,' Daniel now said. 'A romantic pilgrimage.'

'I will love you forever,' Nina said that evening as they toasted their twelfth anniversary and their thirteen years together.

Daniel took over: the future was, after all, his domain. 'I will love *you* forever,' he said. 'Because I've done the research and I'm in charge of predictions.'

Forever lasted exactly five months. There was no explosive stroke, no spectacular heart attack. Daniel, at sixty-one years of age and in the best of health, arrived home from a meeting in Cape Town and told Nina he was leaving her. There was no need for discussion, he said, his mind was made up. Indeed, if left to him he would have packed his bags and left without another word. Nina was in shock, her brain had jammed, yet she managed to remind him his decision concerned her as well. He conceded her point and sat down.

In brief, and he was very brief, four months earlier he had met someone –

'Who?'

Daniel's face was clad in discomfort; this was clearly a question he would prefer not to answer.

'Who is she?'

He stood up, crossed to the liquor cabinet and poured himself a Scotch. The fluid hitting the glass was loud in the silent room. She watched him raise the drink, she heard him swallow, she heard him take a breath. She heard him say Sally.

'Sally?' She didn't believe this was happening. 'You don't mean your research assistant Sally? Sally who's about to move in with her boyfriend?'

Daniel turned to face her. 'Obviously she's not any more.'

'But she *is* still thirty.' The words just slipped out.

'You can be such a bitch, Nina.'

Never in all their years together had he sworn at her. In fact, he had always appreciated her sharp tongue, had often said with admiration that she knew exactly where to land a verbal punch. She looked at him standing stiffly in front of the liquor cabinet, so familiar but obstinately out of reach. He might have been a photograph, this man, her husband, this person who for the past four months had been having an affair with his research assistant.

'Former research assistant. And it's not an affair. I'm going to marry her.'

Daniel, so reluctant to speak just moments ago, seemed to be warming to his topic. But Nina did not want to hear about his future. She didn't want to know about the marriage that was to follow hers, nor the babies they planned to have, nor their home or summer cottage. She didn't want to hear about his future without her. Her heart was shredding; she wanted to vomit.

'Are you absolutely sure?' Her voice was – miraculously – steady. 'You've thought it through and you're absolutely sure about this? Leaving me, leaving our marriage, our life, to start afresh.' She wanted to add 'at your age', she wanted to say 'with someone young enough to be your daughter', but while there remained a skerrick of hope she would not attack him.

'Absolutely certain. Not a doubt.' Daniel was staring into his drink, gently rocking the fluid in the glass – an intricately cut crystal from Waterford and an early gift from her. He stared into his whisky and he looked happy. He'd done the hard part, he'd confessed, and now he was eager to get on with his future. He put his drink down and took a step towards her. 'I'm sorry, Nina, I really am. I didn't plan this.'

'But neither did you stop it.'

He didn't finish his drink. He tossed a few things in a suitcase, returned to the living room and went to kiss her goodbye as if he had forgotten that everything had changed. She turned away. From the hall he said he'd be in touch. She heard the door open and close, she heard him leave.

Alone now in the silent house she might have turned to stone for all she could feel. Outside the wind stripped the last leaves from the trees, rain turned to sleet, the day closed down. At some point she turned on the lights, some hours later she extinguished them. She remained seated on the couch in the dark, paralysed and numb. She remained locked in limbo, outside time, outside geography. She remained there until dawn, the dawn of a future she did not want.

3.

The winter came and went. As one month moved into the next, Nina did not notice the profusion of crocuses and daffodils, nor the bright young leaves on the trees. A succession of bloodless days and jangling nights carried her forward. She moved her winter clothes into the hall closet and her summer clothes into the bedroom cupboard; she woke, she ate, she slept, she worked. She marked her birthday alone, she spent the Easter holiday alone. She avoided favourite walks and favourite restaurants, she could not bear to go to the cinema or the theatre; all she once shared with Daniel was ruined. Even the pigeons. 'Any creature that can survive Arctic wilderness as well as Trafalgar Square deserves our admiration,' Daniel used to say as he tossed crumbs to the marauding throng. Now she would look at the scrabbling pigeons and hate them. And all of these occurrences, the doing without him or the not doing at all, in the period following Daniel's departure felt like falling through thin ice.

Friends took charge of her, mutual friends horrified at Daniel's behaviour invited her for home-cooked meals and weekends in the country. And Zoe, her sister, flew in from Melbourne, a short visit taken in school holidays. It helped to be with people who loved her when Daniel didn't. And two months after Zoe's visit, Sean and his partner on a rare trip together kept her occupied for a week. But when she was alone, Daniel's absence remained a raw wound.

She bought prepared meals from the supermarket and ate them out of plastic containers. She watched American sitcoms and happy-ever-after Hollywood romances. She checked her phone every few minutes. She searched for useless facts online; she spent hours on Facebook; she read blogs – trivial, interesting, proselytising, it didn't matter; she set up home in YouTube, anything to use up time and stifle thought. And email, twenty, thirty times a day, email with all its false positives, for if you don't send them you don't receive them. Morning, afternoon, and all through the hours she used to sleep curled around Daniel's body she sought artificial connection to treat her disconnection.

'Ravaged. You look ravaged,' Jamie said one morning when she arrived at the office.

He drew the truth from her and then he forced her to go cold turkey. He confiscated her phone and iPad, he disconnected her wireless connection at home. The only item of communication technology he permitted was a mobile phone, circa 2000. It allowed phone calls and nothing else.

She had cleared Daniel from view: his clothes and books, his whiskies, his rocket-shaped champagne opener, his armchair, his bowl for olives bought in Sicily, his special asparagus dish, as if by removing these things – mementoes of a lover, a husband – she could kill off memory. She wanted to remember neither the good times nor the bad. She removed every vestige of him with the exception of those objects that connected to her as much as to him – paintings they had chosen together, their collection of Penguin paperback coffee mugs, the tattered two-seater, the hand-crafted pasta bowls they'd bought for their fifth wedding anniversary. To remove these would render herself homeless.

On one of their visits to Australia she and Daniel had included a side-trip to New Zealand. They took long walks through the volcanic region of the North Island, hiking over extinct volcanoes and dormant ones and others that were very much alive. The most powerful eruption in the North Island in modern times occurred at Tarawera in 1886. The series of craters at Tarawera has formed a huge long fissure thickly clad with red scoria. As they walked from the rim down the slope of the main crater, their feet sank into the scoria, and they would find themselves sliding on a raft of pebbles towards the crater floor. With each step Nina would lose her footing, and she would know she would lose her footing. The only way of stopping the slide was to flex her knees, bend at the hips and sit. Step, sink, slide with the shifting ground, sit. After Daniel left, Nina felt as if she were back on the slopes of Tarawera, slipping and sliding over volatile ground.

Tolstoy famously wrote that happy families are alike in their happiness, but every unhappy family is unhappy in its own way. Let's forget these are the words of the great Tolstoy and consider whether unhappy families, along with the individuals they spawn, really are uniquely unhappy. And the fact is there's a sour monotony to unhappiness wherever it occurs in the well-nourished West. Wives and husbands are dumped every day. They are miserable, angry and resentful. They eat too much or not enough, they drink, they take drugs, they become promiscuous or swear off sex forever, they socialise to excess or become reclusive. Unhappiness's repertoire is finite, limited, and bereft of originality. No need to provide a detailed account of Nina's misery in those first months without Daniel. The pain was high voltage, it was twenty-four hour anguish, Nina knew nothing to compare. But others do. Anyone who has been tossed from a shared life and cast adrift knows exactly what she endured.

Another winter arrived, there was snow and plenty of it. The garden looked like one of those sparkly scenes on the Christmas cards from her childhood – always so exotic in the red heat of an Australian Christmas. The lawn was lushly white, snow smoothed the low shrubs into giant cauliflowers, and the yew that dominated the small patch at the back of the house captured the snow in drips and sods. Nina would go outside via the kitchen door and stand in the brilliant whiteness, and not even Daniel's absence could quash her pleasure.

His removal from her life had been swift and total. In the week following the end of their marriage he had sent her an email informing her he would be collecting his belongings; he'd do so, he wrote, while she was at work so as not to disturb her. She actually laughed at this – as if the removal of his own self had not been of such critical disturbance that, in comparison, anything else was a mild rippling of the waters. He had contacted the property agent and had his name removed from the lease; as for the furniture and household goods, she could keep the lot. This was not guilt nor generosity, how much less hurtful if it were; rather, all the things that made a shared life, a shared domestic space, all the things that comprised the evidence of their years together, he no longer wanted. And it was this action, the ease with which he reduced their thirteen years to a sentence in an email, that obliterated any hope he would return. He made no mention of the cottage in Hampshire, nor had it been raised since. The place was poisonous as far as she was concerned, but she guessed he still used it: he'd always loved it and she was sure he would not be averse to recycling any appealing aspects of their marriage. After all, during their thirteen years together, whenever he presented her with copies of his favourite books or DVDs of his favourite films or took her to special places both in England and abroad, she knew that the first wife had been similarly treated. So why not wife number three? Not that they were married yet; Nina expected the divorce papers any day, would leave the mail scattered on the mat where it fell, sifting through the letters with a hesitant toe. Any likely items she would eventually open, hours or even days later, handling them as if they were radioactive.

Now that a full year had passed, the push and pull of his absence allowed much of life to proceed, if not as previously, at least affording some pleasure. She worked, she dined out with friends, she went to concerts and the theatre, she maintained her weekly lunch with her mother-in-law, Shirley Ryman, eighty-five years old and still seeing patients, a woman of such resilience that even after her beloved son's delinquency – 'He goes off with a child! What could he be thinking?' – she had picked herself up and got on with things. 'What else can one do?' she said, not expecting nor indeed wanting an answer. And music: Nina listened to music whenever she pleased, she filled the house with music. She began a collection of requiems, such rousing compositions, and with over two thousand written she would never run short. It was not so much that life was looking up, rather it was moving again: there was a future without Daniel and she was living it.

One morning, a few days before Christmas, Nina left home early, and after a moment's dithering on the snowy verge, decided against the bus and walked instead through the dawn towards St. John's Wood tube station. Despite living through more European winters than Australian temperate ones, she had never lost her enthusiasm for snow. Although a few minutes later, having slipped several times on the icy pavement, she considered turning back – just a moment's hesitation before the lovely brittle air reminded her this was her favourite time of day in her favourite season of the year. Melbourne was in the middle of a heatwave – she took perverse pleasure in tracking the summer weather on the other side of the globe – and here she was surrounded by ice and snow.

She headed up Primrose Hill, stepping off the path to crunch along on the grass – something reassuringly solid about the sound and texture of iced grass underfoot. She exchanged nods with the local power walkers and stopped to talk to her neighbour who was out walking his Airedale. On the St. John's Wood side of Primrose Hill the streets were well covered with grit and the walk to the station was much easier.

The station smelled of damp and cold. She picked up a newspaper and rode the escalator down to the train. She changed at Baker Street and arrived at King's Cross St. Pancras at the rush period. It was all so different here since the 2005 attacks, with shiny new shops, including not one but two M&S food stores (since she had stopped cooking she noticed these places). As she made her way to the exit she was aware of a stiffening of the spine, an alertness she did not feel at other stations. Not that she had been caught in the bombings, she was not even in Britain at the time, but Kings Cross was her station, she passed through here daily, and the Eurostar to Paris took off from St. Pancras International.

Paris by train. She and Daniel had loved the romance of it. Every summer they would make at least one day trip across the channel, leaving home at seven in the morning and arriving back late at night. There would be the Paris lunch, a gallery visit, shopping in the Latin Quarter or the Marais, promenading along the Seine. And the train journey itself – such a brilliant mix of the old Orient Express adventuring spirit with modern speed and ingenuity. The Paris trip made so many times, but since Daniel's defection going to Mongolia would be more likely.

When a Paris job arrived on her desk a few months back, Jamie had tried to reason with her. The job was tailor-made for her, he said, an uncomplicated single-issue affair, no massacres, no bombings, no competing interests, just a single monument to honour Foucault. 'You could do it in your sleep, it would get you back to France, and –' his trump card, 'you've actually read Foucault.' But Paris was synonymous with Daniel and she did not tender for the job.

She exited the station, crossed the Euston Road and entered the narrow streets. This area was a long-time favourite: North Bloomsbury, she called it, the bluestocking's wild sister who drinks too much and stays out late. The last fall of snow had been a few days ago, and in typical British fashion the authorities had run out of grit. Clearly the good burghers of St. John's Wood had acted quickly, but here, after several days of freezing temperatures, the pavements were crusted with ice; it was lethal stuff and nothing short of crampons would make it safe. She trod gingerly, trying to find those patches cleared by pedestrian use. Certainly no one had been out scraping the footpaths as they would in the litigious United States.

Ahead of her, moving slowly but steadily was an elderly woman, her body bent over a walking frame, her gaze fixed defiantly to the ground. So many old people had been forced to stay indoors during the cold spell, making do with whatever food was in the cupboard and the kindness of neighbours. Nina popped across the road daily to see Harvey, bringing him food and checking the heater was on and the stove was off. Harvey said it wasn't necessary; he was of the old school, a Depression-era baby who grew to maturity during the years of rationing. But these days Harvey's memory held much truer to the past than to current events, and Nina worried about him.

The old woman with the walking frame was approaching the intersection. Nina quickened her pace as much as she dared and reached the lights in time to cross with her. Safe on the other side the woman looked up. 'You can't just stop because of a bit of weather,' she said before trundling off. Her gloveless hands had been blotchy with cold, she'd been wearing a wedding band. Nina wondered about the old woman's husband, whether he was alive and in good health, for what husband of long-standing would let his aged wife negotiate these lethal pavements alone?

Nina continued her careful walking past the familiar shops and houses, making her usual detour via Tavistock Square – an automatic response seriously at odds with the treacherous conditions, but worth it when she saw that a caring soul had decked out the bust of Virginia Woolf in a hand-knitted purple scarf and beanie. A few metres away in the middle of the square, hardy Gandhi had no such luck: he was his usual semi-naked, cross-legged self, the bronze now slick with a layer of ice.

She retraced her steps and entered Marchmont Street. Here it looked as if some of the ice and snow had been cleared, the work of the shopkeepers, she assumed, to bolster trade at a time when the weather and the national economy mitigated against it. She quickened her pace, only to lose her footing a moment later on a patch of black ice. She grabbed a street pole, caught herself mid-fall, and proceeded more slowly.

Jamie was already at his computer when she arrived at the office, and with two empty cardboard cups on the desk had clearly been here for some time. Jamie was her wonderboy; he was also colleague, business partner and dear friend. It was her great and good fortune he had stood his ground all those years ago when she did everything to push him away. She'd advertised for an assistant and he had pestered her to hire him. In the end she spelled it out: she doubted the male capacity to handle the detail of office work generally and her work in particular.

'Try me,' he said. 'Give me a month's trial.'

And she did because she needed someone urgently, someone to handle all the everyday tasks while she finished a submission, a vital submission if she was to be noticed in the post-9/11 world. Jamie moved in, he reorganised the office, and within a week he was running it. At the end of the month if he hadn't wanted to stay she would have resorted to bribery or kidnapping to keep him.

He was only twenty-one at the time, a history major fresh out of university. He had seen her advertisement and knew this was the job for him. Five years later he married Greta, and at Nina's suggestion he started to buy into the business. He and Greta were now expecting their first child.

He looked up from the computer. 'What brings you in so early?'

Couldn't sleep, couldn't bear the empty house, couldn't stand the wail in her brain, couldn't be still. None of which she said. People expect you to get on with your life; it was a marriage break-up after all, not a death, and you're expected to be doing just fine, in fact, better now that the two-timing bastard is out of the way.

'I want to send off the final paperwork on the Lise Meitner monument,' she said.

It was the truth, not that it had occurred to her until a moment ago. The official unveiling had happened the previous month and her own work on the project had finished long before that, but she had been reluctant to let go of a project that had started when Daniel and she were still together. It was a commission she had fought hard for, not because of its importance or uniqueness, but because it was Lise Meitner, a great scientist and one of the significant names in nuclear physics, a woman who like so many other women scientists had missed out on the Nobel when her male collaborators had not. Nina hung on to the project because she clung to Meitner, as if Meitner's extraordinary strength and focus could somehow help her find her own. The monument was not in the US where Meitner had lived after the war, but in Austria where she was born and grew up. The location added to the project's significance.

New monuments invariably have double allegiance: they recall significant people and events from the past, but at the same time they have to satisfy current concerns. In working with commissioning groups, Nina often had to employ complex and delicate manoeuvres to expose these concerns and thereby clarify the project, while ensuring she did not do herself out of a job. But the fact remained, because of their allegiance to the present, monuments often give history a cut and polish. So while shameful events are easily buried beneath attractive structures, contemporary values have become quite expert at digging up neglected or forgotten pieces of the past. As a result of her own research on Meitner, Nina had discovered all the uncomfortable truths omitted from the committee's briefing notes. These Austrians had made life so hard for Meitner, firstly as a highly intelligent girl, then as a young female physicist and lastly as a Jew. But with the worldwide rush to memorialise admirable events in a nation's murky past as well as its significant sons and daughters – even if these have only been recently acknowledged – Meitner was an Austrian hero.

Nina had felt a heightened commitment to this project, made all the more special when Daniel accompanied her to Austria for the foundation ceremony. They returned home and a few weeks later he was gone. She had clung to this project that straddled her old life and the new a good deal longer than was necessary, but now, this morning – she had no idea how these things happened – she was ready to let it go.

Jamie was leafing through a pile of mail. 'It's a good thing you're making space in your workload,' he said, handing her a letter. 'Your home town wants you.' He looked at her in that knowing way he had, eyebrows raised, his mouth pursed in a wry grin. 'Not that you'll want the job; it sounds like the project from hell.'

She read quickly. Jamie was right. It was one of those vague, feel-good projects which, in the abstract, promises to fix the evils of the world: a multicultural, inter-faith committee proposing a monument to promote religious tolerance, unity in diversity, individual courage, and freedom for all. A heap of stone with a water feature and a few well-chosen words to right the wrongs of the world – as if that was all it required. The naivety of what this monument was to achieve was irritating rather than touching, and the camaraderie enjoyed by the organising committee in regular meetings and tours to religion's hotspots wouldn't survive the first stage of a project like this. The committee, made up of a handful of moderate religious and social leaders, appeared to have ignored all other interest groups from liberal-minded atheists to hard-line fundamentalists. They called themselves the TIF group: Together In Freedom. The project from hell didn't start to describe it.

She stared out the window to the building opposite. Snow had banked up on the pediments and formed channels in the roof angles. According to the weather bureau more falls were expected: London would be white for Christmas and possibly the new year too. Melbourne was stifling in one of the hottest summers on record and Nina hated the heat. Yet suddenly, and without prior warning, she yearned for the people, places, objects and events that filled her first memories; she longed for space and parrots and eucalypts and the Australian coast; she wanted the environment that was hers before she met Daniel.

'You're surely not considering it?' Jamie looked incredulous. 'You're not going to accept the job?'

She shrugged and there was a brief weary smile. 'I know the project is awful, but I want to go home.'

She booked her flights that morning. She would be in the air on New Year's Eve, saving her the bother of making plans for a night that shouldn't matter but did. Later in the day she rang her sister who was thrilled at this unexpected visit. She invited Nina to stay with her. Elliot was finishing his book, Zoe said, and was largely absent, and the children had a hectic holiday schedule. 'And I'll not be teaching so we'll have lots of time together.'

Nina explained about the TIF project that, unlike Zoe, she would be working and therefore better to have a place of her own. In truth, relations between Zoe and Elliot had become so bitter, that Nina determined on her last visit never to stay with them again. Indeed, it was her plan to see as little of them together as possible: she'd had more than she could bear of wrecked marriages. She booked a serviced flat near the Botanic Gardens, she corresponded with the TIF committee, and by the time she left London a meeting had been scheduled.

During the long flight to Australia, as she hovered in that aeroplane twilight of not-quite-asleep, thoughts of Daniel slipped in unbidden. Vague and fleeting thoughts mostly, with one exception: the possibility that this time, with this relationship, it was not she who had failed but Daniel. It was a faintly disturbing notion, yet at the same time curiously enticing.

Chapter 2. **Mugged by the Past**

1.

Despite one of the hottest summers on record and jetlag more stubborn than any she had ever known, Nina was glad to be home. The familiar roads, the shops and buildings, the clatter of trams, the squawk of parrots, even the nasal twang of Australian speech all settled her, shedding an anxiety that had become so entrenched she had worn it without question.

The serviced flat was modern, functional and beigely anonymous; its air-conditioning was pleasingly arctic. She made her usual slow start to the day: coffee, reading, and an early walk in the Botanic Gardens. For so long, caught as she was in the grip of Daniel and her lost marriage, she had been unable to look ahead, but since she'd been back in Melbourne, just a few short days, she was already making plans.

She had been wanting to explore the still untapped area of virtual memorialising, something that went beyond blogs and Facebook posturings; now she felt an urgency to get started. And there were changes to the Primrose Hill house and garden that would make the place more her own. Nothing major, it was a rental after all, but she'd buy a new armchair made for her body not Daniel's, and a new crockery set with a jazzy geometric design, not the plain white of Daniel's preference. And she would demolish the bed of suffering succulents that had been a pet gardening project of Daniel's. And travel, too, to the Amazon or to Greenland, she hadn't yet decided. Both trips had been planned with Daniel, but now they looked tempting even when envisaged alone.

Until mid-January, when her first meeting with the TIF committee was scheduled, she was on holiday. She had hired a car and each morning she made her way across to Zoe's house. Although they were in close contact no matter where in the world Nina happened to be, they were relishing this face-to-face contact, the most they'd had for years. When she arrived, Zoe would make fresh coffee and they would talk through several cups. They had visited their great-aunt, their cousins, a former neighbour; they'd been to an art exhibition (the artist was a distant relative); they'd had lunches and dinners with friends; there'd been a bush walk and shopping expeditions. And through it all they talked as always, about work, music, their parents (somewhere in Far North Queensland swimming with reef sharks, according to a recent email), Zoe's children, films, fashion, politics.

Only one topic was out-of-bounds: Zoe's marriage. Rotting beneath a thin crust of convention, it was never referred to, not with Nina, nor, Nina suspected, with anyone. Although she hoped that some time in the next month it might be discussed, but with a week already passed she had her doubts. On those occasions when she had nudged the conversation in the direction of the marriage, Zoe had leapt to safer ground, and leapt so adeptly that Nina guessed she was well practised in avoiding the swampy bits of her life.

The house itself was an accessory to the sad deceit of Zoe's marriage, or so it seemed to Nina who lived with what she believed to be a healthy amount of mess. No mess in Zoe's house, not a chair out of place, nor bowl nor flower arrangement, no jacket flung over a couch, no cup left on the sink. The kitchen was of a style Nina expected to see only in magazines. All appliances, free of the scratches and drips found in her own kitchen, were satin-finished chrome. Benchtops and floor were white marble, the splashback was ebony-coloured glass; Zoe's vast collection of utensils was arranged inside smoothly sliding white drawers; the pantry, as neat as a freshly stocked supermarket, was located behind folding doors. Zoe's kitchen looked as if it was never used, but in fact she was an enthusiastic cook, turning out lunches and dinners for family, relatives, friends, her children's friends, sick colleagues, neighbours.

The entire place was a study in elegance and convenience. The furniture upholstery, a dove-grey suede-like material, actually repelled stains; the TV could be viewed from any chair in the living room; the sound system was linked by Wi-Fi to iTunes and piped via discreet ceiling speakers throughout the house, a design feature, according to Zoe, rendered obsolete by teenagers with ear-plugs fixed permanently to their ears; each bedroom was equipped with its own ensuite; the carpet felt like tufted silk. And surprising the white, grey and black colour scheme was the occasional burnt orange or rust-red cushion, an abstract painting in red-earth tonings, a splash of yellow in a glass sculpture. Outside was a solar-powered swimming pool, surrounded by a garden with separate modules – Australian native here, flowering bushes there, fruit and vegetable patch, white garden, private grotto – all of it designed to complement a variety of moods.

Zoe's house was a domestic paradise; so much comfort, so many state-of-the-art utensils, but no one, as far as Nina could determine, wanted to be there. Hayley and Callum were at an age when home and parents were embarrassing encumbrances; Elliot divided his waking hours between the university, the gym and his AA work; and Zoe, here in her own home, was a match for the designer homemaker an advertising agency would hire for a photo shoot of this perfect place.

And there was the nub: there was something unreal and contrived about both home and mistress, or so it seemed to Nina. When they were growing up Zoe was the one to leave her clothes on the floor, dirty mugs would litter her desk, and she never made her bed or hung her towel on the bathroom rail. But then back in those days there was no messy marriage to endure, no husband who would fly at her without provocation. Nina couldn't help but think that Zoe's clinging to all this external order was a means by which she strove to imprint sense and predictability onto the private and chaotic aspects of her life.

Zoe was only two years away from fifty, but looked younger in that stretched way of thin people. Both sisters were tall, but where Nina was dark-haired and dark-eyed, Zoe was fair with white-blonde cropped hair and blue eyes. And there were the bodies: whippet-thin Zoe and nicely cushioned Nina. And the clothes: Nina's bright and flowing garments compared with Zoe's chic black. Zoe selected her clothes with care, but the care showed, so Nina thought, and so, too, the Sunday-best personality Zoe wore in company. Always her smooth, competent disposition, her nothing-is-too-much-trouble attitude, and a particular smile that flashed huge and vivid, just for a moment and then it was gone. Not faded, but

33

instantly gone. Too brief to imply pleasure in the moment, it was programmed: *Zoe smile. Smile now.* And she was always busy. Despite a full-time teaching job, Zoe managed to be active in so many lives. She was available to her son and daughter, and to her husband, that charming (although never to her) brittle man; she attended to the sick neighbour, the needy friend, the distant acquaintance whose mother had just died. Zoe was social worker, psychologist, empathic listener and efficient personal assistant.

This past week when Nina had met people in Zoe's world, all had remarked on her kindness and generosity; Zoe, they said, was always available to lend a hand, a shoulder, a sympathetic ear. But beneath the perfect surface of both house and person what misery lurked? How could her sister not be miserable living in such a hostile marriage?

With Callum away at music camp and Hayley holidaying at the coast, there was nothing to dilute the poisonous atmosphere at home. Zoe and Elliot were excruciating to be around; she was polite and cool, while he, always heavily armed, bombarded her with criticism and derision. Nina used to count herself fortunate to have a husband like Daniel rather than Elliot, but the fact was the good husband had absconded and the bad one was still around. How to explain it? She wanted to discuss this with Zoe, she wanted to unzip this sister who was so emotionally guarded about her own deeply emotional matters. But while Zoe never tired of hearing about Nina's failed marriage, she was quick to deflect any questions about her own.

A few days after her arrival, Nina had approached from the front. 'Your marriage, Zoe, it's a shocker. To my mind it's never been worse. And ignoring it won't make it any better.'

Zoe hardly missed a beat. 'Dwelling on it, as you'd have me do, doesn't help either. Elliot and I manage, otherwise we wouldn't still be together.'

'Don't you want more than merely "managing"? Don't you think you deserve more?'

Zoe shrugged. Her face was blank.

That Nina was prepared to talk about marriage was further evidence she was feeling much more her old self. It was, she decided, being back home with its reminder of who she used to be. How twisted out of shape she'd become in the aftermath of Daniel's desertion, and how quickly it happens that an abnormal state can assume the norm. But now she was back inside familiar skin, she felt not only the relief of it but a recognition, like stumbling across an old friend not seen for a long time and realising how much you have missed her.

The impersonal serviced flat helped, coming as it did with neither history nor demands. Zoe had a guest room, she actually had a guest wing, and as soon as Nina had arrived she'd begged her to reconsider. Briefly Nina hesitated, she hated refusing this sister who was herself endlessly obliging. But five minutes in the company of Zoe and Elliot on that first day had revealed tensions so intense and the threat of breakage so great that Nina couldn't leave fast enough. Afterwards, guessing why Nina had departed so abruptly and still hoping she might reconsider the guest room, Zoe insisted that things between her and Elliot were fine. But what Zoe considered to be fine in her marriage was, from Nina's perspective, unbearable.

The situation was made worse, sadder, because except with his wife, Elliot was good company. He was a nicely put together man in that American clipped and polished way: tall, well built with large white teeth and dark wavy hair. He wore a closely clipped beard which was, unlike the hair, shaded with grey. He liked women and was easy in their company, probably because he was not tempted to stray; and despite his being a non-drinker, his humour and athleticism won him plenty of male friends. Women described him as a woman's man, men described him as a man's man. As one friend said, being with Elliot was like taking a holiday. But not for Zoe. Elliot bullied her, he goaded and attacked her, and his behaviour was made worse by his being so charming with everyone else. At any time and without warning he would fire off an arrow at her, always with bull's-eye accuracy. Target practice for his own frayed ego? Nina neither knew nor cared, for he could wound.

Nothing Zoe did was right. Elliot criticised what he saw as her lack of ambition: 'Who stays in the same job for twenty years?' He criticised her intellect: 'My wife prefers jigsaws to books.' From Nina's perspective he never missed an opportunity to run Zoe down. Last night before dinner, when she and Zoe were having a glass of wine, Zoe had stumbled. Elliot had leapt forward and saved her from falling, then, in that nasty tone he employed only with her, he said, 'You don't even know how to drink properly.'

Nina knew firsthand how devastating a marriage break-up could be, yet you survive, you get over it. But the incessant ridicule that Elliot meted out to Zoe, the scorn with which he spoke to her, the growling derision despite the perfect home and her perfect appearance, all this must eventually break her. And once this happened Nina doubted Zoe would have the capacity to put herself together again.

At least Elliot was out of the house most of the time. Despite it being the summer vacation, he was working hard. There were consultations with his doctoral students, but his main energies were directed towards finishing his biography of Elizabeth Hardwick. He was, he had told Nina, under pressure. Frances Kiernan, who had written such a wonderful life of Mary McCarthy, was also writing a biography of Hardwick. Kiernan and he were taking different but, he believed, complementary approaches, with Kiernan drawing on her vast knowledge of the *Partisan Review – New York Review* milieu. Her Hardwick biography would encompass twentieth-century American letters, while his focused more specifically on the Hardwick life and the marriage to Robert Lowell. But still, whoever published first would have a distinct advantage, so he was pushing himself. Despite a fully equipped office at home, Elliot preferred to work at the university. He left home early for the gym, spent the day at the university, went to AA a couple of evenings a week, and returned home in time for dinner. For her sister's sake, Nina was pleased.

Yet how much more was Zoe willing to suffer in this marriage? And what kept her there? Callum was already at university, and Hayley at sixteen was mature for her age. The children could not fail to see the situation with their parents; they'd understand if this marriage was brought to a close. Why did her sister stay? And Elliot? Why did he stay with a woman he appeared to despise?

It is a truism that you can never understand a marriage not your own – and even your own can deceive you. Nina tried a couple more times to get Zoe to open up, and then decided to leave it alone. Her lost marriage was no reason to be meddling in Zoe's. And besides, she was happy to be seeing so much of her sister. She was happy to be home.

When Nina left Australia in her early twenties, she had
given her leave-taking surprisingly little thought; a similarly
casual connection had characterised her several trips back
to Melbourne. But this particular homecoming seemed
weighted with significance. She had put down roots in New
York and more firmly in London, but her attachment to this
place, this Melbourne, seemed now to penetrate far deeper
than both. So it happened one morning that she responded to
an unpremeditated urge to visit Raleigh Court and the house
where she had grown up.

The heat was fat and leathery by the time she left the
apartment, and the sky that matt violet blue reserved for the
hottest days. It would have been far more sensible to spend
the day beside Zoe's pool, but the pull of the past, or pumped-
up nostalgia, or the simple attraction of home was propelling
her towards Raleigh Court.

The traffic was light and the journey short, and soon
she was standing alongside her car at the neck of the court.
Stretched before her was the pale cement road surface, the
clipped verge cupping the curves, the uniform trees planted
in the grass, the eleven solid family dwellings. And then with
deliberate slowness as if that might soften the shock – her
initial glimpse had already alerted her – she directed her gaze
to the old family home. The red brick had been plastered
over and painted cream, windows sufficiently large for the
Jameson family had been replaced by mammoth panes of
glass, an upper storey had been added and all the walls were
blocked and squared off. A 1950s triple-fronted brick home
was now brazenly *au courant*.

Nina was last here a dozen years ago with Daniel – she had wanted him to see where she came from, the *me-before-you* was how she put it – and at that time fewer than half the houses had been renovated. But now only the house next door, the Blake house, remained unchanged. It was located at the top of the court, the prime position according to her parents; Marion and Michael Blake had modernised it when they moved in with their two boys in the 1970s and, if the exterior was any guide, it had not been touched since.

She looked again at her old home. There was something troubling, even wrenching about the juxtaposition of familiar memories – this court, the houses, her own house in particular – and the strangeness of what presented itself. And she wondered if it was always the case that when long-established memories were undermined, not by another person but by uncompromising reality, one was tripped up, knocked sideways.

The Blake house was just the same, no unnerving quiver when she turned her gaze on it, just the old cloudy disquiet that had long accompanied any thought of this place and its current occupants. And yet it had not always been so: for many years the Blake house had been her second home, and Raleigh Court itself had provided a storybook environment in which to grow up. Sean and Ramsay Blake had been the brothers at number six, Zoe and Nina were the sisters at number seven. The other children in the court were older, with playgrounds far removed from parental gaze, leaving Ramsay and Sean, Zoe and Nina the run of the street.

They played together as a foursome, ballgames in the court and endless hare-brained schemes, but as so often happens with groups of children, special alliances developed. From the very beginning, Nina claimed Sean as her best friend and he felt the same about her. And Zoe had always adored Ramsay – it was the open secret of their childhood – and not just Ramsay's music, which, being musical herself, mattered to her; she loved everything about him, including all those qualities that others found off-putting.

Ramsay was not predisposed to love anyone, with the single exception of his brother, but because Zoe played the cello he was happy to be called her best friend. It was clear though, in those long-ago days, that Sean came first. 'Sean is my brother,' Ramsay would say, 'and my number-one music partner.' And a remarkable duet they made, Sean with his violin and Ramsay at the piano. But even at number two, Zoe claimed a special place in Ramsay's life. And Nina and Sean did as kids do, spying on them and playing endless tricks, and teasing them with soppy love songs – all of which was received in good spirit by Ramsay, because even as a child such things washed off him, and Zoe, because she basked in any reference that acknowledged her special relationship with Ramsay.

For seven years after the Blakes moved next door theirs had been an idyllic childhood. They even had their own secret gang. It was Ramsay's idea, Ramsay, who wasn't yet totally self-absorbed proposed they form the Raleigh Posse with a closed membership of four humans and two dogs. There was a lot of make-believe after that, and like kids in books and films they had wild adventures that took them way beyond Raleigh Court. The two fathers built them a club house in the Blakes' sycamore tree; there were rules and private codes, a secret food stash, and special audio equipment for communication with extra-terrestrials. And so they played through the years under the watchful eyes of the Blake parents, and the more lax, indulgent gaze of the Jamesons.

Then it all fell apart. Sean, the devoted brother and violinist, was shunted to Siberia and Zoe was ensconced in his place. And while Sean had remained Nina's friend, her only lifelong friend, relations between Sean and Zoe had never been properly repaired. As for the brothers, they remained estranged.

Nina, the youngest of the four, was five years old when the Blakes moved into the court; next in age were Zoe and Sean, both seven. Sean was only fourteen months younger than Ramsay, but being all sharp angles and lanky limbs Ramsay always looked much older than his nicely compact sibling. In those days Sean loved his big brother with a devotion reinforced by blindness. Others were less enamoured, but Ramsay's music was so remarkable and his willingness to share it so keen that people overlooked his failings. Even the children at school, perhaps alerted by their parents to the extraordinary boy among them, were kinder to Ramsay than children tend to be with kids who stand out. Certainly that was the case with Nina, for she would never have chosen him as a friend; in time she realised she did not like him at all. But during those first few years, Ramsay being the oldest claimed a certain respect, and people were impressed when she said she knew him; he was well stocked with fun ideas and a cracker at poison ball, but most important of all, he was the boy next door and you can't be on bad terms with him. Yet these reasons notwithstanding, his less attractive qualities were rarely obscured.

He was a boy with a peculiar detachment. Often his gaze would be set to the middle distance: he might respond if spoken to or he might not. He could be silent in a boisterous group or he could rattle on about his latest arcane interest – the geometry of the pyramid, writing scripts of the world, cemeteries, taxonomy – a series of bizarre obsessions about which Ramsay knew everything to the point of tedium. But at the piano he was irresistible, at the piano even Nina was seduced; music made sense to Ramsay in a way people did not. Ramsay Blake with his prodigious talent was, everyone said, marked out for fame.

Ramsay was performing regularly while still in primary school. He won a slew of piano competitions and attended master-classes with visiting maestros. By the time he reached his mid-teens there was little space left in the cabinet displaying all his trophies and medallions and gold-lettered certificates. And always close by were the proud parents: Marion Blake directing his career from the moment she noticed a musical aptitude in her infant son, and Michael Blake who worked hard to give both sons the advantages he himself had lacked. And Sean, the brother with his sweet disposition ideally suited to being a second son when the first took up all the oxygen. If you could create the perfect family for a genius you would use the Blakes as a model.

Such fame as a boy and, with the passage of years, Ramsay had not disappointed. Most people in the musical world would include him in the top twenty contemporary pianists, all would locate him in their top forty. And how much more fortunate had he been than those other gifted boys and girls who had once shared his world. So many prodigies but so few geniuses, Nina had often thought, and perhaps people – parents – should contain their enthusiasms until the gifted youngster has lived sufficiently for experience either to deepen the gift or let it drift away. 'Whom the gods wish to destroy they first call promising' as Cyril Connolly observed. Of all those child prodigies who had rubbed shoulders with the younger Ramsay in 1970s Australia, only Ramsay occupied the world stage as an adult.

Zoe and Nina, Ramsay and Sean were all connected by age and geographical proximity, but the other three shared music as well: Ramsay with the piano, Sean the violin, and Zoe her cello. Nina loved how music made her feel, and she loved the way in which it whisked her into imaginary places, but she was a hopeless musician. She failed first with the violin, then the flute, and when the clarinet defeated her she accepted the hard truth and settled for books instead. The unfairness of the situation was not lost on her: the others could have books as well as music, but her creaky fingers barred her from ever playing an instrument.

'I don't know how you missed out,' her mother would say, holding Nina's wooden mitts in her own musician's hands. It was said with incredulity, never criticism, but when everyone speaks a language that despite your best efforts eludes you, it's hard not to feel an outsider, hard not to feel that you lack something – more so when one of your circle is a prodigy and the other two are considered talented.

Sean said it didn't matter to him she was unable to make up a quartet, and after the rupture between him and Ramsay he told her he was pleased she was not musical, he was finished with musical friendships. As for Zoe, she would have loved Nina no matter what she might have lacked. 'You're my sister,' she said simply.

I was formed here, she thought, a woman in her forties and a preserver of memory standing at the top of the court.

She loathed the old Jesuit maxim, 'give me a child until he is seven and I will give you the man'. Even as a girl, planning her future with Sean and living with the best parents in the neighbourhood, the ones who took the four of them to the local pool on hot days, who annually took them to the Royal Melbourne Show, who arranged tickets to the circus and visits to the museum, she still wanted to forge her own future. And she had – although the primary motivations had not been entirely of her choosing.

Yet she was pleased with the path she had taken – her career, living overseas and now that the pain had settled, Daniel too. But if not for the death of Michael Blake and the arrival of George Tiller as Marion Blake's new husband, if not for Ramsay Blake and those slowly massing toxins, if not for the alliance formed between Ramsay and his stepfather, she might have remained in Melbourne as Zoe had done and made a life here.

She can't remember when first she acknowledged she didn't like Ramsay, although it was definitely after the arrival of George Tiller. No great gash felled the friendship, no cataclysmic wrongdoing. Ramsay was rude to her, but then he was rude to everyone. He was selfish, but again he was selfish with everyone. There was only one identifiable incident: Ramsay stole four of her best feathers and used them to start his own collection. But while the theft was terrible at the time, it was insufficient to explain her dislike of him.

As a child, Nina read English novels about spoiled children, and Ramsay, in her opinion, was typical of a spoiled child. But unlike the spoiled children in novels, Ramsay never got his comeuppance – he might have emerged as more likeable if he had. He occupied his world fully, and treated other people –

Zoe, Sean and herself included – as revolving satellites whose primary purpose was to maintain his central position. He was, Nina eventually decided, a genius at the piano but a half-baked human being in every other respect. Ramsay wasn't a brute although he could be brutal, he wasn't deliberately cruel though he was often hurtful, but anyone who is uninterested, even unaware of other people except when they are personally useful to them, anyone who is so narcissistic that they could walk over you and their only complaint is about the uneven ground, anyone like this demands a fair degree of suspicion.

By the time Nina reached adolescence she wanted nothing more to do with him – not so difficult because by then everything had changed. Partly it was due to what was happening to Sean – shunted to the outer in his own home and family, but there was an event as well, the pivotal event as it turned out, that banished any thought that a return to the foursome was possible. On that day, the last day of the old order, they had all gathered as usual at the Blake house for a concert. Over a period of an hour, a brief sixty minutes, it was as if she was watching a movie in which the main players shifted across the screen until they finally took up the positions they would occupy forever.

It was a Sunday, and like so many other Sundays Nina and Zoe together with their parents had been invited to the Blake house for music and afternoon tea. These gatherings always took the same form: Ramsay would play, then there would be a duet with Sean, and very occasionally they would finish with a trio that included Zoe. Nina always attended, often under sufferance, but she didn't want to miss out on what the others were doing, and depending on the music played she was happy enough to daydream. And the afternoon tea was a party: fairy cakes decorated with Smarties, chocolate brownies, Twisties, green lemonade, the sort of food that would never be found at the Jameson house.

She can't remember the weather on that particular day, nor the time of year, but it must have been warm because Zoe was wearing shorts and the boys wore singlets with their jeans, and the sun was streaming in through the bay window of the music room. Everyone took up their usual positions, her own parents on the couch, she and Zoe on the floor, Sean by the piano ready to turn pages for Ramsay, Marion in the single armchair, and George fussing when fuss was not required given that the Sunday-afternoon concerts had been happening long before he arrived on the scene. Marion looked tired, not that Nina noticed it then, slumped and shrunken in her chair and pale against the maroon upholstery; it was only later that Nina guessed she was already sick – certainly that would explain why she didn't intervene.

Ramsay stood by the piano and announced his piece as he had been taught to do. 'The *Moments Musicaux*,' he said. 'Schubert.'

'For next month's Young Performers series,' George added. 'Ramsay's to open the programme.'

'George acts like he owns Rams,' Sean had complained to Nina on numerous occasions, and now, with George standing alongside Ramsay, his hand on Ramsay's shoulder, Nina saw that Sean had every reason to be peeved.

Ramsay sat at the keyboard, Marion smiled wanly, the others clapped, and Sean pulled his chair closer to the piano. There was no music on the stand.

'You don't need to be there,' George said. 'Ramsay has the work in memory.'

46

Sean didn't move. 'Ramsay likes me here. Don't you, Rams?'

Ramsay might have nodded, he might have shrugged. George, however, was unequivocal. 'Get away from there, Sean. You'll disturb his concentration.'

'Never have before.'

In the silence that followed, George stared at him with a horrible expression on his face. Scary, Nina thought, George was scary. And then George threatened with a single word.

'Move,' he said.

Sean looked to Ramsay for support, but wherever Ramsay's attention was it was not on his brother. Sean stood up, he stepped away from the piano, he moved to the back of the room, and there he remained, separate from everyone else, his face a study in hatred. Ramsay had already started to play.

Schubert's *Moments Musicaux* – there are six of them – are like short stories. That's how they seemed to Nina then and she still hears them in the same way. They are played over thirty minutes, six distinct pieces that vary in tempo, colour, mood and tone. And here is Ramsay, who away from the piano sounds only the single note of himself, playing with such expressiveness, such sublime understanding that he wraps you in each piece and transports you to places far away; in spite of everything, Nina cannot help but admire him. Next to her Zoe is transfixed; her expression is glazed like she's on drugs or in heaven. Not even when the music is finished does Zoe move, it's only when Nina gives her a shove that she joins in the applause. Nina notices she's blushing.

Ramsay takes a bow and then beckons to Sean to join him for their duet. Sean looks happy enough as he makes his way across the room. He's either forgiven George, which Nina thinks is unlikely, or decided to ignore him.

But George won't be ignored.

'No, Ramsay,' George says. 'Not Sean. Give Zoe a turn.'

'Zoe can join us for a trio,' Ramsay says. 'Sean and I've been practising the Brahms.'

Zoe is already on her feet. She looks from George to Ramsay, then back to George. Sean does not exist for her.

'Fetch your cello,' George tells her.

Zoe races next door. Sean is standing in the middle of the room looking helpless. Marion in a quiet voice reassures him that it's just this once and it's kind to share. Nina is torn: she feels sorry for Sean but she's happy for her sister having the opportunity to play a duet with Ramsay. And as Marion said, it's only this once, otherwise everything else will continue as usual.

It didn't. Nina couldn't recall what Zoe and Ramsay played on that first day, but a couple of Sundays later the two of them played Beethoven's Fourth Cello Sonata in C. It was a memorable performance and the last occasion she remembered Sean in the music room for a Sunday-afternoon concert.

Sean was an unnecessary extra in his own home and, increasingly, a presence in Nina's. As for Zoe, George seemed to push her and Ramsay together. She was now Ramsay's duet partner, she went to concerts and the cinema with him, she played cards and electronic games with him, she joined him on visits to taxonomists and cemeteries. Fearful that if Zoe was forced to choose between her sister and Ramsay she would choose Ramsay, Nina tried to disguise her antipathy with indifference.

It wasn't simple dislike, Ramsay actually made her nervous, and George and Ramsay together were frightening. There was something about George Tiller that was needy – never a quality children want to see in an adult – yet at the same time powerful. Great need and great power, such a dangerous combination, and what will stop such a man from seizing what he believes he has a right to possess?

She did not understand her reaction; after all, George had done nothing specifically aimed at her, no threatening or scary episodes. In the end, because fathers, and, she assumed, stepfathers too, were mostly trustworthy and kind, and Ramsay Blake for all his foibles was a genius, she concluded there must be something wrong with her; it was best, she decided, to keep her feelings private. Long after she had grown up she wondered at this common response of children that have them keeping their pains to themselves. So many bitter secrets, and all the while you are thinking that if you can just hang on, manage a little longer, things will improve.

They never did – not that it mattered to Nina. At the age of eighteen she left Raleigh Court for university in Sydney, she left Ramsay and her childhood, and now as she stands on the street where she used to live, as she trains her gaze on the Blake house, even as she recalls the fear of those long-ago days, she's aware of feeling nothing uncomfortable or disturbing; in fact, not a flicker of the old jittering remains. In London, should she cast her mind back, Ramsay always dominated her childhood's folklore, Ramsay and George. But now, being here, she realises she doesn't give a toss about Ramsay Blake any more.

With Ramsay out of the way she is filled with warmth and nostalgia for those long-ago days, for her parents now both retired and seeing Australia via campervan, for her sister, and

Sean too, her only lifelong friend. It's the pains and barbs of childhood that tend to occupy the largest space in memory, almost as if good times come equipped with weak knees and faded complexion. Ramsay was only a small part of her life in Raleigh Court, yet she gave him a leading role. She's shocked that someone like her, whose work constantly struggles with the perfidy of memory, could have offered so little resistance to that age-old snare.

I had it wrong, she wants to tell Daniel, I made far too much of Ramsay Blake and the invading stepfather, they mean nothing to me now. She wants to share these understandings with him. And she wants to ask if there was a child in his past who scared him, and if there was, how does he feel about that child now? It makes her sad: these questions unasked and unanswered, the parts of the other they will never know.

She brushes the thoughts aside – her past was with Daniel, she doesn't want to predicate the future on him as well – and is about to leave when a movement at the top of the court stops her. The door to number six is opening, the door to the Blake house. A figure steps into the sunlight.

It is Ramsay: tall, angular and unmistakably Ramsay. She does not move, does not want to be seen. She wills him to turn, to go back inside, but he is not moving either. Another figure appears, another man just behind him, a man in his shadow: George Tiller, the stepfather, whose arrival here changed everything. George moves forward, he's now standing alongside Ramsay. They used to be the same height but George has shrunk, his head seems to rest on his shoulders, his legs are bowed.

The two men are looking straight at her, not that they can see her, not with the sun glaring at them. Still she does not move. She sees them turn to each other. Ramsay speaks, they both laugh. George walks to the gate, he's slow, he shuffles. Nina is frozen. George collects the mail, he hobbles back to Ramsay. They re-enter the house together.

Nina has been holding her breath, the air now plunges in. She stifles a cough, but they can't hear. And who is she anyway? Just a woman in the street with a catch in her throat. She sucks in another breath, the juddering eases, a few more breaths and it subsides. Soon she feels the familiar contours of herself. She's made a life, a good life far from this place, she could have approached them, she could have made herself known. They can do nothing to her, but more crucially, she now realises, they could have done nothing to her when she was a child.

She turns around and opens the car door; it's stifling inside. She starts up and drives away. But long-held memories refuse to be dismissed so easily; the past, the remembered past, like all habits has such entrenched roots. You might come to realise that long-held fears have no foundation, that long-held dislikes simply don't matter any more; you might well conclude you should have off-loaded these old scores long ago. But as she drives the familiar roads, a scornful explosion escapes: she of all people knows that deliberate forgetting is a loaded act. Deliberate forgetting rides the waves of a past still waiting to be lanced.

Chapter 3. The Failure of Dreams

1.

Nina didn't cross the world to attend tea parties with strangers, and certainly not one hosted by Ramsay Blake.

'I'd no idea you were on party terms with Ramsay,' she said to Zoe.

Zoe muttered something about Facebook and email contact before returning to the topic of Ramsay's afternoon tea. It would be just a small gathering, she said, mainly people from the music world – Ramsay's friends, she added.

Even as children, Nina had doubted Ramsay's capacity for friendship: he was drawn to people for what they could do for him, not for affection or enjoyment. That Zoe counted herself a friend of his suggested she supplied him with a good deal more than the occasional email or Facebook post. Nina, in contrast, had no intention of wasting her time on Ramsay, but mindful of not hurting Zoe and practised in old habits she chose to side-step the truth.

'Since Daniel cleared out I've rather lost my party mood.' And not wanting to manipulate too vigorously added, 'I'm sure it'll return.'

'Not if you continue to avoid the party situation.' Zoe, it seemed, was less mindful of her sensibilities.

She and Zoe had taken up their usual positions in the kitchen, filling in an hour before meeting Sean for lunch. Now Zoe leaned across the bench, her face was close, her expression stern.

'Please Nina – do it for me.'

Zoe pressed a little harder and of course Nina capitulated: Ramsay didn't matter but her sister did. And a couple of hours one afternoon for a sister whose life was so short on pleasure was, she decided, a small concession.

With the decision now made and with a firmness that not even Zoe could oppose, she shifted the conversation away from Ramsay on to the more congenial ground of the children. Callum was still at music camp and Hayley was staying with a friend down at Torquay; both had telephoned that morning.

'It's Hayley's summer of being a surfer chick,' Zoe said, returning to her side of the bench. 'She's having the time of her life. Just like we did.'

'You're not worried?' Hayley was only sixteen.

'We weren't any older and we managed.'

And of course Zoe was right, but today's sixteen-year-olds seemed far less equipped to deal with the world than they had been.

'It's true about most of them,' Zoe said. 'But Hayley's sensible, and Elliot and I have put in a concerted effort to provide her with experiences beyond the digital world.' Zoe was rubbing a smudge on the brilliant marble. Now she looked up. 'Whatever Elliot's shortcomings, he can't be faulted as a father.' And returned to her cleaning. 'Hayley's formed a band with some of her friends – she plays lead guitar, and she's got quite a pretty voice.' She laughed. 'We've used the same approach with Callum and utterly failed. He's fine as long as there's a piano or a computer in reach, but deprive him of a keyboard and all he can do is sleep.' In the silence that followed she reached for her cigarettes. She was fiddling with an unlit one when she said, 'Ramsay considers Callum very talented; he thinks he'll go far.'

There was so much implied in Zoe's comment – Ramsay was constantly on her mind, Ramsay was involved with Callum's music, Ramsay's opinion mattered to her – and Nina assiduously ignored the lot.

'I suppose there's no chance of Sean coming to Ramsay's tea party.' She and Sean could be outsiders together. Then she shook her head. 'No, I suppose not.'

She had seen Sean several times since her return to Melbourne and he'd made it clear that nothing had changed between him and Ramsay. They continued to avoid each other, any communication being mediated by lawyers and accountants. At the rare family gatherings they both attended, they kept their distance. No contact to speak of for more than half a lifetime, yet Nina was in no doubt that Sean still suffered the loss of his brother.

'I don't know how I want things to be with Ramsay now,' he had said the other day. 'I just wish I cared less.'

As for Sean and Zoe, they met only when Nina was in Melbourne and always at her instigation; they wouldn't bother with each other if not for her. What, she now asked herself, was she hanging on to? What absurd hopes? What useless nostalgia? Surely it was time to accept the situation and let them both off the hook. She was about to suggest to

Zoe that she needn't come to today's lunch when Zoe's mobile rang. Zoe glanced at the screen, grabbed her cigarettes and went out to the patio.

Nina sat alone in the perfect kitchen. She could hear the low burr of Zoe's voice but couldn't decipher the words. She worried about Zoe and she worried about Sean, but that was no reason to force them together. Sean, like Zoe, would be relieved if the threesome lunches were to cease; after all, what was Zoe to him now other than an unnecessary reminder of his losses?

Of the four of them, it was Sean who had been most affected by the events of their youth. If not for George, he would have remained in Melbourne, studied music and lived out his days as Ramsay's devoted factotum. But George did arrive and he did take over Ramsay, and Sean couldn't get away fast enough.

Nina had witnessed it all, and as George's crimes mounted up – Sean described his takeover of Ramsay as a con and a theft – the more strenuously did he contemplate his own escape. She and Sean would hang out in her bedroom with the *Reader's Digest Atlas of Australia*, while he weighed up various options. He might head up north to Queensland or the Northern Territory, find work on a property, or perhaps he'd try fruit-picking on the Murray; as his final exams drew closer he decided to hitch a ride on a boat – anywhere would do. In the end it was Sydney and a journalism cadetship that removed him from Raleigh Court. Nina still had a year of high school and Sydney might have been Timbuktu for all the freedom she had. What about me? she had said, begging him to reconsider. What about me? But he remained uncharacteristically firm.

'You don't have to stay here either.'

Twelve months later and equipped with a scholarship to the University of Sydney she had joined him. She needed to get away too, not from George and Ramsay, but Zoe and Ramsay. For the next four years she and Sean lived together. They were each other's best friend, confidant, bullshit detector and family. Sean still played the violin and would pull it out after a boozy dinner with friends, or play just for the two of them when the night was advanced and the rest of the world was quiet. He played, but not seriously. He said he was finished with music, he said he was finished with the past. 'All except you,' he said to Nina. He never mentioned his brother. Indeed, Ramsay might have ceased to exist for all he entered their daily lives, yet being so assiduously avoided he was ever present. And he never mentioned Zoe either. Not then, nor now.

He was shockingly promiscuous in those days and, Nina realised, extraordinarily lucky. By the time everyone was advocating safe sex, he had already feasted on all that liberated gay sex had to offer. It was as if the single grand passion of his childhood – Ramsay – had fragmented into the frenetic, short-lived pleasures that characterised those years. He kept odd hours owing to both work and play, but unlike her he needed little sleep. He would come home very late and thump and rattle through the flat. In the morning she'd be grey and grumbling because of her disturbed sleep and he'd be fresh and apologetic. It seemed to her that no matter how much he imbibed and how little he slept – and they did bear a relation to each other – he wore his excesses lightly. Compact and perfectly proportioned Sean, with sleek hair, golden skin and features that could grace a classical Greek statue. 'My Aussie Adonis,' Nina called him.

AIDS and an expanding career had both contributed to a tapering off of his tart years, and by the early 1990s that period of his life was over. She was already living in London. Sean had several postings in the Asia–Pacific region. Why can't you get sent to London? she said. We could set up house here, you and me together in one of the world's greatest cities. And just when she thought she had convinced him, just when she thought he was on his way, he met Tom.

It was Sydney, early 1994, during a sabbatical in which Sean planned to write a book on Asian political and economic alliances. He met Tom and his life changed. He never wrote the book. Later that year, he returned to the paper and at last received a European posting – the Central European desk and, as history would prove, the place to be. Europe was far closer than Asia, and Nina was pleased for that; but Australia, because of Tom was now home. Tom said he would keep the home fires burning while Sean flitted about the world – with the one condition that their base be in Melbourne. It was not Sean's preference, but given everything else was on his terms, he had little choice but to agree.

For Sean, both the relationship with Tom and his career, firstly as a foreign correspondent and later as a travel writer, had endured, the career more smoothly than the relationship. There had been a couple of years when Sean and Tom had separated, during which time both men had explored their freedom and found it wanting. Their home continued to be in Melbourne, and Sean still intended to write a book, although the topic had changed with the years. The latest was to focus on South America.

It was quiet now on the patio. Nina leaned back on her stool; she could see Zoe standing near the steps. She was smoking and staring out at the garden, deep in thought; this had been no breezy chat with one of her friends. Nina checked her watch, they'd need to be leaving soon, and probably too late now to change their plans. But this would be the last time, she told herself again. No more threesome lunches.

When Zoe returned to the kitchen she made no reference to her phone call. Instead she asked whether Tom was joining them for lunch.

'He decided to let us wander memory lane without him,' Nina replied. A shame, she now thought: Tom would have helped defuse tensions between Zoe and Sean.

A cool change had been forecast with a blustery southerly and a plummeting of the temperature. The sky had already clouded over, and while as often as not in this blazing summer the predicted cool change petered out, this one might actually eventuate. Nina was wearing a slip of a sundress, and she and Zoe went upstairs to find her a jacket.

There is something private about marital bedrooms, or so Nina had always felt, and she hesitated at the doorway. Yet she could see that Zoe and Elliot's private space was as cool and impersonal as the rest of the house: white walls, white carpet, a touch of blue in the bedspread. There was a large glass sculpture perched on a chest of drawers, two bedside tables each with a chrome lamp and a short pile of books (hard to imagine her sister and brother-in-law sitting up in bed together reading), a seascape in rough seas' impasto on one wall, and on the opposite wall a large black-and-white photograph of Callum and Hayley. The entire space was as tidy as a hotel room.

'Come in, come in,' Zoe called from her dressing-room.

Nina crossed the pristine carpet, stepped into the alcove, and was pulled up short. The mess was breathtaking. The dressing-room – similar in size to Nina's entire bedroom at home – resembled the pavement outside a Salvos store after a weekend of neighbourhood spring-cleaning. There were heaps of clothes on the floor, clothes shoved onto shelves, bras, singlets, shirts, dresses, pants, everything tossed in together, shoes, handbags, even jewellery.

Zoe was not in the least embarrassed. 'Excuse the mess,' she said off-handedly, and burrowed into one of the drawers.

This then was the foul rag-and-bone shop of Zoe's heart. There was something both sad and exciting about it. Her sister was not the complete tidy object. Not yet.

2.

Just over an hour later Nina and Zoe were sitting with Sean Blake in a riverside trattoria drinking Chianti ('It's the cocktail hour somewhere in the world,' Sean said) and making swift work of a platter of antipasto, or at least Sean and Nina were, Zoe confined herself to the wine. Sean, once so neat and compact, was now a swollen, slapdash version of his former self.

'I'm afraid my mountain-trekking days are over,' he said, tucking into a pile of fried anchovies and aioli.

Nina smiled affectionately at him. 'I'd suggest even a walk around the block would test you.'

There was nothing remaining of her Aussie Adonis. His skin hung in jowls, there was the glimmer of a dewlap, his colour was pasty. Long days and late nights, too much food and booze all had left their mark.

'I don't know how you keep going,' she said.

He shrugged as if to say he didn't know either. 'Tom says it's time I settled down. Gave up my wanderings. Grew up.'

'Does Tom think travel writers are caught in an arrested stage of development?' Zoe asked.

'Not all of them, but in my case, yes. Boys' own adventures. Escaping adult responsibilities. Hanging on to the golden years.'

They'd been talking non-stop from the first hello. There'd been no need to worry about Sean and Zoe, they seemed entirely at ease with each other – a fact that underscored the weight of early friendship, of the period prior to George Tiller's entrée into their lives. They decided on another bottle of Chianti and more antipasto. Sean added fries – 'For a well-balanced meal,' he said.

'The Rasputin of Raleigh Court', Sean had dubbed George all those years ago. First he'd conned Marion Blake, there was a short-lived period when he courted Sean, but really it was only Ramsay he ever wanted. And Ramsay, who needed someone to organise his life while he played the piano, was easily acquired.

When the wine arrived, Zoe filled the glasses then sat back in her chair, separate from the conversation.

'Are you ever tempted to contact Ramsay?' Nina asked.

Sean shook his head. 'It'd be pointless. The person I miss is my teenage brother, and after years of George and fame I expect there's little of him left.'

Nina glanced at Zoe, but there was nothing to be read in her face.

Nina mentioned Ramsay's afternoon-tea party. 'It'd be much more pleasant for me if you came too,' she said to him, with another glance in her sister's direction. Zoe made no response.

Again Sean shook his head, his pudgy face looking sad and aged. A moment later he excused himself and went to the bathroom while Zoe took the opportunity to go outside for a cigarette. When all three were seated again, Sean asked Nina if she ever heard from Daniel.

She tried to keep her face unreadable, her emotions under the skin. 'Never.'

'You two were my model for domestic happiness,' he said. 'You showed me it was possible without having to spend half the year abroad.' Sean breathed an exaggerated sigh. 'Romance, it's such a tease.' And then more seriously: 'I emailed him, emailed Daniel soon after he absconded with the research assistant.'

Her grievance must have shown for he reached out and took her hand. 'There was no point in mentioning it to you unless there was something to report. And there wasn't. Daniel didn't even reply. And yet,' he nodded to accentuate what he was saying, 'I can't imagine this has worked out well for him. And not just the new girl, but all he's lost.'

'That's if he appreciated what he had in the first place.' Despite her sitting back from the table, Zoe was clearly following the conversation.

'Loss is an excellent teacher,' Sean said quietly.

It was a loaded statement from someone more inclined to joke about emotions. But then he had witnessed so much as a journalist – of loss, of brutality, of suffering. It took a few moments before Nina realised he was probably referring to Ramsay not his work, but by then the conversation had moved on.

'So tell me about the job that brought you home.' Sean spoke in a sprightly, let's-change-the-topic tone of voice.

And so she launched into the TIF project, beginning with the group itself. 'They're dedicated to human rights. They're idealistic people, undeniably good people. But,' she frowned and shook her head, 'they're so naive, a pack of innocents. They don't have a clue of the trouble they're inviting.'

'What's the problem?' Sean said through a mouthful of fries.

'The group itself is the main problem. It describes itself as diverse – there're Catholics, Jews, both Shia and Sunni Muslims, Hindus, Buddhists –'

'The complete box of Smarties,' Sean said with a laugh.

'Yes,' she said, grimacing rather than laughing, 'there's one of everything. But while their religious beliefs and cultural backgrounds are different, they all share the same liberal humanist values, the same commitments to social justice.'

'Who exactly are they?' In all the time Zoe had spent with Nina this was the first question she had asked about the job.

'There's a core committee of six to eight people, all of them people of faith, different faiths. Some are members of the clergy, more or less equal numbers of women and men. Then there's a larger group of supporters that includes educators, artists, writers, performers, athletes, more clergy, politicians, each of whom, I suspect, are jostling for a piece of the action – should the project ever come to fruition.'

'They sound like an agreeable crowd to me,' Sean said. 'The sort of people the world needs.'

'You're probably right, but not for this job. Entirely absent are representatives from the orthodox arms of the various religious groups. Although of far greater concern are the ultra-orthodox. All those zealots punchy with militant piety aren't the sort to remain silent.'

'And the monument?'

'To diversity and courage, to freedom of expression and a common humanity. They want a monument to the best of human qualities.'

'And what might that look like?' Zoe asked.

Nina shrugged. 'I've no idea.'

'But is this really a monument project?' Sean's question was more in the way of a statement because he didn't wait for Nina's response. 'Monuments are erected to remind us of significant people and events in the past. Wars, soldiers, earthquakes, 9/11, genocide, independence movements, Mother Teresa, Nelson Mandela, monarchs and leaders. Monuments are an aid to remembering. This isn't the case with the proposed TIF monument.'

'It's to recall all that's best in us,' Nina said. 'All that unites us – or rather should unite us.'

A smile spread over Sean's face. 'Well I think this project is one of your better ones.'

She detected the criticism in his words. 'You don't approve of what I do?'

He topped up his drink, he topped up all their drinks before he answered. 'I'm in no position to approve or disapprove. I hardly know why you do as you do.'

'But the results,' she heard the defensiveness in her voice, 'the monuments, you know about those.'

He nodded. 'And the ones I've seen are attractive and moving. But to me at least, rather than being true to history they often side-step it.'

Nina did not respond immediately. It was an aspect of her work that made her uneasy too. The Lise Meitner project she'd just finished was a prime example. And so many grand war memorials that were paeans to nationalism rather than tributes to the fallen. And there was a surprising number of post–World War Two memorials in Central Europe erected to victims of fascism that failed to mention the main victims, the Jews, a neglect that suggested the widespread anti-Semitism of the past had a good deal of breath left in it. She helped herself to some feta, spread it with studied care on a heel of bread. There was no simple defence: she truly believed that a knowledge of the past enriched understanding of the present; at the same time she also knew the past was an ever-changing country.

'Monuments tend to be as voluble about the present as the events and people they're intended to commemorate,' she began. 'The preserving fluid of history, of all memories come to that, is constantly topped up with fresh supplies.' Sean smiled at one of her own favourite metaphors. 'History often gets a bollocking, you're right about that, but people want remembrances, they want to honour the past.'

Sean was quick to respond. 'But remembrance and history aren't the same thing. Remembrance selects from the past, it appropriates a snippet of history for a purpose, perhaps to justify a grievance or a recent act of aggression, and ignores practically everything else.'

Nina was about to say it was better for some remembering than none at all, but he was not finished.

'During my journalism days I reported on history in the making, I saw the damage justified by remembrance. Today's violence often has roots in a single powerful event in history while the rest of the past simply withers in its shadow. In the mid-nineties the Serbs justified their slaughter of the Bosnian Muslims because of a battle fought in 1453. As if nothing else had occurred in five-and-a-half centuries.' His face wore an expression of disgust. 'And over in Israel–Palestine, all those settlers are prepared to fight for land they say was promised to them in biblical times. Biblical times! Remembrance so easily reduces history to nationalism, and nationalism is a thug. Less nationalism means fewer wars, and fewer wars means fewer war memorials.' He started to giggle, sounding remarkably like his twenty-year-old self. 'But no need to worry about your livelihood, Nina. You can build monuments to peace instead.'

There was nothing funny in what he said, she felt under attack. 'But there *are* monuments to peace, hundreds of them across the world.'

'But the peace they promote is peace that comes after a particular war. The peace is cemented to war. You don't fight for peace. It makes no sense. You can defend it – with values, with laws, even with customs, but not with weapons.' He leaned across the table; she thought he was reaching for food, but it was her hand he wanted. He pressed it between his own. 'When it's peace you're defending it's moral territory you're concerned about, not land, not ridges and valleys, not villages and towns, not an enemy.' He emphasised that last word. 'If you lose sight of the values, the moral territory, you become a barbarian. Just think of all those young boys wielding guns and machetes, turned into killers before they're old enough to acquire a moral compass.'

He squeezed her hand more tightly and then released it. In the silence that followed he popped a cold chip in his mouth and washed it down with wine. When next he spoke his voice had lost its seriousness. 'Fewer memorials to war, I say, fewer monuments to heroes, and more that focus on peace and ordinary human qualities, the things that unite us. And build them quickly, before what's good in us becomes vestigial.'

He reached for the bottle and refilled his glass. 'I'm coming to think we need more forgetting – or now that I know they exist, more people like your TIF group.'

He sounded quite jaunty, but Nina was aghast. 'You surely don't believe that deliberate forgetting is possible?'

He nodded. 'I do. Before post-traumatic stress disorder was invented it happened all the time.'

'And shell-shock in the Great War?' she said. 'That was just PTS by another name.'

'Yes, it was. But how do you explain all those other soldiers, the majority of them, who survived the trenches and went on to lead satisfying lives? And what about those survivors of the Nazi terror who lost everything, their families, their communities, who suffered unimaginable trauma yet managed to forge productive lives in countries far removed from Europe? And the Vietnamese and Cambodians who despite experiencing indescribable terror in their own countries left it all behind and built successful futures elsewhere. And all those Armenians, suddenly homeless and scattered across the world, yet managing to make their mark.'

Sean was on a roll. 'People are remarkably resilient, or at least they used to be – they don't have much opportunity these days. When some terrible violence occurs, a massacre, an air-crash, 9/11 itself, one of the first responses is to send in the trauma counsellors. The same occurs when there's a natural disaster – earthquakes, floods, tsunamis. I think it'd be wiser to wait, let the dust settle, see how the people fare. Forgetting is an effective means of moving forward after trauma. And if you're still in any doubt, how else to explain all those Nazis who supervised massacres and herded Jews into the gas chambers, who after the war enjoyed long, satisfying and contented lives? Forgetting works equally well for perpetrators as well as victims.'

He sat back, finished at last.

'I think you're tough on human suffering,' Nina said.

He shrugged. 'Or perhaps I've faith in human resilience.'

'But won't the truth seep out at some later time?' Zoe spoke quietly.

He didn't look at her as he replied. 'It might, and it might not. The fact is most people manage. Even with the catastrophic Japanese tsunami of a while ago, the experts estimated that post-traumatic stress might have occurred in twenty per cent of those affected. That means eighty per cent managed to move ahead using other resources. Resources like community, family, cultural traditions –'

'And national pride and traditional notions of honour,' Nina interjected.

'Yes,' he said turning to her, 'those too. But I'd prefer to lay the emphasis on community and a determined looking-forward.'

Clearly Sean was not averse to a little cherry-picking of his own. Nina smiled at him. 'You're as selective in argument as others are selective in remembering and forgetting.'

'Yes,' and he was laughing. 'But all in a good cause.'

The two of them had always enjoyed a good stoush. And they probably would have continued, but waiters were moving around them, setting up tables for the evening meal.

'You're welcome to stay on,' one waiter said. 'But Thursday's a busy night so you'll need to book.'

'Occupation doesn't grant any privileges then?' Sean asked.

The waiter laughed. 'I'm afraid not.'

Sean looked first at Nina and then let his gaze linger on Zoe. 'I've learned that from direct experience.'

A few minutes later they settled the bill and left the café. Out in the street Zoe dashed off, muttering something about an appointment. It was the first Nina knew of it and decided her sister just wanted to get away.

Nina gave Sean a hug. 'Even when you're impossible I love you.'

He smiled and kissed her loudly on both cheeks.

As he turned to leave she tried one last time. 'You won't change your mind and come to Ramsay's tea party?'

Sean twisted around, she saw his smile fade. 'I once had a brother who was everything to me. I'll not get him back over tea and scones.'

3.

Sean arrived home in time for the evening news. He switched on the TV, made coffee, changed into tracksuit pants, the only clothes that were comfortable these days, and was waylaid by a text from Tom: *Don't forget, not home for dinner. Viewing tie king's collection!* By the time he settled on the couch with his coffee the news bulletin had moved to sport. He lowered the sound and stared at the parade of footballers, rugby players, basketballers and swimmers as they moved over the screen. Several minutes passed before he realised he'd been watching these well-buffed, under-dressed men with what could only be described as habituated, mindless appreciation. He turned the TV off – he was becoming a pathetic old perv – selected the music cache in his phone, set it to shuffle and popped it on the dock. He lay on the couch and closed his eyes, although remained alert. It was a game he played, a musical Russian roulette: chance would select Ramsay from his music library, but he, Sean, would not.

He had not enjoyed the afternoon with Nina and Zoe; his body felt leaden and his mind was running on the spot. He had eaten and drunk far too much, as if food and drink could dispel the tensions between him and Zoe. Nina seemed unaware. She was always so keen for the three of them to get together – just like the old days, she said. And rather than a long and murky explanation of grievances he should have off-loaded years ago, he had agreed to the lunch. The plan had been to float through the meal. The plan had failed.

It was not that he held a grudge against Zoe, although he did in fact hold a grudge, or that she and Ramsay were still close, which he resented as well; Zoe reminded him of the loss of Ramsay and all the other losses that flowed from it – music, family life, a sense of home. He didn't want to remember, he never wanted to remember, but there were times when he simply could not help himself. He, who had kept strong amid violence and mayhem, remained thin-skinned when it concerned his brother.

It could have been worse, a lot worse if he had chosen a different life. Tom criticised him for being continually on the move, but it had worked for him; it had helped cloister his pains, and in the process he had made for himself a successful career – two careers: foreign correspondent and travel writer.

Yet now he was beginning to doubt his choices, now he was wondering if he had failed.

Someone, it may have been Auden, coined the phrase 'the well-stocked mind'. His was not. This was not a result of sudden looting; rather there'd been a gradual depletion over time so that now, beyond the unwanted thoughts and longings that sloshed about his head, there was little to feed the future.

He had planned to take a sabbatical until April. Tom had insisted they spend more time together – 'If we don't we might find we can't abide each other when we move into the old queers' home' – and he had decided again to tackle his book. He had been unsure which would be more difficult: writing something longer than a couple of thousand words or staying home for longer than a month. But there was no doubt that at this moment, with disquiet and disgust churning through him, he wanted to toss in the book, risk Tom's dire nursing-home scenario and fly far away.

Although he was going nowhere. He lacked the energy to cross the room much less the world. He'd never slept so much yet he was always tired. What he really wanted was to stay right where he was and actually enjoy it, but he had never acquired the knack. He needed, he expected, to be more like Tom.

Whenever he had compared Tom's life with his own, Tom's, with its simplicity, its day-to-day routines, came up poorly. But now, these past few weeks, he was coming to think differently. He felt bound by a sense of monotonous sameness: so many extraordinary travels and adventures, yet he might as well have stashed each in identical cardboard boxes for all the distinctive impressions they had left. As for Tom, he was happy, at this very moment Tom was elated. And even if the tie king's collection was not up to scratch, there would be the story – imagining the possibility, the chase itself, the first glimpse, the silks, the seams, the facings, the provenance – and Tom was a virtuosic story-teller. It was one of the qualities that had attracted Sean when first they met.

At the time Tom worked in the theatre, in costumes – just the sort of job one would expect of a gay man, Sean had joked. Stereotype or not, Tom adored clothes, particularly vintage clothes, and most of all neckwear: ties, bows, cravats, ruffles.

Nearly a year later, with Sean about to take up the Central European desk, Tom announced he was leaving the theatre and moving to Melbourne.

'I'm going to be a neckwear specialist. I'm going to be *the* neckwear specialist. And Melbourne's the place for vintage clothes.'

Sean had tried to change Tom's mind; anywhere, he said, not Melbourne. But as Tom was quick to remind him, Sean would be away most of the time in locations that enabled him to pursue his career. And Tom needed to be in a place that provided him with similar opportunities.

Tom was a large, flamboyant man, and an enthusiastic ambassador for his passion. He had bow-tie occasions and cravat occasions, there were even Texan shoe-string tie occasions. And parties, usually all-gay affairs, when he would wear one of his prized Swanky Yankees, wide gaudy silks sporting a scantily clad image of a woman. Of all clothing, as far as Tom was concerned, there was none as nuanced nor as expressive as neckwear.

He kept his collection of several thousand pieces in a showroom located in the old garment district of Flinders Lane in central Melbourne. Specially designed cabinets housed most of the collection, but at any one time there would be several hundred items on display. Friezes of ties adorned the walls, protected by sheets of clear plastic – not your common Perspex, Tom was quick to explain, but high-clarity, non-reflective material with an in-built UV factor. 'The same stuff's used in the Louvre,' he said. 'My ties and the *Mona Lisa* are equally well protected.' His neckwear had played in major theatre and opera productions; it had appeared at the Victoria and Albert Museum; it had featured in retrospectives at the major silk manufacturing centres. Tom had forged a living out of his passion for neckwear.

Ties for Tom, the world for Sean, and Sean had never been in doubt about whose work was the more fulfilling. But with him tired and hung-over at seven o'clock on a Thursday evening, sprawled on the couch waiting for his music library to produce Ramsay, and Tom at an appointment that had him sizzling with excitement, he was no longer so sure. Perhaps Zoe was right, that no matter how proficient you might be at deliberate forgetting it will seep out some way.

Sean made fresh coffee and took it to his desk. He opened his laptop, glanced at his email, nothing urgent, leaned back in his chair and closed his eyes. How deeply he had loved his brother, more than he loved anyone, more than he had loved his parents, different from how he loved Tom. He would have done anything for him. Plenty of people thought they understood Ramsay, but only Sean really did. Or at least that was what he believed in those long-ago days. But he didn't understand him, because he never thought Ramsay would choose anyone over him.

He didn't want to think about Ramsay, and yet there were times like this when he was helpless at holding him at bay. How different his life would have been if Ramsay had loved him better. And he knows he should be grateful he had not. For without Ramsay's rejection there would not have been friends, there would not have been a career, and there certainly would not have been the long relationship with Tom. If Ramsay had loved him better, there would have been only Ramsay. But it's hard to be grateful when you have suffered such a loss. And like a death, the loss persists. All those years, all the life Sean had accumulated since, it made no difference to the loss. And where did he place the blame? Where does he still place the blame? On George Tiller. George Tiller arrived and everything changed.

4.

'I hate him,' Ramsay said. 'He's old, he's ugly and he's a know-all. And he sells stuff to dentists. What sort of job is that?'

Sean wasn't sure how he felt about this new man in their mother's life, a man she described as special, but with Ramsay so certain and Sean terrified of the dentist the issue was soon settled.

'I hate him too, Rams,' he said. And after a moment, 'If she marries him, do you think he'll make us go to the dentist more often?'

Ramsay ignored the question. 'How could she choose such a loser after Dad – and so soon.'

The two boys were hiding out in the tree-house with a packet of Tim Tams and a stubby of beer. Their father had died just four months previously, died in his sleep of a heart attack. He'd checked on the boys as he always did before retiring to his divan in the study. He had watched the late news, again his usual habit, and then he went to sleep.

He never woke up.

'There was nothing wrong with his heart,' Marion said. 'Parts of his body,' she shrugged, 'they'd given up the ghost years ago, but his heart was just fine.'

A post-mortem examination revealed a congenital heart fault, something which, according to the doctor, could have killed him at any time.

This was a week after the death, and the publicly grieving widow had become a bottomless trough of anger and tears at home.

'He might have done things differently if he'd known,' she said. 'Might have put his heart under less strain.'

Their mother's voice was quiet and cold, resentment was plastered over her face. At the time the boys, just fourteen and thirteen and not yet aware of the subtle signs of grown-ups that reveal the true state of their feelings, read nothing in her words or indeed her raw moods. A couple of months later, however, just before she produced George, she told them their father had kept a girlfriend, not 'a brief weekend affair' but a relationship that had lasted four years.

'Four years,' she said. 'A whole other life.' She seemed to drive a spike through each word. And it was odd, Sean found himself thinking, how she managed to look angry and sad at exactly the same time.

She told them the girlfriend had revealed herself in a telephone call a few days after their father's death. She wanted to meet Marion, she said, 'in order to discuss the future'.

'I'd no intention of dignifying their liaison with a meeting,'

Marion said, with that haughty attitude she assumed whenever she was hurt or sad.

So the boys came to understand that their parents had not been so happy after all; certainly their mother was very unhappy with their father now he was no longer around. But that was no reason to inflict George upon them.

'I think we should make it so miserable for him,' Ramsay said, 'that he packs up his dental instruments and looks for another widow.'

Despite the seriousness of the situation, Sean could not help laughing. Ramsay was about to embark on one of his campaigns, and once Ramsay put his mind to something it was sure to be successful. It was the way his brother was, and Sean different from him in this respect, in practically all respects. Ramsay's determination whether applied to music, his protection of Sean against the school bullies, or getting rid of their mother's new boyfriend was a quality Sean truly admired.

Ramsay's plan to make George's life a misery went into immediate effect. They feigned deafness when he spoke to them, they pretended he didn't exist when he entered their mother's conversation. Should they answer the phone when George rang they would not fetch their mother as requested, instead they'd leave him dangling on the end of the line. At every opportunity they exchanged 'isn't he a dickhead' expressions, exaggerated and unambiguous facial contortions always in full view of George himself. When George began to stay overnight – in their father's house if not his actual bed – they would pinch single socks, one shoe, and knowing how much their mother disliked body odour, his deodorant.

'He shouldn't keep his stuff in our bathroom anyway,' Ramsay said.

After several lost objects, George was given his own cupboard in their mother's bathroom, one of the few in the house with a key.

'He's so pathetic,' Ramsay said. 'He doesn't even have the guts to fight us.'

And then George moved in. George's possessions replaced their father's: his daggy clothes, his assortment of teas – 'He's more grandma than man' – his two bikes, his war books, the photo of his dead son, his reclining armchair. The boys refused to talk to him, they refused to eat with him. In the end Marion allowed them to have their meals in the kitchen in front of the small TV while she and George ate in the dining-room.

'Do you think we should give him a taste of Dad's rat arsenic,' Sean said one day. 'Not to kill him, just enough to make him sick.'

'Good thinking, little brother.' Ramsay was clearly impressed.

Out they went to the garden shed. At the end of the highest shelf was the tin; Ramsay climbed the small step-ladder and retrieved it. Across the lid and again on the side their father had written: ARSENIC! POISON! DO NOT TOUCH!

Ramsay levered the lid off and studied the contents. 'I wonder how much you'd need to make him sick but not poison him to death.'

Sean watched and waited.

'There are no instructions,' Ramsay said. 'Although Dad never used much for the rats, maybe a teaspoon.' He thought for a moment. 'A teaspoon to kill a few small rats couldn't possibly kill a grown man like George.'

But something else must have occurred to him because a few moments later he replaced the lid and pulled out a large bag of blood and bone. It was nearly full and he buried the poison deep within.

'No one will find it there,' he said, and shoved the bag at the very back of the shed. He piled some old junk in front so it was completely hidden. 'Only you and I know where it is,' he said. 'We'll use it when we have to.'

The campaign to remove George went up a notch after they pulled back from the poison. The piano became a primary site of persecution. George had simultaneously confessed to a love of baroque music, of Bach in particular, and an inability to tolerate atonal compositions. Ramsay, rather partial to Bach himself, now requested his teacher set him modern works, the more discordant the better. Mr Orloff was thrilled. He had always said it was a matter of maturity, that there would come a time when Ramsay would understand the power of contemporary music. At the time of asking, Ramsay had not, but he was prepared to put up with his own discomfort if it caused greater discomfort for George.

When George was not home Ramsay would play the music he fancied, although it was curious, he said to Mr Orloff, how learning a piece, taking it inside yourself, opened out the work to you in a way that would not happen with more cursory contact. And he loved the challenge of these ferociously difficult works. Mr Orloff could not have been more pleased. As for George, he kept his silence, but he must, so Ramsay thought, be finding life at the Blake house increasingly irksome.

Sean certainly was. This new music sounded like traffic noise, or a factory filled with clattering machines, but he knew it was all for a good cause. So rather than suffer as he was sure George must be suffering, he escaped next door to Nina's place whenever Ramsay took to the moderns. There was one piece by an Australian composer that was particularly awful. He told Ramsay it sounded like a flock of cockatoos squawking for fifteen drawn-out minutes. At first Ramsay said nothing, but gradually a smile appeared and a nodding of his head. The piece was called 'Flight', he said, only now did he understand why.

'You surely don't like it?' Sean was incredulous.

Ramsay was still smiling. 'I do rather.'

It didn't matter what Ramsay thought of the music, Sean decided, as long as George continued to hate it. But this new music seemed to be growing on him too. He would stand outside the piano room and listen while Ramsay practised, and he had bought a compilation tape of the best of the moderns – Sean had seen it in his car.

The months passed and the boys maintained their assault on George, although in retrospect Sean realised the sting had gone from Ramsay's attacks. One Saturday afternoon Sean overheard George talking about Ramsay on the phone, describing him as extraordinary. Of course Ramsay was extraordinary. Rams had played on all the major concert platforms in the country and later that year he was going overseas to play for music's most important people. Of course he was extraordinary. But that was beside the point. George had no right to talk about Ramsay. Ramsay wasn't his son.

It was the night following the phone call when Sean first realised that he and Ramsay were out of kilter. Sean had hopped into Ramsay's bed and was scratching his back in the way Ramsay liked. He told him about George's phone call.

'He was talking about you to some stranger, Rams. Acting like he was your dad.'

There was a long pause during which Sean assumed Ramsay was devising a new horror to inflict on George; it might even be time for the arsenic. So it came as a shock to hear Ramsay say that perhaps they should lighten up.

'I don't think George is as bad as we thought.'

'Of course he is.' Sean's hands left their stroking and clenched into fists. 'He's taken over our mother and he wants to take us over too. Or at least he wants to take you over. I've seen him watching you, Rams.'

Ramsay twisted around. 'Forget him, Sean. We've got better things to do.' And when Sean didn't move he said again, 'Forget him.'

Sean went along with their usual fooling, but he was worried: Ramsay was losing his perspective and George was winning him over. In the end Ramsay kicked him out of bed. 'You're hopeless tonight,' he said.

'And you've lost your mind if you think that George is okay.'

'Grow up, little brother.'

That night Sean lay awake for hours. He might be younger than Ramsay, but it was only by fourteen months, and while Ramsay would always be best when it came to music, with his own violin going so well he was no musical slouch. And as good as Ramsay was at maths, Sean was better. Ramsay told him to grow up when it came to George, but Sean had no sense of lagging behind. It was Ramsay who had changed; Ramsay for some inexplicable reason was being sucked in by George in the same way their mother had been.

From that night on Sean took every opportunity to help his brother see who George really was, not a single fault escaped comment. But increasingly Ramsay failed to respond. As the months passed Sean was forced to watch his brother and George become friends. It was George now who sat in the music room while Ramsay practised.

'And Ramsay lets him,' Sean said to Nina. 'He's letting the bastard stay in there. He's actually performing for him, showing off.'

How many times can you beg someone to notice you, to love you like they once did? Sean tried but Ramsay would hear no ill spoken of George. Sean soon came to realise it was either him or George, but if Ramsay refused to hear criticism of George, how then to put forward his own case? 'I miss you,' Sean would say. 'Don't you miss the fun we used to have? Our music? The Raleigh Posse?'

'Grow up, little brother,' was Ramsay's response.

Ramsay had far more important things on his mind. He was planning to be the most famous pianist in the world, more famous than Glenn Gould, more famous than Brendel or Horowitz, he wanted to be as famous as Liszt. And George, he explained to Sean, shared his dream. George believed in him, George was as driven as Ramsay himself. And so, it seems, he had remained, although with George, now over eighty, he must surely be slowing down.

Sean had never found it in himself to be kind about George, yet now he wondered how George would judge his own life and achievements. For several decades he had lived for Ramsay; he clearly thought it was enough or else he would not have stayed. And, if given the chance, Sean would have done the same, so perhaps it was fortunate that Ramsay had denied him. But still he missed his brother, felt a fierce longing for him, wished he could have his work, his life with Tom and a portion set aside for Ramsay as well. He knew it was impossible: it was either full-time Ramsay or nothing at all, but it didn't stop him from wanting it to be different.

It was eight o'clock and hours before Tom would be home. Sean opened YouTube and clicked on to his favourites; he watched his brother at the piano. His heart quickened, his spirits soared. Ramsay at the piano was sublime. No one could help but love him.

Chapter 4. The Old Prodigy

Nina and Zoe were seated on a small couch in Ramsay Blake's living room, the same couch that had occupied this spot when they were children. Directly in front, but with a low coffee table between them, was Ramsay himself, perched on a stool with an aged black-and-white spaniel at his feet. Surrounding him in a semi-circle were a dozen people, all associated with the music world. Since their arrival twenty minutes earlier Ramsay had not paused for breath; not even when George ushered in a new guest did he stop talking. Ramsay was holding court, so it seemed to Nina, and everyone appeared content in their subordinate roles.

She, in contrast, felt detached, bemused and, impossible to ignore, resentful. It was not simply an afternoon given to Ramsay when there were so many other people she would prefer to see, there was all the effort she had wasted on him over the years, skirting around that toxic pool in her memory where she had dumped him. Ramsay Blake was still the spoiled child, still so self-centred as to be impervious to others, but now, watching him at the centre of this group yet oddly sealed off from it, all she registered was a mild distaste. And George too, while he continued to manage Ramsay's life with masterful disregard for anything other than Ramsay's gain, this ageing retainer and mindful host was infuriatingly benign.

Ramsay was very neat – had he always been so neat? – a man who took care of his appearance, or someone did. He was still slender, with a pale angelic face, and despite its being the middle of the afternoon, he had that polished just-shaved look, easily achieved by twenty-year-olds but usually beyond the scope of more mature skin. His hair, satiny and straight, was parted casually to the side in floppy public-schoolboy style, and, like the skin, a nostalgic longing for most men in their late forties; the hair was darker than it used to be, more burnt butter than the blond of her memory. He was dressed in a flowing white collarless shirt open at the neck and tucked loosely into washed-out jeans.

An attractive man who was the focus of this group but not part of it, he was, it seemed to Nina, a mixture of innocence and blind narcissism. Most curious of all was that Ramsay did not seem to be aware of his attractiveness. In fact, he was a man entirely without sexual allure. Even when he looked at Zoe, and of all the people in the room she was the only one he looked at, he was more watchful than connected, more observant than engaged. Although every now and then when their gaze met, something passed between them and she saw them both soften, her tensed sister trapped in her impossible marriage and Ramsay caught within the strain of being Ramsay Blake.

Earlier in the week when she and Zoe were preparing dinner, Zoe had said that life was stressful for Ramsay. 'Just to know what to do, what to say, what's humorous, what's insulting, is hard for some people. It's always been hard for Ramsay.'

Nina had long believed that Ramsay's oddities veered towards craziness, and said as much.

Zoe wore a sad little smile. 'Not crazy, more under-cooked in the ways of human nature.'

Half-baked in human sociality but an ancient when it came to music, and not the first time Nina had witnessed how genius stunts growth in all but its own specialty.

'Genius doesn't know how to wash the dishes, nor does it care,' Zoe had continued, adding sliced tomatoes to a salad. 'In fact, genius is uninterested in everything outside itself.' She grabbed a carrot and started to chop. 'None of which matters as long as genius is served by a reliable and competent handmaiden, someone willing to negotiate the ordinary demands of life.' Now she was slaughtering the carrot. 'And for Ramsay, George Tiller fills that role to perfection.'

'Is George indispensable?' Nina had asked.

Zoe tossed the carrot into the salad bowl, and started to vent her discontents on a cucumber. 'Ramsay thinks he is.'

Surely Zoe wouldn't want to be handmaiden to Ramsay, Nina had thought at the time. Yet now, observing her in Ramsay's house, seeing how captured by him she was, she felt afraid for her sister.

It was possible that any handmaiden would suffice, as Zoe had implied, but for George, hovering round Ramsay, ministering to him as he had for decades, it was only Ramsay he had ever wanted. Why, Nina wondered, as she had so many times in the past. Why would a grown man with two surviving children of his own, grandchildren, friends, interests, toss it all in to devote himself to a piano-playing social infant? If George was born to serve, he already had ample people in his life to meet that need. And if it was a simple matter of a son replacement, he could have had two for the one who died, he could have had Sean as well. Why then had he homed in on Ramsay? They lived together, they travelled together, they took their vacations together, never was there a more compatible couple, both of them united in their devotion to Ramsay and his career.

Under George's guidance the career had sky-rocketed, gathering new audiences in traditional and not-so-traditional places. Ramsay had a huge YouTube following: music lovers able to watch him perform in Rome, London, St Petersburg, Uluru at sunset, and at the rim of the great Ngorongoro Crater. Each year brought new projects in exotic locations. But at home familiarity appeared to be the theme. There was the same furniture that Nina remembered from her youth, the same curtains, the same swirling orange and green carpet, all a little worn but clearly well maintained. Everything in the house down to the bulbous, mustard-coloured light-fittings locked the place in the seventies, a decade sadly lacking in style Nina had always thought. Only the walls rescued the house from dowdiness; these were so white and clean, Nina guessed they were freshly painted.

There was a large glass of water on the low table in front of Ramsay and a dish of crisps; he dipped into these while his guests tucked into coffee and cake. There were no side conversations as he talked about contemporary recording techniques, how a technician could substantially change a performance long after the musician had left the concert hall or recording studio without using any actual takes. 'And a technologically inclined schoolboy could take recordings from Brendel, Arrau and Richter, cut, slice, interweave and truly come up with the recording of the century – the last century,' he quickly added. 'Although you'd plunge headlong into the twenty-first if you drew on recordings from Hamelin, Hewitt –'

'And Blake,' someone said.

Ramsay shot a brief smile in the direction of the speaker before continuing. His human weight was a mighty thing in this group; everyone was riveted as so often happens when someone exceptional is in the spotlight. It's as if the light shining on the esteemed figure reflects back on to admirers, showing them to great advantage. Ramsay's guests felt good just by being there. Desultory exposition notwithstanding, Ramsay could talk about the secret life of ants, he could read from the telephone directory, he could relate the history of recording from the beginning to the end of time and his audience would be eagerly attentive. As she absorbed the reverence which surrounded him, Nina realised that Zoe was right: there were many people willing to cater to Ramsay's needs, but George being so cleverly efficient made sure Ramsay wanted only him.

While Ramsay guided his guests into every nook and cranny of contemporary music recording, Nina saw not a shred of the irascible, impatient, lively boy who had once been the undisputed leader of the Raleigh Posse. Here was a cool, passionless man, detached, still childlike, and with a fanatical disregard for opinions not his own. He kept his gaze pitched to the wall just above their heads; he might have been talking to an empty room.

Just one significant remnant of the old Ramsay remained: his smutty jokes. As children they had thought them hilarious, now they were simply embarrassing. Ramsay would tell one of his jokes and laugh uproariously, and his guests would laugh too because the jokes were Ramsay's. The jokes and his laughter were a weird accompaniment in a person so disconcertingly absent.

Zoe took advantage of a rare pause to shift the monologue

to Ramsay's forthcoming trip to China, his seventh tour to that country.

'They love our music,' Ramsay said. 'Western music.'

As he talked about the technical virtuosity of young Chinese pianists, unmatched, he said, anywhere in the world, suddenly but just out of reach Nina knew Ramsay reminded her of someone, a person who had crossed her path recently. She travelled back over the time she had been in Melbourne. When she found no candidate she deliberately returned her attention to the gathering, knowing the lost connection would surface if she stopped searching for it.

A conversation had at last ensued – this was a musically literate group, after all – with others providing their observations of the Chinese scene. Still Ramsay made no eye contact, there was no emotional colouring to his speech, he made hardly any gestures and barely changed his facial expression; though when he talked, the muscles of his forehead constantly tensed and flickered as if he was studying a puzzle and trying to determine how the pieces fitted.

Now that everyone else was talking, Ramsay spoke only occasionally and always in a louder-than-necessary voice. His comments were relevant so he must have been listening despite appearing distracted. He had taken a paper serviette and torn it into strips. He lay the strips in front of him on the coffee table, and as the conversation surged around him, he took each strip and twisted it into a pellet. He piled the pellets in a heap on the table, smoothed it into a tidy cone, then once he was satisfied with the shape, he squashed the cone with the palm of his hand and started the whole process again. No one commented on what he was doing, no one even showed they noticed.

'The man's hardly human,' Nina whispered to her sister.

Zoe shook her head. 'No, he's an exaggerated human. Every quality is more pronounced.'

And again Nina was made aware that this was no casual acquaintance between her sister and Ramsay. In fact, it was dawning on her with some horror that the same attraction binding them as children was still operating – at least it was for her sister; what went on in Ramsay's heart was anyone's guess.

She leaned in closer. 'Do you still play music together?'

Zoe's face was fiercely blank. 'That stopped years ago. When Elliot and I were married.'

No heated duets, just the old romance of them. And email. Email would allow for a Ramsay without the smutty jokes, the paper pellets, the prolix soliloquies, the blatant disregard of everyone else. Email would provide the best of this peculiar man, email, YouTube and recordings of his music. But as much as email can hot-house emotions and as wonderful was Zoe's decade-long duet with Ramsay, surely these were insufficient to maintain a love through twenty years. And what would it say about Zoe if she had hung on to such a futile passion?

There are many people, and perhaps her sister among them, attracted to those with obvious frailties. Zoe did, after all, marry an alcoholic. And perhaps Ramsay's frailties enhanced his appeal. As Zoe had said, the usual aspects of daily life, the sorts of things most people manage without a moment's thought, were not easy for Ramsay. It was his music that held him together. She said he'd die without music.

There had been a period, Nina remembered it well, when Ramsay had lost his music. It was after George moved in with Marion Blake, around the time Sean was side-lined. Ramsay said he had lost his drive; he said his passion for the piano, his desire for music and his confidence to play had deserted him.

Sean tried to help. Zoe tried. His teacher tried. Even Nina, responding to the havoc Ramsay's plight was causing on both sides of the fence, tried to help. But the crisis continued. Then George stepped in and took control, and within days Ramsay's talk of giving up the piano ceased. According to Zoe, George gave Ramsay back his future. It was easy for George to become indispensable.

With several conversations now surging around them, Nina leaned closer to Zoe. 'Does Ramsay know we never liked George?'

Ramsay suddenly looked their way and Nina paused, continuing only when one of his guests claimed him. 'George wasn't a proper parent, yet he behaved as if he was. And there was something else, something –'

'Sleazy?'

'Not sleazy, more that he seemed to be running the show. Running us.'

Zoe said that she and Ramsay never mentioned George. 'He's just there, a fact in Ramsay's life. And besides, you need to be careful what you say about a friend's beloved.' And catching the disbelief on Nina's face, added, 'No, no, nothing like that, but Ramsay's greatest intimate.'

It was hard to think of anyone being Ramsay's intimate, but it was clear her sister knew better, that from the battlements of her own intimacy-starved marriage Zoe knew how Ramsay functioned. And perhaps she always had. How much, Nina found herself wondering, had she not seen in those long-ago days of their childhood? How much was she not seeing now? She observed Ramsay and her sister, she felt the bond that connected them, and it occurred to her – chillingly – that caught between a hostile marriage and a toxic devotion her sister was endangered, like a rare animal, the remnant of its species, eking out an existence in a zoo.

'Will you play for us, Ramsay?' Her sister's voice was barely audible, but Ramsay immediately rose from his stool, smiled at Zoe, his gratitude obvious, and led the way to the music room.

It was a largish room, although smaller than Nina remembered. In contrast with the rest of the house, the paintwork here was peeling and discoloured, and cobwebs dangled at the angles of the walls and windows; the carpet around the piano was threadbare, but beyond the instrument the psychedelic swirls were so bright the carpet might have been newly laid. There was the bay window with a seat built into the curve, and the maroon armchair with the varnish rubbed from its wooden arms, and the couch where her parents used to sit for the Sunday concerts; poised off-centre and catching the light from the bay window was the concert-sized Bechstein. The only decoration in the room was a frieze of photographs that documented Ramsay from child prodigy to premier league, a series of different pianos, different concert platforms, Ramsay in short pants, Ramsay in trousers, Ramsay posing with conductors, other musicians, his mother and father, with prominent people from the arts, and, in so many of the images, with George.

Propped against the wall were several fold-up chairs. People helped themselves and in less than a minute everyone was settled.

'Ravel, *Le Tombeau de Couperin*,' Ramsay said, and began to play.

No matter what she might think of Ramsay as a person and no matter how much she used to resent the hours spent in this room, from the first fall of notes in this, one of her favourite Ravels, Nina was gripped by his music. Ramsay's tempo was quick, although not disconcertingly so – when versions differ too dramatically from the familiar there can be an almost unbearable grating. There was nothing histrionic in his playing; his stiffness, his coolness, his detachment simply slipped away. All fragments just a moment ago, there was now a coherence to him, a completeness, and such vibrancy in the sound produced, even in this Ravel, with the trickling rush of the prelude (it reminded her of a waterfall, not of Niagaran force, but a late spring waterfall, light and tumbling and every drop clear). Ramsay plays the prelude softly, but with such clarity, his touch deft and delicate, and even as the prelude passes into the slower fugue – a walk round a calm lake as against the prelude's splashing water – there is a physical presence he instils in the music that makes her forget, improbably makes her forget. Come the skip and swing of the jazzy forlane and she is whisked away from this room, this house, this suburb, this Australia. This music could put her back in the arms of Daniel if she allowed it.

As he plays, Nina is aware of feeling envious of half-baked Ramsay, for he is at home here – and this would be the case wherever there was a piano. Half-baked Ramsay doesn't need a partner, he doesn't need close friends. So lacking in an integrated self that to be with him is a strain, at the keyboard he is complete. And suddenly it comes to her, who he reminds her of. It is John Coetzee, the central character in J.M. Coetzee's *Summertime*, a novel she read on the long flight from London to Melbourne. The same confusion, the same muddied longing, the awkward hold on the normal movements of a life, that simultaneous presence and absence, Ramsay Blake reminds her of a character in a novel.

Chapter 5. **Borders of Belief**

The Together In Freedom Coalition – TIF – had formed about five years earlier. It comprised the steering committee Nina would be meeting today, and a group of several hundred active supporters. According to the briefing notes she had received, the core members had come together in the post-9/11 world, concerned that the laws and regulations enacted to protect against terrorism were actually inhibiting much that was good in humankind. From the TIF perspective, societies were being shaped by their basest fears and around their basest elements, while the majority of citizens with their qualities of openness and generosity were being stymied.

The briefing notes had been surprisingly informative – often, Nina had found, with the more amateur groups they were not. The committee members had made several study tours, including a month in the Middle East encompassing Israel, the Palestinian territories, Egypt, Jordan and Lebanon. They had also visited India and Pakistan and several African countries, witnessing firsthand the horror of sectarian violence – different regions and different grievances but, according to their notes, the brutality and torture distressingly uniform. They had forged strong links with moderates in these countries, and had sponsored trips to Australia by a number of them. These visits had included lectures, seminars and discussions, ensuring that the reason of the moderates was for once heard more clearly than the shrill voices from the extremes. Every second month TIF sponsored an evening seminar devoted to a topical issue: a co-ordinated international response to asylum seekers, for example, or commercial exploitation of third-world resources. Annually they held a day-long conference, the most recent being shaped around the statement, 'No one chooses exile.' The TIF people had been surprisingly effective; their briefing notes listed some impressive achievements, and much more would be possible, Nina believed, if they maintained their current focus rather than redirected their funds and energies into a monument project.

Under normal circumstances, which is to say in her Daniel days, she would not have pursued this contract, and certainly not as an excuse to return to Melbourne. It was as if she thought it would be a weakness to come home without a job, without a legitimate reason. Of course no justification had been needed, she knew this now, nonetheless the job remained. She was committed only to an initial meeting with the group, but knowing as she already did that the TIF monument project had little likelihood of success, she felt uncomfortable – these were people of conscience, all of them activists for a better world – weighed down by false pretences and bad faith.

She had worked in the field of memorialising long enough to know which projects were likely to progress smoothly and which would bring trouble. A single event about which there was little controversy or a single person to be honoured would, aesthetic considerations aside, proceed without a hitch – a monument to Weary Dunlop, for example, or a commemoration to those killed in the Port Arthur massacre. But when the event or person, or, in the case of TIF, the values were contentious, and if, in addition, certain stakeholders with competing views had been excluded, such an enterprise would struggle to make it beyond the early stages.

Until the planning for the 9/11 memorial project on the site of the Twin Towers, Maya Lin's Vietnam Veterans Memorial in Washington took the prize for monument controversy. Nina was still at school when it was dedicated in 1982, but the uproar was so great that even schoolgirls could not fail to be aware. Nina had long wondered if the germ of her future career took hold at that time: she was intrigued that a monument, a sleek wall of granite carrying the names of the fallen, could arouse such passions.

Lin was Asian, female and young; her monument was black, abstract and lacked the usual heroic depictions of war. The protests, angry and aggrieved, approached from two fronts: the modernist memorial itself came under attack, as did the war it sought to remember. In the US at the time there was no national memorial for World War Two, nor was there one for the Korean War, yet Vietnam, a war that continued to inspire *Sturm und Drang*, a minor war from the perspective of the veterans of other wars, had been honoured. Why Vietnam? Why not us?

From that time no military campaign was to be ignored. In the aftermath of the Vietnam Veterans Memorial fracas, two new national war memorials were planned for Washington: the huge sprawling overwrought landscape of the World War II Memorial, in Nina's opinion one of the ugliest and shamelessly nationalistic memorials on Western soil, and the ultra-realist yet strangely moving Korean War Veterans Memorial, with its larger-than-life steel soldiers burdened with military clothes and hardware, each man essentially alone in the dreadful landscape of war. As for the abstract contemplative structure designed by Lin, two additional Vietnam monuments were added to the same site – placatory monuments to silence the protests in that both depicted realistic, life-sized figures enacting traditional war postures and narratives.

Washington was monument city and Nina visited regularly. She was present when the Korean War Memorial was opened to the public in 1995 – decades after the soldiers came home; and again when the World War Two Memorial was dedicated in 2004 – nearly sixty years after the war ended. She visited recently to see the Martin Luther King Memorial, a mammoth statue erected a full forty-three years after King's assassination. Even to the casual observer, something other than the worth of a person or an event is relevant when monuments are proposed. Indeed, as Nina well knew, history as embodied in enduring monumental form is a slippery enterprise. In the break-up of the former Soviet Union, one of the first acts of the liberated peoples was the tearing-down of Soviet-inspired monuments across the entire Eastern Bloc. And it did not surprise her that one of the most powerful symbols of the fall of Baghdad in 2004 was the huge statue of Saddam Hussein bound by ropes and pulleys crashing to the ground. Yesterday's shrine readily becomes today's scrap heap.

Over and over again, Nina was reminded that history has little capital these days unless it bolsters values, attitudes and beliefs currently in vogue. The challenge to her – to anyone planning a memorial – was to keep as narrow as possible the gap between the historical event or figure and its modern appreciation. In recent times, a popular means of closing the gap has been to render history as a personal experience by inserting the viewer into the representation. So there are Holocaust museums where visitors enter cattle cars, and World War One installations where they get down into the trenches.

Nina loathed these experiential memorials. To domesticate the persecution and slaughter of millions was, she believed, a travesty of the magnitude and impact of those atrocities. But memorial personnel were quick to defend the approach; they said that most visitors arrive with no personal connection with the event being portrayed, yet they leave shocked, challenged and in many instances changed by what they've seen.

No defence had yet convinced her. As far as she was concerned, the experiential approach was in the same vein as those reality TV shows where people swap wives or houses or countries for the duration of a six-part series; or return to nature or the nineteenth century, or live like a pauper or an aristocrat. As for imaginative empathy, or any form of abstract understanding, it was not simply discounted, it was actually heading towards extinction.

There was something in the TIF proposal that suggested they might be wanting an experiential approach. They wrote that their monument would help people 'reconnect with what is best in human nature generally, and, at the same time, what is best in themselves'. The TIF monument would prompt people 'to know what it is to be part of a world community that simultaneously embodies diversity and common hopes and values'. Even if by some miracle the TIF proposal shed all its other problems, if it was an experiential approach they were after, Nina wouldn't want this job.

And yet it was not so simple. While she did not share their religious beliefs, she certainly shared their other values;

she might even have become a TIF member if she lived in Melbourne. But to build a monument to an idea, or rather several ideas, for it to possess a pedagogical dimension as well – as if any single object could teach freedom or courage – and then to exclude from the planning process well-organised and voluble stakeholders was to shunt the project into the realm of the impossible. As much as she might admire their principles, it was only right, Nina decided as she rode up in the lift, to be forthright about her concerns before the project advanced any further.

Her resolve was shaken as soon as she came face to face with those who formed the TIF steering committee. Seven people sat at one end of a large elliptical table in the board-room of C.G. and C.K. Holdings. Seven people smiled at her as she entered the room. Charlie Goldstein and Cate Killeen, a Jew and a Catholic who had met young and acquired their wealth together, sat next to each other on one side of the table. They rose as Nina entered. Both were in their late forties. Cate, dressed in black, was tall and elegant with a mess of red curls; Charlie was short, bald and rumpled. They directed her to a vacant chair and made the introductions – out of courtesy rather than necessity: the committee members knew who she was and she had been sent a list of their names and credentials.

Immediately to her right was the Uniting Church minister, Reverend Elizabeth Featherstone, a large, attractive woman with dark features and pillar-box red lipstick whose mother had been one of the stolen generation. Seated next to her was the political historian, Professor Karim Qureshi: forty, maybe fifty, clipped greying beard, Semitic features, and wearing a surprising pale pink T-shirt. At the end of the table was

Rabbi Lorrie Aarons who looked hardly old enough to be out of high school, and between her and Cate Killeen sat Father Jamie Gray, who, with his spiky hair and black casual clothes, resembled the front-of-house in a chic restaurant rather than the Jesuit priest and social commentator he was. The last member of the steering committee, sitting next to Charlie and opposite Nina, was Nadirah Harvey, the Iraqi-born human rights lawyer, married to an Australian, an out-spoken critic of Australia's refugee policies and an ardent defender of asylum seekers. With her grey head-scarf and neat grey jacket she looked as if dressed for court.

Cate Killeen welcomed her on behalf of the group and then launched straight into the project.

'We want to create a monument to diversity and social inclusion,' she said. 'A monument that reflects Australia as a compassionate, multicultural society, one not merely tolerant of different races and religions but actually embracing the differences. We're keen,' she explained, 'to differentiate ourselves from the so-called melting pot of America.'

Cate nodded to the young rabbi to continue.

'Despite its well-sung myths, America would prefer to eliminate difference,' the rabbi said in American-accented English. 'Everything has to become American. Italian-Americans, Jewish-Americans, African-Americans, Irish-Americans, Italian-Americans – the emphasis is always on the American side of the hyphen. Bleach out the differences. Fit in.' She paused before adding, 'But you'd be aware of this, you'd have observed it yourself.'

They all knew about her work at the UN of more than twenty years ago. 'Felix Hovnanian's one of our most valued supporters,' Charlie Goldstein explained. 'He's adviser, key advocate and friend all rolled into one. In fact, it was Felix who recommended you.'

Felix Hovnanian, her MA supervisor, her first boss and first lover. Nina quickly established he was living here in Melbourne, attached in an honorary capacity to the university. He was as active as ever, according to Charlie, lectures and keynote speeches, regular media commentary, several high-profile committees, and, it emerged, recently divorced – from the same wife he was married to when he was having his affair with her. Extraordinary, Nina thought, that a divorce should happen at this late stage with Felix's most active philandering days surely well behind him. She slotted all the information into memory before guiding the discussion back to the TIF project.

'Our monument is to remind us what we set store by as Australians,' Nadirah, the lawyer, said. 'What permits so many of us to make Australia our home.'

She glanced around the table taking in the rest of the group. Her smooth brown face framed by the scarf was, Nina found herself thinking, beguilingly ageless.

'These days,' Nadirah continued, 'people have little opportunity to reflect on their beliefs. We believe a monument will help to concentrate thought. A monument will provide a safe and peaceful place for people to step out of their busy lives and recall what's truly important to them and to this country of ours.'

'"To remember is to safeguard something."' Cate Killeen quoted Seneca's well-known maxim.

Nina encouraged them to talk, to explain their rationale for the monument. She did not want to be seen to be diminishing their project by attacking it or injecting damp realism into their ambitions. She hoped that if they talked long enough, guided by strategic questions from her, they would eventually come to see not the folly of this project – never folly, not with such admirable intentions – but the impossibility of it.

Although the more she heard, the more she realised that the force of this group was something to be reckoned with. So strong were their beliefs, they blanked out other competing factors. She wanted to remind them that people are driven by envy and fear every bit as much as by goodness; she wanted to say that one person's goodness is another's selfishness. At one point she did mention the American religious right, their belief that wealth was a sign of godliness and poverty a self-induced punishment for wrong living. And a short time later she brought up race riots. 'They've occurred here in Australia,' she said. 'People who are different are seen as threatening. Outsiders are demonised, and everyone becomes more firmly rooted in their own primary identification group – their own gang – which they're prepared to defend at all cost. And the gulf between groups widens.'

Several voices were raised in protest. Look at us, they were saying, we reflect different backgrounds, different religions, and we're enriched by our differences, our group's strengthened by them.

'That's true,' Nina said. 'You see the need for this project, you agree on what it should symbolise and, aesthetic tastes aside, you'll agree on the form it'll take. But already from your own accounts you've experienced opposition from the more orthodox members of your communities. They say you don't represent them. They've told you to stop TIF or let them in. Either way your project collapses.'

'Two projects then?' the young priest suggested.

There was a pause before the professor, Karim Qureshi, spoke. 'It's exactly the sort of response we're receiving from the orthodox quarters, or rather the ultra-orthodox, that makes our project so important.' He spoke with an accent, different from Daniel's, but with a similarly pleasing effect. 'We want to reinforce our shared values.'

'I've absolutely no quarrel with what brought you together. But already there's been trouble and I'd anticipate a good deal more.'

'Why are you so hostile to what we want to do?' The rabbi's voice was loud, she looked disgruntled. The others nodded in agreement.

'I'm not hostile,' Nina said, annoyed she'd been so transparent. 'I'm simply exploring your project. You think you represent diversity, but values, attitudes and beliefs are at least as important as religion and ethnic background when it comes to loyalties and personal identifications, to what unites and divides people. I'm introducing some dissent into what I see as a homogeneous and consensual group.'

These words were greeted with astonished silence. Finally Elizabeth, the Uniting Church minister, spoke. 'I see what you mean.' She looked around the table. 'I think we all see what you mean, and it's useful to be reminded of who we are and what we represent. But we don't think for one moment that a lack of diversity in our interfaith, multicultural group,' – she loaded 'interfaith' and 'multicultural' with emphasis – 'is any reason to weaken our resolve. If anything it strengthens it. If we can draw on our similarities in the light of seemingly great diversity, others can too.'

Nina was about to respond but Elizabeth was not finished.

'We've often joked that the orthodox branches of our various religions would have much more in common with one another than they would with each of us, moderate practitioners of their own faith.'

'And what would happen if you were to include orthodox believers in your group?' Nina asked.

The rabbi answered. 'We'd introduce competing views, views that couldn't be assimilated with our own. We're all well aware of this.'

'But if you can't convince your co-religionists, how do you propose to convince atheists and half-strength believers and just plain ordinary pragmatists more concerned with their everyday comforts than anything disturbing or inconsistent in their beliefs? What monument could possibly have such power?

'The world is small these days,' Nina continued. 'You can connect with anyone anywhere. You can read breaking news in dozens of countries while riding the tram. If people want to look and learn beyond their own sphere it's very easy. But I'd suggest most people would prefer to catch up on episodes of *Big Brother* and *MasterChef* when they go online, and that's after they've chatted on Facebook and checked out their friends' postings on YouTube. The wider world's at our fingertips yet many people choose to look away.'

Several voices sounded in unison: this was the very reason they wanted a monument, something to concentrate attention on beliefs and values and attitudes that were easily overlooked in the rush and tumble of modern life.

'And your monument is to remind us of freedom, social inclusion and a common humanity?' Nina said. *Your monument*: it sounded as if she were deriding it.

'Yes, but also to inform those who've never considered such values before,' Cate said.

'With a pedagogical function as well?' Nina continued.

There was much nodding around the table.

'And there's more,' Nadirah Harvey said. 'Here in Australia, people of different ethnicities and religions live in harmony.'

Nina was tempted to interject: if there's so much harmony then why the need for a monument, but kept her silence.

'There's no sectarian violence here,' Nadirah continued. 'No centuries-old religious arguments, and we want it to remain that way. So our monument will have a pre-emptive function. It'll send a message to would-be terrorists not to bother with us, that Australia offers freedom to all its citizens.'

'Our monument will be like the Statue of Liberty,' Elizabeth said.

'Exactly,' the rabbi was smiling, 'but with aesthetic merit.'

Nina reminded them that when the Statue of Liberty was dedicated back in 1886 it carried very different cultural capital. 'It was actually a gift in friendship from the French to the Americans to commemorate the centennial of the signing of the Declaration of Independence. No one thinks of that now.'

In the silence that followed Nina thought she had at last made an impression. Then Charlie Goldstein reminded her again this was not a group willing to change its mind. 'It's what the Statue of Liberty has come to represent,' he said, 'that encourages us a monument can embody complex abstractions like freedom and hope.'

'You don't think that the monument you're planning might be over-burdened with symbolic freight?'

Charlie smiled. 'No. We'll choose our designer carefully. We'll choose our site carefully. Our instructions will be absolutely clear to those whose job it is to transform our dreams into a reality. And when the monument's unveiled, we'll ensure ample information is available so that our ideas and ideals are brought into easy reach of everyone.'

There was a scatter of applause around the table, and an array of relieved faces. Nina had detected a let's-bring-this-meeting-to-a-close tone as Charlie spoke and she decided there was little more to be done today. She thanked them all and apologised if she'd caused any offence.

'It did feel rather like an interrogation,' Nadirah Harvey said.

Nina knew this woman had lost family members to interrogation and torture under Saddam; hers was a comment aimed at putting Nina in her place. But she didn't react, she knew the reasons for her questions.

She suggested they discuss the form the monument might take at their next meeting. 'And before then I'll circulate a paper on trends in memorialising and monuments to help frame the discussion.'

The words were out before she could stop them: the professional wrapping things up. There was to have been only one meeting and now she was setting herself up for another. In the past she would not have made such a mistake.

There was a stiffness as Nina left the room. It didn't surprise her: often when working with groups she was the first person to question a seemingly worthy project. But even before the door was closed she heard them, not the words, but small explosions, and then one clear voice. She recognised it as belonging to the young rabbi.

'Do we have the right person?'

*

It was hot, too hot to remain outdoors, but neither did Nina want to return to the flat. She was unsettled, irritated, and the tiny box of her temporary home would plunge her deeper into the mire. The fact was she was better informed than the good people seated in the boardroom of C.G. and C.K. Holdings, and was burdened by this in much the same way as if she were privy to hurtful information that would be damaging to a close friend. She wondered, not for the first time, whether any of her friends had known about Daniel's infidelity before she herself found out. And if so would she have wanted to be told? She needed to know, but would she have wanted to know? The TIF people were, she believed, in a similarly vulnerable situation. They were corralled by their goodness, and their vision so narrow that even if they wanted, they could not see all the troubles ahead. And there was something else, something harshly personal; it was the couple at the centre of the group, Cate and Charlie, partners in every aspect of their lives. Why them? Why not her and Daniel?

She took a tram back to the centre of the city, it was far too hot to walk, and then on a whim she caught another tram to the university.

It had always excited her that nothing, barring disease or trauma, is ever forgotten but is locked away, often behind steel-plated doors, not because the memories are injurious – although that can be the case – but for the simple reason that life has bolted off in another direction. Then something happens at a very particular time and the doors are suddenly opened. If someone had mentioned Felix Hovnanian a few years ago, Nina expected that after a brief nod at the past she would have let him slip away. But now, today, she turned her back on a less-than-satisfactory meeting and headed towards the University of Melbourne, perhaps to front up at his door twenty years on, or perhaps not: she was yet to decide.

She took out her phone and searched the university website. Felix was an honorary fellow at one of the new institutes that had replaced so many of the traditional university departments. She walked across campus to the location, found that it was more virtual than actual, but there was, quaintly, a pigeon-hole for each institute associate. She found Felix's name – her heart was thumping – scribbled a note with her phone number and email address and put it in his slot. She left quickly before she could change her mind and caught a tram back to the flat.

She switched on the cooling, stripped down to her underwear and flopped onto the couch. She was tired, and it was not just the meeting with the TIF group, hers was a tiredness that stretched all the way back to Daniel's departure. It takes a great deal of energy not to think about someone, and it's impossible to do the job properly. She could monitor her thoughts with the diligence of a fundamentalist but just by being who she was, the woman who for thirteen years had shared her life with Daniel, condemned her to failure. If she'd been asked before his dumping how long she thought it would take to recover from a spouse's defection, she would have naively answered six months maximum, that such betrayal simply would not warrant any more energy or time. But some things, it seemed, were beyond control.

And maybe it was these thoughts that steered her into her email archive, for one minute she was making herself a cool drink and the next she was scrolling through the emails in an ancient file titled 'Daniel', untouched since his return from that fateful trip to Cape Town. So many loving messages, hundreds of them saved over the years, his emails to her, hers to him. Nina dipped in at random; she could actually hear his voice in the words he wrote. There were emails sent by him from Argentina, Canada, Ireland, America, and by her from Russia, Vienna, Paris, Australia. There were emails written at his desk in Primrose Hill and others from her desk in Bloomsbury. *Billets doux*, they called them and she'd kept them all. She loitered in their correspondence, let herself roll with the current of his words, down down down the list until she was reading the emails from their last months together.

When someone owns up to deceiving you for four months, they may as well own up for six months or eight; she'd been inclined to believe his timeline, primarily because she simply could not believe he had been lying all through their anniversary weekend, that loving weekend when the storm raged and the two of them had never been closer. But as she scrolled down the email list, she began to doubt. This was a man who could hide behind words.

I love you. Don't forget that. I'll toast my beautiful
girl tonight from the plane. You toast me too.
You are a great blessing. Please look after yourself
while I'm away.
And DON'T run yourself into the ground ... for anyone ...
much love and missing you already
Your dxx

Daniel was off to Japan, a meeting in Osaka with a few days' holiday tacked on the end. She would have joined him but she was in a delicate stage of negotiations with a difficult group, so difficult that if she had not been so interested in the proposed project – a monument to the Jewish presence in London's East End – she would have withdrawn from consideration. So Daniel went to Japan and she stayed home. But the date of the email would have put him, according to his confessed timeline, in that first exciting flush of the affair with Sally. Loving emails sent to his wife and, she now assumed, wild passionate emails to the new lover. Unless, that is, the lover travelled to Japan with him.

If words come easily to you, as they did to Daniel, how simple to use them to conceal your deceits. Did he pause for a moment and think what he was writing to her, his wife, during those four months, or longer, he was cheating on her? Or did he simply sit at his computer and let the familiar words and loving expressions roll off his fingers. And for each email he sent to his wife, how many arrived in the girlfriend's inbox? Nina read every email written to her during their last months together. All those loving and familiar words, and all of them lies. As for the happiness she experienced during that time – it was corrupted, it had been a sham.

She had thought Daniel to be a man of good faith, for thirteen years she believed he had a horror of self-deception. So what was happening here? Either she'd been wrong for thirteen years and all his loving words were no more meaningful than a football commentary. Or he had really loved her, in which case might he have made a mistake in leaving her? She wondered if he was happy in his new life – a momentary lapse before calling a halt. You can't afford to think like this, she told herself. Allow him even the possibility of a mistake and you let in hope. He's not coming back to you, he's not coming back. If he's made a mistake, it's no business of yours.

Chapter 6. The Frailty of Monsters

Nina would have floated a raft of excuses to avoid a whole day in the company of her sister and brother-in-law, but Zoe's blunt honesty silenced her.

'It'd be much more enjoyable for me if you joined us,' she said. 'Easier, too.'

A day trip was planned down to the coast to the Jameson family beach cottage. Zoe had lent the place to friends the previous week; the wife was undergoing treatment for breast cancer and the couple had needed a break. With her normally efficient and reliable friends clearly squeezed by the stresses of cancer, they'd left a few of their belongings behind. Zoe offered to collect them and at the same time check that all appliances had been turned off, the rubbish bin emptied, the house secured.

Please come with us, Zoe said, and of course Nina agreed – for Zoe primarily, but also to see the old beach house. It was here the family had holidayed throughout her childhood, and where her parents planned to retire when they were, in their own words, 'too old to move'. Until such time, Zoe and Elliot used the house more than anyone else; Elliot, in particular, loved the place and would often go there by himself to work.

How much easier it had been to manage the tensions between Zoe and Elliot when Daniel was around, she found herself thinking, which was, she realised, dangerously close to wishing Daniel was here with her now. She was quick to remind herself that if Daniel hadn't deserted her she'd not be in Australia at all. Instead the two of them would be on an adventure in the Amazon Basin, or watching the northern lights in Greenland, or tracing the footsteps of Bruce Chatwin in Patagonia – they had promised themselves all these trips when their future stretched forever.

How mindlessly does happiness trade in forevers, she thought.

She grabbed a shopping bag, shoved in jumper and shoes, bathers and a hat, hesitated over a book and in the end included it: if the tensions between Zoe and Elliot escaped so would she, to a shady spot on the rocks with her book as she had done so many times as a girl. She locked the apartment and walked down the four flights of stairs rather than rely on the old slogger of a lift. The building had been recently renovated, but for some reason the lift had been left languishing in the 1980s. Her brother-in-law was not a man to be kept waiting and she wanted to be standing on the pavement when he pulled up.

Elliot drove one of those monster four-wheel drive vehicles with tinted windows and a don't-mess-with-me bull bar. Nina, who had never owned a car much less one so dangerous, was appalled when she first saw it.

'He loves it,' Zoe said. 'It makes him happy.'

Elliot was a biographer and academic, Zoe taught music at an inner-city school, both were committed urbanites whose children were fast approaching the age of independent mobility; they had no need for such a vehicle. But if it made Elliot less prickly and disagreeable, and if life thereby became a little easier for her long-suffering sister, then let him have his monster.

It was while she was waiting for Elliot that Nina noticed a man standing at the edge of the footpath, just a few metres away. In one hand he held a cigarette, with the other he steadied himself against an electricity pole. He wasn't wearing shoes and there were holes in the heels of his socks; the exposed skin was not soiled as she would have expected but a vulnerable piglet pink. His white shirt was creased and there was a large brownish stain between his shoulders. But the sleeves were folded back in that fashionable way of businessmen relaxing after work, and his trousers, while in need of a press were, to her eye, stylish and well cut; his hair was neatly cropped, suggesting a recent visit to the hairdresser.

The man finished his cigarette and threw it in the gutter. Then he turned around and she saw his face. The orbits of his eyes were so swollen that the eyes themselves were reduced to sad black slits. His cheeks were bloated and the skin mottled with wine-dark blotches; his mouth hung loosely open. The man was thirty, perhaps a little older, impossible to know in a face so ravaged.

Suddenly Elliot was by his side. 'Do you need some help, mate?'

The man mumbled something and brushed him away.

Elliot persisted. He offered to call a taxi, he offered to ring the man's family, to telephone a friend, he offered to find him water, shoes, a clean shirt. The man now pushed past him: he was fine, he said, and staggered towards the apartment building. He had almost reached the entrance when he stumbled, an arm jerked towards the door frame and missed, and down he slumped, first to his knees then on all fours.

Elliot was again by his side. 'You can't stay here, mate,' he said. 'I'll help get you home.'

'This *is* home,' the man said.

He tilted back on to his knees then, using the wall for balance, managed to drag himself upright. He fumbled with his wallet and with the slow deliberateness of the drunk withdrew a key card; he nearly lost his footing again as he tried to insert it in the slot. Finally the card connected, the door opened and he was inside.

An hour later and hurtling along the road out of Geelong, Elliot was still trumpeting on about the man. He could pick an alcoholic at one hundred paces in poor light (a short-sighted teetotaller could have picked this one, but with Elliot venting his expertise on alcohol dependence, Nina decided to remain silent); Elliot could predict the man's future, obviously still in work judging by his clothes, but not for much longer given the state he was in. Without help this man would end up in the gutter. Elliot knew the man's drinking patterns – steady daily drinking with binges on weekends; he knew the man's drink preferences – Scotch, he could smell it on his breath; his personal supports – the family had thrown him out otherwise he wouldn't be staying in a serviced apartment. And while it occurred to Nina that the man might be visiting from interstate or overseas, he might be staying at the flats while his house was being renovated, staying there with his wife and children, the man might be renting a well-appointed serviced apartment close to the city centre for a host of different reasons, but again she kept her silence because alcohol and its dependence were Elliot's specialty. Elliot could speak with the greatest authority because he, Elliot Eugene Wood, had been there.

It was not until the first glimpse of the ocean just past Anglesea that Elliot's rant slackened and finally abated. It didn't mean that he'd said all he wanted to say, or that he needed to concentrate on the winding road, rather an ocean panorama was one of the few known panaceas to his fevers. The water today was glassy with a gorgeous swell, the surfers were tiny blots on the shining sea, the sun shot sparks off the water, the water was fabulously blue. Elliot opened his window and inhaled the salted air.

'Glorious,' he said. 'Heaven on earth.' And no more was said about the drunk man.

The Jameson cottage was one of the last old-style homes in the hills above the Great Ocean Road, the byway of twists and curls that traced Australia's south-eastern coast through Victoria all the way to the South Australian border. Most of the old cottages had been mown down in the construction stampede of the past few decades, replaced by huge houses, two and three storeys high, sheathed in glass, with wrap-around balconies for 360-degree views of ocean and inland bush, houses that had cost millions to build and by the time the paint was dry were worth a great deal more.

The Jameson cottage was a quaint low-lying structure nestled within a clotted garden of tea-tree, agapanthus and aged she-oaks. The beach was just a short walk away, and the ocean a perpetual and peaceful white noise. With just a few kilometres remaining before they reached the house, Nina felt exactly the same excitement and anticipation as she had as a child, the same happiness too.

Childhood memories are so indulgent of nostalgia, Nina was well aware of this, but the fact was those long-ago days spent by the ocean were among her happiest memories. Every summer for several years both the Jamesons and the Blakes would pack up the cars and drive down the Great Ocean Road where each family rented a cottage for the summer; later, when the Jameson rental was put up for sale, they bought it. For the entire holiday the two families shared their days. They took long walks together, they shopped together, cooked and ate together, played numerous games of Monopoly and table tennis together. Only when both Michael and Marion were gone was the pattern broken. Sean continued to spend the summer at the coast with Nina's family, while Ramsay remained at Raleigh Court with George.

Before George wrecked it, those stretched summer days were perfect. Away from home and humdrum routine, whatever divided the four children melted away. They'd rise early, pull on their bathers, and after a quick breakfast head straight to the beach. There they would pass day after easy day, swimming and surfing, building sand sculptures, and playing endless games of beach cricket, regularly disrupted when one of the dogs ran off with the ball. For lunch the four of them would go to the Blakes' or to the Jameson house, or one of the parents would bring sandwiches down to the beach. On overcast days they'd explore the coastal bushland, collecting spiders and insects, geckos and one summer a magnificent blue-tongue lizard. They'd pretend to be ship-wrecked, the Raleigh Posse forced to live off the land and daring each other to eat plants that might be poisonous. Once they came upon a man and a woman naked on a rug in a small clearing; they'd watched in hushed fascination at what looked like violent combat, and afterwards all of them were too embarrassed to discuss what they'd seen. Those summer days were filled with thrills, and when the holidays were over and they returned home, Ramsay to his music and the others to their sophisticated city pursuits, they'd partition off their childish fun until the next summer.

How fresh those memories were. The lunches on the sand, comparing and sharing Christmas presents, the salt-tight skin after swimming, the dangerous undertow, sand mixed in with sticky white sunscreen, squishing jellyfish between your toes, pruney fingers and blue-tinged lips after hours spent in the water, and the friends who were the best part of her world. Friends for life, they pledged back then, forever friends.

It's ironic that childhood, the period of life that's all change, so readily assumes permanence. This is, perhaps, the most trenchant of childhood's delusions. And it occurs despite blatant evidence to the contrary: school friends change from year to year; favourite subjects, favourite sports, even hopes and ambitions regularly change; families move house, a father dies; the body grows and reshapes; there are new fashions – in clothes, in music, in possessions; childhood's pains – bullying, neglect, shyness, acne – all eventually pass. But the immediacy of childhood experiences and the smallness of the child's world result in the child assuming – there is little reflection on these matters – that these friends, these moments, these possessions, these sufferings will endure.

As Elliot drove the coast road, the glistening ocean to the left, the scrub and cliffs to the right, Nina was aware of the warmth and happiness emerging from those ancient days and filling her now. And she was struck with the power of childhood, how it manages to seize the better part of memory for itself, and no matter how far you have travelled, it can ambush you and pull you back.

*

The first part of the day passed predictably enough. Zoe's friend, exhausted by cancer and its treatment, and her husband exhausted by everything else, had left the house in a mess.

'I've told you not to lend the place,' Elliot said to Zoe. 'Not that you listen to anything I say.' He made himself a cup of coffee and collected the morning papers. 'You clean up,' he said. 'It's your fault not mine.' When Zoe reminded him her friend had cancer, he merely shrugged as if to suggest the cancer was irrelevant. He called to the dog and he and Adelaide headed out to the verandah.

Nina helped Zoe restore the house to order. They took their time, and when Elliot yelled out he was hungry, Zoe said he should help himself to a snack. It was another hour before they joined him on the verandah. Zoe had made sandwiches at home that morning, perfect sandwiches of several varieties, one large platter and another in the kitchen, sufficient for a party.

Nina praised the sandwiches: they were delicious.

'Most people aspire to more than the perfect sandwich,' Elliot said with a glance at his wife.

Nina, too, looked at Zoe, but if the insult had registered, her sister hid it well. As for Elliot, he was happy enough to eat the maligned food, tossing whole triangles into his mouth one after another.

They sat in silence, eating the perfect sandwiches and sipping Zoe's home-made lemonade. There was a sea breeze that eased the summer heat, from the distance came the flop and purr of the surf, and at the bottom of the garden scrub wrens darted in the brush. A sweet, gentle day, Nina was thinking, and turning out much better than she had anticipated, when she heard it, they all heard it, the crunch of tyres on gravel, and each looked towards the driveway.

Adelaide barked and raced down the slope. A car, an ordinary white sedan, came into view. Nina did not recognise it, but Elliot certainly did. He turned on his wife.

'What have you bloody done now?'

The sun shone on the windscreen, it was impossible to see who was in the car. The vehicle mounted the drive and pulled into the parking area below the house. The engine was extinguished. Elliot stood up, silent and bristling; he glared at his wife. Zoe, also on her feet, was turned towards the car. She was smiling.

The passenger door opened and Ramsay bounced out. He waved, shouted a greeting and strode towards the house. His old dog waddled over to Adelaide and the two animals threw themselves at each other with much boisterous yelping. George unfolded from the driver's seat, steadied himself against the side of the car before moving round to the passenger side and shutting Ramsay's door. Then he started up the rocky path. He was listing to the left; his shoulders, hunched forward, were pathetically shrivelled. George was an old man, Nina was thinking. Ramsay should be looking after him, not the other way round.

Zoe welcomed them warmly, Elliot was slower to come forward; more time to calm himself, Nina decided. Although a moment later she was marvelling at his control, for when he did speak, his furies were well coated with hostly courtesies. As for Nina, the day that a short time ago had found its satisfactions was spoiled.

The new arrivals were quickly settled, drinks were dispensed, the second platter of sandwiches appeared, and after that came cake and fruit; these guests had been catered for. Nina was appalled at what her sister had done. Ramsay might still be her great weakness, but it was such an old weakness and Zoe in all other respects so sensible, Nina would never have thought she would indulge it in so public a manner. And so carefully planned, too, even down to Nina's own presence.

As for Elliot, for the first time in all the years she'd known him, she felt sorry for him. Once he had loved Zoe, probably still did, but how very distressing to love someone whose own passions are directed elsewhere. Not that Ramsay would ever return the feeling – romantically, sexually or in any other way, but that made it even worse for Elliot. There are many forms of infidelity, and adultery – the very fact of sex providing something concrete to anchor your fight – is far from being the most painful. Emotional absence is far worse, and while this is bad enough when a spouse dumps you as Nina well knew, how much worse to have to live with the absence day in and day out, suffer it while you sleep with your absent lover and eat with her and go about your daily life together. This was Elliot's plight, and whether he still loved his wife or not, and Nina assumed he did or else he would have left her, Zoe's detachment and her emotional hoarding must confine him to an internal exile, a form of home detention without reprieve.

Just the previous day when Elliot had lashed out at Zoe over some minor slip-up, Nina had asked Zoe how she put up with his constant bruising.

'I'm used to him,' Zoe had replied. 'We're used to each other. I'd never leave him.'

Watching her sister chatting with Ramsay, lively, engaged and responding to him in a way she did not her husband, it was not difficult to understand Elliot's attacks on his wife: this was a man burdened with his own hurts and seeking to armour himself against more of the same. It didn't excuse his behaviour, but it did explain it. What masochistic hunger would make people party to this sort of deal, Nina wondered.

'I suffered his drinking days,' Zoe had said several times over the years, as if that would justify any poor behaviour of her own.

Zoe believed Elliot had already dealt her a full hand of harm, but how much more, Nina wondered, did Elliot think he owed his wife? Or was his drinking a debt that could never be properly repaid? Elliot had been a shocking drunk: angry, unpredictable, threatening, a man beyond reason and control. But he had given up alcohol when Hayley and Callum were toddlers and both were now nearly adults. Zoe, it would appear, had never given up Ramsay. How to measure and compare two entirely different wrongs?

Daniel had been a brute at the end, but for all the years they were together theirs had been a warm and affectionate marriage. They would touch each other as they passed in the house; they held hands in the street; they left loving notes for each other on the kitchen bench, on pillows, in the car, on desks. She had kept all his notes, and even now one would occasionally turn up, flimsy memorials to a past love, she called them, but still she could not bring herself to throw them out. There was a trip she'd made to Sarajevo, never had she been so nervous about a job nor so doubting of her abilities to pull it off, and Daniel, recognising her fears, had slipped notes into her luggage to bolster her during the trip, 'I love you and think you are wonderful' notes slipped into her wash-bag, between the pages of a book, in the cup of a bra, the toe of a sock, a dozen notes that sustained her through the week she was away. She would prefer to be by herself than live cold like her sister and Elliot.

If Zoe was universally cool it might be more tolerable for Elliot, but she demonstrated great warmth to everyone else – a suspect warmth, Nina had often thought, given she dished it out so indiscriminately. She was glowing with Ramsay, and friendly with George, a man she did not much care for; she was a loving and affectionate mother, a loving and affectionate sister too; with her friends and colleagues, with acquaintances, even with strangers working in shops or travelling on the tram Zoe was generous, responsive and empathic. And again Nina wondered about Elliot, denied what his wife gave so readily to everyone else and, she suspected, hungering for it.

With lunch finished, Elliot called to Adelaide and took himself off to the beach. George settled into his chair, closed his eyes and soon a faint, irregular snoring showed him to be asleep. Zoe and Ramsay chatted together about the relative merits of the latest Xbox (Nina was coming to believe that Ramsay could talk about earthworms in India and her sister would be a willing participant), there were a couple of his crude jokes, and then he turned to her.

'So, are you still making your memorials?'

If Ramsay had ever asked her a question it was so long ago she had forgotten. As for her work, she was surprised he even knew what she did.

She nodded. 'Although I don't make the memorials. I help people bring their projects to fruition.' And was about to continue when Ramsay launched into one of his lectures.

Ramsay was an expert on memory. 'It's what makes me a pianist – not the only thing of course, but crucial. And it's got nothing to do with statues or monuments or any concrete reminders. It's here,' he tapped his head, 'and here,' he held out his hands. 'Memory's physical, it's in the body. Memory's a matter of will. Practice and willpower. If people forget, it's because they're lazy, or they lack concentration, or they lack determination.' He went on at length how he memorised his pieces. 'I play them over and over. I analyse the notes, the phrases, the tempi, the interaction between the musical lines, the key changes; I listen to the music, and as I come to understand it, it settles in my body.'

'But what about remembering events and people from a nation's past, things about which you mightn't have direct experience? Remembering as against memorising?'

He shook his head. 'You've got the web for that. Everything you want to know is online – you don't have to remember things from the past, not any more. But that aside, I don't agree with your distinction. Memory, remembering, lodges in the body; it's always personal.'

'And history?'

He shrugged. 'What about history? History is history, it's not memory.'

Zoe was listening, shifting her gaze from one to the other, a faint smile on her face. Nina should have left him to his opinion, she knew this even while she argued on.

'You're reducing memory to a process without intelligence,' she said. 'But what would happen to human progress without our ability to step out of the here and now? We need memory and imagination for that – reasoning too.'

Ramsay would have none of this. 'I don't know about progress, but I do know about memory.'

He subjected her to yet another account of how he learned complex pieces of music. Nina persisted for a bit longer before giving up: it was like arguing with one of those mechanical talking toys programmed with a finite collection of statements.

His lecture continued unabated. She looked towards Zoe – how do we stop him, she was wanting to say – but Zoe was so enthralled she was not even aware of Nina's gaze. In the end it was Ramsay's dog that silenced him; Horo was barking at something down near the bushes.

'Quick,' Zoe said. 'It might be a snake.'

Ramsay was out of his chair, down the steps and running over the slope with Zoe following close behind. He grabbed Horo and peered into the bushes. And then he started to laugh.

'The great guard dog,' he said, 'is protecting us from a piece of foil caught in the banksia.'

'He's protecting us from the big bad banksia men,' Zoe said, and she was laughing too.

They were pushing each other towards the snake in the bush and carrying on like kids, and foremost among Nina's thoughts was how fortunate that Elliot did not have to witness this.

When the laughter stopped and with the foil added to the garbage, Zoe suggested they join Elliot on the beach. George roused himself and then decided to stay behind; Horo exhausted from the excitement settled himself in a patch of shade. So it was just the three of them who set off, Nina and Ramsay with Zoe in the middle.

There was no sign of Elliot down on the beach. The wind had picked up and the sea was now messy with foam; most of the surfers had called it a day. Ramsay set a rattling pace, and with the hurtling wind and the churning sea it was impossible to talk. Soon Nina dropped behind, dawdling at the edge of the waves, digging her toes into the cool soggy sand. As she ambled along she slipped into that dream-like state that a raucous sea can produce, and it was some time before she was aware of having fixed on the two figures striding ahead of her, tall and slender and surprisingly similar from behind. The two of them were walking close enough to be touching, their heads bent towards each other. Zoe and Ramsay looked like a long-established couple.

In the distance, sitting high on the beach in the low dunes was a man with a dog; too far to be seen clearly, Nina knew it was Elliot. Directly in front of him down at the water's edge, walking in step with each other were Zoe and Ramsay. Elliot must be watching them, how could he not? By the time Nina had drawn level with him he was sitting with his head in his hands, a drooping, dejected figure, monumentally alone. She slowed down, hesitated, then walked up the beach. Adelaide stood up, her tail wagging.

'Elliot,' she said.

He raised his head. His eyes were hidden behind sunglasses but his mouth exposed him.

Pointing to the sand next to him, she said, 'Do you mind?'

He shrugged, an almost imperceptible movement, yet the futility was unambiguous; this was a wounded man, a man of aristocratic sadness. Nina loved her sister, the only person in existence she loved unconditionally, but she felt sorry for Elliot, desperately sorry for him. How much better it would be if he did not love his wife.

She sat close to him on the sand, gazing at the sea. The waves surged and rolled forward, tossing themselves on the shore. Her own marriage was dead and Elliot's marriage was a wreck. He was wrong to let the steam off his misery by attacking Zoe, he was wrong to run her down the way he did. But Zoe was wrong to take for granted a husband who loved her. As for Zoe's attraction to a man incapable of loving anyone, it defied all reason.

She and Elliot remained together in the dunes, without speaking – there was nothing she could say – until the two specks that were Zoe and Ramsay reappeared in the distance. Without a word they stood in unison and hurried down to the water's edge. With Adelaide chasing waves they walked along the beach well ahead of the other two, and then up to the house. Nothing was said while Elliot poured them fresh lemonade, and when ten minutes later Zoe and Ramsay arrived, Elliot was so composed he might have spent the past hour with a book.

It was not quite five when they left the coast, firstly George and Ramsay, and thirty minutes later Zoe and Elliot with Nina and the dog in the back seat. She dreaded the drive home; she had seen Elliot's anger in the past, more significantly she had seen his hurt now, and both, she believed, would translate into a vitriolic attack. But nothing of the sort occurred. Zoe scrolled through the music library in the car, settling on the soundtrack to *Rent*. She explained to Nina that this musical was one of Elliot's favourites. By the second track Elliot was tapping the beat on the steering wheel, a short time later he was singing along. Zoe gazed out her side window, so still and silent she might as well not have been there. And from her position in the back seat, Nina looked at them, her sister and brother-in-law, their two bodies cupped by the car seats, two people married for more than twenty years, no warmth between them, hardly any visible connection at all, yet bound together by bonds so strong that not even misery could cut them free.

Chapter 7. New York Snowdome

1.

The year 1989 has become emblematic of fundamental change. Panel by panel the Berlin Wall came down, European communism was drawing its last breath. With its superpower status on the rubbish heap, Russia became a target for nation states hot for recognition, hungry for Western lifestyles and pumped up with long-stifled pride and patriotism. Thousands of kilometres further east, peaceful protesters were mown down in Tiananmen Square. Over in the US the first Bush became president, ushering in a new political family that was more parody than actual dynasty. In Australia, two of the worst bus crashes in the nation's history occurred on the notorious Pacific Highway two months and a couple of hundred kilometres apart, and the year ended with an earthquake in Newcastle that left thirteen people dead. This was the year the Ayatollah Khomeini pronounced a fatwa against Salman Rushdie for his novel *The Satanic Verses*, the second edition of the twenty-volume *Oxford English Dictionary* was published, and Nintendo's first handheld Game Boy entered the market.

In New York City, Nina and Zoe Jameson together with Ramsay Blake were the subjects of change every bit as momentous as the social and political events that exploded about them. In the space of a few weeks, long-held dreams collapsed, hopes disintegrated, futures were rewritten; there were disappointments and cruelties and – surprisingly – a stock of enduring love. In 1989 the world changed, and so too the lives of Ramsay Blake and the two Jameson sisters from Melbourne, Australia.

Nina had arrived in New York in the summer of the previous year. Her MA supervisor, Felix Hovnanian, a specialist in twentieth-century conflict, had been appointed as convenor of a UN working party charged to prepare guidelines for use in suspected cases of genocide. He accepted the job on the condition he could bring his own research assistant. Nina, an efficient combination of top graduate student and highly satisfactory lover, was his choice. With a free trip out of Australia and a working visa in the US, Nina was happy to comply with both briefs.

By the time Zoe joined her in New York fifteen months later, the UN job was nearing its end and from Nina's perspective the affair was well and truly over – although she thought it best to maintain the status quo until the job was officially finished. And then? There were several options, each with drawbacks. She could find another job in the US with the usual green card hassles; she could start a PhD at Columbia with accompanying scholarship hassles; she could blow her savings and travel, thereby delaying any decisions about the next phase of her life. She was even considering a return to Melbourne; she could rent a place in the inner city and live much as she did here in New York. She'd been surprised at the extent to which she missed her family, Zoe in particular. And Melbourne itself. And the coast and the bush. She missed breathable air and wide open spaces. She missed home.

So when Zoe telephoned to say she was coming to New York – no prior warning, she'd made the decision and would be arriving in a matter of weeks – Nina was thrilled. Zoe had taken extended leave from her teaching job, her intention was to stay several months. But Nina's joy quickly evaporated when on the very day of Zoe's arrival, her bags still unpacked and Nina planning to show her the neighbourhood, Zoe shoved the dollars Nina had given her as a welcome-to-New-York gift into her wallet and said she was off to meet Ramsay.

'Ramsay?' Nina said. 'Ramsay here? In New York?'

Zoe was already at the door, her explanation was rushed: Ramsay had arrived a couple of weeks earlier to take up a position as pianist-in-residence at one of the New York music schools. He'd be in Manhattan for several months.

'With George?'

Zoe shook her head. 'George needed some sort of orthopaedic surgery. His knees or maybe it was his hips. He'd been on a waiting list for ages, and when he was finally given a date for the operation, he had to accept.' She shrugged. 'Bad luck for George, bad timing.'

So that was it. Ramsay had separated Zoe from her teaching, Ramsay had caused her sister to leave Australia for the first time in her life, Ramsay Blake was the reason for Zoe's shedding her sensible and considered self and flying across the world. Ramsay, not her. And because she was hurt and disappointed, Nina attacked him. What sort of person would bolt to the other side of the world when the man who was *in loco parentis* as well as minder, manager and friend was undergoing major surgery? What sort of man was Ramsay that he would leave George, seriously restricted in mobility, to cope alone?

Zoe's defence came easily: the New York residency had been scheduled for more than a year. Everything was locked into place. And besides, George wouldn't have wanted Ramsay to cancel.

'But Ramsay himself, wouldn't he have wanted to be with George? This is major surgery after all. And during the long rehabilitation, no thought of looking after George – as George has looked after him these past many years?'

Zoe continued to defend Ramsay, and Nina, now more angry than hurt, decided on a different approach. 'What would you do, Zoe, if our father was having major surgery?'

'I'd stay with him, you know I would. I'd want to help. But it's different for me.'

'In what sense different?'

'I don't receive invitations to work in New York.' Her head was cocked to the side, her eyebrows were raised, her hands were thrust forward. Her entire demeanour suggested the answer was self-evident. 'I'm no genius.'

You're beautiful and you're smart, Nina wanted to say, and you have your own musical talent, just how much more of your life do you want to give to this guy? But reason was a bloodless exercise when it concerned Zoe's feelings for Ramsay so she said nothing. All that she'd planned for the two of them, theatre, bars, concerts, exploring this great city together; all the trips she'd envisaged, to Charleston and New Orleans, across to Chicago and the great lakes, to the desert and the west coast, all they might have done together slipped quietly away. She had no desire to watch her sister in this doomed crusade. As Zoe closed the door behind her, Nina suspected she would be leaving New York a good deal earlier than she had anticipated.

Ramsay's apartment was only a dozen blocks from Nina's. Zoe sped down West End Avenue, floating was how it felt, 98th, 97th, 96th, the streets even closer than they appeared on the map. She'd never been in New York before but she knew exactly where she was going, in a sense she'd been heading this way all her life. When she reached Ramsay's building and the doorman said Mr Blake was expecting her, and when she took the rickety lift to the eleventh floor and stood outside Ramsay's apartment, she felt the blissful inevitability of her being here, both she and Ramsay far from home, away from work and colleagues, away from George most of all.

Ramsay must have shared her excitement for he opened the door even before she knocked. Ramsay, dressed in his customary white shirt and jeans, a smile filling his face, his hands stretched towards her. Ramsay, with a black curly-haired dog at his side.

'Well, here I am,' she said quietly.

He stepped forward, wrapped his arms around her and hugged – just a moment before pulling her inside.

'And here's my place.'

The apartment was a similar layout to Nina's and small by Australian standards. A short narrow passageway led from the front door past a kitchenette into a living room; there was an upright piano against one wall. On the opposite side and through an open door was the bedroom with a neatly made bed. There were books on shelves and weavings on the walls, a framed collage of leaves and bark was propped on a TV, ethnic knick-knacks were displayed on flat surfaces, and a rug in reds and browns was cast across the parquet floor. There was a sofa bed – where George would have slept, she assumed – and an armchair plump with cushions. The place was comfortable, bright and warm, very different from the Blake house in Melbourne. It appealed to her, appealed greatly.

'None of this is mine, of course,' Ramsay said, waving a hand at the living room. 'It belongs to one of the horns at the college – she's on sabbatical somewhere in Europe.' He bent down and scooped up the dog. 'I don't care for her taste in interior design, but she can't be faulted when it comes to dogs. This is Lotte.'

Zoe knew all about the dog. A couple of months earlier when his New York accommodation was being arranged, Ramsay had been offered the choice of two apartments. As soon as he learned that one came with a dog, the amenities of the places became irrelevant. So wooden when it came to people, Ramsay lavished a vast range of loving emotion on dogs. When they were children, his dog, Schnabel, was his constant companion. And once he started touring it was the separation from his dog that he found most difficult.

Lotte, he said, was made to order. 'She's perfect. Musical, with a preference for the classical repertoire, obedient, a favourite with other dogs in Riverside Park. And she couldn't be more attached to me if we were from the same litter.'

If dogs took over the world, Ramsay would be one of the few humans to feel entirely at home, although a quick glance around the small apartment showed him to be quite at home here. Maybe Ramsay was about to learn he could manage without George.

Zoe nodded at the piano.

'It's adequate,' he said. 'And I have a lovely middle-aged Steinway at the college.' He crossed the room and beckoned to her to join him. 'This building is full of musicians, in fact the entire Upper West Side is awash with us.' He leaned out the window and raised his voice over the traffic. 'Music's everywhere. The Lincoln Center and Juilliard are in walking distance, so are the Manhattan School of Music and Mannes. Everything I want is right here.' His hands took in the whole neighbourhood, then he pulled back inside and, uncharacteristically, seized her by the arms. 'It's heaven, Zoe. And everyone's so friendly. I've invitations most nights for dinner and music. And I never have to go far,' his smile broadened, 'often just a few floors in the elevator. It really is heaven.'

He truly looked as if he had landed in paradise.

'So you're managing without George?' She kept her voice casual. What she really wanted to say was how are you getting on without the man who has choreographed your every move these past dozen years?

Ramsay's face filled with delight. 'I was nervous at first, but you predicted that, so I wasn't surprised. I just went about my business and the nerves disappeared.'

Zoe had deliberately warned him. Ramsay had rarely been thrown on his own resources and never for longer than a few days. She was terrified he would flee New York before she arrived and rush home to George.

'I *was* nervous,' Ramsay now continued. 'After all, George looks after everything, he looks after *me*. But I knew you were coming, and you did promise to stay until George arrives.' He paused, and when he again spoke the words came more slowly. 'If George arrives. Apparently he's had a pretty rough time. Some sort of infection. He's okay now, but you said you could stay until the residency finishes – the full five months.' Anxiety had now transformed his face. 'You said five months, if George can't make the trip. You haven't changed your mind?'

She shook her head and immediately he relaxed.

At the college he had been welcomed as an honoured guest. His teaching load was light: a weekly master-class with some remarkable young musicians, and office hours on Friday afternoons. He had a practice room with superb acoustics, and access to a performance space for which he was to understand – as did everyone else – he had priority use. If he needed a secretary, there were secretaries; if he needed other musicians to play with he could choose from the best in the country.

'Everyone's been so helpful, both here in the apartment building and at the school, so helpful that –' and he dashed into the bedroom, 'look what I've managed to get for you.'

Ramsay returned with a cello. 'It's no Stradivarius, but it'll do.'

When they were children together in Raleigh Court, Zoe used to imagine playing house with Ramsay, their own place, just the two of them, no adults, no other children. She envisaged it as a miniature castle, with turrets and a conical tower, a moat with a bridge, and a central garden in which lived chimpanzees and macaws (she would have liked a unicorn too but that was stretching her fantasy too far). Inside the castle was a special food room – not a kitchen, a kitchen was her mother's domain – with shelves of chips and chocolate, a cupboard with a perpetual supply of orange cake and chocolate biscuits, a fridge which never ran out of green lemonade or icy poles, and an oven that always contained hot pies and sausage rolls. Their own place, just the two of them, with a new TV and the latest video-game console, Ramsay's piano and her cello. There'd be duets every day, and a single bedroom like the one Ramsay shared with Sean, and every night after lights out they'd talk for hours. And here they were exactly as she had always wanted, but better, so much better because they were adults, and in faraway New York. The freedom, the possibilities, the future itself were far more wonderful than ever she could have imagined.

She took the instrument from Ramsay and ran the bow over the strings. She looked up at him. 'I'm so happy to be here,' she said.

And he laughed and said he was happy too.

Their time had come, Zoe knew it and she was sure Ramsay knew it too. He opened all the doors of his life to her. He produced the cello so they could play together, and over the next few days he showed her around the college and introduced her to his new friends. Everyone assumed she was Ramsay's girlfriend because invitations were now extended to her as well. Soon there was dinner and music every night, and while she knew Nina was disappointed to be seeing so little of her, when it all worked out, as she knew it would, her sister would be happy for her.

How often it happens that a lover is given precedence over a sister – or a brother or a close friend. It's as if you know the sister will withstand all manner of slight, even blatant neglect. Certainly the sister will be there with her sisterly love long after the lover has departed – not that anyone thinks that today's lover will ever join the ranks of ex-lovers: one always embarks on a new love wearing forever's rose-coloured glasses.

In retrospect, and there was plenty of retrospective replaying of those early weeks in New York, Zoe should have allowed more time for Nina, but the fact was she could not have too much of Ramsay. And he clearly felt the same. There was the cello and the dinner invitations, and then he produced two bicycles so they could ride the boroughs together.

'A different borough for each month we're in New York,' he said. That she was a nervous bike-rider even in the quiet streets of suburban Melbourne was suddenly irrelevant: Ramsay would look after her.

On that first morning of their New York adventure, Ramsay was full of his new life.

'I love it here, Zoe. The work at the college is light, I eat when I want, I sleep when I want, I practise when I want. And now you're here as well.'

He sat down at the piano and launched into Liszt's *Grand Galop Chromatique*, an exhilarating dash that had always been one of his happy pieces. As Zoe watched him at the tatty upright, his hands speeding over the keys, she knew that wherever he was going he was taking her with him.

When he was finished there was no need for words, rather she took his hands and held them between her own, his skin warm against hers, just a moment before he pulled free.

'Play with me, Zoe. Let's play our Beethoven in Manhattan.'

He meant the Fourth Cello Sonata in C, the very first duet they had learned together. Our Beethoven, he had always called it. She placed a chair to the right of the piano where she could see his face and hands, tuned up and with her opening notes guided him in.

Some duets have a gladiatorial rumble but not this Fourth. From the beginning so close in the tiny room, she could hear his breathing but would have felt it anyway. She leaned into the long bowing of the solo opening, the sonata's key phrase, only a dozen notes but located in the cello's favourite register, and when she handed the melodic line to the piano, there was Ramsay, eyes closed, face euphoric, feeling exactly what she was feeling. Then the two of them together in the sweetest dialogue, two different voices but echoing each other, handing the melody back and forth in perfect synchronicity, one, two, three minutes and then suddenly – how they thrilled to the drama of the mid-movement change – with a clarion of unison notes and they're leaping and swooping together, swirling around each other, the connection so strong and intense that the piano – Ramsay – falls to a murmur at exactly the right moment, followed by a change of tempo in unison as if some magical thread joined their thoughts, their very selves. They're sitting a metre apart yet they might be inside the same skin; every movement of his prods her own muscles, every movement of hers and he adjusts to fit. She feels him, the freedom and happiness, the past and the future, it's all here in their music.

Nina said that Ramsay could never walk inside another's heart, nor indeed open the door to his own. Emotions for him existed only in the music. But Nina was wrong. Music and emotions were inextricably bound, that much was true, but music was the only way to Ramsay's heart.

'I like playing music with you more than anyone else,' he had said when she was fifteen years old, then eighteen, then twenty and twenty-two. And now here in New York. It was, Zoe believed, an admission of love.

They were only children when first they performed this piece. It was in front of their families, she remembers the occasion so well, the shock of it, guiding him in with the solo entry from the cello, the ensuing dialogue, the stunning intimacy. And when they were finished and prickling with the certainty of their partnership, she saw in his face the wonder she herself felt.

'Aren't you both marvellous?' her mother had said.

'They were made to play together,' George added.

And so they did, year after year. And while she felt sorry for Sean, if Ramsay could have only one of them, she wanted it to be her. Joined in the music, that was how it had long been, and now joined in New York. So much music over the years, complex, knotty music, flamboyant pieces, restrained pieces, combative pieces and gentle pieces, together they have cracked the code of human experience. And now as they play their Beethoven in New York, the happy perfection of C major and George half a world away, she revels in the attainable future.

They reach the end of the sonata, they are holding on to each other, and their gaze is holding on, and still holding when the sound fades to silence. Aren't we marvellous? She hears the words although neither has spoken. Some musicians speak of telepathy, but it's not telepathy; what she and Ramsay share is deep knowledge. You see each other, you feel and hear each other, you can't move without the other. The air you breathe is suffused with your extravagant togetherness.

Zoe walks into his apartment and within minutes they are settled in their unique and familiar intimacy. They've been waiting all their lives for this.

There are periods in a life when immediate experience becomes your entire world; every one of your actions is full strength, every moment inflamed. Pain can bring on these times, so too can grief, but by far the most tantalising are those threaded by bliss. You don't follow the news, you don't notice your neighbours, books remain closed, the TV is turned off. Whether days be hot or cold, whether you're crushed on the subway or lounging in the park, whether confronted by louts or angels, this time is immune to anything toxic, this time is sublime.

Zoe Jameson arrived in New York and was living her dreams. She and Ramsay binged on music, on the city, on like-minded people, on each other; they were never really sober, never firm-footed enough to see themselves clearly. For five whole weeks their shared life was the only life. So rich was the present that they were not waiting for something to happen, it was already happening.

Every morning Zoe would leave Nina's apartment and walk the dozen blocks to Ramsay's building. Ramsay would be waiting for her in the lobby with the dog. Together they made their way to the bagel shop where Ramsay would wait in the street while she went inside. Sometimes the queue stretched almost to the door, and there was always someone loitering at the entrance, hand outstretched for small change. Initially she bought just two bagels, still warm in the paper bag, and by the time they arrived back at Ramsay's apartment the bagels, gorgeously gluey in the mouth, were half eaten. And they would turn to each other, laugh, and go back for more. After the first couple of mornings they bought four bagels.

'Bagels,' Ramsay said. 'Edible Bach.'

'Surely not Bach,' she said with a questioning smile. 'More like Brahms.'

'Wanna Brahms?' he'd say when she arrived each morning.

After breakfast and a morning of music they'd walk down to Riverside Park where Lotte would play with the other dogs.

Standing there with other couples, Zoe felt as if they were a family, she and Ramsay with their dog. Then it was back to the apartment to collect the bikes, and off they'd ride, through the noise and bustle of the daytime city into the quieter residential streets; there they'd dismount in order to talk more easily. Most college days she'd accompany him to the campus and practise while he practised or sit in on his classes. And most evenings there was dinner and music with friends.

Her sister didn't complain – she had always known how it was between her and Ramsay. And when Nina stopped trying to make arrangements with her, Zoe couldn't be sorry; she had never known such happiness.

2.

Nina gazed out the office window. The flags of the UN member countries tossed and twisted in the wind; down at street level tourists wrapped in coats posed for photos. On First Avenue the traffic surged and lagged, held up by frequent traffic lights and pedestrians of every age, shade and style. So much was happening down here. There were several overseas missions in the area, a bevy of tugs and barges on the East River, an ever-changing theatre on United Nations Plaza, and Zoe, who had been in Manhattan nearly a month, had not found time to make a single visit.

Zoe was occupied full time with Ramsay.

Nina had wanted her sister to absorb with her the sheer energy of this amazing city. And she had wanted to bring her here to the UN, show her around, take her into sessions, share her own hopes and optimism about all these nations congregated together. Nina could not have said where she thought she'd be in her early twenties or indeed the work she'd be doing, but never in her wildest dreams did she imagine being in New York and working at the UN. Of course she wanted to share this with her sister.

When first she arrived, she had fallen for the city instantly and totally. There was something about the place that enabled her to be as she had always wanted – not that she could have defined what that was exactly, it had taken New York to show her. The city had magically peeled away her outer layers to expose parts never before glimpsed. Felix said her response to New York was nothing other than the common sensibility of the traveller, that away from home and released from the constraints and expectations of family and other familiars, she could slice off huge chunks of her history and replace them with more desirable influences; she could, like all travellers, make herself anew.

She resented that he would so easily dismiss her passion for New York: the city wasn't ordinary and neither was her response to it. But as so often happened with Felix, she kept her irritations to herself. Felix Hovnanian was a married man and she was the affair; there was no future to invest in – there was, in fact, no future. Although Felix behaved as if there were. He talked about trips they would make together, not one or two but several; and the previous winter when he'd seen how much she'd enjoyed the Olympics on TV, he promised to take her to the next winter games. In four years' time. Four years!

He had wanted Nina to live with him in New York, be his 'holiday wife' as Nina herself termed it. And what, she asked, was she expected to do when his permanent wife telephoned from Sydney? And when he talked to his sons? She didn't want to be skulking in the background, nor did she want to be homeless when his family visited in the school holidays. But mostly she didn't want to live with him, and certainly not in New York. Felix had no intention of leaving his wife, but even if he were available Nina could not see him in her long-term future. He said she made him feel young, she refrained from telling him he made her feel old. He said he loved her, but Nina was of the opinion that spousal bedrock provided him with the rope he needed for his extra-marital affections to fly loose and free.

And besides, she had been offered an apartment, a sublet on the Upper West Side at 100th, which came fully furnished with added extras of rent control and two cockatiels. With Felix at E 62nd the location was perfect, and she was amused by the idea of living so far from Australia with two Australian parrots. She was nervous of dogs – Ramsay always had a dog and none was particularly friendly to anyone other than Ramsay – and she was allergic to cats, so the cockatiels were ideal. She cut short any further discussions with Felix by moving into the sublet.

While there was a vibrancy throughout Manhattan, and an edge and an insouciance to its inhabitants, these qualities, it seemed to her, were more pronounced on the Upper West Side. Here the shops were always open and the pavements always crowded. There were beggars begging and psychos singing, there were wealthy matrons and lumpy bag ladies, there were blacks and Hispanics, Asians and Jews. Central Park was a few blocks to the east and Riverside a few blocks to the west, and dotted through the area were galleries, bars, concert venues and museums. If she were to inscribe a circle from her apartment with a radius of two kilometres, this small area would supply everything she had ever wanted. And while the apartment itself was tiny, with the parks so close and street-life so plentiful she never felt confined.

Each morning she travelled from the Upper West Side down to the UN; from neighbourhood to world community was how she experienced it. She believed in the ideals and promises of the United Nations. It didn't matter to her that there were interest groups jostling and lobbyists lobbying, that there were deals being done every day; it didn't matter that any achievements came slowly and invariably diluted. She appreciated what the UN stood for. Felix ascribed her idealism to youth, he said she'd grow out of it. She told him she'd prefer to remain an unreconstructed idealist than become a sour old cynic like him.

'Your generation has made such a mess of things,' she said. 'And rather than admit it you damn the world and its people as a bad lot. This immature observer thinks you and your contemporaries could benefit from a few youthful ideals.'

It was a regular argument and not one on which they were ever likely to agree.

Australia was so far from anywhere, a huge blob of land suspended in splendid isolation from the rest of the world. But here, in the thick of things, in the rush, the passion, the multicultural mix, she was learning what she truly valued. And the New Yorkers themselves with their devil-may-care attitude, their bluntness and confidence, it was how she wanted to be – and would become if she lived here long enough. But the job was finished and although Felix had not accepted it, they were finished too. He wanted her to return home with him; he wanted his mistress, far more portable than his wife, to go wherever he went. He said he would find her a tutoring job at Sydney University while she completed a PhD, he painted what he regarded as a rosy future. Rosy for him but dead-end for her. She would not be going home with him. But now with Ramsay in New York, she didn't want to stay here either, watching her sister whirling ever closer to the edge of a perilous cliff.

The fax machine rang. It was a message from Felix's wife confirming her flights to New York. *I've missed you so much this time*, she wrote. *We must never again be apart so long.*

Nina placed the fax in the centre of Felix's desk. She checked her watch, he would be back from his meeting soon and she didn't have much time. She took a sheet of UN paper. She would not be returning to Australia with him, she wrote, nor would she be staying in New York. A job in London had come up and she would be leaving for the UK soon. She wished him and his family well. *I'd prefer not to see you*, she wrote. *It's better this way.* She put her note alongside his wife's fax, collected her few belongings and left the office for the last time.

Exactly five weeks after Zoe arrived in New York, Nina left for London. In the space of a week, she resigned from a job that was already finished, and left an affair that was already over. She told Zoe the same story she had given to Felix. But there was no job in London and distressingly few contacts – although she would manage, and better than if she stayed in New York. With another four months on the sublet, Zoe would live there and take care of the cockatiels. Nina embraced her sister and in that embrace tried to impart the strength and common sense that romantic love shies away from.

Zoe was full of elder-sister concern. 'Write to me as soon as you're settled,' she said. 'And remember, if things don't work out in London you can always come back here. Though goodness knows where Ramsay and I might be.'

At the time of her leaving, Nina wanted to believe it was not cowardice that drove her from New York but selflessness. As she boarded the red-eye to London she hoped this was the case. But more than anything, she hoped she was wrong about Ramsay, that Zoe would be the exception in his otherwise narcissistic existence.

3.

Nina left for London and Zoe now had her own place. Stretching ahead were four months in New York, just her and Ramsay together. They had already established a routine, one they both relished, but if their relationship was to move forward as it was clearly ready to do, some adjustments needed to be made. Knowing Ramsay as well as she did and her own shyness notwithstanding, Zoe knew it was up to her to guide them into the next phase.

On the third morning after Nina's departure, when Zoe met Ramsay in the lobby of his apartment building, she proposed that after they bought the bagels they should walk Lotte in the park and then go back to her place for breakfast.

'I want you to see where I live.'

'And our music?' he said. 'What about our music today? And our touring?'

He had planned a ride up to the Cloisters, and while she assured him there'd be plenty of time later in the day he was clearly uncomfortable with the change. But he did manage it, as she hoped he would; he did it for her.

They bought their bagels and walked to the dog-run in Riverside Park. Later it occurred to her that Ramsay had deliberately delayed at the park, talking to other dog owners at greater length than usual and letting Lotte play until she did not have a run left in her. And it was a slow walk back to the apartment although, again in retrospect, what she had attributed to Lotte's being tired may have been Ramsay's stalling. She showed him round the tiny apartment, white and minimalist and shiny-surfaced modern, except for the cockatiel corner which had been transformed into an Australian diorama. He talked with the birds while she prepared coffee and laid out bagels, butter and jam. He settled the dog on the couch and as soon as the food was on the table he began to eat. She put on the Barenboim–du Pré recording of the Brahms first cello sonata – in lieu of our music, she said – and joined him for breakfast.

What then followed was her doing, all of it was her doing. They ate their bagels, they listened to the Brahms, and when the music was finished she led him to the bedroom. She undressed him and placed him between the sheets. He lay on his back, he did not watch her remove her own clothes, he did not watch her slip in beside him. He did not speak as she kissed his face, his eyes, his forehead, his cheeks, his lips. Not speaking nor moving as she kisses his neck, the rim of his ear. She runs her mouth over his chest, the flat stomach, her arm brushes his penis, and as her tongue traces the fine hair down to his navel and her lips trace the definition of his ribs she touches him again with a nonchalance that is anything but inadvertent. She kisses the hard smooth skin of his belly, his penis is erect, she's in no hurry, runs her tongue from hip to hip, and suddenly he's springing forward, he's grabbing her under the shoulders, his fingers dig into her armpits, his penis is hard in her gut, he drags her up his body, tosses her to the mattress, leaps on top of her, pins her to the bed, chains her wrists with his hands. Stop, she shouts. Stop. Her legs are thrashing, he shoves his knees into her thighs, her muscles recoil in pain. Stop, she cries, but he's pumping the air out of her and her voice is only a whimper. It feels like a fist inside her, he's tearing her apart. And then a single clear moment when she knows that the only way this will stop is when he's finished, and the end will come sooner if she gives up the struggle. He plunges into her over and over again, she is silently pleading for him to come. But his rhythm doesn't change, he could pound on for hours. When she can't stand any more, and with a strength powered by desperation, she rolls them both over and now she's atop of him, she's doing the work. It's like having an out-of-body experience, she's separate from him, from all that's happening, up and down and watching his face, the face that tells her everything: Ramsay is utterly absent, his eyes are vacant, she could be anyone, she could be a mechanical device for all it matters to him.

At last he's finished. Deep within she's raw and hurting. She leaves him on the bed and without looking back goes to the bathroom. She leans against the closed door, her wrists are red with his grip, his neat pianist's nails have left red crescents in her armpits.

She hears the bed creak and a minute or two later the sound of shoes on the timber floor. The cockatiels whistle, he calls the dog, the footsteps grow fainter, the front door slams. After he has gone she lies on the terrible bed. She listens to the traffic outside, the constant burr broken by the battering of motor bikes. There's the occasional screech of tyres; people shout. She pulls the quilt over her body. Her skin burns, her vagina feels like it's been hollowed out with sandpaper. All of her lacerated, her dreams most of all. She lies on the bed. The pain reminds her of all she has lost.

It is dark when she finally rouses herself. She fills the hipbath, lowers herself in, drapes a towel around her bare shoulders, and there in the cramped space hunched over, her knees pressed into her breasts, she struggles. She doesn't want to think evil of him, she doesn't want to steep his heart in blackness; it's a torment to know what to do, but her body hammers home the hard truth: her dreams have crumpled, her memories have changed colour, she is not Ramsay Blake's beloved.

In the years to come Zoe held on to those five weeks with Ramsay in New York as her sojourn in Eden. Brief and complete, that time together remained perfect, a snowdome to be taken out when life weighed in with trouble.

Years of hopes buoyed along by all the music they'd played together had drowned out Ramsay's lifelong message: he needed only music and any people he permitted into his life were there by virtue of what they contributed to his music. She didn't know if he was aware of this, but with her hopes now hushed to an embarrassed whisper the message was very clear to her. She had been so stupid: the way in which he had responded to her advances was nothing more than what she deserved. She knew Nina would be horrified, would insist that such violence could never be justified. But even if Nina were still in New York, Zoe would not have told her, would have hidden her physical bruises and silenced the emotional ones, would have kept quiet about the shocking loss of the only future she had ever wanted. *After great pain a formal feeling comes –*. She read Dickinson's poem until it was lodged in memory. And then she repeated it like a mantra until her own hour of lead had been transformed by the strange alchemy of pain.

There will be many who find Zoe's response incomprehensible. All that can be said is that such people have never loved selflessly – not that there's anything to recommend selfless love: the lover is left undernourished and the beloved is deluded. But it is bewilderingly common. Zoe, far from being alone in transforming violence perpetrated on her as her own fault, joins a crowd. That she continued to love Ramsay might be difficult to explain, but it's not all that surprising.

What Zoe most wanted was to return to Australia, to immerse herself in her familiar job, to be surrounded by her kind, unquestioning friends. And from home she could resume contact with Ramsay from a safe distance. But there were the cockatiels to be looked after, and she had promised Ramsay she would be in New York until George arrived, or for the entire period of his residency if need be. When Ramsay telephoned her three days after the incident (this was how she referred to it on the rare occasions her mind took her there) wondering where she was, she realised that from his point of view nothing had changed.

The next day, with her body still bearing his fingerprints, she and Ramsay rode their bikes up to the Cloisters. They walked through the buildings together, gazed at the tapestries and other exhibits and afterwards had coffee in the outdoor café. Sitting at the table, her thoughts kept swerving back to the terrible day. She fought the thoughts, wanted to forget, wanted to be in this beautiful garden with the only man she had ever loved. Shut up shut up, she told her mind. But her mind refused to listen.

And suddenly his hand was upon hers, he was struggling to speak but unable to shape the words. He squeezed her hand and drew it close to his heart, held it there for a long time.

Back at his apartment – she had wanted to go home but he had insisted – he sat her on the sofa and he played for her, one beautiful, sad piece after another. And every phrase told her he understood he had hurt her and he was sorry. By the time she returned to her own apartment her mind was made up. She was in New York for four more months. She would see Ramsay during that time and support him as promised. She would listen to his music, she would explore the city with him, she would accompany him to concerts and dinners, but she would not play music with him. In fact, she doubted she would ever play with him again. Too dangerous. She would tell him she had found a job, a morning teaching job; the cello he had borrowed for her she would keep at her apartment. She would manage.

The next day saw the start of her new routine. She rose early, pulled on tracksuit and trainers, slipped water, money, cigarettes and a book into a small back-pack and went for a run in Riverside Park. Then she found a seat facing the Hudson to watch the rising sun light up the buildings across the river. And there she would remain, reading or just gazing into the morning as New York limbered up for the day. Around eight, she would return to the apartment via a different bagel shop from the one she and Ramsay had frequented, eat breakfast, practise for an hour or two and then visit one of the museums. She would meet Ramsay in the early afternoon after he had finished his own practice. She would manage. It was the type of person she was.

4.

It was a struggle to drag himself out of bed, but now that Elliot is in Riverside Park jogging through the fresh morning air he is pleased to have made the effort. More particularly, he is pleased with himself: how much easier to have remained at home, nursing his head and regrets. But he is a disciplined person, a man of muscular determination – he may have borrowed that phrase from Virginia Woolf – and being out at dawn running off the excesses of a misspent night is much more the Elliot Eugene Wood he believes himself to be, than a miserable waster curled in a quilt.

He takes the left-hand path over the pedestrian bridge, conscious of maintaining his pace despite the steep rise. Ten minutes of exercise and he still feels dreadful, but soon he'll be on the mend. It invariably works: a night's damage can be offset by a morning run, and with an hour in the gym after his last class he should be fully restored. But now his head is pounding, his mouth is foul, his lungs sodden, his legs leaden, and each step punches his stomach and he wants to be sick. He slows down, takes a swig of water, drains the bottle and refills at a water fountain. When he sets off again he is feeling a little better, and he reminds himself that, therapeutic value aside, he actually enjoys a run at this time of year. There's a crispness to the air, and the trees so recently wilting in the suffocating New York summer are now brilliant with fall colours, and on the ground swaddling the trunks lies a changing patchwork of russets and coppers and yellows. Of course he's feeling better.

The Hudson is a broad strip of steel in the early morning shade, and on the other side of the river much of New Jersey is still lit up. He never tires of this view, always feeling more firmly rooted in Manhattan when gazing across at New Jersey. Not that Manhattan isn't home, but he likes to experience it as home, experience it consciously. He spent his first twenty years in Illinois and the last twelve here, but Manhattan is home in a way Peoria never was. Peoria does what cities are meant to do, its concern is with practicalities not sensibility. It's where he grew up, where he was educated, where his family still lives. Not a dream-like city in the way of Paris or Prague, its very ordinariness powered his own dreams. He was always going to leave.

He returns to Peoria for Thanksgiving and birthdays, weddings and other family occasions, stays with his parents and sleeps in his old bedroom, now set up for his sister's children but retaining vestiges of his own boyhood. While he enjoys these visits, he feels nothing in the way of nostalgia. He used to think he was not the nostalgic type, but give him a book from his childhood and he is rushed with bittersweet yearnings, present him with an old girlfriend with whom he parted amicably and there are the same soft tuggings. He's just not nostalgic about Peoria. As for his parents and his sister, he loves them but that has never satisfied his hunger for a world beyond their lives.

Manhattan was that world. He arrived at Columbia for his post-graduate studies and all about him were people he wanted to know: blacks, Jews, Italians, Greeks, Asians, Argentines – girls as well as guys, and within this mix he, a white Protestant American male, experienced a sense of belonging he had not in the Mid-West. As he wandered the streets of New York, as he discussed and argued with his new friends, he felt the contours of himself sharpen. By the end of his first semester he was resolved to make Manhattan his home.

He has always lived on the Upper West Side; this is his New York and he cannot imagine living on the east side or downtown, and with tenure at Columbia he doesn't have to. Of the two parks that border the district, he has a particular fondness for this one, Riverside, just a slender strip of green tracing the Hudson, a neighbourhood park as opposed to the tourist magnet of Central Park. Even during the rush hour the traffic noise from the Parkway is manageable, and a good thing too, for while his legs have settled into a steady rhythm his head is punished by each step. Another few minutes and he knows the pain will have eased, and again he congratulates himself on getting himself out of the apartment when his body was screaming to be left to rest.

He has no idea what time he arrived home last night. He has a vague notion that Bob saw him to his door, he'll check later at the faculty meeting. Not that he feels particularly beholden; after all, none of it would have happened if not for Bob's determination to celebrate his divorce. In fact, before Bob persuaded him to come for a freedom drink, Elliot's plan had been to stay home for an alcohol-free evening and a new biography of Peggy Guggenheim. But Bob insisted on a celebration and said he couldn't do it alone. In the end, a group of them had started out from Columbia – he can't remember who nor the exact time, though it must have been after his five o'clock class. He assumes they worked their way downtown through the bars, they'd done that in the past, and there must have been food at some stage judging by the ketchup on his shirt. He can't remember any aspect of the night; in fact, as he passes the Soldiers' and Sailors' Monument at 89th, as he tries to glide rather than jog to spare his head, he realises that not only has last night disappeared but the day before as well.

It is light now and he pulls his cap lower to shade his eyes and spare his head. The dog-walkers are out, and women pacing in pairs, and plenty of other joggers, too; his head is definitely clearing although his chest still squeals. He pushes himself harder, he knows it will do him good.

And then he sees her. On a park bench beside the path, about eighty yards away. Later he will wonder how it is possible to see someone, actually select her from the surroundings, how you can know with neither evidence nor other prior warning that this woman is important, that you are, in fact, facing your future. She holds herself like a dancer, straight back, long neck, the figure so slight. She has a book in her lap. There is something about her even at a distance, not just her beauty, it's the tranquillity of her, this woman reading on a fresh fall morning in Riverside Park. He slows down, his headache forgotten. She is without a Walkman, just her book and the trees and the sound of birds, and utterly rapt in her own thoughts, for as he draws closer he sees her eyes are closed and the book is turned face down. He recognises it as Mary McCarthy's autobiography, *How I Grew*, the volume that covers McCarthy's college years and first marriage. He passes at a walk and stops a couple of yards further on. He cannot help himself, he has to speak to her, at the same time he doesn't want her to think him a freak or a pervert. He decides on the book.

'Excuse me,' he says.

Her eyes spring open. They're blue, swimming-pool blue. He apologises, he hadn't meant to give her a fright; it was her book that caught his attention, he says. He sees her relax, there's a delicacy about her, in the white skin, the closely cropped blonde hair, the brilliant eyes. He points to Mary McCarthy's book and hears himself say: Hannah Arendt.

'No,' she says, 'not Arendt, but Mary McCarthy.' Her accent is not American. 'She died this week. Mary did.'

Again he apologises and quickly explains his habit of shorthand. 'I think the first part of a sentence but only utter the latter part. It means I often make no sense at all, or, as in this case, I say entirely the wrong thing.' He tells her he is writing an article on Hannah Arendt. 'And of course they – Hannah and Mary – were such close friends.' The words are cascading out of him. 'I'm tempted by the story of that friendship, to write a book of it. They left a huge cache of letters. And yes, it's all past tense now. Both of them gone.'

There's something about communication with strangers met on a plane, or a holiday, or by chance in Riverside Park, something that elicits not only blithe confidences, but eye-opening, heart-pounding revelations. After all, you don't know this person, there's nothing to be lost. But there was everything to lose, Elliot reminds himself, so better if he holds himself in check.

The woman observes no such caution.

'I'm reading Mary McCarthy,' she says, 'because of the love affairs.'

'Yours or Mary's?' The words are uttered before he can stop them. Too direct, he tells himself, and far too personal

The woman smiles, she's clearly not affronted. 'Mary's. She fell in love regularly, and she fell into bed rather often.' She turns the book over and flips through the pages, not reading, more a filtering through the life. 'So many achievements, but it's love I'm interested in.' She smiles again. 'I rather hoped I might learn something.'

'Biography as how-to manual?'

'Why not?' she says. 'Only so much scavenging in the lives of real friends and family is acceptable – not that Mary paid much heed to that: she filched whatever she needed for her fiction. But with the dead, and the subjects of most biographies are quite conveniently dead, you can leap into their private life with equanimity, no fear of backlash, no guilt over prying.' A woman of wit and irony, Elliot is thinking. This woman is perfect. 'And when there's a rich written record as well,' she continues, 'diaries, letters, and in Mary's case her life-based fiction, biography's a rich source of information for life's amateurs.'

'And you? Are you an amateur in love?'

She glances up at him with those extraordinary blue eyes and then looks away. He hears a derisory little snort, sees the faint shake of her head. 'I hardly qualify as a novice.'

Elliot finds this hard to believe. With looks and clearly brains as well, this woman could have any man she wanted.

She's standing up, she's about to walk away. He has to stop her. 'Are you English?' Not the most original of lines.

Not English but Australian, she says. A couple more questions and she is sitting down again and he joins her on the bench. He discovers she is in New York visiting her sister who unexpectedly was called away to London. She'll be here alone for several months. He cannot believe his luck. Her name is Zoe Jameson. She's a teacher and a musician, beautiful in that fine-carved, boyish style that has always appealed to him, an excellent conversationalist, a reader, obviously a traveller and, like him, a poetry lover.

'It's the meeting place of language and music,' she says. 'Poetry is lyrical language.'

'So poets could save opera from extinction?'

She laughs, her whole face laughs. 'I rather think composers would disagree.'

There follows a delighted swapping of their favourite poets. There's some overlap – Auden, Plath, Dickinson – but most of her favourites – Wordsworth, Coleridge, Larkin, Emily Brontë, Judith Wright, Bruce Beaver reflect her Australian schooling, while his – Bishop, Wallace Stevens, O'Hara, Whitman – are firmly rooted in America.

They're sharing their love of poetry and then in a pause she is standing again.

'I really must go.'

He plunges in – no time for hesitation, no time to rehearse options – and invites her for dinner that night. To his surprise she accepts.

During the next eight hours, in between classes and student appointments, Elliot made Zoe Jameson a book: *Poetry for Zoe*. He selected poems about New York from Walt Whitman, Wallace Stevens, Sara Teasdale, Hart Crane, Langston Hughes, Elizabeth Bishop, Adrienne Rich, Frank O'Hara, Nikki Giovanni, Grace Paley and a smattering of Ginsberg. He photocopied each poem onto heavy white paper and bound the sheets into a cardboard folder decorated with sepia-toned pictures of old New York. The hours sped by, Zoe's book grew. He only had two classes, but never had he taught so well. And his memory had returned, for he found himself elaborating his lectures from a cache of quotes suddenly in easy reach. He had known this woman since the morning, a mere handful of hours, yet he felt as he had when he first arrived in New York, with energy so abundant he might never stop.

He left his office at five-thirty and walked the few blocks home. He showered and dressed, took a small beer from the fridge and leafed through *Poetry for Zoe*. Would she think his gift foolish? Might she think *he* was foolish? Or perhaps she'd think the book inappropriate, too much too soon? Although if she had been able to track his mind today she would have discovered far more flamboyant gifts, including a weekend in Paris, a city she said she longed to visit. And beyond gifts, she would have discovered his plans for an entire future together. So pre-occupied had he been he had forgotten about the faculty meeting and he hadn't asked Bob about last night. Not that Bob's account mattered any more, he was finished with bar crawls. Zoe was in New York for the next few months and he wanted to spend every night with her.

It had been Zoe's suggestion they meet at Ivy's Bookshop. 'I'm never late,' she said. 'So if we meet in a bookshop it won't matter if you are.' He didn't bother to say there was absolutely no chance of his being late, instead he told her he made exactly the same arrangement when he was meeting someone. 'Thank God for bookshops,' he said.

'So you think God's a bibliophile?'

'Without a doubt – if, that is, he were to exist.'

The entire day had been full of her, it was only now, as he was preparing for their first evening together, that it occurred to him she might not show up. These things happen: a casual meeting, a close connection, and then you never see the person again. In fact the closeness is possible because you'll never see them again. He quickly finished his beer, slipped the poetry folder into a carry bag, checked his wallet, and headed off down Broadway. It was only a dozen blocks and he practically ran all the way. He arrived at the shop with fifteen minutes to spare.

She was already there, standing at the rear of the shop reading. She raised her head as he entered, a smile filled her face; she replaced the book on the shelf and walked towards him. She was dressed all in black except for turquoise loops in her ears. She was still smiling when she reached him.

'The colour of your eyes,' he said, pointing at her earrings.

He had chosen a neighbourhood trattoria, a place with good food and an alcove set apart from the main dining space. He had booked a table in this area; quiet and private, it was as if they were alone on their own small island. They talked through two courses and a bottle of wine. He was about to order a second bottle when she said she never drank more than a glass or two, she was what they call in Australia a two-pot screamer. He decided against another bottle and instead ordered a single glass of the house burgundy, forcing himself to sip slowly as she talked about her family, her sister, Nina, now in London, her music, her work as a teacher, and a childhood friend currently in New York, a pianist who was apparently among the best. Elliot decided to check out the concert program in the city over the next couple of months, find a Ramsay Blake performance and surprise her with tickets.

With the drink finished and an urge for another he decided it was time for his gift. He handed the book to her, saw her surprise and, when she opened it, her pleasure. She looked across at him; her gaze, so steady and intense, held him fast. Such a thoughtful gift, she said, a beautiful gift.

She leafed through the book; she knew most of the poets, but nearly all the poems were new to her. 'New York in a folder. It's wonderful.'

'Poetry for Zoe.' He tried to introduce a lightness to his voice, but he stumbled on her name.

'Read me one of your favourites.'

He took the book and turned the pages to Nikki Giovanni's 'Just a New York Poem'. His hands were shaking, blood was thrashing in his ears, his legs wouldn't support him if he were to stand. He had given lectures to audiences of several hundred, but he had never been so nervous as he was now. He hardly heard himself say the title or the poet's name, and then suddenly the jittering dropped away and he and Zoe truly were on their own small island.

> *i wanted to take*
> *your hand and run with you*
> *together toward*
> *ourselves down the street to your street*
> *i wanted to laugh aloud*
> *and skip the notes past*
> *the marquee advertising "women*
> *in love" past the record*
> *shop with "The Spirit*
> *In The Dark" past the smoke shop*
> *past the park and no*
> *parking today signs*
> *past the people watching me in*
> *my blue velvet and i don't remember*
> *what you wore but only that i didn't want*
> *anything to be wearing you*
> *i wanted to give*
> *myself to the cyclone that is*
> *your arms*
> *and let you in the eye of my hurricane and know*
> *the calm before*

and some fall evening
after the cocktails
and the very expensive and very bad
steak served with day-old baked potatoes
and the second cup of coffee taken
while listening to the rejected
violin player
maybe some fall evening
when the taxis have passed you by
and that light sort of rain
that occasionally falls
in new york begins
you'll take a thought
and laugh aloud
the notes carrying all the way over
to me and we'll run again
together
toward each other
yes?

He could not say at what point in the poem she put her hand
over his, but it was there when he finished reading, and so it
remained for the rest of the evening.

The next three-and-a-half weeks passed in talk and laughter,
private poetry readings and love-making. They would go to
one of the local eateries and it felt new, the neighbourhood
shops were new, the streets and parks he had criss-crossed
for twelve years were new, conversation was new, poetry

engraved on him as only memorising can do was new. He read to her, she read to him, they read together.

'Reading poetry like this,' she said, 'is like musicians playing duets.'

And the sex was unlike anything he had ever experienced. He had always held that sex was a purely physical activity, supplying much the same sort of satisfaction as a good meal or a run in the park. He used to deride the expression 'to make love': to convert sex to an emotional state, he had long believed, was oxymoronic. But with Zoe he changed his mind. She kissed him after their second date and again at the end of their third – both lunches. The fourth date was another dinner. He walked her home, and instead of the expected kiss in the lobby, she invited him up to the apartment. That night and again in the morning he made love for the first time in his life. He made love nearly every day for the next three weeks. To touch her was to show he loved her, to be touched by her fuelled his love. She was a strong and vigorous lover, yet she could be slow and gentle and almost unbearably arousing as well. Zoe Jameson ran love's repertoire of emotions.

And then she went away.

He could not believe she would leave, and once she was gone he was terrified she wouldn't return. She was visiting a friend, she said, a school friend from Australia on holiday in San Francisco. And even when she explained that this had been her very best friend at school, it made no difference. Elliot did not want to be away from her, not for a week, not for a single day.

'Your friend might persuade you to return to Australia.'

Elliot knew he sounded pitiful but he couldn't stop himself. And when Zoe explained she could not possibly leave New York for who would look after the cockatiels, it was not the response he wanted. Who would look after him? Desperate to maintain any connection with her, he offered to look after the birds, but she had already arranged for her pianist friend to do that. This Ramsay Blake could go to her apartment whenever he liked, wander her space, sit in her chair, drink her coffee, stare out her window. Her old friend, Ramsay, could spend the entire week in her apartment; while he, her new lover, was severed completely.

Zoe left for a holiday with one old friend, leaving another in charge of her New York life, and Elliot slumped. It would have helped if he could telephone but she said she did not know where she would be staying. She would call him, she said. But – and her voice was firm – it was only a week. A lost week as it turned out. It coincided with the Thanksgiving break. He had thought she would be in New York so he had told his parents he'd not be spending the holiday with them; by the time she revealed her plans it was impossible to get a flight. And besides, he didn't want to be with his family in Peoria. If he couldn't be with Zoe, he wanted to be alone and miserable in New York.

He had his first drink contemporaneous with her flight taking off. There followed the bender to beat all benders. He bought the day's booze in the morning and returned to the apartment. He didn't leave until the next morning when he went again to the liquor store. He drank bourbon, he drank vodka, and he kept a supply of the white wine Zoe favoured and drank a bottle of that each day too. He didn't bother with running off the damage, he didn't go to the gym. There was no point. The lost weekend stretched into a week.

She called him two days before she was due home. He didn't make it to the phone in time – and fortunate for him, as he lacked the capacity to form words much less make any sense. Her voice on the answering machine was sunny and loving; she sounded everything he was not. He replayed the message again and again. He drank faster than his usual fast and finished the day's quota by six o'clock. He went out for more. And there in the street outside the liquor store he paced and battled. His booze-battered brain couldn't argue, his booze-battered brain had been silenced. His body was straining towards the store, but something kept him dithering on the sidewalk – afterwards he would say it was the basic human drive for survival – and eventually led him home.

It took all of two days to sober up; he remembered nothing of the time except that sobering up required every ounce of his energy. He swallowed a slug of vodka before he took a cab to La Guardia to meet her. It was Dutch courage, he told himself, and then a promise uttered aloud: *my last Dutch courage.*

Fall moved into winter, Zoe thrived in the icy days. She would spend hours outside, walking through wind, sleet and snow.

Elliot laughed at her. 'The weather's keeping all sensible people indoors –' he was trying to rub the warmth back into her body, 'and the mad Australian's flirting with frostbite.'

Sense, she said, had nothing to do with it. After a lifetime of boiling Australian Januarys, New York in winter was not simply novel, it was actually exciting. As she walked the wintry streets, her face freezing, her body camouflaged in New York winter clothes, she had a sense of being inside a Woody Allen film: it was fun and it was liberating.

One day after a fall of snow, she and Elliot were walking together in Riverside Park and suddenly he went down on one knee.

'Marry me,' he said to her. 'Please, Zoe Jameson, be my wife.'

There was an eagerness in his face, and love too – this man loved her – and his grip on her hand was strong, all of Elliot was strong. She looked into his shining face and everything seemed possible.

Four months after their first meeting, Elliot and Zoe were married. If she'd had her way, the wedding would have taken place early in the morning in a frosty Riverside Park. Instead they settled for a quiet civil ceremony with dinner afterwards, just a small gathering with Elliot's parents, his sister and brother-in-law and some friends from the faculty. Zoe didn't invite Ramsay; she could not have married Elliot or indeed anyone if he was present. But with George now arrived and the two of them in Boston that weekend, Ramsay couldn't have come anyway. Zoe had told him a week earlier she was to be married. He'd been curious enough to ask about the groom, but showed no surprise nor, she noted, as if to drive the truth home, did he show any regret. He wished her well, and he sounded genuine. He wanted her to be happy, he said.

The evening before the wedding Zoe rang her parents in Melbourne. She had mentioned Elliot a few times in her letters but nothing to suggest the relationship was serious.

'Are you sure?' her mother said. And – 'What's the rush?' asked her father. But given her parents had married within months of meeting each other, their questions, despite their underlying concern, carried little weight.

And she rang her sister in London. Nina was far more direct. 'What about Ramsay?' she said. 'You've loved him your entire life. You came to New York to be with him. You'd have followed him to the ends of the earth if he'd asked you. What's happened with Ramsay?'

Zoe pulled out her prepared response. 'Ramsay's married to his music,' she said. 'We're each other's best friend and that won't change. He's happy for me.'

'So he and Elliot have met?'

'Of course they've met,' Zoe lied. And then lied some more. 'Ramsay's going to be our witness. Our best man.'

Elliot and Zoe flew to Paris for their honeymoon, ten days in the city of romance. It was during this first extended period together that Elliot learned of Zoe's practice of slotting her life into compartments; he learned too that some of those compartments were closed to him. They would spend the morning sight-seeing, then stroll to one of the Paris gardens for a makeshift lunch of bread, cheese and fresh fruit. And then she would disappear; off by herself for a couple of hours and he had no idea where she went or what she did. Later, when he realised the situation between her and Ramsay, he guessed her time alone was actually time spent with Ramsay: in her thoughts, her daydreams, postcards, letters, even the occasional phone call. But this was much later. When she left him during those afternoons in Paris he felt hurt: this was their honeymoon, every minute in her company would not have been too much for him. He suffered but he cautioned patience: they were at the beginning of their marriage; as they grew closer, as they built their own shared life, so she would invite him into all that mattered to her. The reasoning meant he didn't badger her but neither did it make the hours alone any easier. He'd mute his hurt with coffee and cognac, but his mind wouldn't stay away from her, his body wouldn't either;

he wanted her, he wanted her all the time. And he needed her to want him in the same way.

Then she would return and everything was perfect again. In fact, the first two years of their marriage, the New York years, were happy. Although again, when he finally realised the situation with Ramsay, the happiness might have had less to do with himself and more to do with Ramsay's being elsewhere. And he was at the university every day; Zoe could have her couple of hours alone, longer if she wanted, without it impinging on him. But when they were together it was as if nothing could separate them. He loved her, he believed there was nothing he did not want to know about her. And she loved him. Later he would question if she'd ever loved him, but at the time he felt her love, and in its glow he grew in his own estimation.

He published his biography of Elizabeth Bishop during their first year together and finished his article on Hannah Arendt. He gave up the idea of writing a book about the friendship between Arendt and McCarthy, and began instead his research on Djuna Barnes. He had never been so productive. And he and Zoe travelled, not only in the US, but places in Africa and Central Europe where he'd never been before. And in all that time there were no prolonged benders, although the occasional lost night – nothing to worry Zoe, nor him, for that matter – but increasing in frequency as the months passed. It was one of many reasons that made the job in Australia attractive.

Centres for biographical studies were being established in universities throughout the Western world. Tom Wolfe's 'me decade' had spilled into the 'me and you decades': it seemed people could not get enough of other people's lives. Specialist celebrity magazines devoted to gossip filled the newsstands, and there was a host of new TV shows that took the rather innocent *Candid Camera* of the sixties and seventies, tizzied it up and aimed it at the lives of anyone keen to notch up fifteen minutes of fame. Biography was booming and universities seized on this as a means of boosting dwindling enrolments in the humanities. Australia was following the trend.

In 1992 Elliot and Zoe arrived in Melbourne where Elliot had been appointed director of the newly established Centre of Biographical Studies. Zoe was pregnant and keen to be home, and Elliot was keen to be wherever she wanted to be. And it wasn't a bad idea to put some distance between himself and his old drinking mates. Impending fatherhood, a new job and a new country would put him on the wagon and keep him there. These were his thoughts as he and Zoe settled into their new life in Melbourne. Zoe's parents embraced him, Zoe's friends warmed to him, his colleagues welcomed him, the future stretched ahead with neither blemish nor shadow.

Chapter 8. Cravings

1.

It is just after nine in the morning and Elliot is seated in his study. His Elizabeth Hardwick lies in a neat stack on the desk. He rests his hands on the manuscript: five years of work and at last it is finished.

Once he would have shared this milestone with Zoe. It was French champagne and oysters when his Elizabeth Bishop was finished, and a night spent at a swank hotel when the contract was signed; there was more champagne when the proofs were corrected, and a meal at New York's finest when his advance copy arrived. With the first complete draft of his Djuna Barnes, there was a celebration to mark that too, but he ruined it – his drinking was off the rails by then. The evening had ended with Zoe grabbing the manuscript and throwing it at the wall.

'Drink with your famous dead women,' she had shouted. 'They liked booze as much as you.'

By the time Djuna was finished he had stopped drinking, but he didn't know how to celebrate without alcohol, and besides, by then Zoe wasn't living with him.

Hardwick wasn't a drinker, he'd like Zoe to know, but she isn't interested in his work these days; Zoe isn't interested in him. And in this, as with most things, they're poles apart. For no matter where he is, whether alone or in company, working or not, yesterday or tomorrow, and as his laptop slips into the photo library screen-saver, at this very moment, he feels the pull of his wife.

Photos float across the screen and he tightens with anticipation as images of the children, friends, colleagues, picnics, parties pass in front of him. He's willing the photos of Zoe to appear, pictures from their early days in New York, photos taken on the honeymoon in Paris, on their various vacations, at their first house in Melbourne, Zoe with the babies, Zoe with her cello, with her students, but the Zoe pictures are mixed in with all the others and he's too impatient for chance to produce her. He opens his photo library and selects the special Zoe folder he has made: three hundred and ninety-seven photographs and every single one of her. He sets his preferences to slide show and sits back to watch his wife.

Almost immediately one of his favourites appears, the two of them sitting together on the bench in Riverside Park where he had first seen her. There'd been a fall of snow and they are framed by the crisp white cold, the two of them swaddled in their winter coats and Zoe's red scarf looped around both their necks; and a short time later when they resumed their walk, he'd knelt in the snow and asked her to marry him. Here's a photo taken in Paris, a crisp spring day, the same red scarf and the two of them – newlyweds – embracing beneath the marvellous metal of the Eiffel Tower. And a lovely sequence of photos taken during an afternoon on the Chobe River, idyllic at the time but in retrospect ... and he shakes off the thought: enough of retrospective wisdom, he doesn't want to lose the happy times. That trip to Botswana was particularly special because Zoe, far more interested in cities than nature, had planned it knowing how much it would appeal to him. And it was during their cruise on the Chobe River that she'd turned to him and said how happy she was. 'Happier than I ever thought possible.'

It had been a perfect day in a week of perfect days, the water calm, the sky a rich African blue, the air sweetly warm. A herd of elephants walked in single file through the shallows on one shore, on the opposite bank gazelles grazed peacefully in the late afternoon sun. He remembers every detail. Zoe leaned against him, her hand clasping his as the boat meandered along. Up ahead in a broad cove a cluster of large smooth stones broke the surface of the water, and as the boat drew closer Zoe had started laughing. 'Not stones,' she said, 'but hippos.'

They watched the great beasts sink into the water and rise up again, eggcup eyes appearing and disappearing; and when the guide switched off the motor they heard splashing and snorting and a gentle roaring as the huge domed heads broke the surface. One of the creatures opened its marvellous mouth revealing a gigantic cavity with fist-sized teeth, another followed suit and then another. 'We're seeing a minuet of hippos,' Zoe whispered.

As the boat continued up-river, they saw another family of elephants trekking up the bank, some fully grown, others youth-sized, and two babies nudging the baggy legs of their mothers. Buffaloes were feeding on the lush grass, their massive shoulders bent forward, pale heavy horns outlined against the rich green turf. Fish eagles swooped through the air and dived into the fertile waters, and in the shallows they saw the sculpted hillocks of a crocodile's back.

The sun sank lower, yet the sky remained a brilliant blue, the river a deep green, everything intensified by the African light. As the boat sailed on through the tranquil water, he and Zoe settled into the gentle movement. The sky was turning a streaky red and the waterbirds were sounding a noisy chorus when suddenly they were hit by a putrid smell, a rotting flesh smell, and there in the shallows – they both saw it at the same time – lay the bloated body of a dead buffalo. The creature was on its side, its head concealed in the long reeds at the water's edge; its right fore and hind legs, stiffened by death, poked crazily into the slack warm air. Nearby, perched on the bank, were several vultures; they stood motionless and menacing, watching the dead animal.

'What's happening here?' he'd asked the guide. 'Why are the vultures just standing there? What are they waiting for?'

'The hide of the buffalo is very tough,' the guide had replied. 'Too tough for the vultures. So they must wait for the crocodile to come and tear the hide apart. These vultures, they are waiting for the crocodile.'

He had felt a sinister shadow – not a sense of foreboding about his own life, but something confined to those waiting vultures. It took a couple more years before he saw the personal warning in the benign beast and the patient, cruel vultures, an omen of what would become of his life and his marriage. But in the days of happiness nothing was a warning.

About twelve months ago he had scanned in the photos from their early years: the African photos, their other travels, and so many pictures from those first wonderful months in New York when he fell in love and he thought she did too.

Life before Ramsay, is how he thinks about it, although he knows that for Zoe and by extension for himself, there has never been life before Ramsay: rather it is life before he, Elliot, learned about Ramsay.

Zoe truly looks happy in the pictures taken in 1990 and 1991, before they returned to Melbourne, before his drinking unravelled. Here she is in their apartment on West End Avenue, here she's running in Riverside Park, here tobogganing in Central Park, here with her cello. And of course the trip to Paris – no one could refuse Zoe's 'We're on our honeymoon, will you take our picture?' The best ten days of his life, and twenty-four hours after they returned to New York she saw him drunk for the first time, the first of so many times. And how he wishes he could erase the sore points of a life in the same way you can delete photos or, and he looks at the finished manuscript to his side, polish a life not your own. Yet would it make any difference? There was a weird germ in the mind that drove him to drink, and a thirsting of the heart that drove her to love where no love was returned. Yet he has been sober for a longer period than he drank; she, on the other hand, is still hooked on Ramsay.

Zoe and Nina are in the living room. The previous evening the two of them had met up with old friends and Nina stayed overnight. He can hear their voices, the two sisters chatting together in comfortable rushes of familiarity, talking in a way he does not experience with his wife, nor with anyone. Or rather, anyone living. For he knows that hushed closeness with Lizzie Hardwick, and before her Jean Rhys and Djuna and Elizabeth Bishop. Biography, so close and intimate, the ultimate peering through keyholes and rummaging in closets not your own. The ultimate, controllable 'we', your subject and yourself, and such a contrast with his life here, his sense of living alone in the house. Even his children have exiled him. When they were young they pulled him into the rhythm of their days, they loved having him around; now all he is good for is as a chauffeur with deep pockets. Zoe has never needed him, although she used to want him. 'I prefer being with you to anyone else on this planet,' she once said. Another life. Another self.

He watches to the end of the slide show, three hundred and ninety-seven photos all of his wife. The happy days are long gone, preserved only in pictures, yet he can never have enough of her; still and always it is Zoe he craves.

Cravings, his whole life rent by cravings. And if the cravings suddenly stopped, what would be left of him? Was there something about those hard-wired longings that he clung to? Was it the cravings themselves that held him in thrall and not what he craved for? Booze, his wife, the perfect biography – all of them impossibilities, but still the cravings persist. Although not for booze, not any more. For years he craved alcohol, for years after he'd stopped drinking still the craving. You go to the edge time after time, sometimes you slip over and have that one drink because you're convinced you can control it; then the bottle is empty and soon it's next week and you have to start all over again. Years of sobriety shot through with craving and then a day comes, or at least it did for him, when he realised the craving was gone. No longer did alcohol fill his mind, no longer did he bargain silently with himself, with the liquor shop, with the pub, with this friend or that (just one drink, a small beer or whisky, a small anything); the cravings for alcohol had gone quiet. He wanted to tell Zoe, he wanted her to know this miraculous happening, but by then their communication had been drained of life and he simply could not risk her looking bored or disinterested. He shared it with his AA group and how supportive they had been, but that didn't replace the acknowledgment and praise he wanted from his wife. Wanted unreasonably, he suspected. After all, it's your wife who suffers the greatest when you're drinking; your not drinking, such an achievement for you, is only what she always deserved.

The voices from the living room have stopped. There are footsteps in the hall, his wife's tread. Either she is coming to his study or she will continue past to the laundry. He bargains with himself: she'll stop, she'll enter. Let's go for a walk, she'll say, let's go to Paris, let's shuffle the cards and draw out all aces. The steps draw nearer. The door is slightly ajar, it is never shut. He's had nothing to hide since the day she packed bags for herself and the children and moved in with her parents.

'Come and get us if you stop drinking,' she had said.

If. You. Stop. Drinking. She carved out each word. 'Otherwise don't bother. There's nothing to discuss. It's either your family or your alcohol.'

That night, the night she took the children and left him, he drank. He drank at the pub, he drank at home. He drank beer, he drank rye, and when the rye was finished he moved to vodka. He didn't remember drinking Zoe's cooking sherry, but the empty bottle was on the floor when he awoke the next morning. He felt terrible: his head, his mouth, his gut, his miserable life. His wife was gone, his children were gone. Coffined by alcohol, he lacked breath for insight, but somewhere in the dark hole of himself there was some primitive urge for life.

He rang AA and was told of meetings in his area that evening. No, no, he said, this afternoon. He travelled to Bentleigh, a suburb he had never been to before. It didn't matter, he had plenty of time, his wife had left him and he wasn't drinking. That night he attended a meeting in his own area. The next day he drove to Ivanhoe, in the evening he went local. Time and misery, both of them usually placated by booze, were blocked out now with AA and the complete works of Jane Austen. The days passed, he longed to contact Zoe, he ached for his children, but forbade himself until he was sober for a month. In the past he'd cut down, he'd changed his drinking habits, but never before had he given up alcohol entirely. This time he did, a whole month and not a single slip-up. It was hard, at the time he thought it would be the hardest thing he would ever do. But he has since learned that living with a woman you love who does not love you is harder.

Although does he still love her? He has the habit of loving her, of adoring her, and he has the habit of craving her love. At the same time he's desperate to be free of this implacable longing. Yet still there's that leap of the heart as she knocks on the door. Quickly he shuts his laptop and obliterates all those lovely images of her; the door swings open and she steps into the room. His heart rate has increased. It's this thirst for her still. The rough edge of wanting what you can't have.

Zoe says Nina's off to her apartment to do some work before meeting Sean, and she's about to leave too. He doesn't ask where she is going. He's sure it wouldn't concern Ramsay, not on a weekday morning, but still he suffers the cut of this possibility. The knife sharpens his own reply, excises all warmth and love, leaving only the stockpile of disappointment and longing.

'Why bother to tell me? You'll do as you like. You always do.' Cold and corrosive, he barricades his need. He hates what he has become with her.

She says she is going shopping and then to June's place to cook a few meals. With June back in hospital, she continues, Edward doesn't have time to cook. (June? Edward? More of Zoe's lame ducks, he supposes. Perhaps if he was ill she'd care for him too.) She explains that if she cooks at June's place she can look after the children or at least be available should they want to talk. She does not smile. She certainly does not touch him. They will never again go to Paris.

She leaves his study. He hears the front door shut, he hears the car start up, he does not move. The house is still. He forbids thoughts of his wife, he forbids criticism of his own coldness. This sense of being an automaton is a familiar state these days: flick a switch and he doesn't feel anything; pull down the blinds and life on its knees slips into the darkness.

He reaches for his manuscript of Lizzie Hardwick, the fourth of his big women and the one he loves best. In her foreword to Mary McCarthy's *Intellectual Memoirs*, Elizabeth Hardwick mentions the drinking of the 1930s. 'The cocktail age, how menacing and beguiling to the sweet tooth, a sort of liquid mugger.' It was insights like this, soaring on breath-catching imagery, that made Elizabeth so wonderful. (Drink was everywhere in those days. When Mary McCarthy won the English Horizon Prize for her novel *The Oasis*, Horizon's editor Cyril Connolly, author of *Enemies of Promise*, whose own promise was swamped by food and fine wine together with a surfeit of sloth and self-pity, added a dozen bottles of dry sherry to the £200 prize.) But it was not just Hardwick's language and insights that attracted him, it was also her love for Cal, her husband, the poet Robert Lowell. She loved him through their difficult marriage and afterwards when he married someone else. She loved him when he came back to her in the last year of his life. Lizzie said he was the only genius she had ever known, and she was in a strong position to judge given that she mixed with New York's intelligentsia. Robert Lowell – Cal – was of course impossible in his madness but, as far as Hardwick was concerned, he was a genius mad or sane.

As for his own work, Elliot hopes she would approve. She was dismissive of biographers. 'Biography,' she said to Darryl Pinckney in a 1984 *Paris Review* interview, 'is a scrofulous cottage industry, done mostly by academics who get grants and have a good time going all over the place interviewing.' Yes, he is an academic. Yes, he wins grants, and yes, he enjoys the travel and the interviewing. But biography for him is so much more: not simply a job in the way that teaching is a job, but something he is driven to do. He adores his big women, he hungers to know everything about them, and curiosity when given plenty of space to spread its tentacles is brilliantly liberating. Curiosity allows him to lose himself, lose that irritating demanding 'I'.

He wonders how different his marriage might have been or how different a husband he might have been if he had not involved himself with these other women. He's passionate about his work, a passion as intense as any libidinal urge, and more reliably satisfying too. Life without his big women? He expects he'll never know.

E.M. Forster once considered what happens 'when death becomes a gesture'. But what, Elliot wonders, if *life* becomes a gesture? Every day the same hopes, the same losses, the same resentments, the same silences. This was not the way of his big women; never for them the ruts of habit. Mountains and chasms, clouds and ice floes, his women tried them all – and always with courage. He suspects he lacks courage, that other men would have left Zoe years ago. Perhaps courage is his by proxy, via his big women.

He changes his big women every few years, his wife in contrast endures. Perhaps he should write a biography of Zoe, alter the facts, make her love him best. If he could contain her in words, in a form solid and concrete, he might be able to move forward. A type of memorialising, it occurs to him, and – might all biographies be monuments of sorts? He is infatuated with each of his subjects when he begins – could he still be in the infatuation stage with his wife? – and as he breaks through their crust and works deeper into their life he comes to love them. But by the end there is always a curl of dissatisfaction that propels him to the next subject. No dissatisfaction with Lizzie yet, but it will come.

Dissatisfaction has great energy and it has moved his work along. His marriage has been drowning in dissatisfaction yet nothing has changed: he still loves his wife, while Zoe is still besotted with Ramsay. Dissatisfaction, which promises a future that is an advance on the past, has had no such effect on his marriage.

2.

'I don't understand, Sean. What about South America? You spent months there last year. For the book, you said, the book at last. Those were your very words. And now you say you want to go to Cuba.'

Nina stopped in the bustle of Brunswick Street, she caught Sean's arm, forced him to face her. 'What about your book on South America?'

He shrugged. 'I've missed the boat. South America's old hat.'

He knew he sounded pathetic, he *was* pathetic. But rather than see him as such, Nina simply looked concerned. Her voice was low when next she spoke, and gentle like a mother with her child.

'One day you'll have to stop moving, Sean. One day you'll need to stay at your desk until the work's done.' In the pause that followed he saw her deliberating whether to continue. 'That's if you truly want to write a book.' She put her arm around him and bent her head close to his. 'Sometimes the message to be taken from not doing something is that you never really wanted to do it in the first place.'

She was being kind in her plain speaking, but all he could think was he should have kept his new plans to himself. Though perhaps he wanted to be challenged, perhaps a deep, out-of-reach part of himself wanted someone – not him – to produce an argument that might convince him to change his life.

Nina's arm was still around him. 'Let's get out of this heat and find a café with air-conditioning. We've a lot to discuss.'

Did he want to talk? Had he left himself any choice? And what sort of man was he that he could walk through toxic wastelands alone, trek mountains by himself, explore Naples' back alleys with enough swagger to keep danger at bay, yet he lacked the courage to stay in Melbourne for longer than a couple of months with his partner of many years, working on the book he had always intended to write? He was exhausted from endless movement, and knocked about by the lurching dissatisfactions; he wanted to drop to the pavement right here in one of Melbourne's busiest streets and sleep. Or cry. But Nina was steering him into a café and sitting him at a table. She seemed determined that he have the conversation he had avoided for years.

She waved aside his request for wine. 'I want you on the ball,' she said. 'No escapes, no excuses.' And went to the counter to order coffee.

That morning he had booked a flight to Cuba. Rather than the South American project that had occupied him these past twelve months, he had decided instead to write about twenty-first-century communism, a book shaped around Cuba, China, North Korea and a few of those former Soviet states that had ditched the democratic promise. The airfare was a special fare; it needed to be paid in full within twenty-four hours of booking. He'd be leaving Australia in a month.

There was a queue of people at the counter. Nina would be a while, but she kept her gaze on him, holding him in his seat as if she knew that given the slightest opportunity he'd escape. He turned away and stared out the window at the passing parade. It was a mid-week afternoon but Brunswick Street was buzzing. This strip never closed. Food, drink, books, records, weird gifts and weirder homewares, hats, jewellery, vintage clothing, bondage gear, high-end guitars and exotic flowers: everything you needed for an edgy, cool existence could be found in these couple of blocks.

People had shed their clothes in the stifling heat. There were swathes of toned skin in singlets and shorts, sundresses no bigger than scarves, and a Yakuza's delight of tattoos. These people hanging out in Brunswick Street on a Tuesday were laughing and talking and seemingly without a care. And with money to burn if their shopping bags were any indication.

'Do you think these people have jobs?' Sean asked, when Nina returned to the table.

She laughed. 'That's the sort of question I'd expect from a man in a suit.'

Her comment opened up yet another kitbag of worries, this time about the middle-aged values he seemed to have picked up. 'They look so happy. Carefree.'

'When did you last feel that way?' Nina asked.

'When did you?' he replied.

'A question in response to a question? I'm not so easily put off, Sean. Though I will answer: when I was married.' She grimaced. 'Actually I'm still married, so, to be more accurate, I was happy and carefree when I was living with Daniel. What about you?'

He considered lying, but what would be the point? 'A long time ago,' he said. 'I was happy when we were children.'

'When you and Ramsay were close.' She shook her head slowly. 'What is it about you and Zoe?'

'It's the wrong question.' He spoke quickly, he wanted it to be the wrong question.

'So tell me, what's the right question?'

He was reluctant to feed this conversation, and desperate for a drink.

'What is the right question?' she said again.

His stomach was heaving, he felt quite ill, but he knew Nina wasn't about to let him off the hook. He took a deep breath to settle his nerves. 'What is it about Ramsay that keeps us attached? That's what you should be asking.'

Ramsay he was running from. What sort of middle-aged man still suffers a loss inflicted on his fifteen-year-old self?

He stayed in the bathroom until he heard a gentle knock and Nina's voice. She wrapped her arms around him as soon as he opened the door. 'It's because I'm worried about you,' she said.

'You've always worried about me.'

'I'm particularly worried now. You're not twenty any more, and you've already given up too much of your life to Ramsay.' He heard her snort, it may even have been a sob. 'I said the same thing to Zoe just the other day.'

They stood in each other's arms in the doorway of the bathroom until a man appeared, wanting to use the toilet. When they returned to the café Nina immediately rolled out a stream of innocuous chatter – Tom and his ties, the beigeness of serviced apartments, a trip she and Sean had made to Las Vegas, and soon harmony was restored. He was about to suggest that with the serious talk over it was time for a bottle of wine, when she looked at her watch and said she had to dash. She was meeting up with her old university supervisor later in the week and she needed to buy something eye-catching to wear.

'You're surely not planning to restart things with old Felix, are you?' Sean retained an image of a man impossibly old and revoltingly lecherous. He never understood what Nina saw in him. But then heterosexuality had never been his forte.

She shook her head and laughed. 'But I am curious to see him, and I need to look my best – this is an old flame after all. I'd ask you to join me, but I know how you hate shopping. Tom would be a far better prospect.'

She kissed him goodbye, one cheek then the other. 'You know I love you,' she said.

As soon as she was gone he ordered a glass of wine and a bowl of fries. It didn't make him feel any better, and it didn't silence unwanted thoughts. He toyed with a newspaper, turning pages but not reading. The wine was quickly finished and he ordered another – he should have bought a half bottle – and sipped more slowly. Gradually he became aware of a man seated at a nearby table. This man was in even worse physical shape than he was and at least ten years older. This man was eyeing him off.

His communism project had collapsed, he had lost interest in South America, and a fat old queen was leering hopefully at him. He had no idea what to do for the rest of the day much less the rest of his life, and for a moment he was tempted, anything to kill some time. He met the man's gaze, then quickly looked away, swallowed the rest of his wine, gave the man a 'Sorry' shrug, paid at the counter and headed into the heat.

The crowds surged around him, the voices and laughter were loud in the hot still air. He wished he was twenty years younger, he wished he was twenty kilos lighter, he wished he was anywhere but here. Damp with sweat and breathing heavily, he caught a tram to the city. Ten minutes later he disembarked and headed for the nearest cinema complex. An action movie was about to begin. He bought a large popcorn and an ice-cream and sat alone in the dark, eating junk and watching athletic guys leaping across the big screen.

Chapter 9. Against the Grain

Life is a capricious business. For months, a year, you limp through the days, then one morning you wake up and you know even before you leave the bed that you feel different. There's no identifiable explanation, no event or unexpected meeting, you just know the smog has lifted. Nina awoke on the day of her second meeting with the TIF group and she felt – the word actually burst from her mouth – brilliant.

A cool change had blown in overnight and a breeze from the west wafted in through the window. The sky was blue, the sun was shining, and in the plane trees beyond her balcony a flock of rainbow lorikeets was raucous in the fresh morning air. Shortly there would be breakfast with Felix Hovnanian, followed by her meeting with the TIF group, then an afternoon to do whatever she fancied, and finally dinner with Zoe.

Well-intentioned friends had tried to console her with platitudes. Time heals all wounds, they said, eventually she'd recover from Daniel's desertion. Such comforts had always struck her as nonsense: time alone did nothing for your pains, you had to work the time, fill it, make changes – it was these that produced the healing. But the fact remained that inexplicably, on this late January morning she awoke feeling like her old self. It wasn't Felix, she expected nothing from him other than a pleasant couple of hours reminiscing and catching up. As for the TIF meeting, the uneasiness she had experienced when first she met the group had not diminished. There was no obvious reason for her change of mood, and in the end she stopped searching for one. Just be grateful, she told herself, that finally you've moved on.

She settled at the table with her computer and coffee, scrolled through her essay on recent memorialising trends, made a few insignificant changes, and wondered why she felt so unsure about a document she circulated to prospective clients as a matter of course. While the TIF monument had a different focus from her other projects, the result the committee wanted – an enduring structure emerging from current interests, designed to impart information and understanding to contemporary populations – was the same. She had promised to send the document before the meeting, now she decided against it – for no good reason she could determine, just a vague sense of not wanting to restrict or influence the proceedings, vague and illogical, given her job was all about influencing and shaping proceedings. The fact remained that the project *was* impossible and she *was* uneasy, but there was something about the TIF undertaking, or perhaps it was the committee itself, that nudged at her. A week after a meeting that had been unequivocally negative, rather than withdrawing from the project as she'd intended, she was actually looking forward to seeing these people again.

She gathered her things and left the flat. After weeks of heat, the fresh breeze was blissful; she soaked up the cool air as she strode to the shops. It was peak hour at the South Yarra eateries; tables were full, people clustered at counters waiting for takeaway coffee, and as she passed the open doors she was rushed with conversation, the wheeze of espresso machines, a jangle of music. Outside and clogging the footpaths were more tables and chairs. Here sat business people and school kids, parents with babies, and plenty of tight-skinned, blonde-haired, lycra-clad women who looked as if they'd been turned out by the same factory.

She found the café where she was to meet Felix and chose an outdoor table; it would be hot again by the afternoon and she was determined not to miss a moment of the heavenly respite. She pulled the table into dappled shade, had scarcely settled herself when she saw him. Unmistakably Felix. His walk and carriage hadn't changed, twenty-plus years appeared to have left him unscathed. Although as he drew closer she noticed the lines on his face and the thinning hair, and the hands he stretched towards her were mottled with age. And when they embraced, the skin was loose beneath the fine material of his shirt, and she smelled that must of age that no amount of cologne can entirely hide.

'Let me look at you,' he said, holding her hands and stepping back.

They took each other in. Lines and thinning hair notwithstanding, Felix still looked a good ten years younger than the seventy-something he must now be.

'You're as gorgeous as ever,' he said.

His facial expression – unambiguous appreciation – was as familiar as if she had seen it yesterday. In fact, being with him, being with him now, it was as if the intervening time had collapsed.

She hugged him again. 'And you look so good I'm suspecting a pact with the devil.'

He laughed. 'A pact with a personal trainer is more like it,' he said. 'And a new woman in my life.'

'How old is she?' The question just slipped out. She saw the sudden shift in his expression.

'You always knew where to land a punch.' It was not a compliment.

'That's what my husband says.' She noticed her use of the present tense and decided against retreat. 'He likes it, considers it one of my finer qualities. So? What's her age?'

Mandy was thirty-one and a mature-age student. Not so mature, Nina thought, but kept that to herself. In fact, realising that Felix's Mandy and Daniel's Sally were of a similar age she decided to slot Mandy into a no-go folder as she once used to do with Felix's wife. She should pop Sally in there as well. As for her present-tense husband, it surprised her that he came more easily to her lips than the ex who had so heartlessly dumped her.

A waiter arrived to take their orders and effectively closed the topic. Felix chose a yoghurt-based health drink and a bowl of fresh berries. She decided on French toast and a large cappuccino. Felix looked aghast, but she didn't care, she felt like indulging herself. Every Sunday morning when she was growing up, her father would cook French toast for the family, often for the Blakes as well; it was not simply his speciality, it was the only meal apart from barbecues he ever cooked. When Daniel heard the story he decided to take over the role of French toast specialist. He appointed Nina chief taster and after some dedicated experimentation arrived at the perfect recipe. Thereafter, every couple of weeks he would make his French toast for their Sunday breakfast. This past year the mere thought of French toast had made her want to vomit, but today that too had changed. And when the food arrived she lavished it with maple syrup under the disapproving gaze of Felix.

That gaze of his, it was different. Something about the eyes she had once so admired, no longer heavy-lidded with the world-weary dark rings, they were smoother and smaller, the lids tighter and the orbit paler. And the chin looked different as well, far too chiselled for the sagging neck. Surely not cosmetic surgery? Yet how else to explain his appearance? Felix was entering old age with a thirty-year-old, even a man with less vanity would be tempted by surgery. And Felix had always been vain – she wasn't the first student he'd slept with and clearly, given young Mandy, she wasn't the last. His luckless wife (Janet? Jill? June?), what a lot she'd had to contend with. And now she inquired after her, how the poor woman was faring with this rupture so late in life.

Felix said her sympathy was unwarranted. 'The divorce was mutual.' He hesitated, then he shrugged, 'What the hell – I'm past caring. Julie was two-timing me. She'd had someone else for years. A *girlfriend*.' He spat the word out as if it were mouldy food. 'My wife has decided she's a lesbian.'

Nina burst out laughing. 'It serves you right.'

'She'd been cheating on me for fifteen years.'

'With just the one woman?'

'Of course there was only one woman.'

But Nina could see by his troubled expression that it had never before occurred to him that his wife might have been a serial adulterer, just like him.

'Fifteen years,' he continued. 'Although it would have been far worse if she'd been cheating with a man. In fact,' and now he was smiling, 'I saw no reason why we shouldn't continue: she could have her girlfriend and I could have mine.' He dipped his voice to a confidential low. 'I imagined some rather tantalising possibilities. But Julie had other plans. She and the girlfriend are hiking somewhere in South America as we speak.'

From his wife, 'the ex-wife' he corrected, the conversation moved to his honorary work at the university, then an itemising of recent lectures and consultancies, accounts of his sons (both married, both successful lawyers), to political and social issues. And all the time she was feeding him questions he did not ask her a single thing. Although he did offer the information that he'd noticed she had failed in her bid to manage a memorial project to the Armenian Genocide. 'I think it was somewhere in America,' he said, and she didn't bother to correct him.

They differed on what to do about global warming, they differed on the troubles in East Africa; he wanted to export democracy everywhere, she wanted to make the case for other forms of political organisation; he supported the lesser evil approach to troublesome regimes, she did not. They argued about the future of memory in an age of on-tap information, they disagreed on the new directions in university education. There was not a single issue on which they agreed.

He said she'd acquired a certain hardness. 'You used to be such a sweet girl,' he said.

But it was not hardness, rather she no longer hung on his every word.

Their breakfast lasted less than an hour. There was no warm spontaneous embrace when he left, just a peck to her cheek before he hurried off.

Nina lingered at the café for another coffee. Perhaps if this meeting had occurred earlier in her visit she would be feeling sad and disappointed, but on this *nova vita* day – that's truly how it felt – she was greatly amused, and satisfied too: one of the best means of confirming you've not wasted the years is to revisit an old lover. The affair with Felix had come at the right time but, more importantly, she had moved on at the right time.

A few minutes later, after settling the bill (Felix had paid only for his share), she made her way back to the apartment. There she prepared herself for the TIF meeting, including a jacket and proper shoes rather than sandals. She felt protected by the clothes, and then wondered why on earth she should feel exposed in the first place.

She had not checked her email earlier and with plenty of time to spare she opened her laptop. Later she would tell Sean it was as if she expected the email, for there was no shock when his name appeared in her inbox.

Daniel, the first message in more than a year.

> *You used to say I found it difficult to admit to my mistakes.*
> *You used to say I was appallingly reluctant to apologise.*
> *So let me be absolutely clear.*
> *1. I made a terrible mistake in breaking up our marriage.*
> *2. It was entirely my fault.*
> *3. I am so very sorry.*
> *I very much want to see you. Please – will you see me?*
> *I love you even better than before.*
> *D*

She stared at the screen. The email had come in at four in the morning Melbourne time, corresponding to five o'clock yesterday in London. Had he dithered over it all day before deciding to send it? She read the email again, she read it several times. She left the computer, she paced the flat, she went out to the tiny balcony. Her mind was on hold, no thoughts, no hopes, just his words turning over until they might have been Sanskrit for all the meaning they had.

Then she returned to the screen and read again. And suddenly her mind was thrown into aggrieved and critical overdrive. 'A terrible mistake' he wrote. Only one mistake? There was the initial mistake of falling for his research assistant. Then: he carried on a secret affair; he deceived his wife; he lied to her every day for four months; he dumped her to pursue his new love; he destroyed their past; he scuttled their future; he treated her as if she had never mattered. The mistakes were many and profound. And now he's sorry. For which bit? He says nothing about regretting the affair. Nothing about ending his marriage. And if he's not sorry about Sally then he could run off with a twenty-year-old next time. He could run off with a wombat if he were so inclined. And sorry for whom? If young Sally has dumped him as Nina suspects she has, he's most likely sorry for himself. And even if he's done the dumping, he'd still be feeling sorry for himself in his suddenly solitary state. Nowhere in this email is there any concern for her, any acknowledgment of what she, Nina, has been through. Of course 'I love you better than before' wants to suggest he's learned by his mistakes, but she remains shocked he could have acted as he did in the first place.

Her laptop is open, she is fuming at the screen when, just after eleven – midnight London time – another email appears. It's a copy of the first email with the question: *did you receive this?* Then a couple of minutes later there's another message.

What I did was unforgivable. But you always said that
far too much is made of forgiveness – that some actions are
forever unforgivable but not reason enough to break up a
marriage. You may have found someone else, I wouldn't
blame you if you had. I'm so sorry. I never loved her like I
loved you – like I still love you. The time with her and the
time without you has shown me what I've lost. Will you
please let me know if I have any hope.

Hope? She's an aficionado of hope. Hope dampens pain that would otherwise be unbearable, hope soars on currents of longing, hope keeps you going when circumstances would bring you to your knees. Hope is a house of straw.

She is not thinking as she leaves the flat, she doesn't know what to think. Although with the TIF meeting just an hour away she needs to keep her husband quiet. She knows you can numb a small defined portion of mind – if not for this skill she would have been unable to work since Daniel left – and that's what she needs to do now, a squirt of anaesthesia to blank out the events of the previous hour.

Twenty minutes later Nina entered the city precinct. Daniel's email was still throbbing, like a drumbeat at odds with the main tune. She made yet another attempt to silence him, pull her mind into line and orient herself to the task ahead. When the meeting is over, she said aloud, I'll attend to you. But now I have to work. Now I need to focus on monuments.

Monuments. So many of which she had first seen with him. Perused, analysed and argued about with him. On his first visit to Melbourne, Daniel, with his stranger's eyes, had observed how there was insufficient history in the city for the sort of jostling for space on street corners that occurred in central London; but nonetheless, he had been surprised at how many monuments there actually were. 'It's as if you Australians are making a deliberate effort to fill out your flimsy past.' She'd defended Australia's history, both black and white: it wasn't flimsy, she said. And besides, she'd added, monuments were a British tradition and Australia was simply following that heritage (although he did start her wondering about the tendency of the second league to acquire both the muscles and garments of the first). They had stopped in front of famous men at intersections and outside neoclassical piles and perched on plinths in the city's public gardens. So many explorers, jurists, politicians and military leaders great enough in their time to warrant a monument, and since forgotten. 'Do you know who these people are?' he had asked. She hadn't, and now as she again read the names, there was still no recognition of the men, although the monuments themselves were vaguely familiar. She found it interesting that the pile of stone had more impact than who was represented; it was the sort of conundrum she and Daniel would have grappled with together.

The TIF people were expecting an overview of trends in memorialising – the topic of the paper she hadn't sent. As she made her way through the city down to Docklands, she made a last attempt to shift Daniel from her mind. She recited Blake's 'Jerusalem', and a few verses of 'The Highwayman', followed by the 'La Marseillaise', and then John Masefield's 'Sea Fever' and by the time she had finished with Auden's 'Tell Me the Truth about Love' her mind was free of Daniel and ready to work.

She decided to begin her talk with the sponsored chairs
found in the city parks of many major cities, including
Melbourne's Botanic Gardens; just ordinary park benches
overlooking paths and lawns and lakes, each bearing a
plaque on which was engraved a remembrance of a person or
sometimes a couple – personal tributes yet strangely powerful
in the way they reached out to strangers walking past.

Experience had taught her that setting up her presentation
with such modest memorials was an effective way of
counteracting the often huge monoliths people had in
mind for their own projects. In memorialising, size tends
to reflect significance and influence. Lenin, Stalin, Saddam
Hussein, Mao, Lincoln, Jefferson, these sorts of leaders all
had towering statues. Then there were massive memorial
structures like the Victory Monument in St Petersburg with its
powerful narrative of the siege of Leningrad, and the colossal
over-wrought Il Vittoriano in Rome to Victor Emmanuel II;
even the Vatican itself, a conglomerate memorial to God and
the Catholic Church. But huge monuments can mute and
crush those who stand in their shadows; huge monuments
can actually make individuals disappear. Nina was wary of
whoppers and she tried to direct her clients away from them.

She expected many of the TIF committee to be familiar
with the Diana, Princess of Wales Memorial Fountain in
Hyde Park. This was an interesting project, one she had been
determined not to like given all the hoopla surrounding the
princess's life and death. But on her first visit there – yes, with
Daniel – she was captivated by the huge ring of moving water
in the middle of a large park in the middle of a major city.
The two of them had stood at the highest point of the water
ring, and just like music can draw you into itself, so too this

flow cascading down the slope in two directions. It was lively yet hypnotic; she could not have deflected her gaze even if she wanted. Slowly they had walked together down the slope, the channel of water sloshing and hissing over the small rock falls and sluicing into the granite walls, down down down to the lowest point where water from both sides of the ring met in a suddenly calm pool. They crossed one of the bridges into the central open space, the heart of the monument, and there they sat on the grass. The sound of the water, the breeze, the trees, the broad sky, even the muffled sounds of the other visitors created a rare peace.

She had returned to the monument several times since Daniel's defection and had experienced the same tranquillity. She had only fleeting thoughts of Princess Diana during these visits, or none at all; rather the monument had her reflecting on her own life, and less personally although more profoundly on life and death and the need to eschew the sort of conveyor-belt existence that would confine you to the same path from start to finish. It was during a visit to this monument that the possibility of a satisfying life without Daniel first entered her mind.

The TIF group was wanting a similarly meditative effect for their monument – a monument, she reminded herself, that probably would not and should not be built. But the committee needed to come to this decision themselves, an outcome more likely the better informed they were. The Princess Diana Memorial Fountain was a good example, and she could contrast it with the more spontaneous monument to Diana on the parapet above the Paris tunnel in which the fatal crash had occurred. Whenever she was in Paris, she felt compelled to visit this site, yet she always came away irritated.

The hand-written messages left by bereft Diana pilgrims in French, English, Spanish, German, expressed love and loss and appreciation of the beautiful young princess, while at the same time revealing gaping absences in their own ordinary lives. Similarly the mountains of flowers in central London in the immediate aftermath of Diana's death. These offerings by strangers, Nina believed, said more about their own unexamined lives than the recently dead princess. (How different from that single bunch of drooping flowers taped to a roadside telegraph pole marking the spot where a person was killed in a motor accident. A spouse, a child, a parent, a sibling, a friend, a lover, someone who actually knew and loved the deceased person wanted to mark the spot where a life had ended and their own life was forever changed.) And then there was the Diana and Dodi Memorial at Harrods, a shrine-like installation that marked a new high in kitsch memorialising. The centre-piece consisted of a bell-jar under which stood the actual unwashed liqueur glasses that held Diana and Dodi's last drinks. Whenever Nina came down the escalator and saw the shrine she had to stifle a laugh. But many were the times she had witnessed people weeping in front of it.

'You're hard on the ordinary person,' Daniel used to say when she railed against flowers or teddy bears or dolls left by strangers at a significant site. And she'd reply that there would be no ordinary people if everyone gave more thought to what they did.

'These displays are examples of mass behaviour,' she said. 'And it's not hard to move the masses. We see a Hollywood romance and we cry – dozens of us, all strangers, crying together. We go to a football match and together we yell for our team and hurl abuse at the opposition. We attend a pop concert and throw ourselves into the general hysteria. We line The Mall for Diana's funeral, we go to Ground Zero in New York, and in all these places we are part of a great mass movement of incontinent emotion. It feels so good.'

Although kitsch by itself, Daniel had reminded her, was insufficient reason for her to condemn a monument. He had laughed uproariously when she showed him the Animals in War Memorial in Park Lane, considered by many to be mawkishly sentimental, but one of her all-time favourites. Only in animal-mad England could such a memorial have been built, and on prime real estate too, and in 2004, so there could be no blaming nineteenth-century bleary-eyed romantics. It was a large monument with two life-sized, heavily burdened donkeys, together with a dog and a horse; and in bass relief on a curving wall was an array of animals from elephants to carrier pigeons to the glow worms used to light the trenches in the Great War. As for the caption, THEY HAD NO CHOICE, sentimentality did not begin to describe it. And yet she loved this monument – for what it said about the English, what it said about animals too.

If she was to describe the Animals in War Memorial to the TIF group then she ought to balance it with a more abstract structure – perhaps the 1962 Memorial to the Martyrs of the Deportation in Paris, a solemn construction weighty with symbolism located behind Notre Dame Cathedral. You tend to visit it after you've been to the cathedral, so you approach the Martyrs monument overheated with Gothic splendour. By the time you've walked down a long flight of narrow steps to the open space below, you feel as if you've entered a different world. The sky is overhead but you feel cut off from the life of the city. Whenever she has visited, she's either been the only person there or one of just a handful, further exacerbating the sense of isolation and contemplative mood. The underground structure feels like an underworld; all cement, granite and metal it is made up of long passages, and cells – compartments – with triangular shapes used in abundance, symbolising the one hundred and sixty thousand people deported under the Vichy regime. They were mostly Jews, including eleven thousand children, but also political dissenters, members of the resistance, gypsies and Jehovah's Witnesses. Engraved on the walls are words from a number of French luminaries, including Jean-Paul Sartre and Saint-Exupéry; but it is the quiet profound poetry of Robert Desnos that particularly moves her.

This place of solitude and reflection doesn't convey the overwhelming factual information of the Holocaust museums; instead it provides a meditative space in which to ponder the human capacity for evil – boundless and horrifying – and acknowledge the human spirit for survival. It's long been one of her favourites.

There were many more monuments she might mention (European, American, African – the locations of her own work – and none, she was well aware, drawn from the Asia–Pacific region), but as she made her way through the Docklands precinct towards her destination, she decided to hold back, listen first to what the committee had to say and then improvise from there. It was not the way she usually worked, but nothing about this day or this project was usual.

By the time Nina arrived at the offices of C.G. and C.K. Holdings she was eager to begin, and, not surprisingly, the meeting proceeded very differently from the last. She let the group talk about the sensibility of their project, prompting only with an occasional question. They all contributed except Professor Karim Qureshi. As the conversation surged around him, she could not help but notice the extraordinary range of expression that shaped his broad dark face. And then she saw his hand, the right hand: it had no fingers. How could she have not seen this at the first meeting? And on the back of the hand, running over the wrist and disappearing beneath the cuff of his shirt, was a ropey swirl of scars. He wore a T-shirt last time; his arms were bare. How could she have not noticed?

She must have been staring because he moved his hand from the surface of the table and, with a pause in the discussion, he spoke for the first time. 'How do you balance art with the purpose of the monument, the monument's message?'

That rich resonant voice with its lyrical accent: she expected he was a mesmerising teacher.

She addressed the group. 'All monuments are public art. And you're right,' she glanced at Karim, 'the challenge is to get the balance right. Often there's conflict between the more artistically inclined citizens and the general community.'

She pulled up some photos of the Sibelius Monument in Helsinki. 'This organic, pipe-like structure is an early example of an abstract monument, selected by competition in 1961. When it won there was an uproar, not dissimilar to the controversy surrounding the Sydney Opera House design. But eventually, as with the Opera House, public taste caught up with the artistic vanguard and the monument's now highly valued by both Finns and tourists alike.'

'All those metal pipes don't evoke Sibelius for me,' Father Jamie Gray said.

The Uniting Church minister, Elizabeth, was smiling. 'They do for me. The pipes look like the rise and fall of sound.'

'That's because you already know the monument honours Sibelius,' Father Jamie persisted.

'Everyone does,' Elizabeth said. 'There are signs in several languages, and one of the compromises to placate the literalists was to add a realist bust of Sibelius alongside the abstract sculpture.' She paused before adding, 'I visited Finland with my husband a few years ago.'

'Surely you can have both art and message,' Nadirah Harvey said.

Nina nodded. 'But literal, figurative structures often don't receive an aesthetic imprimatur, while abstract structures can muddy the message of the monument. To get the balance right is difficult. And the issue's further compounded by the fact that art can date.'

'Great art doesn't date,' said Charlie Goldstein.

'But it takes time for great art to reveal itself,' Elizabeth said. 'And in the process much of what was thought might become great has lost its kudos.'

Nina showed them slides of the Martyrs of the Deportation monument in Paris. She explained why this was one of her favourite monuments: its use of poetry, the solitude, how the abstraction and symbolism of the structure provide ample cognitive space for observers to draw on their own experiences and understandings.

'I think all those sharp metal triangles look passé,' Jamie said. 'And the lettering is so last century.' He would, by Nina's calculation be one of the youngest members of this group.

'Art aside, even literal monuments can date,' the rabbi said, rearranging herself in her chair. She was pregnant, Nina suddenly realised, Lorrie Aarons was heavily pregnant. 'Has anyone seen the scouting monument in Washington DC?'

A couple of people smiled and nodded.

'It consists of a huge naked man and a scantily clad goddess-type woman flanking a small boy in full scouting regalia,' Lorrie continued, shaking her head in disbelief. 'With paedophilia such a hot topic these days I'm surprised it hasn't been ripped down.'

Nina riffled through her photo library and found an image of the monument. There were gasps and laughter and Father Jamie, so recently critical of the modernist Sibelius Monument said, 'Give me abstraction any day.'

'There's art and message to consider,' Nina continued, 'and abstract and figurative forms. And there's another interesting phenomenon too: when a structure never intended to be a monument acquires monumental force.' She told them about the spacious, well-appointed bathroom at Theresienstadt concentration camp in what is now the Czech Republic. 'This bathroom with its large white basins, its taps and mirrors, its clean walls and floors was built for display purposes only; it was never used. When members of the Red Cross made an official visit to check that the Jews were not being maltreated, they were shown the sparkling bathroom and not the filthy rat-holes where the Jews lived and died in overcrowded and insanitary conditions, weakened by disease and starvation rations.

'My husband and I were visiting Theresienstadt for the first time, we'd not heard about the unused bathroom before. Yet for us, this bathroom was far more expressive of the brutality of the Nazis and the terrible deprivations suffered in the camp than the various monuments that have been specially erected on the Theresienstadt site.' And again she registered a flare of pleasure at her present-tense husband, as she had with Felix that morning.

'It's the same with the Warsaw ghetto,' Cate Killeen said. 'We visited Poland during the papacy of Pope John Paul II.' A smile filled her face. 'It was a life-changing trip. While we were in Warsaw we went to the Ghetto Heroes Monument built to honour those who opposed the Nazis.' She looked at her husband and put a hand on his arm. 'Remember?'

Charlie nodded.

'During the 1980s, the Ghetto Heroes Monument became the rallying point for members of Solidarity, and since then it's become the location for all manner of protest and anniversary. I could give only a vague description of the monument and the surrounding grassy area. But what I can describe in detail is the remaining piece of the wall of the Warsaw ghetto.'

Again she glanced at her husband, again he nodded.

'Tall, tarnished and made from rickety bricks, this small portion of the ghetto wall stands among apartment buildings, across from a clock tower counting out the minutes, the evenly paved paths, the people going about their daily lives. I looked up at that wall, we both did, and we recalled the Jews who suffered and starved there, and those who managed to survive only to be killed in Auschwitz. We remembered those Jews in their daily struggle for survival, while around them, beyond the wall, life went on.' She paused, and then a quiet final comment. 'I'll never forget what that piece of wall means.'

Nina observed the TIF members. All their faces were glazed with faraway expressions as if they were actually seeing the ghetto wall. She allowed a moment for Cate's story to settle before continuing.

'So memorials don't have to be monuments, and some of the most powerful are not.' She showed them a series of roadside memorials. There were wilting flowers and toys, faded photos and weathered sporting equipment, and one memorial she'd seen in Queensland with a miniature surfboard at its centre. She talked about churches being types of memorials, to God, to faith, and how ruins like Pompeii and the Acropolis could be seen as memorials to past civilisations. And she talked about the collapsing of time when first she walked through the Forum in Rome, her simultaneous sense of being a modern wandering the ruins, and an ancient inhabiting what was an extraordinary metropolis.

'But someone with less imagination, someone whose thoughts were on the McDonald's outlet they'd noticed on the way to the Forum, would just see stones and rubbish and weeds and priceless land going to waste,' Charlie said.

She agreed. 'All the best monuments require a willing and open imagination. As for the worst,' she shrugged, 'there are, unfortunately, too many examples, and no amount of imagination will save them. The poet Robert Lowell wrote that some monuments "stick like a fishbone in the city's throat", well, here's one of them.' She brought up photos of the bombastic World War II Memorial in Washington DC. 'This is a huge neoclassical and Deco hotchpotch of bad art and hefty jingoism. There are waterfalls and fountains and mammoth granite columns and arches, all proclaiming American might and American victory. As for the Europeans and Commonwealth citizens who fought in the war, they hardly warrant a mention.'

'But it might be that in our increasingly ephemeral world, history needs the solid reminders of monuments – even the bad ones,' Nadirah Harvey said.

Nadirah was wearing a cream head-scarf today; it set off the pale brown eyes, the light olive skin. And even though her mouth was not quite symmetrical and the eyebrows were too heavy, Nina saw an unusual beauty in her face. As for the point she made, Nina had herself argued much the same.

'And yet memorials serve the ever-changing present as much as the past,' she now said. 'You need only observe which monuments haven't endured, like all those destroyed when the Soviet Union collapsed. And decades earlier, when Stalin was discredited, so many statues were brought down then. The Stalin Monument in Prague, the largest representation of Stalin ever constructed, was completed in 1955 and destroyed a mere seven years later.'

'And in the Arab Spring a while back,' said Karim Qureshi. 'There was an avalanche of falling figures.'

Nina nodded. 'And even when monuments endure, the meanings attached to them may not.' She projected the Bremen Elephant on to the screen. 'This ten-metre high, red-brick elephant was unveiled in 1932 to celebrate Germany's colonial conquests in Africa.'

They all looked horrified.

'We forget how recently colonialism was a source of national pride,' she said with a wry smile. 'All colonisation of Africa was brutal but the German colonisation was particularly brutal, and no more so than in Namibia – not that anyone was concerned about that in 1932. Fifty years later when colonisation was viewed very differently, the statue had become such an embarrassment there were calls to have it removed. By 1990, when Namibia gained its independence, the Bremen Elephant was re-dedicated as an *anti*-colonial symbol. And then in 2009 another monument, flat and organic and in direct contrast to the hefty flamboyance of the elephant, was erected nearby in remembrance of those tens of thousands of Namibians who perished in the German colonisation. This one monument and so many different meanings.'

'It's terrible,' Charlie said. 'It's racist and it's patronising. The meanings attached to it may have changed, but the image –' he threw his hands out wide. 'It's no different from those appalling plaster blackboy figures holding up letterboxes in so many gardens in America's deep south. The Bremen Elephant simply by being what it is still harbours all those old colonial values.'

There was some agreement around the table, while others said that too great an emphasis on political correctness would erase much of history and culture. Nina listened with interest, all of these people so thoughtful and well read, well travelled too. It was only when she noticed Nadirah Harvey checking the time that she moved the discussion on.

She talked about gravestones as a type of memorial. 'And cemeteries themselves can have monumental force,' she said.

'Like the Jewish Cemetery in Prague,' Lorrie Aarons said. 'Thousands of old tombstones crammed in together all higgledy piggledy. The whole area's neglected, no one's left to take care of it. All the Jews are gone. Dead.'

'And Cambodia's killing fields,' Karim Qureshi said. 'And practically all of Afghanistan.' He was staring through the window to the sky beyond. His next words came slowly. 'So ... is it the monument, or what you bring to it?'

Nina smiled, it was a crucial question. 'It's both.' She paused a moment before continuing. 'What do you think people will bring to your monument?'

'Those who share our values will feel confirmed in their beliefs and enjoy a sense of inclusion,' Karim said.

'And those who differ will either pass it by or throw a bucket of paint over it.' Jamie Gray gave a wry smile.

'Well, there it is: your challenge is to reach the paint-throwers before they reach for their cans,' Nina said.

Everyone laughed.

'So, memorials speak to those willing to listen, who have a reason to listen,' she continued. 'But what they say, the information they impart, the understandings they promote, tend to speak to an individual's life and experience as well as their needs and longings at the moment they stand before the monument. Monuments,' she said, 'are like books. A book read at a particular time can leave you untouched, and yet at another time it can strike at the heart of you.'

'So how do we produce a state of mind that'll make people receptive to our message?' Elizabeth Featherstone said.

There was silence as everyone pondered this question. Those facing the window stared out at the sky, those on the other side of the table fixed their gaze on a wall of paintings. Cate Killeen closed her eyes. Such an easy silence, Nina was thinking, and she, too, shut her eyes. Deliberately she brought to mind – she could see it as if it were in front of her – the 'private memorial to our love' (the words were Daniel's). There had been a problem with the water pipes near their home. The road had been ripped up together with a small section of the footpath. When the pipes were repaired, fresh bitumen was laid on the street and a pale concrete slab poured onto the footpath. The whole job took only a few hours. When the workmen were finished, Daniel had come inside and pulled her from her book. Down the street they went to the new patch of concrete, still damp and shining and unblemished, except in one corner where Daniel had engraved *D.R. loves N.J.* and a heart – a rather wonky heart drawn very quickly, he said, because he didn't want to be caught defacing council property. By evening, his private message on the public pavement had been joined by four other messages, each much larger than his but, to Nina's eye, not nearly as elegant.

That patch of concrete quickly became a significant landmark in their relationship. But after Daniel left she would have ground it out altogether if she'd not been too afraid of being caught. Now, however, she brought it to mind and held it there, this private monument, not simply to better times, but more generally to happiness.

There was a rustling of paper. She sprang back into the room; everyone was looking at her, everyone was waiting. She repeated Elizabeth's question. 'So? Any ideas about how to produce a state of mind that will orient people to your message?'

Cate Killeen was nodding. 'The surrounding environment is all-important,' she said. 'The environment sets the tone. Without the park and trees and sloping terrain the Princess Diana Memorial Fountain would be nothing more than a stream of water. Without its Central Park location and the nearby Dakota Building where John Lennon and Yoko lived, the Strawberry Fields monument would be just another engraving on a path.' She spoke slowly, with care. 'I think we need to look to our environment.'

'Perhaps,' her husband said, 'our memorial will be all environment.'

'Yes, yes,' Father Jamie said. 'Like ancient Japanese gardens.'

'Or Tasmanian old-growth forests.'

'Or the Nile Delta after rain.'

And suddenly all of them were talking of bush and rivers and lakes and cliff tops, birds and pagodas and viewing seats.

Then Karim Qureshi was speaking. 'All environment? Or all words?' He looked across to Nina. 'I'm thinking of your response to the Martyrs Memorial in Paris. What affected you most? What's remained with you?'

She thought for a moment. 'The words,' she said. 'Robert Desnos's words.'

'So perhaps,' he continued, 'what we're wanting is a collection of inspirational sayings. Words from Nelson Mandela, Gandhi –'

'And Roosevelt,' Lorrie said, tapping into her phone. 'There are quotes all through the FDR Memorial in DC. "The test of our progress is not whether we add more to the abundance of those who have much; it is whether we provide enough for those who have too little."' She scrolled down the screen. 'And here's a peace statement: "The structure of world peace cannot be the work of one man, or one party, or one nation ... It must be a peace which rests on the co-operative effort of the whole world."'

'What wonderful sentiments,' Elizabeth said. 'If only our present-day leaders demonstrated such wisdom.'

Nina stood up. She was smiling. 'This all sounds very promising. But before we go any further I'd like to add just one more element to the mix. It's the notion of a counter-monument.' She explained how the counter-monument concept arose in opposition to the plethora of huge awe-inspiring memorials. 'And the most effective of these counter-monuments is, in my opinion, the Harburg Monument

Against Fascism in Hamburg. The creators, a husband and wife team called Gerz, designed a monument that was self-effacing and impermanent.

'Harburg was a rather rough area of Hamburg,' she continued, 'well off the tourist track. The location was an important consideration in the Gerz concept, as you'll soon see.' She projected an image on the screen. 'And here it is. A twelve-metre-high, one-metre-square aluminium pillar coated in soft lead. An obelisk type of structure. People were invited to engrave their names on the pillar – special styluses were attached – and in this way add their names to those who'd remain vigilant against fascism. When the accessible space was filled, the pillar was lowered a little way down a twelve-metre shaft sunk into the ground.

'The monument was constructed in 1986. Every few months it was lowered until in 1991 it disappeared altogether. All that remains is a burial stone marking fascism's grave.'

'I wonder how many people visit there now,' Elizabeth said.

'I'm not sure it matters. Over the five years of its existence a huge number of people made their mark on the monument. And they took photos and they'll show them to their children and grandchildren. More significantly though, it continues to speak of an absence – and not just of fascism but also the vanished Jews of Europe. But most important of all, it creates a space for dialogue, for debate, for analysis. I'd guess it has a more lasting effect than many of the mammoth war memorials built around the world.'

'And graffiti?' Nadirah Harvey said. 'You're surely not going to tell us the graffitists and vandals stayed away.'

Nina smiled. 'There was graffiti and plenty of it, including fascist symbols like swastikas and death's heads. But despite the protests it was permitted to remain. This was a monument to reflect the range of human responses, and the good and the repulsive jammed up against each other actually added to the monument's power.'

'And it no longer exists,' Karim said.

'But nonetheless,' Charlie added, 'we're talking about it.'

Soon after, Charlie Goldstein wound up the meeting. He realised time was limited, that Nina would be returning to London shortly. He checked with the rest of the group that they were able to stay and discuss the project further, then, amid a chorus of thanks, he saw Nina out.

The cool change had dissipated and the heat rushed at her as she left the building, yet, unusually, Nina was not bothered by it. Rather than the tram, she decided to walk a while and crossed to the other side of the road into a sliver of shade. She slipped off her jacket and would have removed her shoes as well if the pavement had not been so hot.

Invigorated, that's how she felt, and liberated too, as if she'd been encased in plaster for a long time, and suddenly the plaster had fallen away leaving her free to emerge, whole and fully repaired.

It was these people, these TIF people, they were unlike any she had ever worked with before. It was not simply their passionate engagement with ideas and beliefs – she was accustomed to working with people when their passions were inflamed – rather they struck her as uniquely outward-looking, the opposite to self-serving (she was unable to find the right word), a combination of benevolence, selflessness, optimism and faith in humankind. So much for 'the project from hell'. She had needed the TIF project, she had needed these people.

She arrived back at the flat and went straight to her laptop. No new message from Daniel. She was disappointed, and angry at herself for being disappointed, then furious with him for making her feel this way. But as quickly as the emotions flared so they settled, and what she most wanted was to ring him and hear his voice. Instead she dialled Sean's number. He'd been avoiding her since she questioned his communism project; but she wanted to tell him about Daniel's emails, and at the same time prevent herself from acting precipitously. As the phone passed to message bank, it seemed he was still avoiding her. 'Ring me,' she said. 'And remember, Sean, no matter how much I upset you, I'll never stop loving you.'

She was hungry, she hadn't eaten since the French toast with Felix; now she made herself a snack of cheese with a sliced peach. Daniel lingered in her thoughts, but rather than being distressed by this, she remained quite cheery. It was the new possibilities with him, and while she was far from making any decision, it appealed to her that the human psyche would make a beeline for happiness as soon as it became an option.

She settled in a chair out on the balcony, ate at leisure, and must have dozed off because she awoke to the sound of her phone. She ran inside and grabbed it just as it rang off. It was Zoe and she called back immediately.

There was no greeting.

'George is dead.' Zoe spoke loudly and in a rush. 'A heart attack. And Ramsay's alone. No dinner here tonight. Sorry, I know you'll understand.' And she hung up while Nina was mid-sentence.

George was dead and dinner cancelled and what exactly was Nina supposed to understand? That Ramsay had lost his closest intimate and was helpless with grief? That Ramsay had lost his manager and organiser and did not know what to do from one hour to the next? That with George out of the way her sister finally saw an opening for herself in Ramsay's day-to-day life? That her sister, still obsessed with Ramsay, was planning to leave home and family to set up a life with him?

This last option was so awful that Nina quickly pushed it aside. And yet it was a possibility. You can put desires in storage because circumstances prohibit their address, but as soon as the situation changes, out they come, ten, fifteen, twenty years after their use-by date, still magically fresh and in perfect shape. And it was not as if her sister's marriage had provided a viable alternative, it should have finished years ago. But not this way. George was dead and her sister was rushing to Ramsay's side.

Chapter 10. At the Crossroads

1.

The heat dragged on. Temperatures had lodged in the high thirties and low forties; the day of George's funeral had been one of the hottest on record. With unremitting humidity, it was a heat more inclined to the tropics than temperate Melbourne. There was something ominous about it, Nina thought. It threw everything off kilter.

The school term had begun and Zoe had returned to work, although it was hard to know exactly what Zoe was doing as she rarely answered her phone. According to Hayley, her mother left home around seven – early enough, Nina realised, to stop by Ramsay's place before work. When Zoe appeared for dinner, again from Hayley's account, she would dash in with chicken and salad bought from the local rotisserie, pastas and casseroles from the local deli, racks of lamb and roasted vegetables from the local carvery, food as ominous as the weather given Zoe's pride as a cook. Once the meal was finished she would dash out again and not return until late.

'I hear her come in,' Hayley said. 'It's never before midnight and once it was after two. Two o'clock in the morning!'

Her eyes were glassy and she swiped at them. 'I can't believe she'd do this to Dad.'

Nina couldn't believe she'd do this to her children.

'And even when she's home she's not actually present,' Hayley continued. 'I could shave my head and cover my skull in tattoos and she wouldn't notice. And why? Because of Ramsay Blake. Bloody Ramsay Blake.' Another swipe at her eyes. 'I've never liked him. He's always been weird. And I don't mean cool weird. He's bad.'

Elliot, too, had been absent since the funeral, a quick trip to New York, so he said, for some final research on his Elizabeth Hardwick biography. Nina had thought the book was finished and had said as much to him. There was a long pause – he had phoned her before he left – and when he answered his voice was heavy. 'I need to get away for a while.'

During the hot, claggy days, Nina passed most of her time alone. All those afternoons spent with Zoe, all the dinners, all the hours of late night talking, these were things of the past. Zoe was consumed by Ramsay, as it seemed she had always been, but now with no obstacle in the way she was indulging her hunger. Nina would have thought her marriage and children constituted obstacles – but clearly Zoe did not. Nor, apparently, did Elliot, whose sudden trip back to the States seemed to be facilitating the passage of his wife into Ramsay's arms. And before he left he had changed, softened towards Zoe, as if he had given up the battle. Perhaps the marriage had finally broken him, or perhaps he no longer cared.

Since the second meeting there'd been no contact from the TIF people, nonetheless Nina's thoughts kept returning to them. They seemed to have latched on to an aspect of her grown slack through lack of exercise. These people, it occurred to her, were out of step with the rest of society; their very goodness struck her as radical, their actions as oddly subversive.

Her parents had not subscribed to any religious belief, but the school she and Zoe attended for their entire education was a Protestant school. Every morning they recited the Lord's prayer, they sang a hymn, and there would be a reading from the Bible. Nina grew familiar with most parts of the Bible, core passages she knew by heart. Now she reread the Beatitudes; in fact she read the entire Sermon on the Mount, not with bored schoolgirl eyes, nor with the cynicism of the secular, but as a thoughtful, culturally sophisticated, twenty-first-century woman. The meek and the poor would rise up and inherit the earth: what could be more subversive than that? What could be more radical than loving your enemies? And if you leave out the Kingdom of Heaven, the Beatitudes as a way of being in this life would see the poor and down-trodden, the peacemakers and the persecuted as the most admired members of a community. She reread Genesis and Milton's *Paradise Lost*. She had always sided with Eve against God. Without curiosity, without pushing the boundaries of the unknown, we'd still be living in caves. Eve, Nina believed, had received a raw deal.

She was revisiting books not read for decades and reconnecting with values and ideas that were hers when she was working at the UN, and all because of the TIF people. She didn't know where this change might lead, nor was she worried it might suddenly stop. Each day was sparked by surprising new thoughts, each day was fuelled by an energy that carried its own momentum. And it occurred to her that it was exactly this vibrancy that Sean was missing. Steeped in sameness, day after dismal day, no wonder he was exhausted.

Each morning, before the heat became unbearable, she would walk in the Botanic Gardens. This was her Daniel time, and different from remembering. Before he started writing to her when all she had was memory, a memory sadly polluted by bile and longing, she would recall her marriage piece by piece from the milestones of their thirteen years. And it was as if it had shrunk, become matted and tough like a woollen garment put through the wash. She would hold it up and although it no longer fitted she could not bear to part with it. Memory was a spoiler but until Daniel made contact, it was all she had.

After his first message he had been sending letter-like emails, written as if he was talking to her. He was desperate to talk to her, but she refused: not simply that she didn't want him to know she was not in London, she wanted to digest his words at her own pace. She replied to his emails, not immediately and always briefly. And she remained extremely cautious, for it would be so easy to succumb to the Daniel-ness of these long communications.

The previous evening she'd taken her drink out to the balcony and there she'd stood in the heavy heat of dusk, the traffic noise a constant, the tops of the trees in the Botanic Gardens engraved against the deep blue of the late sky. She had spent the day trying to arrange her thoughts about monuments and their embodiment of abstract qualities like freedom and tolerance. She'd considered the Statue of Liberty, Berlin's Holocaust Museum, the Arc de Triomphe. And iconic places like Robben Island, a prison that became a monument to the human spirit, and Ground Zero prior to any reconstruction, a sacred place symbolic of courage and freedom as much as tragedy and loss. Memory was involved with all these sites, either personal memory or received memory, but what gave them power was the human ability to imagine and empathise with those who actually experienced the events being memorialised. It occurred to her for the first time – although she expected there was a wealth of literature devoted to it – that memory, far from being a discrete cognitive process, was actually a subset of imagination.

When she remembered something, like the facets of her life with Daniel, she was actually imagining how things used to be. Imagination, she decided, was essential to remembering – and why memories were so unstable, so slippery. All memory, then, required the imagination, but not all imagining involved memory. And somewhere between memory and the imagination was a cloudy cognitive stretch where memorials found a place.

It was difficult to pin her thoughts down, and it occurred to her that the person she wanted to talk to about these issues – memory, the imagination, the texture of a marriage, even goodness – was not Daniel but Elliot. She was surprised. Until that day on the beach, never had she felt the desire to draw closer to this man who treated her sister so poorly. But now, with Zoe's feelings for Ramsay unequivocal, an attraction that poor Elliot must have been aware of throughout his marriage, Nina wondered at his extraordinary loyalty. Elliot had remained with Zoe through years of wreckage – his wreckage but hers as well – and Nina wanted to know how he had managed it. She wanted to talk with Elliot, but Elliot had disappeared.

2.

Elliot is becalmed.

He has set up home in a van, not in New York but in Melbourne, a short fifteen-minute drive from his home. The van is equipped with a bench-bed, a single-burner stove, microwave oven, foldaway table, reading light and kitchen utensils for one. Daily he swims at the council sports centre and uses the facilities there. At night he parks in a street alongside the Merri Creek Trail, a corridor of bush and parkland that follows the main waterways of Melbourne from the outer suburbs to the city centre. He has a few companionable books, his laptop for emailing Zoe, his phone to text Callum and Hayley. He also has a sizeable cache of video downloads, but so far he's had little inclination for them. And with vague thoughts about his next project, he included a few of Arthur Koestler's novels in e-version, for which he's felt even less inclination. He sleeps surprisingly well, tranquil, floating, worry-free sleep; the whoosh of passing cars might wake him, or the flurry and squeal of possums, but soon he is asleep again. In the morning he carries cereal and coffee into the park and, seated on a wooden bench, he eats his breakfast.

He took up his van life a week ago. Each day has been much the same. He's in the park by seven, the sun high and condensed into blinding rays by the branches of the trees. The grass is sizzled to straw and soon the bushes, spry after the cooler night air, begin to wilt. There's not been even a wisp of cloud to feed hopes of a cool change – not that it's bothered him; unlike Zoe, he thrives in the heat.

At home he always reads over breakfast, but here in the park he leaves his book in the van and instead watches the birds: rainbow lorikeets darting in the trees, red-rumped parrots pecking the dry ground before the heat drives them away, and magpies – such glamorous creatures – just a metre from where he sits, waiting for crumbs. He's fascinated by birds, always has been. Zoe's indifferent to them, always has been. Perhaps this should have been a warning back in those heady days of New York, together with all the other warnings. He remembers talking to her about birds: they were walking in Riverside Park a week or two after they met, the air was brittle, sparrows were rummaging for food in the icy earth. Birds, he said, are the most splendid of all species. He talked about their colour and design, their staggering variety. 'And perched at the pinnacle of the bird kingdom are parrots. And –' he was triumphant, 'Australia has more types of parrots than any place on earth.'

He remembers it still, how at that moment he saw himself in Australia, watching parrots in their natural habitat with this woman who had miraculously entered his life. But Zoe fails to notice birds.

The parrots are lively in the early morning, and the cavalcade of dogs too; their owners, in contrast, move slowly through the hot damp air. He knows it is a cliché that owners resemble their dogs, but it's true. Pale reddish humans tend towards pale reddish dogs; humans with dark curls have dark curly-coated dogs; there's a Labrador-type of person and a small-white-dog type who is often very large. He is missing his own Adelaide, but how to collect her and install her in the van when he is supposed to be in New York? And suddenly, on the seventh morning, the whole ruse seems pointless. What does it matter if he's in New York or here in Melbourne? His leaving so suddenly following George's death and Zoe's mercy dash to Ramsay is unambiguous. He decides to forgo the charade. He'll email Zoe and text the children; he'll let them know he's not gone far, that he'll be home soon, but for the moment he needs some time to himself. And he'll fetch his dog.

He resumes his breakfast. He might feel nicely cocooned but he is not invisible. He sees furtive glances cast in his direction and no one lingers in his vicinity. He's a middle-aged man living in a van on an inner-suburban street – not the sort of behaviour to instil ease and comfort in passersby. Yet he has seldom felt so relaxed. His oddity protects him, or what would be perceived as oddity. And he's reminded of a long-ago incident, his early days in New York, a small-town guy alone in the world's most exciting city, and a particular evening in Central Park when he wandered away from the main paths, away from the running tracks and the tennis courts and became lost in the rough undergrowth of the North Woods. He'd been told about the gangs that lurked in this area, and it was growing dark – how could he have been so stupid? The more nervous he was the more disoriented he became: even if he could see the lights of buildings he wouldn't know if he was looking north, south, east or west. He seemed to be walking in circles, kept finding himself in the Ravine. It was darker down there, frightening, and he would scramble up again, only to find himself a few minutes later in what appeared to be the same area. Where to hide if he needed to hide? He wished he was taller, stronger, he wished he was armed. He wished he was one of those crazy people he'd seen on the New York streets that everyone gave a wide berth. And suddenly he had his solution. He started to sing, he sang the only songs he could remember in his fear, hymns from years of family church attendance. He waved his arms wildly, fanning the music; he was running and singing boisterously, keeping to the high ground as he galloped towards the lights. And if anyone was lurking in the brush they left him alone; no one wants to mess with a madman.

And that's how he feels with his van life: insulated by what others would regard as crazy behaviour. It makes waiting for Zoe bearable; so, too, the separation from his children. The miniature home with everything in reach seems to have muffled his body's cravings, and after a few days they've disappeared. The truth is he has always enjoyed being alone.

When Diana Trilling published her memoir, *The Beginning of the Journey*, the book that chronicled her childhood and the first half of her marriage to Lionel, Elliot had been horrified to learn of her terror of being alone. The neurosis (that was her terminology) eventually passed, but until her middle years she could not bear to be solitary – a fatal liability for a writer and perhaps the reason she came to her work rather later than most. In the early years of her marriage, when Lionel was supporting them both as well as his parents on an instructor's salary at Columbia and articles published in various low-paying periodicals, he contrived to be with her as much as possible. Lionel was working flat out, he was exhausted, he would write while she was sleeping, he would come home to be with her when he had obligations out in the world. And what was she doing? Nothing much. In the end she hired a companion – she'd come into some money by then – which lightened Lionel's load.

Elliot did not care for Mrs Trilling and it was her own account that prejudiced him. This neurosis of hers was a fate not to be endured, and anyone with more than a kilo of intellectual weight would make sure to be rid of it – unless of course the neurosis was a contrivance to avoid serious work. Sartre often left Elliot cold, but his play *Huis Clos*, with its famous pronouncement that hell is other people, had always spoken very clearly to him. Diana Trilling's neurosis condemned her as selfish, lazy, undeserving of respect, the sort of person he abhorred.

He is well aware that other people don't have such strong reactions to characters in novels or subjects of biographies and autobiographies, but for him, the people he finds in books are as real, as complex, as confusing and as beguiling as his own wife. And if they are more reliable and more predictable, it is only because he has read to the end of their story. Although Zoe's future is not entirely unknown. He's in no doubt that George's death and the hiatus it has left spell the end of Zoe's devotion to Ramsay – he is loath to call it love. He has always believed that if he can only wait it out, Zoe will not only return to him, she will embrace their marriage and embrace him in a way she has never done before.

Zoe has been gripped by Ramsay, or rather her idea of Ramsay, ever since childhood. Blind to the gaping tears in his human fabric, she might well dive in to fill the void left by George, but George, having no needs of his own, could devote himself fully to Ramsay. In contrast, Zoe's love (there, he has used the word) is a needy beast. Desperate, hopeful, pumped up by years of dreaming, she'll charge in and run smack into Ramsay's disinterest in everything not Ramsay. She'll take another run-up, and another, but it won't be too long before she sees how things are, how they've always been. Crippling disappointment? Elliot cannot predict. Relief? He hopes so. But the spell will be broken. How could it not with someone who away from the piano is a miserable runt of a man?

Someone in the future will write Ramsay Blake's biography, someone who admires the musician sufficiently to put up with the disappointing man, and Zoe will warrant at most a couple of paragraphs. Elliot knows what drives the biographer. With his own big women he can't know too much about their passions – the people they adored, the work that claimed them; but the hangers-on and the lovesick fans, they don't interest him and they don't make good copy.

Each of his women has become as familiar as a lover, and in many respects far more satisfying. Biographical subjects never demand that you change, adapt, open old wounds and then close them up again. In fact, during the biographical process your own life's failings and disappointments are hushed as you find another cache of letters, conduct your interviews, travel to places your subject visited, the very same hotels, the same houses and apartments; you cannot acquire too much of their life.

He owes so much to biography, the single reliable pleasure of his adult years. With one's own life so much is forgotten or deliberately repressed or, for smoother passage through the days, actually redrawn. But with biography there's the unequalled satisfaction of knowing an entire life: its obstacles and setbacks, mistakes and injustices, as well as the achievements. His big women, how they've sustained him. Lizzie Hardwick, Djuna, Elizabeth Bishop and the only non-American, Jean Rhys, all of them except Hardwick as much in thrall to alcohol as they were to literature, and all demonstrating a perfect pitch – an innate, indestructible talent that he adores.

It is possible his work might have traversed another path if his marriage had been different, not just male subjects but maybe biography itself may have been less compelling.

Although he doesn't think so: he can't imagine any work he would prefer to biography.

With his Lizzie Hardwick now with the publisher, he is already considering his next subject – Cynthia Koestler, a wife not a writer. But it's early days, more nudging interest than full-blown affair, and his time would have been spent waiting for Zoe to come to her senses if he had not sought refuge in the van. Although initially he thought he could wait it out, be patient with her, try to be kind. But she was hardly ever home and when she was she looked as if she might break. He did his best not to aggravate, not to niggle, but it was unbearable to watch her self-destruct. So he invented some additional research on Hardwick – Zoe didn't know the biography was finished – packed a bag and left.

And here he is. No classes, no project on the go, no family life, and with all his yearnings in limbo he passes the hours nosing around in a mind released from all restraints. He has driven to the bay, the ocean, the hills, the wine-growing district in the Yarra Valley, the zoo, the sculpture park on the far side of town, returning each evening to the same spot beside the park. He has a sense of himself as thickly varnished – not iced over, not that extreme numbness when the mind is drumming and you're paralysed, a frightening feeling that seized him when he first realised his wife's feelings for Ramsay. The varnish feeling actually muffles his internal voices and mutes unwanted emotions, leaving him free to absorb the hush, the gentle tug of the present moment, the houses and streets, pedestrians, other drivers, dogs, the broad sky, the end-of-summer gardens, the bush, gaudy lorikeets, gorgeous magpies.

On his fourth morning at the local pool he met a man who had made a lifestyle of van living. This man did not have a wife he loved, he'd abandoned his children, and he'd never had a job he found endlessly interesting. Elliot's situation is vastly different: it's primarily because he knows his van-time is limited that he's able to enjoy it. Daily he writes supportive and loving emails to Zoe; he wants her to know he remains steadfast. Sometimes she answers, mostly not. And he ponders his long loyal love for her. He realises that to an outsider it might appear he has loved his wife as fruitlessly as she has loved Ramsay. But that would be wrong: Ramsay is a figment of Zoe's imagination, a sculpted desire which, if tested – as must be happening now – would be rudely shattered. Like all obsessions hers has been mindless, all-consuming and staggeringly deluded.

His love, on the other hand, has spared him none of the truth. He knows Zoe's flaws all too well, her capacity for indifference being the hardest to bear. He knows all about his wife, and a vastly different woman she is from the one who first captured his heart. He doesn't blame her, nor does he blame himself, after all, how could he know, how can anyone know when they meet and fall in love with a stranger, that this adorable person is their usual self? Who even considers the question? He saw how she fizzed and popped, he saw her leap without a safety net. One night she dragged him to the Greyhound bus station, she wanted to see Niagara Falls at dawn. The experience was like no other, witnessing one of the great wonders of the world with this woman, this wonder, who had streamed into his life.

She would dance until three in the morning and make love until six and still leap into the new day. She leapt and laughed and he loved her. The beautiful face, the Australian accent, the slender body, a mere touch of her hand would set his own skin dancing. And he married her, this woman he believed to thrive on change and excitement, who lapped up days streaked with passion. He discovered all too soon that far from free, she hefted around a cement wall to which she was firmly chained. And far from relishing change, she wanted things to remain exactly as they were: her music, her job, her home in Australia, Ramsay.

Zoe, in her own defence, would say she did not realise the man she married was a drunk. But he hasn't touched alcohol for years, while Zoe continues to squander herself on Ramsay. They might have lived anywhere in the world but she wanted to settle in Melbourne. Ramsay's home city. She could have played in a trio, a quartet, a chamber group as well as teaching, but she wanted to have free time. For Ramsay. She has neglected him, her husband, because of Ramsay, and she has defaulted on their marriage. Yet he's always given her another chance, he's been well stocked in other chances. Only now, and it's a reluctant thought, Elliot wonders if the supply might ever run short.

Coming towards him is a couple he has seen before. They are much the same age as he and Zoe, they always walk with their arms linked and they always have plenty to say to each other. Their two old dogs waddle along, stopping to sniff tree trunks and clumps of dry grass; every now and then one or other of the couple calls them to heel. These two people look so comfortable with each other. Both carry a little too much weight, both are dressed in T-shirts and baggy shorts, both wear a wedding band and no other jewellery. This couple looks happy.

3.

Zoe has been up since five preparing the day's lessons. Just before seven, with Callum and Hayley still sleeping, she

227

leaves the house. She's exhausted, but she'll collapse only if she stops, and she doesn't want to stop. So she'll do her work, she'll maintain the house, she'll attend to the kids, and she'll care for Ramsay.

She cannot help herself. It's the way it has always been with Ramsay – and different from those high-flying women you hear about, a company CEO or a top medical specialist who risks all for a man, usually not her equal, with whom she is reduced to sand and water. Her feeling for Ramsay is not like that – for a start he's a genius – yet she knows she is fixed on him in a way that is disturbing. Not that she has time to dwell. Ramsay can't cook or clean, he can't shop or drive, he can't wash or iron, he can't organise appointments or work commitments. And overriding all these practical concerns and despite keeping his feelings to himself, he must be missing George who was, after all, father, companion, manager and friend, the central figure in Ramsay's life.

A number of other people have put themselves forward as George substitutes, but Ramsay has been quite clear.

'You know me, Zoe. Not like George knew me, but second to George.'

And given George is not here any more, she wants to say: I'm the only one to look after you.

Occasionally she has sounded a warning to herself: remember what happened in New York, remember how it was then. And while she acknowledges it could be like that again, more than twenty years have passed since that terrible mistake, years in which they both have grown in maturity and wisdom.

As for Elliot, she doesn't want to think about him. And neither is it so difficult. For most of her marriage, with cast-iron determination she has hollowed out two separate spaces: her Elliot compartment and her Ramsay compartment. Days, even weeks can pass with her entering one of the spaces and staying there; at other times she'll swing back and forth in a single day. Now, however, she locks the door on Elliot. It will be opened again: Elliot grounds her, Elliot is home and she can't imagine life without him. As for Ramsay, such a long-time resident in her heart and mind, she would shut down if he was to disappear from her life.

A couple of days before George's death and without any prior warning, Elliot had raised the topic of Ramsay.

'Me and Ramsay,' he said. 'In relation to you.'

For her, both men endured like faith endures; there was nothing to discuss. But Elliot had persisted; he had not forced the issue for years, he said, but now he needed some answers. In particular, he wanted to know why she stayed with him, a man she clearly did not love.

She insisted she did love him.

'Like you love Ramsay? Is that your idea of love? No sex, no physical contact. Like a nun loves Jesus.' His laugh was bitter. 'Only one Jesus in your life and that's Ramsay Blake. As for me, I'm your wayward priest, your one-time whisky priest. You sleep with me, have occasional sex with me, we have children, a house. You live with me after your fashion.' He looked simultaneously angry and resigned. 'But if your definition of love is what you feel for Ramsay, then you clearly don't love me. So – why do you stay?'

They were sitting at the table, just the two of them, the remains of dinner in front of them. He picked up a fork and dragged the tines across the table surface, back and forward, repeating the same question: *Why do you stay? Why do you stay?*

But it was the wrong question and she knew this at the time; it was not why she stayed but why he did.

The conversation was interrupted by the children coming home, but Elliot said he wanted to return to it. And then George died and Ramsay needed her, and Elliot, far from pursuing a conversation she would prefer not to have, became quieter, kinder, more understanding; he let her do as she felt she must. And then he said he needed to fly to New York for some final research on his Elizabeth Hardwick. At first she thought he really had taken a trip back to the States, not for research for she knew the book was finished, but rather a leave of absence from a painful and complicated situation. But his passport was still in his desk and all his winter clothes were still in the wardrobe. It was clear he needed to get away, in his position she would have done the same. But he has not gone far – he told her this in a recent email; more importantly, he told her he'd be returning.

For now, she is grateful for his absence. She wouldn't know how to accommodate him in these days when she hardly knows how to manage herself. How to explain morning departures of seven o'clock and evening homecomings right on dinner time? How to justify twenty-minute meals of takeaway food and then out again till all hours? How to defend an existence stubbornly blind to the future? She couldn't bear to have him observing her as she dashes here and there, never stopping. And that's the trick: don't stop, don't even pause, and don't think.

She turns into Ramsay's driveway at twenty past seven; with a nine o'clock class she can only stay an hour. She lets herself in with the key he has given her. He's not in the kitchen, nor the living room; she peers into the bedroom, it is empty and sour smelling – she must remember to change the sheets. The music room door is open and as she approaches she hears him crying. Ramsay didn't cry in the days after George died, he didn't cry at the funeral, she's not seen him cry since then; in fact in all the years she has known him she has never seen him cry. She rushes into the room. He's still in his pyjamas, unwashed and unshaven. She wraps her arms around him, soothes him as she did the children when they were young. There, there, she says, I know you miss him, I know how terrible this is; but it'll get better, I promise you, it will get better.'

'I can't do this.' The words catch in tears and spluttering.

'You don't have to. I'm here. I'll help.'

'But you don't even know who we use.'

Suddenly the sobbing eases, his voice clears. 'Sean! Sean would know. It's the same piano tuner we've always had.' And now he looks up at Zoe. 'Ring Sean.'

The piano needs tuning and Ramsay cannot practise until it's done. His closest friend and companion, the man who was his entire family has died and Ramsay has not shed a tear; but with the piano out of tune he is inconsolable. Although better now he has the solution: he wants Zoe to ring the brother he long ago rejected, the brother who for all Ramsay knows could be in London, Delhi or Timbuktu. Just ring him, Ramsay says, and find out the piano tuner's name.

In some clearer future Zoe might reflect on what manner of man would behave this way; but now all she hears is Ramsay's distress over the out-of-tune piano. She goes to the kitchen for George's telephone directory: there's no one listed under piano tuner. She checks the address book on George's mobile: again, nothing. In all the urgency, in all Ramsay's panic, at least she knows she can't contact Sean.

'If he's been coming for years,' she says, 'surely you know the man's name.'

'Dinger. His name's Dinger.'

'His real name?'

Ramsay shakes his head. 'Between ourselves, George and me, we only ever called him Dinger.'

She checks again in George's telephone directory and his mobile phone. There's no Dinger.

'Think,' she says to Ramsay.

'I can't think.'

George was an orderly man, an organised man. Zoe goes to his filing cabinet. She riffles through the files in the top drawer, then every file in the second drawer. In the third drawer, in a file marked piano tuning and repairs, she finds what she wants. The piano tuner's name is Donald Singer.

She rings him.

He sounds surprised when she explains the problem. 'I'm due tomorrow. I come every four weeks. I've been coming every four weeks since Ramsay was in short pants. He knows that.'

Zoe asks him to hold while she tells Ramsay the tuner will be there tomorrow.

'I can't wait, he has to come today.'

She returns to the phone. 'Mr Singer –' she begins.

'I heard, I'll be there in an hour.'

She asks how much it will cost, says she'll leave a cheque on the piano. 'And thank you. Thank you very much.'

Ramsay is now calm. And he's apologising. He doesn't know what happens to him. George used to do these things, and without George he just flies into a panic.

'I'm here now,' she says. 'And I'll help you. The piano will be tuned this morning, everything will be fixed. Everything will be all right.'

They move into the kitchen so she can check the contents of the fridge. It's a mess in here even though she left it tidy yesterday evening.

'Could I have a hamburger for dinner?'

She twists around. Ramsay looks like a cast-off engine tossed into this junkyard kitchen. He even smells rusty. Her beautiful man is nowhere to be seen.

'A home-made burger, not those scrawny things in a spongy bun you get from Maccas and Hungry Jacks.'

She pulls herself together. Ramsay's bereaved, of course he's not concerned with his appearance.

'A hamburger with the lot: egg, cheese, cooked onions, beetroot, lettuce, lots of tomato sauce – it has to be Rosella brand – all on a proper toasted hamburger roll.' He walks towards her and for a moment she thinks he's going to embrace her. 'Will you do that for me?'

Of course, she says, and at the same time she'll prepare extra for Hayley and Callum – they'll be thrilled, she would never usually cook such food. She tells him to expect her around five, although she'll ring at lunchtime just to check he is all right.

Through the open window of her car she reminds him the piano tuner will be there within the hour so he needs to shower and dress. He laughs, does a little bow on the front porch and skips off inside as she reverses into the street.

Ramsay re-enters the house and the laughter stops. All of him stops. He leans against the wall and slowly sinks to the carpet. He draws up his knees, rests his head against them and shuts his eyes. Horo nuzzles against him and he wraps an arm around the dog. He could stay like this all day, has spent days in the one spot, unaware of the drifting hours, ignoring hunger and thirst, only moving when his bladder is full. And after he relieves himself he returns to his possie to wait through the next few hours. He has no idea how to occupy himself.

The piano has deserted him.

He can still play, his technique is not the problem, and he knows how the mood should sound and can replicate it; but he feels like a foreman rather than a pianist. It is truly awful, and so upsetting he'd prefer not to play.

Music has abandoned him.

Once before this happened, only fifteen years old at the time, and he truly believed he was done for. George saved him then, George guided him back to music, and any hostility towards the man who had married his mother and replaced his father disappeared. But who will save him now when the cause of the trouble, George's death, thwarts its solution? That other time there had been no clear cause, the rupture was sudden, a haemorrhage in the piano-playing part of himself. One week his life was running normally – early breakfast, practice, school, more practice, dinner, TV, bed – and the next week he never wanted to play the piano again. What had been natural became a penance.

And now again. Ramsay Blake, defined by music even before he could walk. Ramsay Blake, the person who sits hour after hour, month after month, year after year at the piano. Most people are an alphabet of qualities – Australian, bike-rider, clown, dishwasher, energetic, flat-footed and so on down to x-ray vision, yachtsman and Zen – but he can be summed up almost entirely by 'p' for pianist and 'm' for musical. Any place he finds himself, any time, any crowd, it is music that defines and protects him.

And he doesn't have it any more. His music's soul has shrivelled; playing Bach is no different from playing scales. And in the hard chill of that sad space he realises that rather than the soul feeding his music, music has filled every nook and cranny of his soul. Suddenly he is no different from a boot or a ball or a piece of paper wafting in the wind. He may as well be dead.

No one must know, he keeps telling himself. No one must know, he told himself that other time. But George knew, George saw what was happening. George was kind, he was understanding, he stepped in and guided him back to music. George believed in him, and his music returned.

There's no one to save him now.

He has retrieved the arsenic buried in the bag of blood and bone. On one of his teaching days at the university he took a small sample to the chemistry department to be assayed. He told them he had a rat problem, that the arsenic had sat for years in the shed; he wanted to know if it was still effective. The results confirmed it was arsenic, but it was well past its use-by date; he'd need barrels of the stuff, they said, to get rid of his rats. Still he brought it inside and stored it at the back of the laundry cupboard: science had been wrong before and it gave him a sense of comfort knowing it was close at hand.

He has nothing to show for these days without music. He knows it is time to get up when Zoe arrives; he knows it is nearly dinner time when she returns in the afternoon; he knows it is Monday because Mrs Monday turns up, and Wednesday because he is at the university teaching. He exists in a cloud, he moves in a cloud. He wants George back.

He checks his watch. He doesn't want to move, but Dinger will be here shortly. George always said that Dinger was the best in the trade. Can Dinger tell if a piano has not been played? Will Dinger guess what's happened to him? The old terror returns, it has money to burn, and there's no one to save him now.

Chapter 11. The Human Touch

1.

It is the thirteenth morning of Elliot's van life. Nearly a week ago he collected Adelaide, and she has settled into the rhythm of his days. She is a small dog, van-sized, whose ginger and spice coat, snub nose, pricked-up ears floppy at the points belie her grandiose name. With her unconditional devotion, she is in every respect a perfect companion.

The dog-walkers in the park now talk to him. The conversation is strictly dog centred: name of pet, age, breed, temperament. Adelaide revels in the pack of canines. In the park where Elliot usually walks her most of the dogs are exercised on leads while their owners jog, but here the animals chase and sniff and wrestle together while the humans saunter along chatting about the weather and their pets.

The thirteenth day starts as usual: breakfast in the park, followed by a swim and shower at the local leisure centre. After his morning email to Zoe he decides to walk to Dight Falls – the marvel of inner Melbourne he called these rapids when Zoe first brought him here soon after they moved from New York. Dight Falls became their special Melbourne place, much as Riverside Park had been their special New York place. They celebrated their first two anniversaries of life in Australia with a picnic at the falls. Callum was tottering on newly discovered legs the first time, it was a perfect family day. On the second anniversary, Callum, with all the bravado of a two-year-old, made a beeline for the river rocks and nothing would deflect him, Zoe was too anxious to enjoy herself and he was too hung-over.

Since then he has visited the falls often, but always alone. It's a place for introspection, a place where he has grappled with his marriage, his work and, in the early days of sobriety, his not drinking. If he was asked to choose a significant location in Melbourne, just one, it would be this patch of wild water not far from the city centre.

He hurries Addie along the path and soon he is standing on the grassy prominence overlooking the rapids. The foam smashes against the boulders, the sky is a smooth cornflower blue, a breeze rises from the water: how calm he feels among the boil and roar. On the far side, perched on a rock in the shallows, is a white-faced heron, and towering over the water are ancient steep cliffs, history compacted in their lovely layers of rock. On that very first visit, Zoe was pregnant with Callum; they stood where he is standing now, her arm about his waist, his arm draped across her shoulders, and he remembers thinking how fortunate he was, married to this woman, soon to be a father, about to begin an exciting new job. Ramsay was living in Europe at the time – not that he knew about Zoe and Ramsay then – and only booze cast a shadow over his otherwise perfect existence. He resolved that day to bring his drinking under control, once and for all.

They were happy in those early years, or at least he thought they were. Not that he controlled his drinking then; the resolution made as he stood above Dight Falls lasted the usual couple of days, then came the bargaining and soon there was no point in keeping count. He does, however, have a sense of happiness when he looks back at that time. But what if Zoe has never been happy with him? It's a shocking thought, an unbearable thought, and as he stands above the falls, as he watches the heron fishing, the water churning, he forces it to the margins of his mind.

'It's so peaceful here.'

The voice, pitched beneath the water's roar, startles him. A woman is standing by his side.

He glances briefly in her direction then back to the rapids. 'Yes, very peaceful.' And shifts ever so slightly to give himself more space.

Addie trots over and sniffs at the new person then returns to her rummaging in the delicious mud. The woman is tall, much the same height as Zoe, but where Zoe carries an air of fragility, this woman's fullness, her bright loose-fitting dress, the mass of dark hair billowing over her shoulders give an impression of strength.

'I come here often,' she says, turning towards him.

He, too, turns and finds himself looking directly at her. He was intending to say something about the wonder of this place; instead he registers her face, the surprise and pleasure of it.

He takes another step to the side, this time to see her more clearly. 'It's the commotion here, nature's turmoil,' he says. 'Works like meditation.'

She nods, the movement slow, resigned. 'Yes, I know what you mean. Holds you in the present.'

Her skin and eyes are dark, her eyebrows are thick and black. He guesses she's Indigenous, not just her features, but she speaks with that singsong inflection he's come to associate with Aboriginal speech. She's a good-looking woman with her broad, smooth face, and the full mouth that's ever-so-slightly crooked. He expects she's much the same age as he is.

Her name, she says, is Elizabeth.

'Lizzie?' he asks, thinking of his own Elizabeth Hardwick.

'Beth,' she replies.

She comments on his American accent and he gives her a potted biography. 'And you?' he asks.

'Australian.' She smiles wryly. '*First* Australian. Aboriginal. Koori.'

With such emphasis, Elliot is curious about her name.

She explains that her parents wanted her to have a solid English name. 'My father was one of the first Aboriginal pastors.' She is fiddling with her unruly hair. Suddenly she looks amused. 'Things were so different in those days. Different language, different ideas as to what would bring about advancement for Indigenous Australians.' And now she laughs. 'Indigenous Australians! We were all blackfellas back then.' And laughs some more. 'So many girls in Australia around my age, in the entire Commonwealth come to that, were saddled with Margaret or Elizabeth after the princesses.'

The princesses? He realises she must be a good deal older than he first thought. It turns out she is past sixty.

She is shouting to be heard over the roaring water and, without any forethought, Elliot suggests they adjourn somewhere for coffee.

She checks her watch, then burrows in her bag for her phone. She needs to ring work, she says, to let them know she'll be late. He's about to apologise, withdraw his offer, when he realises she wouldn't be changing her plans unless she wanted to spend more time with him.

He rounds up Addie and they make their way along the river path towards the Abbotsford Convent – decommissioned long ago and now used as an arts and community complex. What were formerly the nuns' cells have been converted to studios and leased at reasonable rates to artists and writers. Elliot is familiar with the scheme because several years back, during a period when Ramsay seemed to be continually in Melbourne, he'd applied for one of the studios. The study at home had become too close to his wife and his university office attracted too much passing traffic; he just wanted to be alone with his woman of the moment – it was Jean Rhys – in a small monastic space where he could work and unwind. His application was unsuccessful, and not surprising, after all, he was far from being an impoverished writer or artist.

At first he was disappointed, but soon he realised that the appeal of the convent had little to do with his needing a quiet work-space; rather, what he wanted, what he actually craved, was respite from his usual life. He arranged to go away to an isolated cottage on Kangaroo Island, a week that replenished him far more than a year hanging out in a nun's cell. The sound of the ocean was a constant comfort, the coast itself was a five-minute walk away. The cliffs were high and black, plateaued at the top and dropping sharply to the sea; rocky outcrops the size of small islands had broken off from the land mass and obstructed the incoming waves. The foam was thick, intricate, mesmerising. Such a fabulous changing sea: he spent hours with it every day as life in Melbourne went on without him.

That week on Kangaroo Island was rather like his van existence and perhaps not unlike the drinking binges of long ago. It seems he has always had a need to escape his life. And perhaps this woman, too, who appears padded out with something – solitude? loneliness? When he learns she is newly bereaved – her husband died just a few months earlier – the cladding makes sense.

Within twenty minutes they are in the convent grounds. In addition to the nuns' cells there are offices and seminar rooms, workshops, performance spaces and a variety of eateries. Soon they are seated with coffee at an outdoor table of a bakery café with Addie stretched out in the shade of a nearby tree. They talk without restraint, two strangers who know that after this moment they'll go their separate ways. They talk about dogs, convents, the environment, children, and soon he is telling her about his tattered marriage, his drinking, about Zoe and Ramsay; he tells her the whole sordid story. When finally he stops, his coffee is cold. He drinks the dregs and grimaces, not at the taste but his own bitter life.

'Sorry for rambling on,' he says. 'I don't know what possessed me.'

She brushes his apology aside. 'How do you feel about your wife now? After all that's happened?'

He's about to say he still loves her, but something stops him, something makes him consider what he has always taken on faith. Is it love that he feels? Or habit? Or need? Or a combination of all three?

Beth breaks the lengthening silence with a more direct approach.

'Do you stay with her out of guilt? All those years of your drinking?'

He's quick to dismiss any suggestion of guilt. 'Which is not to say Zoe doesn't think I owe her.' He hesitates, and then decides not to hold back. 'I've always regarded guilt as a useless response.'

'You're clearly not Catholic. Nor Jewish for that matter.'

He shakes his head. 'Just an ordinary Protestant atheist.'

She leans forward, smiling. 'This might be an appropriate time to tell you I'm an ordinary Protestant minister.'

He should feel embarrassed but he doesn't. 'We've managed well enough so far, no reason we shouldn't continue.'

She relaxes into her chair, smoothes her dress of many colours. 'Okay then, back to guilt.'

'Firstly, it comes too late, the damage has already been done. Secondly, while you're feeling guilty you're not doing much else. Guilt becomes an excuse for inaction.'

'Paralysed by guilt, that sort of thing?'

'Exactly. And for those with masochistic tendencies who like a bit of self-flagellation, it can be quite pleasant.'

She laughs. 'You've clearly given this some thought.'

He nods, suggests more coffee, is halfway to standing when she stops him. 'The coffee can wait. I'm not finished with guilt.'

Was she reprimanding him? And then deciding to take her words at face value, he sits down again.

'I think you're right about guilt, but only in some respects and for some people,' she says. 'For many, guilt's the precursor to a better understanding. And from there it's just a short step to action. People can change.'

'But where was their moral gauge when they were committing the wrong?'

'For drivers over the limit who cause accidents, their moral gauge is doused in alcohol,' she said. 'For bankers or business people who rip off their investors, their gauge has been rusted by greed. My point is that there are plenty of people who rob and deceive and maim and kill who show genuine remorse.'

'But there are a whole lot more who don't, so we've high recidivism for most crimes. You can't tell me they're all psychopaths and sociopaths.'

Her broad brow crinkles, she fiddles with her wedding ring. He worries he's said too much, spoken too bluntly. But even as his anxiety stiffens he reminds himself that they're tourists in each other's life, strangers an hour ago and soon to be strangers again.

'I'm perplexed,' she says at last. '*You* perplex me. You've so little faith in the ability of people to change, yet you've been waiting your entire marriage for your wife to change.'

He meets her gaze, then turns away. He has no explanation.

The café is crowded – new mothers mostly, with babies and toddlers. The chatter is lively, he hears bursts of laughter, two of the women are breast-feeding. How happy he and Zoe were as new parents. He remembers so many occasions, he, Zoe and Callum, the three of them together on walks, picnics, the Sunday lunches with Zoe's parents. He remembers how his son would toddle towards him and put his arms out, how the little body would fold about his own, arms around his neck, legs curled about his waist. He remembers how Callum would fall asleep in his arms, the warm trusting weight of his sleeping boy. And he remembers nothing of Hayley's first years. There are photos of him holding her and photos of him playing with her, but what he remembers are the photos and not the events themselves.

As he observes the women at the café with their babies he feels an ache. It's all too familiar.

Beth has been watching him. 'So,' she says. 'What do you feel for your wife now?'

He meets her gaze. 'I long for her.'

2.

Across town, at Zoe's school, the Friday general arts session was drawing to a close. The guest today was Ramsay Blake, recruited by Zoe when the novelist who had been scheduled cancelled at short notice. Privately, Zoe had welcomed the inconvenience as an opportunity to get Ramsay out of the house and out of the doldrums. And she had been proven right. At the piano, playing for an audience, there was no indication of Ramsay's loss, no sign of the panic she'd witnessed on several occasions since George's death; Ramsay was, as always, at home and happy with his music. And now as the girls asked him questions, he was relaxed and charming the lot of them.

'He's so cute,' she heard one girl say during the break. 'Model status,' said another. And she registered a rush of pleasure that Ramsay, her Ramsay, a man heading for fifty, was pin-up material for a bunch of teenage girls.

A girl in the front row, a violinist with abundant talent but meagre application, had her hand in the air. Zoe indicated she should go ahead.

'How can you bear all the practising?' she said.

Ramsay propped himself on the edge of a table, just a metre or so from the girl; a violin case was at her feet. He spoke loudly enough for everyone to hear but he leaned ever-so-slightly towards the girl, and his eyes – Zoe could see quite clearly from where she stood – his eyes held her.

'I love to practise,' he began. The girl grimaced as if to say: how could you? He cast his arms out wide in a happy, helpless gesture. 'I like the memorising, I like the mastery, I like discovering nuances in the music. It always amazes me that even with a piece I've performed dozens of times, I'll discover an interval or a pause, some small intricacy I've never noticed before.' He shrugged. 'I find that remarkable. And the muscularity of practice, I like that too – much more than jogging or swimming laps.' He paused a moment, folded his arms across his chest. 'And ... I like the orderliness of practice. The hours of solitude, too, just me and my piano.'

'Don't you ever get bored?' It was the same girl.

He nodded. 'Sometimes, but that shouldn't reflect either on the music or the dynamics of practising. Rather it means I'm tired or distracted. I take a break, go online, walk my dog, have a snack, and an hour later I'm ready to return to the piano.'

'That wouldn't work for me,' the girl said.

He cocked his head to one side in a familiar gesture that made Zoe's breath catch. 'Do you love music?' Ramsay asked the girl.

She nodded.

'And do you marvel sometimes at the sound you can draw from that?' He pointed to her violin.

Again she nodded.

'Well I want as much marvelling as possible in this life.' He now took in the whole group. 'You know how it feels to look up on a clear night and take in the entire universe? Or see animals in their natural habitat? These things inspire wonder. And so for me does the sound I can make at the piano. Music's wonderful. And I mean that literally. That I've been given the ability to play is more precious than life itself.'

'Do you teach?' a promising young pianist asked. And when he explained that his concert schedule didn't allow for regular pupils but he took master-classes and mentored young pianists, Zoe guessed that not only the girl who asked the question but all the aspiring musicians in the audience would be applying for future Ramsay Blake master-classes.

With only a couple of minutes remaining, Zoe walked to the front of the room and stood alongside Ramsay. She called for one last question.

'How do you know Mrs Wood?' someone asked.

Ramsay turned to Zoe and gave her shoulder a squeeze. 'We lived next door as kids. We played music together.'

Zoe could see by the expressions on their fervent young faces that his answer appealed, certainly that touch to her shoulder would fuel plenty of gossip. But it was not the response Zoe wanted.

Mrs Wood, how do you know Ramsay Blake?

And her honest reply? I've always loved him.

Zoe shut the door behind her last pupil, sank into a chair and closed her eyes. She'd had so little sleep since George died and in all the rush she had not felt tired. But now she wanted only to sleep – blessed unconsciousness for a month or more in a leave of absence from a life grown too strenuous. The exhaustion had come on suddenly, today, yet nothing in essence had changed. She was still married to Elliot or rather he was still married to her, the children still lived at home and maintained at least a veneer of civility, and there was still Ramsay after a lifetime of Ramsay. But the disappointment with him this morning had scratched an old sore.

How do you know Mrs Wood? We played music together.

How do you know Ramsay Blake? I've always loved him.

The disjunction between their two answers would be reason enough to withdraw quietly with what little grace and dignity she had left. She knew this, had probably always known, but there was something in her that did not want to let go of Ramsay, something in her rather than something about him that stoked her devotion. And while Elliot's daily emails reassured her he had not left her yet, the very fact of his disappearing without any explanation suggested he was at the end of his patience. As for her children, Callum oscillated between cyberspace and his music, picking up food and sleep on the way, and Hayley at sixteen was bristling for independence. Nothing had changed, yet everything had changed.

She wished she could swallow a pill and be whisked out of here, she wished she could hitch a ride on a passing aeroplane, she wished she could leap onto a rainbow and walk its entire length; she wished, in short, her life was different.

She dragged herself to her feet. She didn't want to see or talk to anyone, she just wanted to go home, but Ramsay was expecting her and she knew she wouldn't default. Although just in case he might have cancelled she checked her email; nothing from Ramsay, but heading the inbox was the latest instalment from Elliot. No, he hadn't given up on her yet.

The email was headed REMEMBER? and consisted of a poem by Nikki Giovanni. *The* poem.

i wanted to take
your hand and run with you
together toward
ourselves ...

She reads slowly, each line out loud, all the way down to the end: *and we'll run again/together/toward each other/yes?* Of all the poems he might have sent, he chooses this one. She feels the tears rise, doesn't stop them, is sobbing when her phone rings. A glance and she sees it is Ramsay, probably wondering where she is. She shoves the phone aside, holds her head in her hands and closes her eyes. The call rings out while she's back in New York, not the restaurant where he first read her this poem, but at the apartment not long before their marriage, the cockatiels in their corner, she and Elliot together on the couch. There's cheese and pickles and smoked whitefish on the low table, and fresh bread from the local bakery, and her legs are draped across Elliot's thighs and he is reading to her, reading this poem. It's so real, so vivid, she feels his legs under her own, she can hear his voice. It's like meeting an old lover after a long absence.

She reads the poem a second time, she lives each line, and at the finish she sits silently in the memories. Time passes, and only when the phone rings again does she rouse herself: Ramsay again, and still she doesn't answer. She dashes off a text, *running late, on my way*, and collects her belongings. Slowly she walks to the car. Slowly she leaves the school premises.

During the fifteen-minute drive, lines and images from the poem surface. Could this poem ever refer to her and Ramsay? Would Ramsay ever send this poem? Has he ever sent her poetry? In this as with everything he is so different from Elliot. Elliot loves poetry as much as she does; the first years of their marriage were full of poetry. But those days ceased long ago to feel like her marriage.

She is tired no longer, hard to know exactly how she feels. *I wanted to take your hand and run with you* floats in her mind like a familiar song, she can even imagine the music, is humming a phrase as she turns into Ramsay's driveway. Ramsay is waiting on the front verandah, he's pacing. The music stops, the poetry slips away.

He runs down the steps, opens the car door before she has switched off the engine. 'Where've you been? I thought you weren't coming.'

Whatever he has been doing since she saw him earlier at school he certainly hasn't been playing the piano. His shirt is grubby and covered in dog hair. He's changed his jeans for sweatpants and they too are stained and streaked. His face is ravaged, the normally rosy skin is pasty, there's dirt beneath his nails.

'What on earth have you been doing?'

He looks sulky. 'Waiting for you.'

She glances at his clothes. 'I mean while you were waiting for me.'

He shakes his head, he looks lost. 'I was rummaging around in the shed.' He flings his arms forward in a gesture of helplessness. 'I don't know what I was doing.'

She suggests he cleans himself up while she starts dinner.

'There are emails, Zoe, at least a dozen of them, most of them about China.' Ramsay is shaking his head and shrugging his shoulders. 'The China tour. It's three months away and they want to lock in schedules and hotels and the food I like, all the things George looked after. And they want to do it now.'

She tells him not to worry, she'll deal with it. All the things George did she'll handle. 'You just need to concentrate on your music.'

She ushers him into the house. He's just standing there in the hall, his body drooping, the sinewy hands dangling. He seems unable to move. Seeing him so helpless, a terrible thought occurs to her. 'The program *is* confirmed?'

He nods.

'And you are on schedule with your preparation?' She speaks slowly and clearly – she sounds like a teacher.

He turns to face her. His mouth opens as if to speak, then he presses his lips together, almost violently it seems to her, nods again and marches down the hall.

She collects George's laptop, sets it up on the kitchen bench, and while the food is cooking she answers the various emails, all of them dealing with practical details to ensure Ramsay's comfort in China and the smooth progression of the tour. None of it is difficult and anyone with a knowledge of Ramsay could have responded, but still, and despite the lingering sour taste from the morning, despite, too, the sad intrusion of her lost marriage, she's pleased he asked her to help.

Although he hadn't asked.

She arrived at his house, she saw he was in trouble, she leapt in and smoothed things over. He didn't need to ask for a thing. She'd behaved in a similar fashion with the children when they were young, catching them before they fell or failed. It was Elliot who made her see what she was doing, that she had to allow them to stretch themselves, meet challenges, cope with disappointment. 'If you do everything for them,' he said, 'they'll neither learn nor grow. And they'll certainly never leave home.'

She doesn't want to be Ramsay's mother, she doesn't want to be his housekeeper, she doesn't want to be his nursemaid, although she'd perform all these roles if ... If what? If he'd love her? It was a glorious dream when George was around, but now the position is vacant – George's role and she assumes more besides – what does she really want with Ramsay? The question hammers her and the terrible fatigue pours in again. She needs to get out of here. She calls out to Ramsay that his dinner is in the oven and she's about to leave.

He rushes into the kitchen. He is wearing only singlet and shorts. His face is wet, water drips down his neck, drops glisten in the fluorescent light. No, no, he says. Don't go. Stay and eat with me.

It's an invitation she would normally seize. But not now, not today. She pecks him on the cheek and rushes to the car before she can change her mind.

Chapter 12. Newly Minted Prospects

1.

Hayley stood in front of the open refrigerator. There were several plastic containers neatly stacked on the shelves, some with a smear in the bottom, others with a few centimetres of food. This was what remained of the meals of the past weeks, the period of her mother's madness. The chicken and Chinese mushrooms smelled all right, if she could only remember when it was bought; a spoonful of stiffish fried rice was from the same era. She put both aside and continued her search. She didn't even bother sniffing a piece of hamburger wrapped in plastic and a single triangle of pizza, just threw both into the rubbish bin. In another container neatly arranged were a wedge of roasted pumpkin, a teaspoon of peas, a roasted potato and a single lamb chop, all from the carvery meal of just a couple of nights ago. It looked fresh enough, although meat and three veg was not exactly what she had in mind for an afternoon snack. There were four separate containers of limp and slimy salad, and another with some sour-smelling white stuff she failed to identify.

This frustrating array was her mother's work. Pretence that takeaway meals were real meals, and sufficiently self-conscious about her privileged life to be uneasy about waste, Zoe appeared to have thrown nothing out since her delinquent behaviour began.

Hayley again inspected the old Chinese food; it *was* old, she decided, and shoved it back in the fridge. She found some toasted muesli, the gourmet stuff that tasted better without milk, was eating it from the packet – what did it matter? Callum wouldn't care, and neither her absent father nor crazy mother would ever know – when her phone rang. It was Maddy. Maddy was a texter and a tweeter not a phoner, it must be important.

And it was.

A gig. A proper gig in a pub. With Adam, Maddy's brother, twenty-eight years old, brilliant song-writer, legend on the guitar, seriously cool. A gig, not with his band, not with MagneticBlue, just with him. She knew his music, Maddy kept her up-to-date, and most of his songs figured in her top-rated playlist. And there'd been two memorable occasions when she had jammed with him, casual, spontaneous happenings, singing and playing guitar together. And now he wanted to know if she was available. To sing with him. Tonight.

'His usual partner's been in a car accident,' Maddy said. 'She's fine, or rather she will be. Broken limbs, awful of course, but fixable. And –' she paused both for sympathy and effect, 'what a chance for you.'

Maddy was an average student, she made the B teams in sport, she was musically ordinary, attractive without being drop-dead gorgeous, but she notched up world's best practice as a friend. She was genuinely happy when good things happened to you, happy without a skerrick of jealousy. And she was so

254

sharp about people, she understood you, usually before you understood yourself. In fact, if you believed in mind-reading you'd be convinced Maddy was a leading practitioner.

'I guess you feel a bit like the understudy who gets to play the lead because the star's sick or in rehab,' she now said. 'Your great fortune because of someone else's misfortune. But this is the system, Hay. So it's okay to feel happy.' She paused to allow this to sink in. 'By the way, Sissy's recovery is expected to take months and Adam tells me the band has a great line-up of gigs booked.'

Now Adam himself took the phone. 'We've got about three hours before we're due at "Crossroads"' – her first proper gig and it's at 'Crossroads'! 'I'll pick you up at six.'

She had thirty minutes to turn herself into an enigmatic, hip singer. Hayley had met Sissy twice and both times she was wearing black. In the pigsty of her mother's dressing-room, she found a body-hugging sleeveless jacket made of a black leathery material – it would be perfect with her own black pants and boots. Her hair, straight like her mother's and dark like her father's, she shined up with a bit of product and left hanging loose and long. She ringed her eyes with eyeliner and on a whim added a beauty spot above the left corner of her mouth like an old-fashioned Hollywood star. Definitely enigmatic.

She wrote a note for her mother – band practice, she explained, and was about to add she'd be late, but decided not to bother: as late as she might be her mother would be later – put the note on the kitchen bench and was waiting in the street when Adam drove up with Maddy.

Adam appraised her. 'You look great. You look the part. Now we've only the music to worry about.'

A half-hour later they were tuning up at the house Adam shared with a couple of other guys. His musical influences were retro, the same rhythm and blues singers that were her father's favourites. She and Elliot would regularly adjourn to the turn-table and listen to Ray Charles, Nina, Aretha, Otis, Clapton, Jerry Lee Lewis, all the old greats. Thanks to her father, Hayley knew exactly where Adam was coming from. And thanks to Maddy, she knew all of his work. Adam was impressed. As for her harmonising, 'You're a natural,' he said. And while she already knew this, having been surprised long ago to discover that what came to her naturally did not to most people, she thrilled to his praise.

If they had stopped after the practice session it would have counted as the best night of her life, but that was only the beginning. When they set off for the venue, Adam seemed to think they wouldn't embarrass themselves. In fact he struck her as surprisingly calm.

The pub was a jangle of bodies and voices, and as they moved through the room everyone seemed to know Adam; even Maddy was acknowledged by a couple of people.

'Do your parents know you come to places like this?' Hayley asked, once they were settled at a table reserved for the musicians.

Maddy looked at her as if she had asked the dumbest of questions. 'Of course not.'

There was a band up before them, rhythm and blues covers, good not great, but with a stash of friends in the audience the applause was enthusiastic. Their bracket gave her nerves plenty of time to warm up, so by the time she and Adam took to the stage the blood was belting around her body and she was shaking so violently she doubted she could sing or play a note. While Adam explained Sissy's absence and introduced her as his 'fabulous stand-in partner', he kept a steadying hand on her shoulder. It helped. The first song, deliberately chosen, required only harmonising vocals from her and a bit of strumming. By the time she launched into 'Blueswoman' she was switched on and ready, and when she sang his signature 'Gravel Planet' there were whistles and foot-stamping and calls for more.

Forty minutes passed in a moment. She and Adam left the stage, the applause continued, the shouting grew louder. They returned for an encore and then another. At the end of the last song Adam pushed her forward to take a bow, and the roar of the crowd increased. She looked out at the faces, the waving arms. She loved being here, she loved the crowd, she loved that they loved her.

It was a debut performance of which fantasies were made. Afterwards when they were unwinding over a drink, Adam put his arm around her. 'You're good,' he said. 'You're really good.' And cocked his head to the side. 'So? Are we in business? And not just the duo, but MagneticBlue as well?'

Hayley didn't know how she would arrange it – with her mother, with her father if he ever returned, with her school work – but she knew what she wanted to do with the rest of her life. Only a fool or a coward would pass up this opportunity.

2.

The house is empty and very quiet. Zoe is accustomed to feeling Elliot's presence even though he would rarely greet her; Addie, in contrast, always made a fuss when she arrived home. No Elliot and no Addie. Callum is at a friend's place and Hayley, according to a note left on the bench, has band practice. No need to cook, no one to cook for. Zoe makes coffee and withdraws to the sunroom; she opens the sliding doors, sits on the couch, sips her coffee and smokes. It's not yet dusk but the sun is low and the garden is in shadow. There's a hint of autumn in the air and the leaves look more sprightly than they have for months; even the flowers appear to have perked up. If she had energy to move, she'd sit outside.

On the coffee table is a stack of periodicals, mostly issues of the *London Review of Books*, some going back years. Elliot never manages to catch up, but neither can he ditch an issue until it is thoroughly read. 'I'm an intellectual manqué,' he would joke. 'Can't afford to risk missing out on the goods. Can't reduce my chances.'

Once she would have laughed with him, but not now. Theirs has become a humour-free marriage and maybe doomed forever to be. Although not at the beginning, even the shoddy fortune-teller had predicted a future of laughter and happiness. That fortune-teller down in Greenwich Village … And she wonders at this caprice of memory that it throws up forgotten events when you least want them but perhaps most need them.

It was exactly two months after they met, their second anniversary. They had celebrated with a sandwich and champagne lunch eaten in a chilly Washington Square, surrounded by the usual hobos, junkies and students who hung out there. The plan was to visit a local gallery, but as they were making their way through the Village they saw the shingle, both of them saw it at the same time – they were often in sync like that. FORTUNE TELLER, the sign said. YOUR FUTURE FOR CHEAP.

'I dare you,' Elliot said.

'I dare *you*,' Zoe replied.

'I dare us.' Elliot was triumphant.

The shop was tiny and reeked of freshly fried chips; lurking beneath the new oil was the taint of old fry-ups and greasy carpet. The light was dimmed by a grimy shawl thrown over a lamp. Business isn't booming, Zoe whispered, and turned to leave, but Elliot held her. 'It'll be fun,' he said.

An old woman lumbered in from the rear through parted curtains, just like in a B-grade movie. Up close they could see she was more worn than old; a stink of cigarettes and fried food wafted about her. She was dressed in B-grade movie gypsy garb: full floral skirt, maroon velvet jacket laced across a bulging bosom, scarf about her head. Her accent was pure Brooklyn. They sat on one side of a small square table, she occupied a stool opposite, and between them was a crystal ball. It was as much as they could do not to laugh. The walls were draped in lengths of material oddments, their colours dulled by dust.

They were an easy study: a young couple, obviously happy, asking about their future. She told them she saw much joy and laughter in their lives, and the occasional obstacle as well; she even mentioned a shadowy man who would threaten their relationship. They would enjoy health, wealth and – she must have noticed Zoe's cello brooch – music. The telling of their future lasted no more than ten minutes and she wanted to charge them fifty dollars – a huge amount in those days. Elliot referred to her sign. Fifty dollars isn't cheap, he said. She argued that there were two of them, it'd be cheaper for one. In the end they settled for thirty-eight dollars plus two special stones. Real amber, she said – more likely to be plastic, they decided, although they always referred to them as *our amber stones.*

The stones represented their two souls, she said. 'This one,' she gave a stone to Elliot, 'represents her soul,' she nodded at Zoe. 'And this one,' she put the other in Zoe's hand, 'is the stone of his soul. You must keep them close forever.' As she ushered them out she added as a parting shot, 'They're usually eighty bucks extra.'

They had laughed and laughed, but nonetheless they protected their stones. Elliot kept his in his pocket, moving it with his loose change from one pair of trousers to another. She kept hers in her purse. And once they were living together they each put their stone on their bedside table. The stones made it to the flat they rented when they first arrived in Melbourne, but Zoe has no memory of them after that. Perhaps the fortune-teller was right: the stones had drifted apart and so too had she and Elliot.

She had so wanted to believe that Elliot would come to occupy the space long filled by Ramsay, but now she wonders if she ever truly thought he could, for surely it would have happened. And quickly lets herself off the hook: no one would knowingly distribute disappointment and misery; her hopes back then had been real enough, she really did want to rid herself of Ramsay.

Outside the sun has disappeared, and the air is shuddery with dusk; she sucks hard on her cigarette and watches the garden sink into darkness. Thirty minutes pass before she pulls herself together: how much more pathetic can she get, sitting alone in a darkened house chain-smoking and drinking cold coffee? She pushes cigarettes and coffee aside, switches on a lamp, and pulls a magazine from low down in the stack. Listlessly she turns the pages. She reads headings, initial paragraphs, skims columns. Bret Easton Ellis's latest is canned, a Craig Raine novel is similarly dismissed (why doesn't he confine himself to poetry?), an article on Carthage holds her attention for a full page. Then comes an essay by an Alex de Waal on political deal-making in some of the world's trouble spots.

She is reading because she is sitting in her empty house with time to fill and a pile of old magazines in reach, but something about de Waal's article holds her. Like so many people she'd been horrified at the second Iraq war and even more horrified at its aftermath, not simply the lack of an exit plan nor the shocking suffering of ordinary people, but the absurdity of muscle-bound, self-righteous America trying to impose its own form of democracy on a country where power had long resided in local leaders. Even she knew that these leaders – religious, secular and tribal – operated according to a complex web of authority, patronage and power play.

According to de Waal's article, a similar system of power-broking, exists in the Sudan. She knows nothing about the history and politics of the Sudan, but is fascinated by something the Sudanese call 'Jellaba politics'. De Waal describes this approach to business as 'retail patronage politics', in which the price of an individual's loyalty is calculated, and an offer made – with an eye to the future as to whether the price will rise or fall.

A futures market on loyalty, Zoe finds herself thinking, one which could easily apply to a marriage or, for that matter, any long-term relationship. A futures market for the personal sphere. And in her own small world, who has paid too much? Who too little? Elliot certainly paid too high a price when he married her; he would have made a far better deal if he had settled for a lively, short-term affair. And she – there was so much resistance to even a brief private acknowledgment – she has paid far too highly with Ramsay. As for Ramsay himself, he has shelled out to no one.

She lights another cigarette, sips the tepid coffee, and with her mind bucking against the gathering disquiet she reads on. De Waal refers to another process in brokering agreements in Sudan: *tajil*, or 'delay', and the refined skill of 'tajility', 'strategic delay or the art of procrastinating until one's counterpart is exhausted or removed'. Again Zoe is drawn to the personal sphere. Her husband, wherever he is, is worn to a shard; it is a question of not whether he gives up but when; she is exhausted and feels as if she is eroding. And Ramsay? He'll get over George, she has no doubt about it, leaving him after all these years untouched and undisturbed.

She pushes the magazine away. She wants to run from her thoughts, she wants to run. Common sense is shouting at her. She can see it, she can hear it, she can taste it. All that's now required is to swallow it even if it means admitting that more than half her life has been wasted on Ramsay Blake. But surely, as bad as this would be, it would be far worse to continue the waste.

3.

The woman, Beth, has invited him for dinner.

She and Elliot left the convent café, he to return to the van, she to head off in the opposite direction to work. They had said their farewells and started on their respective ways when he heard her call his name. He turned. She was walking towards him.

'Would you like to come to my place for dinner tonight? A proper home-cooked meal?' She looked doubtful, even nervous, but nonetheless pushed on. 'It'll give you a break from microwaved food. And for me ...' her voice faltered as she searched for a reason, 'for me it'll be a welcome change.'

She took Elliot by surprise. Sociality was not factored into his van life and meals with strange women not an aspect of his life in or out of the van. He did not know what to make of the invitation, and yet he was glad of it.

'It'd make a welcome change for me too,' he said.

The doubt immediately vanished from her face. She told him her address, suggested he arrive at seven, said that he was to bring nothing but himself and Addie.

She waved a goodbye and then hurried off to work; he turned and strolled back along the river path. At Dight Falls he hopped across the rocks, found a smooth one and sat down. Addie soon joined him. Seagulls flew over the water and two pied cormorants fished from a fallen branch. And there he remained until the sun forced a retreat, buffered by wind and water and the unexpected pleasure of a woman actually wanting to cook for him.

He arrives exactly on time. Beth is wearing the same bright dress she wore earlier in the day, but now her feet are bare and the bushy hair is caught in a knot on top of her head. She has applied fresh lipstick and smells of something fresh and flowery. Since giving up alcohol he notices scents. She thanks him for the flowers – bright like her dress.

Her house is a timber Victorian dwelling, and typical of the area. He follows her down a central passageway with two rooms off to each side and enters a large open area at the back comprising the kitchen and living room. Beyond glass doors is a deck and a small garden. He knows from their conversation earlier in the day that Beth has lived here for thirty years, that she and her husband raised their two children here and 'survived two major renovations'. Now she stops in the middle of the living room and with her arms flung wide takes in the house.

'I know it's way too big for one person, but I've no intention of leaving – despite what people advise.' She shakes her head in disbelief. 'People don't understand. I've lost my husband, it'd be a lunacy to get rid of our home as well.'

There are two pillowy couches upholstered in a deep blue corduroy, the sort of seating you sink into and which holds your shape, the sort that has no place in his own home. The walls are covered in an array of paintings, prints and photographs; ornaments are dotted throughout the room. While Beth busies herself with the flowers he wanders around. There is a circle of fossils arranged on a shelf, and nearby stands a cluster of stone animals – a polar bear, a hippo, a crocodile, a blue frog. On top of a bookcase is a gathering of sacred figures – an ivory Buddha, a clay Minoan goddess, a black Madonna and a half-dozen other pieces carved in wood or stone.

'This is quite an extraordinary ecumenical gathering,' he says.

She joins him at the display, her bare feet are silent on the polished floorboards. She picks up each carving in turn, explains its provenance and what it represents. Her favourite is an Inuit spirit made from a dark green mottled stone called serpentine. She puts it in his hand. It has the face and upper body of a woman; from the waist down she is a buxom mermaid. The sculpture is solid in his palm.

'I could believe in the power of this spirit,' he says with a smile.

Beth and her husband bought it in Churchill. 'On Lake Hudson, in central Canada,' she says. 'We were there to see polar bears.'

Each year in late autumn, she explains, after the long summer fast, bears arrive at the shores of the lake and wait for it to freeze over. Once the ice is hard enough to support them they go hunting for seals.

'The ice is forming later and later,' she says. 'The bears are starving. They'd prefer seals, but they're opportunistic feeders and they'll forage for other food.'

'People?'

She nods, 'It's happened. But don't blame the bears. The people were stupid to get in the way.'

'That's not particularly Christian of you.'

'She shrugs. 'We're all God's creatures.'

She has cooked a vegetarian paella. He's a meat man, but these vegetables are not only tasty they're substantial too. He used to enjoy cooking, but it's been years since he joined Zoe in the kitchen and he can't remember when he last cooked for the family. Beth has a nip of whisky and then swaps to sparkling water for the rest of the night. Dessert is fresh pineapple and a hunk of sharp Tasmanian cheddar – his sort of dessert given he does not care for cakes and puddings.

He clears the table as she stacks the dishwasher; she washes the pots and pans, he dries them. While she puts things away and wipes the benches he goes to a display of photos that covers much of one wall. He has wanted to look at these pictures ever since he arrived, but it seemed too personal, too intrusive so he held back. All the photos, displayed as collages in large frames, are of her and her husband. Each large frame contains a dozen or more pictures taken in an exotic location: Central Australia, the Galapagos, on safari in Africa, and somewhere volcanic. He turns round. 'Where's this place? This volcano?' he asks.

'Arenal in Costa Rica. And here,' she joins him in front of the photos and points to the safari pictures, 'here we're in Botswana and Tanzania. And here –'

'I guessed the Galapagos.' He laughs, 'The iguanas are a giveaway.'

'And probably the best trip we ever made, although they were all marvellous.' She smiles at some private thought. 'We always travelled well together.'

Elliot gazes around the room. 'It looks as if you made a home well together too.'

Her eyes fill. She nods and turns away. 'I miss him terribly.' She speaks so softly he only just hears.

The house is full of him. 'Mausoleum' leaps to mind but just as quickly Elliot rejects it. The husband belongs here, he's part of this place. He and Beth would have chosen the furniture together; the paintings and prints and ornaments reflect their life together. As for the photos depicting their travels, Elliot expects they have hung like this, in this spot, ever since the trips were made and the photos printed. This place is their home.

Beth is sitting on one of the couches and he goes to join her. It is a surprisingly companionable silence for two strangers.

The shared meal, the conversation, even the after-dinner chores, it's all been companionable. He has learned to live without this sort of togetherness, but like that single drink for an alcoholic, having a taste of it makes him want more. He has longed for Zoe, how he has longed for her, but what fills him now is wistfulness over what he has missed. They don't take trips together, they don't shop together, they rarely eat out together and when they do it is with a crowd; they don't sit on the couch together, they don't even talk together, they talk past each other like deaf people whose hands are tied. He and Zoe are simply and always not together.

'You look sad,' Beth says.

He meets her gaze, this woman who is mourning her husband. 'My sadness is nothing compared with yours.'

She reaches out and touches his arm. 'Sadness doesn't work like that. Reason may construct a hierarchy of sadness, but whether your sadness, my sadness, or the sadness of the child down the street, every sadness feels bleak and oppressive. Every sadness feels sad.' She shuffles closer and puts her arms around him. He feels himself stiffen, but as she relaxes against him, he realises the physical contact is as much for her as it is for him. He lets himself go and leans into her too.

They remain locked together, nothing is said. He is aware of her breath drawing slower. He relaxes too, holds her gently, and when a few minutes later she pulls away, he doesn't want her to move. She looks at him; her expression is utterly lucid, a combination of inevitability and an acknowledgment that they each understand the other.

'You can stay if you'd like,' she says. And as if to make herself perfectly clear, she adds, 'You can stay here, for the night.'

She installs him on her husband's side of the bed in a room that flagrantly exposes its long-time inhabitants. His and Zoe's bedroom is so impersonal, but here there are two dressing gowns hanging on the back of the door, more ornaments and photos on shelves, and a variety of clutter on the bedside tables. On his bedside table, the husband's bedside table, there are a pair of glasses, a stack of books, mainly modern history and science – the husband, Scott, was a chemist, not the shop-front variety but a university researcher and lecturer – and an old-fashioned handkerchief, one of those medium-blue ones with a border of darker blue stripes that he associates with his own father. An unused handkerchief never to be used again. A man's wristwatch is partially hidden by the handkerchief, and there's a crystal water glass, empty. All these things freighted with meaning are laid out like a shrine. He feels like an imposter: he can't understand how she could put him where her husband has so recently been. And then there's Beth herself. She doesn't have her own church – she works in the Uniting Church's social justice division – but still, he's in bed with a priest, a woman of God. What seemed so simple just a short time ago is fast being overwhelmed with complications.

Stop, he tells himself. Stop. He's here and he's glad to be here. He closes his mind to all intrusions and takes her into his arms. She fills his embrace – Zoe is so slight – and there's a softness to her, no angles and bones, and she smells different, not just her perfume, but the scent of her hair and skin. Her lips are plump and less muscular than Zoe's, her taste so strange, and he's reminded that of all the things two naked people can do together kissing is more idiosyncratic and more intimate than anything else.

When he was drinking there was a tangle of drunken mistakes when he would find himself in the back seat of a car, or a bed in a strange flat, or a room in a hotel with a woman he could not recall meeting and a mouth full of garbage. He could rarely remember the sex and he was always desperate to leave. The guilt was so aggressive he'd try to make amends to Zoe; mostly he ended up grovelling to her. When he gave up alcohol the anonymous sex went too; there has been only Zoe these past many years. Yet as he adjusts to this new woman, he feels again that his current life, his van life, runs at a tangent to his real life, so that having sex with her doesn't strike him as betrayal at all.

But the dead husband, Scott, is another issue. He is a real presence. If Zoe died, Elliot wouldn't want anyone on her side of the bed for a long time – at least he doesn't think he would. And because this situation with Beth is one with neither expectations nor repercussions, he asks her, in the dark and after the sex as she lies with her head on his shoulder, her left arm flung across his chest, he asks about his being here in the bed she shared with her husband.

She takes her time in answering, so long that he's about to apologise for intruding.

'It's as if death turns you slightly mad,' she says at last.

He wishes he could switch on the light, it would help if he could see her.

'You want moments of forgetting,' she continues. 'And you want comfort. And you want not to be alone while sleeping.' Her voice sounds quite calm, but he feels her take two or three deep steadying breaths. 'The absence, Scott's absence, it scrapes like barbed wire. Sometimes I think I'd do anything for respite.'

She moves even closer. Her body is pressed against his, her face is buried into his neck.

'Until now,' she says, 'this night, the only man I've ever been with is my husband.'

Maybe losing a beloved – a husband, a wife, a child – is one of the few things in life that actually needs to be experienced to be understood, for Elliot cannot imagine doing as she is doing. And yet he wants to be here, feels fortunate to be here. She falls asleep, it takes only a few minutes, while he remains awake, strangely contented. The room is lighter than his and Zoe's and a bright half-moon stencils the branches of a tree on to the bedroom wall; a faint breeze ruffles the shadows. Curled on a blanket on the floor, Adelaide snuffles in her sleep, and on his shoulder this sad, sweet stranger sleeps on. After a while he, too, drifts off.

He wakes in the small hours to find himself turned on his side away from her; her body is curved around his, her breasts are soft against his back. He reaches for her arm and pulls it more tightly about him; he falls asleep again, his hand over hers.

It was not that he was embarrassed in the morning, nor did he think was she; rather, whatever they had both wanted had passed with the night. He declined her offer of a shower, he didn't stay for coffee. As they stood in her doorway she seemed unsure what to say. There was a pad and pen on the hall table and Elliot wrote down his mobile number.

'I could come back if you wanted,' he said.

She gave an almost imperceptible shrug, her gaze did not meet his.

'I'd like to,' Elliot said. 'Really. But I'll leave it up to you.'

He stepped forward and embraced her. They stood together in each other's arms. It was she who drew back.

That evening in the van after dinner as he was reading one of Koestler's mediocre books, of which he was beginning to think there were far too many, Beth texted him. He collected a few things, locked the van, and together with Addie walked to her place. The following afternoon she telephoned. After that it was understood they would spend the nights together. There was no sex after the first night, it was not what she wanted, nor as it happened did he. Sex was something he and Zoe had always done with ease: they mightn't talk to each other, but their bodies managed to communicate very well. Affection, however, was quite another matter. Zoe had never been the type to give him a spontaneous hug, she'd never stretch out her arm along the back of his seat as he drove, it would be unthinkable for her to hold his hand in the cinema. She was affectionate with friends and of course with the children, liberal with her hugs and kisses. What about me? he wanted to ask. What about me? But should he reach for her, she would brush him off. As for sleeping in his arms, she said he was far too hot, and would turn away from him to curl up on the far edge of her side of the bed.

Beth was a glorious foreign country. He loved lying with her in the pale night of her bedroom, he loved the weight of her against him, the heat of her skin, her breath on his neck. He loved her hand on his belly, her body snuggled into his back. In the dark, in bed, they talked very little; it was the physical presence of the other they both desired and they grabbed it whole-heartedly. And he came to realise how completely he had accommodated the deficits in his life. His was a marriage in which unhappiness had become so routine he'd ceased to notice it.

There was a book in the stack on Scott's side of the bed that he'd heard of but never read. Called *The Captive Mind*, it was a long essay by the Polish poet Milosz exploring how it could happen that Stalinism had captured the minds of so many. He asked to borrow it, and when Beth hesitated – the book bore her husband's annotations, she said – he assured her he would treat it like a rare manuscript and return it that evening.

He showered at her place and before it became too hot walked to one of the local cafés with a shaded courtyard. There he settled Addie with a bone and himself to Milosz's essay.

That the book bore Scott's annotations was an understatement. Hardly a page had escaped comment. More in keeping with diary entries than a dialogue with the book – there were even references to 'B' – Scott's marginalia were annoying and distracting. Elliot pushed himself through the early pages, but as he was pulled into the current of the book, so the annotations ceased to intrude. Within thirty minutes Scott's jottings may as well have become invisible for all he noticed them.

How can people believe they are blessed with the most humane system in the world when they live in fear of betrayal by neighbours, work-mates, even family, Milosz asks. How can they believe theirs is the most benevolent of systems when their own speech or actions or even their thoughts can have them thrown into prison? How can they believe theirs is the fairest system, when ordinary people are forced to manage without sufficient food, heat and other basics? The propaganda says they enjoy the best of lives, their reality is all about fear and deprivation. What twist of mind and heart can make people deny their own perceptions, their own reason?

Over the next several hours he read *The Captive Mind*. He read slowly, lifting his gaze every so often to reflect on a point or check on Addie. Walking back to the van later in the day he was filled with the book. How easily is the mind captured. Zoe looks at Ramsay and she sees Switzerland. Everyone else looks at Ramsay and sees a desert. And what about him? Did he, Elliot Wood, really love his wife? The very question distressed him. Or had he merely developed the habit of loving? (That phrase, the title of a short story by Doris Lessing, only now did he really understand it.) What indeed was there to love? Zoe was courteous but cold. She had a talent for domesticity, but it was a job not a gift. Yet when he tried to imagine life without her, he could not, nor did he want to. Zoe might well be his habit of loving, but it was a habit he didn't want to relinquish. What he wanted was for her and their marriage to be different.

273

Chapter 13. The Hour of Lead

1.

Zoe is locked in a desultory pacing around Ramsay's garden. The late sun casts dreary shadows across the dusty grass, the air is yellowish and worn. It feels like a lifetime since George died. With his passing, Zoe had hoped for change, some vague yet brilliant replacement of old discontents. And while she hasn't yet buried the future of her dreams, she knows she will have to. Ramsay has left her no other choice.

Inside the house he is with a woman he calls Mrs Monday.

It was to have been a perfect day, a mid-term school break and she and Ramsay were to spend it together. Such a happy prospect had staunched her recent dissatisfactions, so when she arrived around midday the world was still spinning on its axis and she was still locked in fantasyland. A mere six hours ago she had breezed into the house with sandwiches for lunch and a range of suggestions for their afternoon together.

'We'll need to be back by five,' Ramsay had said. 'In time for Mrs Monday.'

'Mrs Monday?'

Ramsay had laughed. 'George named her. Her real name's Vera, but between ourselves, George and me, we always referred to her as Mrs Monday. Monday's her day, she always comes on Monday.'

Which explains why Zoe hasn't met her. The school string orchestra practises on Monday afternoons and she never arrives at Ramsay's before six. Zoe assumes this woman is a not particularly efficient cleaning lady given the state of the house, or an odd-jobbing person, someone who does a bit of gardening and sewing, some minor repairs.

She reassures him they'll be back in time, but for now they have several hours together. She proposes a visit to the beach, the latest exhibition at the National Gallery, a drive to the berry farm for fresh strawberries. Ramsay is interested in none of these. She suggests the zoo, Healesville Sanctuary, the Lost Dogs' Home. He rejects each in turn. She tries a couple more suggestions – a walk in the Dandenong Ranges, a visit to the gold museum – before giving up. And now he leaps in as if he has just been waiting for her to exhaust her ideas: he knows exactly what he wants to do.

'It's an exhibition, Zoe. A model world expo with a huge display of accurately scaled models of the world's major cities. I read about it online. It looks fantastic.'

He says he'll eat his lunch in the car, he doesn't consider how she is to eat hers, but that's Ramsay in a state of excitement, childlike excitement. And while it has its down-side, it's invigorating to see a grown man flaunting what most adults so carelessly discard.

An hour later they are standing in the main hall of the Royal Exhibition Building. In front of them stretch long rows partitioned into cubicles, each space of a few square metres displaying a city or landscape recreated in miniature. This is not an exhibition Zoe would choose to visit, but now she's here she is curious to see these tiny portrayals of well-known places. There's something fascinating about a person or an object wrenched out of its normal proportions: the gargantuan peach in America's peach state of Georgia; the giants and dwarfs photographed by Diane Arbus; the giant- and dwarf-sized people you see in the normal run of your everyday life; even that old film with Lily Tomlin, *The Incredible Shrinking Woman*. Something about this sort of aberration that demands to be stared at, but too often in the real world you can't for fear of giving offence.

Ramsay is eager to begin. He pauses just a moment in the entrance before crossing to a display at the top of one of the long rows; the sign reads Holland. There's a crowd in this part of the hall and Zoe's view is momentarily obstructed; when Ramsay is again visible he is crouched in front of the miniature Holland. How quickly he slips from the world at large, Zoe is thinking, and how much she would like to squat alongside him, loop her arm through his, be with him in his absorption – like when they used to play music together. But she knows it won't happen: he'd shrug her off, he wouldn't even notice it was her. She collects her disappointment, turns away from him and wanders down a different aisle.

Ramsay loves this Holland. Dominating the scene are the tulips, broad stripes of red and yellow and orange, with a tiny turning windmill at the rear. In the channels between the rows are miniature men with spades, and women in weird white bonnets carrying baskets and secateurs. Each figure is wearing wooden clogs smaller than a peanut. Over to one side is a cart already laden with pails of flowers. Dotted among the fields are cottages and small villages, vegetable gardens and farm animals, and beyond the fields the great dykes holding back the sea. The scene is exactly like the coloured plates of Holland in a picture book he had as a child.

He would like to linger, but with so many more places to see, he makes himself move to the next display. He thought it might be Amsterdam but he finds himself staring at Manhattan. It's an odd perspective: rather than looking northwards from where the Twin Towers used to be, Manhattan has been tipped on its side – clearly the cubicles come in a standard size. Briefly he is disoriented (if this were real he'd be standing in the East River) but quickly he rights himself. Brooklyn is part of the display, but without any distinguishing features it's just an excuse to include the Brooklyn Bridge; the other boroughs have been omitted altogether. And suddenly he recalls: New York was originally New Amsterdam, so it makes sense to place it alongside Holland.

He wants to find the building where he lived on the Upper West Side, he wants to find the Lincoln Center and Carnegie Hall too, but there are three boys blocking his view. He moves forward, stands far too close. The boys look at him, they look at each other. They don't budge. Another step and his arm brushes against one of them.

The boy glares at him, shoves him with an elbow.

Ramsay moves even closer.

'Get away from me, you fucker.' The boy sounds more threatening than he looks.

Ramsay makes no response. He certainly doesn't move.

The boy gathers his mates. 'Come on, let's get out of here.' As he pushes past Ramsay he hisses, 'Fucking perv.'

Ramsay now has the view he wants. Again he squats down. And there it is, up near 87th and West End Avenue, his apartment building, the actual building. And twenty-five blocks south, the Lincoln Center with the new forecourt and a working fountain. He peers closer, yes, real water. And real water in the Hudson too. And the Cloisters, they've included the Cloisters the mock castle affair at the northern tip of Manhattan, and all the subway stations too. And there's his local, the #1, with a replica train on the above-ground section.

He jumps to his feet. They've made a mistake: they've got the train emerging at 112th but it doesn't surface until 116th. And it returns underground at 135th, but on this model it stays above ground all the way to the Bronx. There's been a mistake. He has to tell someone. He looks around, hails an official.

'There's a mistake,' he says pointing to the display. 'Over there, with the subway.' He's speaking far too quickly.

The official is not in the least concerned. 'There's a mistake in Santiago, too. That's where I come from. And I expect there are mistakes in Athens and London, in all the places.' He bends his head towards Ramsay and lowers his voice. 'Confidentially, I think it's bloody amazing they got so much of it right.'

Ramsay had been ready to quit the exhibition, but he realises the man makes a fair point. He'd prefer one hundred per cent accuracy, but ninety-nine per cent, he decides, is acceptable. He thanks the official, he calms himself down, he leaves New York and passes on to Ho Chi Minh City. He's never been there, but seeing it laid out before him, he thinks he'd like it. There's a pleasing jumble about the place. The roads are clogged with cars and bikes, the narrower streets and alleys are teeming with people and street stalls. And such a variety of buildings: French colonial blocks that wouldn't be out of place in Paris, a patchwork of bright terracotta-tiled roofs, colourful exotic temples and quite a few skyscrapers too. The city really does appeal. He'd ride a bike everywhere, a week's holiday, maybe longer, although without George how to manage it? Without George, and he shakes the thought from his mind: he lives without George every minute of the day, he needs a break, he wants to enjoy himself, and moves to the next cubicle.

It's London, one of his favourite cities. 'One of everyone's favourite cities,' George used to say.

He inspects the display, ticking off the major landmarks – Trafalgar Square, Buckingham Palace, the Houses of Parliament, St. Paul's. There are clusters of heavy grey buildings heaped between narrow streets, and stamp-sized neighbourhood squares, and double-decker buses and black London cabs, and a mass of tiny figures on the footpaths of Oxford and Regent streets. The green patches of Hyde Park and Regent's Park look to be made of real grass; the trees seem to be fashioned from real plant material, the ducks on the ponds have real feathers. London, unlike New York, is perfect. There are people riding in Rotten Row. He's never been on a horse; he's admired them and petted them, but now it occurs to him he'd like to ride one. George would have forbidden it as too dangerous, but a new experience might help him out of this terrible malaise. He'll ask Zoe to organise it for him, she's good at practical tasks and she wants to help. Perhaps she could look into Ho Chi Minh City as well.

He moves on to the next display, it is the huge bulk of Antarctica. He leans in closer, a chill nips his face: this

Antarctica is constructed from real ice. Mountains of snow and rock plunge to the water, glaciers fill the spaces between the peaks and slide into the sea. Glistening wetly on the lower reaches of the land are ice sculptures with intricate peepholes and bulging curves. He inhales the crisp air. With its clarity and purity this landscape reminds him of Bach.

The water itself is filled with floating ice. In some places the ice looks like thick white marble, in others it looks as perilous as porcelain. And there are icebergs too, magnificent, unearthly structures. One looks like a miniature white Uluru. The water, the icebergs, the cliffs of ice scored with deep cracks, the bulky white mountains create a misty-magical atmosphere, and Ramsay imagines himself standing on the ice surrounded by the white mountains and the frozen sea, wrapped in the cold and shuffling silence. All the angry anxious wind has left him; he feels weightless and at ease.

It is so hard to leave Antarctica but he must see more of these wonderful places. He passes on to Rome, then Hawaii, to the Serengeti, to Casablanca and Edinburgh, Rio, Toronto and Paris; he enters each of these dioramas as if it is the only place in the world, and when he feels a hand on his arm he shoves it off. Don't disturb me, leave me alone. And then he sees it is Zoe and mumbles an apology.

'It's time,' she is saying. 'If you want to be home by five we'll need to leave.'

Zoe watches him surface.

'We can come back again,' she says. But she knows the moment of enchantment will have passed. For both of them.

They are caught in the early peak-hour traffic and when they arrive home, Mrs Monday – Vera – is seated at the kitchen table with a cup of tea. There's no sign of washing or ironing, no cleaning has been done or none that Zoe can see. Vera stands up, gives Ramsay a quick embrace.

'How are you travelling?' she asks him.

He says he's fine, better now she's here.

Vera looks at Zoe. 'He's a man of routine is this one.'

Vera makes fresh tea and the three of them sit around the table. It's clear that Vera has never heard of Zoe for she asks how long she has known Ramsay. With Zoe's 'Practically my entire life', Vera laughs and says 'a little longer than me – although I'm coming up for seventeen years.'

It emerges she is a book-keeper who still works part-time for the dental-supply company that once employed George, and suddenly Zoe realises how she fits into Ramsay's life: she does his accounts.

After fifteen or twenty minutes Vera checks her watch and stands up. She touches Ramsay on the shoulder. 'We'd better get started.'

'Let me know if I can bring you anything,' Zoe says, as Ramsay pushes back his chair. 'More tea. A cold drink. Just give a yell.'

'We won't be long,' Ramsay says, before turning away.

Zoe does not grasp what is about to happen. Not when Vera leaves the kitchen, nor when Ramsay follows her. Not even when they enter Ramsay's bedroom together. If Zoe'd had any idea she would not have walked up the hallway to use the bathroom before she started the dinner, she would not have heard them together in Ramsay's room, seen them too, through the door left slightly ajar, on Ramsay's bed – she couldn't believe she counted so little they'd not even bothered to shut the door. She tiptoes back down the hall and then she runs, through the kitchen and laundry and out to the garden. She's choking, she feels sick, she cannot believe that what is happening is truly happening.

Seventeen years of Mrs Monday and just another facet of Ramsay's ordered life. Over and over again Ramsay has said how George looked after everything. Everything. Zoe can't think, doesn't want to think, lights a cigarette, paces the garden, should get in the car and drive away, can't believe it, a mistake, surely a mistake. Ten minutes later with a fresh cigarette and she is still pacing the garden. She has no idea what to say to Ramsay when Mrs Monday leaves.

But what is there to say? What could possibly be said now? How much more humiliation can she bring upon herself?

Go, she tells herself.

At last a clear and sensible voice.

Go. Go now.

She slips back into the house and collects her bag and keys. She scribbles a note for Ramsay – *Something's come up at home. There's a lasagne defrosting on the sink. All you need do is heat it in the microwave* – and leaves the house, while Mrs Monday attends to Ramsay, as she has for seventeen years.

2.

Callum was sitting on his bed with legs outstretched, his back against the wall. He was threaded to his phone, his head was nodding to music and he was tapping away on his laptop. He neither saw Hayley standing in the doorway, nor heard her call his name. She walked towards the bed – still no awareness –

282

and stood in front of him waving her arms and making faces. At last he looked up with that glazed expression of someone whose gaze has been too long on the screen – a dope-face, her father called it, because it reminded him of people who were stoned.

'Yeah?' he said.

Hayley touched her ears and raised her eyebrows – it was a query as well as a request. Reluctantly he removed one of the ear-plugs.

She assumed by his head nodding that he was listening to rap – he listened only to rap and classical. '*Both* ear-plugs,' she said. 'We need to talk.'

The second ear-plug came out. Her brother did not look pleased.

'This better be important,' he said. 'I'm busy.'

Callum spent half his life on the web. In fact, between his piano and cyberspace there was little time for real face-to-face contact. If he didn't watch himself he'd turn into a Ramsay Blake – not that Callum would regard that as the fate worse than death that she did.

He patted the bed next to him. 'Have a look at this, Hay.' Clearly he'd forgiven her interruption. 'It's a great new site. Been up only a few weeks but it's going through the stratosphere. It's called "Ask Nemo" and it's all about lists.'

She looked at the screen. 'That's not Nemo,' she said. 'It's Mnemosyne, the Greek goddess of memory. Nem-OZ-inee.'

He shook his head slowly, a look of bemusement on his face. 'I don't know where you find such stuff –' nor did he wait for her to tell him. 'You can ask anything.' He hunkered into his topic. 'How many new postage stamps issued in any one month; the number of words in a five-minute rap; YouTube usage by country; people in the world over two hundred and ten centimetres. You ask and the answer appears – usually immediately, sometimes in a couple of minutes. If it's a hard question you might have to wait a few hours.'

'Like why people kill other people? That's a hard one. Or is there a God?'

'No, no, no, not that sort of question. Those questions don't have proper answers, a single answer. For Nemo, there has to be a definite right answer.'

'Okay then. How about asking your online know-it-all if our parents are getting divorced.'

Callum turned to her with an expression that suggested she was crazy. 'Why on earth would they do that?'

Sometimes he was so exasperating. 'Haven't you noticed? Our father has left home, he's disappeared.'

'He sends me texts, there's been phone calls.'

'But he's not here, Cal, in his own home where he's supposed to be. As for our mother, she's not out looking for him, she's hanging around with that cripple Ramsay.'

'He's a brilliant pianist.'

'I don't think he's playing the piano for her. Anyway, it's beside the point. She's not where she belongs, and neither is Dad.'

Callum sat in silence, his lips pressed together, his head now nodding in time to whatever thoughts were passing through. At last he spoke. 'It's not as if they like each other.'

'Exactly,' Hayley said. 'But that's not new – they've never liked each other. This time it's different. It looks to me as if they've separated and haven't bothered to tell us.'

Again he was silent, pondering the possibilities. 'I refuse to live in two places.'

'I don't think it's at that stage yet, after all, Dad's only been gone a few weeks. But I do think we should tell him to come home.'

'From New York?'

'He's not in New York, stupid. Don't you read your texts?'

'Yeah, of course I do – from my friends. But it's different with parents.' He looked vaguely confused. 'Do you read all Mum and Dad's messages?'

Hayley took a deep breath – she had to remain calm, she had to stick to the task. Best just to ignore his question.

'Our father collected Addie, the arrival of his texts show he's in the same time zone as we are. Anyway, even before he told us he'd not gone far – that was one of the texts you neglected to read – I always knew he wasn't in New York; I checked his desk and his passport's still there.'

Callum looked at her admiringly. 'Sometimes you surprise me.'

Actually she had felt very uncomfortable riffling through her father's desk. She'd be furious if she discovered someone had gone through her things. But she was desperate.

'We have to do something, Cal.' And popped a humourless laugh. 'Too bad your Mnemosyne can't help with things that actually matter, things which affect your life.'

There was a long silence. 'I miss him,' Hayley said finally. She was holding back tears. 'I want him to come home.'

Cal mumbled something about missing him too. Then in a clearer voice he said, 'What we need is a plan.'

Finally it seemed she had moved him. And he sounded so purposeful that suddenly the woeful situation of a moment ago seemed less hopeless. With his age and her common sense they should manage to find a solution – although she didn't underestimate the difficulty ahead. There was an awful stubbornness to parents, and kids were rarely able to make them do anything they didn't want to do.

She glanced at her watch. As urgent as the parental problem was, their planning would have to wait. 'I have to dash,' she said to Callum. 'I've got a gig tonight.'

Callum, about to reconnect himself, paused, and again that admiring expression. 'That's great, Hay. Where?' And when she mentioned an inner-city pub, commented: 'It certainly beats an old concert hall.'

She could see he was interested. 'Why don't you come along? Although,' she nodded at his sweat pants, 'you'll need to change.'

He took a moment to consider and then shut his laptop and leapt off the bed. 'You're on.'

Up on stage Hayley was unrecognisable. Sophisticated and so cool, she could be one of those famous, mostly dead singers from the 1960s, huge posters of whom adorned the walls of the pub. Callum recognised Jimi Hendrix, whose soft-brimmed hat looked exactly like the one Hayley was wearing, and Joan Baez, whose long black hair was just like Hay's, and the great Janis Joplin too. And there was something about Hay's soaring, no-holds-barred voice that was reminiscent of someone famous, although he couldn't recall who. In appearance and in her music, his sister belonged with these old singers from the sixties, but Hayley didn't take drugs, or at least not to his knowledge. And it occurred to him seeing her up there, her head thrown back, eyes closed, her body synchronised with the music, there was much he didn't know about his little sister. His parents knew even less.

The crowd was a mass of waving arms and throbbing bodies, he was pleased to have found a space separate from the main pack. The place was not as he expected, more church-hall-crossed-with-ageing-suburban-pub than cool-music-venue – and this place was reputed to be among the coolest music venues around. He'd long intended to check it out but never seemed to find the time nor, for that matter, the company. And now he was here, thanks to his little sister.

There was a small cluster of tables and chairs to one side – 'For any oldies,' Hayley explained when they first arrived. 'Like parents or critics, or impresarios with deep pockets waving a contract at us.' On the opposite side was a bar, and in between and in front of the stage, a space crammed with a couple of hundred people.

His sister and her band were a hit. This was no high-school group.

'Although I did play with a bunch of school friends,' Hayley had said earlier in the evening as the band was setting up. 'So I haven't been lying. MagneticBlue is new for me, I just haven't managed to tell our parents.' She splayed her hands in a gesture of helplessness. 'What opportunities have there been?'

Their parents, Callum was thinking, would be frantic if they knew their daughter was playing in pubs with rock stars twice her age.

'So how did you get with these guys?'

'Adam,' she pointed out the lead guitar, 'is Maddy Stamp's brother.'

Maddy was Hayley's best friend. Maddy was, like Hayley, sixteen. The brother looked to be at least thirty.

'He's twenty-eight,' Hayley said. 'Just not his best at the moment.' She leaned in closer and lowered her voice. She smelled of incense, or at least Callum thought it was incense. 'Adam's miserable. His boyfriend dumped him. He did it on Facebook. Can you believe that?'

Callum could, but his sister looked so shocked he decided to look shocked too.

'Adam also does vocals. He started MagneticBlue with Brenda –' she nodded at the keyboard player, 'and Dude –' she pointed to a one-man band equipped with drums, xylophone, harmonica and pipes. 'The fourth member and lead singer was a girl called Sissy.' Hayley assumed an expression of mock horror. 'If I was called Sissy I'd know my parents hated me.' She explained about Sissy's accident. 'So the band was looking for a stand-in singer and Adam had heard me sing. And the rest,' she suddenly looked her age, 'is history.'

'And Brenda and Dude – how old are they?'

'Thirty, but they don't seem that old. They're an item. Brenda's pregnant.' Suddenly she was struck with an idea. 'We'll be looking for a keyboard player to fill in when Brenda has the baby.'

His sister didn't have a clue. 'Forget it, Hay. You know I can't play modern stuff.'

'Have you ever tried?'

He hadn't – apart from jazz. And not jazz improvisation, he'd be hopeless without sheet music. Hayley was smiling, she was clearly very taken with her idea. 'You should think about it, Cal. Your life lacks balance. I wouldn't want you to turn into Ramsay Blake, just like I wouldn't want to end up a music teacher like our mother.'

No chance of that, Callum was thinking as he watched his sister perform. She was swept up in the rhythms and sweeping the crowd along with her. He didn't know the song, something about love gone wrong and nothing special about the lyrics, but the music was a fist-at-the-throat ache, with a syncopated blues rhythm in the bass, and a fugal treble that played between his sister and tenor harmonica. Something simultaneously sad and sexy about this music – about his sister too; all eyes were on her, girls, guys, she was seducing the lot. And where she managed to acquire that pure, aged voice was beyond him; his mother and father could sing, so could he for that matter, but nothing like this. Her voice was a mix of honey and grit; she didn't play a bad guitar either.

The band moved from one song to the next without stopping for applause, although there were whistles and whoops of recognition with the first notes of each song. Callum was accustomed to respect and admiration when he played, but there was something else happening here. It was not adulation – the audience was too much a partner in the music for that. In fact, so intense was the engagement of the audience, Callum could not imagine the band sounding nearly as good if playing in a studio or practising in someone's garage. As much as Callum enjoyed the connection with an audience, he also knew that some of his best performances happened at home with only the dog in the room. This audience seemed to add to the exhilaration of the music, the euphoria – yes, that was the word he was wanting, euphoria. Just being here was like being high.

MagneticBlue played for an hour then they signed CDs, although not Hayley – 'The next album will have me as lead singer.' Afterwards they withdrew to an adjacent room to wind down. The others drank alcohol, his sister had a coke. When the next band started up, someone ordered another round.

'Not for me,' Hayley said.

'Are you ready to leave?' Adam asked.

She nodded. 'Maths assignment. Need to put in a couple of hours' work before bed.' She turned to Callum. 'Coming?'

He paused long enough for her to tell him to stay. And when still he hesitated, Adam assured him he didn't need help getting her home. 'I'm a seasoned taxi-driver when it comes to your sister.'

'Okay then,' Callum said to Hayley. 'If you're sure you don't mind, I'll hang out a while longer.'

There was a vacant chair at one of the oldies' tables. If he was going to stay he might as well be comfortable. He collected a beer, nodded to the others at the table, settled back and let the music have its way with him.

Chapter 14. A Shift in the Centre of Gravity

At last Nina heard from TIF, a phone call from Charlie Goldstein to let her know the group was rethinking their project.

'We've cooled on the monument idea,' he said. And then he laughed. 'You can count us as one of your successes, even though we never made it to the contract stage.'

She laughed too, but at the same time was disappointed. She'd been looking forward to seeing them again.

'After you left our last meeting we talked for another hour,' he said. 'We were all drawn to the notion of the counter-monument, but at the same time we were struck afresh by the power of words.' He paused, and in the silence she heard a mobile phone ring. 'Since then, there's been a lot of thinking and many emails.'

The group had met again that morning, and all of them had come to much the same conclusion: that their existing program, with modifications to reach more orthodox believers, addressed the group's current values and aims. That perhaps one day there might be a monument, but this was not the time. They would, Charlie said, be circulating their thoughts to TIF's larger group of supporters in the next few days.

'You've done a great job with us,' he said in conclusion. 'And I promise if a monument is ever back on our agenda you'll hear from us.'

The phone rang off. She stood in the tiny kitchen, oddly stilled. She was sorry not to be seeing them again, yet she was aware of a sense of satisfaction about the project. So celebrate, she told herself, celebrate the conclusion of what had been, after all, a successful job.

A celebration warranted company, and Zoe was her first choice. But there was no point in contacting her: Zoe either ignored her calls, or, should they speak, she deflected all inquiries with a light and cheery tone that was meant to disguise the mess she was in. Nina rang Sean instead. He clearly had forgiven her because he picked up on the first ring. But he didn't give her the chance to explain about TIF, he didn't even wait for her 'hello'.

'You're right,' he said. 'I need to make some changes.'

She quickly shifted from TIF to the last time she and Sean met, to his communism book and the trip to Cuba.

'So, what's the next venture going to be?' she asked.

'No, not work. Ramsay. I've been thinking about Ramsay.'

He'd never stopped thinking about Ramsay – which was, as far as Nina could see, Sean's crucial problem. She tried to sound casual. 'What about Ramsay?'

'I haven't decided anything yet, but,' and there was a long pause, 'I'm thinking it's time I paid him a visit.'

'Time to face your demons?' She spoke quietly.

'Time to face my demon. Singular.' Then he spoke in a rush. 'Can't talk. Still deliberating. I'll keep you posted.' And then he was gone.

It didn't matter he was not ready to talk. That he was at

least thinking about the wretched stalemate with his brother was a giant leap forward. She had long feared that being so accustomed to dragging the weight of Ramsay around, Sean would never cut himself loose. But maybe, at last, he might manage to free himself. With such a possibility she did not mind going out for a celebratory meal alone.

She had locked the flat and was waiting at the lift when her phone rang. Her first thought was Sean had changed his mind, that he did in fact want to talk about Ramsay. When she saw it was Daniel, it wasn't so much shock or surprise she felt, more a sense of strangeness to see his name appear on her phone. It had been such a long time. In his emails he'd made it clear he wanted to talk to her, but she'd resisted, not wanting to be caught up in his desires and desperations. But now, with the phone ringing in her hand, she hesitated – long enough for the call to ring out, but a hesitation nonetheless. When the ringing stopped, she turned around and re-entered the flat.

His message was brief: *I'm hoping you might be ready to speak to me. If not now, soon.*

Even at her most hurt and angry she had never stopped wanting to speak to him. She'd got on with her life, a different life from the one she shared with him, but interesting and satisfying enough. And she'd never stopped missing him.

Others might allow a single terrible betrayal to erase all that was good in a marriage, and in the first raw months this was exactly what she did – as a means of moving forward, she expected. But now? She couldn't say what she wanted with him. Although a phone call was just a phone call, it wasn't a promise, it wasn't a commitment; it was contact, contact she longed for.

So why deprive yourself? she said aloud. And laughed, she who had become a specialist in deprivation this past year.

She weighed the phone in her hand, she turned it over in her palm, she stared through the window at the treetops. She wasn't deliberating, she wasn't debating the pros and cons; the decision, she realised, had been made.

She texted him: *I'll Skype you in a few minutes.*

She went into the bathroom and was about to brush out her hair – he had always preferred it hanging loose – then changed her mind and pulled it into an even tighter knot; she refreshed her lipstick and touched up her eye makeup. She was dressed in a lovely wisp of a frock she had bought for her breakfast with Felix. Its marine blues and greens, so light and summery would present a stark contrast with drab, wintry, middle-of-the-night London – it would also suggest she was not at home in Primrose Hill. But as to her exact location, this beige, undistinguished apartment would not be releasing any secrets. She checked herself in the bedroom's full-length mirror, a view well beyond the capacity of Skype: she looked good, and while such things shouldn't matter, they did.

She had bought some Tasmanian cider. Now she poured herself a glass, collected her computer and sat on the couch; if she were a smoker she would have lit up and made sure to have had a full pack close by. Her heart was banging against her stomach, her throat was tight. She selected his name, she heard the connection tone, everything seemed to occur in slow motion.

And there he was, Daniel filling her screen, leaning forward as if reaching for her, Daniel, and the first sight of him for more than a year. She drew back.

'Nina,' he said. 'Nina.'

He had a way of saying her name, it was like no one else. Not simply his accent, but he seemed to sigh on the word.

She had always heard love when he spoke her name, now she heard relief and anxiety, or perhaps she saw these in his face. His forehead, heavily creased, seemed enlarged by the screen; he was blinking in an exaggerated way and there was an odd twist to his mouth.

How greatly had he aged. Only fifteen months had passed, but his hair was now completely grey and the once-thick crop had acquired that old-man dusty appearance; the bushy brows had drooped and there were fatty pouches beneath the eyes. He was wearing a white sleeveless T-shirt they had bought together on a trip to Naxos. She had taken a photograph of him standing on a rock in an all-conquering pose, the sparkling Mediterranean behind, his limbs brown and muscular, a youthful-looking man radiating strength and energy. The same T-shirt now exposed a neck of sinews and channels with the Adam's apple a vulnerable protrusion floating in a swirl of skin; there were crêpey folds in his upper arms (with the biceps so clearly outlined she was reminded of testicles), and his skin was the colour of suet. Time wields a strong arm after sixty, but it had been particularly pugnacious with Daniel.

He put his hand on the screen where her own face would be. It was his left hand and he was wearing his wedding ring.

In the small projection of herself on her own screen she saw her wry, unemotional expression. 'You've disappeared behind your hand,' she said.

His hand immediately sprang back. She saw him raise his eyebrows. 'You've weathered this year better than I have.'

'I'm fine,' she replied quickly, resisting the loaded 'now'. Her voice was strong, the rest of her was quivering.

'Being home is obviously agreeing with you.' And seeing her surprise, he added, 'Shirley told me you were in Melbourne.'

Of course. And if not his mother any number of their friends would have told him where she was, friends who'd dropped him when he took up with Sally but would have opened their arms and homes to him now he was alone. How naive she had been to think he didn't know her whereabouts, yet how essential it had been to believe it.

'And how is everyone?' he asked. 'Zoe? Elliot? The children?'

Nina shook her head, saw the same wry expression spread across her face. 'Far too complicated to explain, and besides, that's not how I want to spend the first conversation we've had in –' she paused, and when she again spoke it wasn't sarcasm she heard in her voice, but there was a twist of something bitter, '– in quite some time.'

He looked worried, if she didn't know him so well, she would say he looked scared.

'So,' she continued, 'how long have you known I was in Australia?'

His face relaxed at her question, and he settled back in his chair, not a chair she recognised; in fact she recognised nothing in what looked to be very ordinary surrounds. Despite his light clothes, his skin was clammy – the place, like so many in London was clearly over-heated. And suddenly it hit her: this must be the flat he moved to with Sally. Nina didn't need to see this, she didn't want to see this, how vile of him to parade the life he had dumped her for. And just as quickly as the fury flared so she stifled it: in the scheme of things the flat was minor, and besides, she found it quite satisfying to see that his love nest was as appetising as a budget motel room. She asked again: 'How long have you known I was in Australia?'

He shrugged, or perhaps slumped. 'Soon after we began emailing.'

A silence weighed in between them. In days gone by she would have filled it, but *he* had called her, *he* wanted to speak with her. She sat back on the couch and took a sip of cider. She could feel her hand shaking but doubted he could see it.

'What are you drinking?' And when she told him, he said quietly, 'Our summer drink.'

There was another long silence, hard for her to bear. At last he spoke. 'I've been thinking about us, of our life together.'

'How long is it since you and Sally separated?' The question shot out without warning. At least her voice sounded neutral.

He sighed. 'Do you really want to talk about that now?'

She shook her head. 'No, just an answer to that one question.'

His eyes glanced away from the screen, just a brief skittering to the left, before he sat forward again his hands clasped in front of him. He was looking straight at her. 'I moved out late October,' he said, 'four months ago. But it was over a good deal earlier. In fact, it never worked.'

'It?'

'A proper relationship.'

'You were oozing hormones when last I saw you.'

'Lust always has a use-by date.' He pressed his lips in an I-should-have-known-better grimace. 'A very short use-by date in this case.'

'You're showing your age.' Again the words just slipped out.

He rested his chin on the palm of his hand, his eyes were lowered. 'Maybe I am, but even if I were twenty years younger

I still would have realised my mistake.' He shook his head slowly, he appeared puzzled. Then he took a deep breath and looked straight at her. 'I realised my mistake very quickly. Punishingly quickly.'

So why did you stay with her so long, Nina was thinking. And with his 'punishingly quickly', surely he wasn't expecting sympathy from her? And she finds herself bristling; just a couple of sentences from him and it all floods back, those miserable months, his terrible betrayal, and all of it, he now tells her, was a mistake. She considers finishing the call, then reminded she can cut him off at any time, cut him out of her life too, she calms down.

'You said you've been thinking about our life together,' she says.

He leans forward again. 'Yes, yes.' And now he's smiling and his whole face lifts into its familiar shape. 'I've been trespassing on your field.'

'Memory?'

He nods. 'I've been reading your Margalit.'

'*The Ethics of Memory*?'

She had searched everywhere for the book even though she suspected she must have left it at the cottage. In the end she bought a replacement copy.

'You left it at the cottage,' he now says. 'You left quite a few interesting books there.'

'And you didn't think I might want them back?'

'By the time I got to reading them I was rather hoping you might collect them yourself – with me.'

She keeps herself absolutely still: impossible to know how to respond to such a loaded statement. She sticks to the topic. 'So, what do you think of Margalit?'

Again he perks up, again his old enthusiasm. 'Margalit writes that "the search for knowledge is ... an exercise in reminiscence".' He nods his agreement in a barely perceptible movement, and then he seems to fall on the screen. 'Oh Nina, I want our life back. I want you back.'

In the silence that follows she hears lorikeets squawking in the trees and the squeal of brakes on Punt Road. The cars outside will be bumper to bumper, they always are during the working week. In winter she can understand people opting for the warmth of their cars but in summer, why not take public transport? So much better for the environment. And she bursts out laughing.

He looks surprised but very pleased. 'I thought it'd take a good deal longer to get a laugh out of you.'

'It's not you,' she says, and is about to tell him how at this highly charged moment she's being a dedicated environmental warrior, when she hears it, unmistakable, the clatter of a tram, not outside her apartment, there are no trams on Punt Road, but coming from the computer, coming from Daniel's flat. She takes in his impersonal surroundings, his summery clothes, there are no lights on in the room, it is not night.

'Where are you, Daniel? Where are you right now?'

Daniel spoke to his mother, he spoke to mutual friends, he was encouraged to contact Nina, to try and persuade her to take him back. He was an old-fashioned lover, a face-to-face man. He reorganised his schedule, packed a suitcase and flew to Melbourne. He rented an apartment in the Docklands development, just a few minutes' walk from the offices of C.G. and C.K. Holdings.

'I could have bumped into you at any time,' Nina says.

He has changed his skimpy T-shirt for a pale blue cotton top with collar and sleeves; while it's an improvement on the computer-screen image, he's still grey and worn. Bright and buoyant in her gossamer dress she feels the contrast. He offered to come to her apartment, but she wanted the safety restraints of the public domain. So here they are at a rooftop bar at the top end of the city, an old favourite of hers sandwiched between a theatre on one side with a Parisian-style grey mansard roof, and on the other, the stone wall of a Victorian apartment building. To the front is a panoramic view of the State Government buildings and gardens.

'I can't believe you've never brought me here before,' Daniel says, gazing about him. 'We could be in Paris or London,' and as a tram rumbled past, 'or Vienna.' He smiles at her. 'But I'm very pleased we're here together in Melbourne.'

She decides not to comment. She's not even sure what she's doing. Indeed, in the time separating their Skype call and meeting him she must have changed her mind a dozen times. She's nervous, she's uncomfortably eager, and she's on her guard.

'Cider?' he asks, a question far more meaningful than what she might like to drink.

She shakes her head, wary of sentiment, wary of special 'us' experiences. She orders a gin and tonic, he a Balvenie single malt. Balvenie was the first distillery they visited together, she chooses to ignore this.

It's a beautiful evening, warm and tranquil, the sky tinged with pinks. All the other tables are occupied – a few couples, but mostly people meeting for a drink after work.

'He's not interested in her,' Daniel says with a subtle nod in the direction of a buffed and stubbled guy of about thirty and an attractive woman draped all over him.

'Gay?' Nina suggests.

Daniel shakes his head. 'Narcissistic. Would prefer to be at the gym flexing in front of a mirror.'

She smiles in spite of herself.

'But one day – I'd give it no more than ten years – Hercules will have started to sag. Even to himself he'll be a disappointment.'

'I expect that Hercules and Achilles, Odysseus, Jason, all the strong and fearless men of ancient times never made it to forty. The ravages of war saved them from the ravages of ageing.'

'Did you see that Achilles has been given a good scrub?'

'Wellington's Achilles at Hyde Park Corner?'

Daniel nods. 'Isn't he one of your favourite memorials?'

She grins. 'He's twenty feet tall, he's cast from French cannon won at Waterloo, he's starkers –'

'Except for the fig leaf –'

'– he's got a ten-pack that makes the usual six-pack look like a plate of sausages, and he's been blessed with a head of thick curls. A favourite?' She's laughing. 'Of course he's a favourite. He's Hollywood circa 1820.'

'And his message? What the statue of Achilles represents?'

'These days no one remembers either Achilles or Wellington –'

'Achilles entered popular culture with that film *Troy*. Remember? Brad Pitt played Achilles.'

'Ridiculous piece of casting. It needed a twenty-first-century version of Charlton Heston.'

'What about our Hercules over there?' Daniel says, again nodding in the direction of the couple.

But before she can answer, both are caught by the drama playing in front of them. The woman is unpeeling herself from the man's body; she looks furious.

Nina leans towards Daniel. 'Feisty suits her far better than fawning.'

He nods. 'It certainly does.'

Now the woman is standing, she's towering over the man. The crowd suddenly hushes; everyone likes a show.

'I think she's going to pour her drink over him,' Daniel says.

'I expect he deserves it.'

Daniel turns to her, their faces are a few centimetres apart. 'I expect he does.'

Nina pulls back and pins her attention on the couple. The woman is wearing an engagement ring, the man looks up at her smiling.

'That's quite a rock,' Daniel says.

'That's quite a smug prick,' Nina replies.

'I think she's about to wipe the smile from his face.'

The woman is tall, suited, stylish, and now she's no longer draped over the man, she carries herself with confidence. She picks up a glass of water – 'I'm not about to waste good wine on you,' she says – and empties it over his head. Then she removes the diamond ring and drops it into a bowl of aioli, gathers her bag and turns to the staring crowd. 'That was a near miss,' she says, before striding to the exit. There's a burst of applause and a shriek of wolf whistles. She turns and takes a bow.

'Isn't she marvellous?' Nina speaks her thoughts aloud.

'No more marvellous than you,' Daniel says.

'I should have done what she did.'

'In a way you did – by keeping your cool.' And then he adds, 'I expect it was very different when I wasn't around.'

'It sure was.' She tastes the bile and with it a torrent of sour words. She keeps her mouth shut.

'I deserve everything you want to hurl at me – and I expect it's far stronger than water.'

She's not sure what she wants to do with him. But in spite of it all – the dumping, the desertion, the despair of that long year spent alone, despite the hurt he has caused and the anger she still feels, she knows that the life she prefers is with him. She can hear her sister say, *Don't take him back*; she can hear her friends say, *Don't take him back*; she can hear people tell her that if he can betray her once there's every likelihood he'll do it again. She knows all the arguments for telling him to get lost, but the facts are clear, and although the facts are drawn from the past, some things don't change. She liked the person he was and she liked herself with him; she had never been bored with him; she was drawn to his values and beliefs, his energy and curiosity, and – this had come as such a surprise – she had felt so fortunate, special, in the way he loved her. As for her own feeling for him, it had an intensity and authenticity that had utterly eluded her in all the earlier disastrous relationships.

She has been staring past him. Now she meets his gaze and sees the question in his expression. She keeps her own face mute; there is no hurry. Daniel is going nowhere and neither is she.

Chapter 15. Awakenings

1.

Ramsay tied up the bag of rubbish and took it outside. He was wearing only pyjama shorts and his skin frizzled in the midday heat. Let it burn, let all of him burn. Trails of ants toiled up the sides of the rubbish bin, criss-crossing the lid before disappearing inside. Ants were supposed to be the most organised of insects so why, he wondered, didn't they take the shortest route to the spoils? He lifted the lid, the stink grabbed his throat, the rubbish inside was black and seething; he threw the bag in and slammed the lid. Back in the house he searched for insect spray, racing from room to room, cupboard to cupboard, at last finding a can in a basket contraption on the door of the broom closet. Outside again to the bin where he sprayed and sprayed, he sprayed until the can was empty. And all the while he hated having to kill the ants, hated they were there in the first place, hated having to manage these chores, hated that George was gone.

He wandered back inside. He wished he could return to the model exhibition, lose himself in the miniature cities. But he'd need to shower and dress and order a taxi, and it was all too much for him. What he really wanted was to sit at the piano and practise the time away. He longed for his piano feeling, felt useless and empty without it.

The house, too, was empty. Empty and suffocating at the same time. Of all the people in his life only George had properly understood him, and because no one knew how it had been, no one knew how he was suffering now. Zoe made his meals, she looked after the practicalities, she thought she was looking after him as George had done. But she didn't know what he needed in the way George did; George knew what he needed before he knew himself. And Mrs Monday came as usual, and Mr Monday too; Mr Monday, who without a proper job was really Mr Any-day-of-the-week, maintained the house. But there were never any ants when George was running things. Nothing was the same.

When his father died, music saved him. When his mother died, music saved him. That awful time with Zoe in New York, music saved him. All those instances when people jostled for a piece of him, music saved him. And now it had cut him adrift. But George would want him to persevere, this had become his mantra, so after washing the insect spray from his hands he went to the piano.

He stared at the keyboard: he didn't want to be here, yet he wanted to be nowhere else but here. He ran his fingers over the keys. His hands were cold despite the heat, his fingers were stiff. Actually it was worse: his fingers were foreign and his left hand felt weak. He tried Bach – Bach who except for that one time when all music failed him had never failed him – but he might have been playing scales for all the effect it had, so he swapped to Rachmaninov hoping the more dramatic music would awaken him. It didn't. From Rachmaninov he tried

Schubert impromptus – a mistake because soon he was crying over the keyboard, fool that he was. Focus on the moderns, he told himself. He wiped his eyes and plunged into Bartok's first piano sonata. He played it fortissimo from start to finish, each syncopated note slammed into his body, he played the piece without wit or whimsy, four minutes of attack, four minutes of battle. He played to the end and returned to the beginning, his left hand picked up, yes, this was better. He blitzed the keys, louder and faster, to the beginning again, he punched the notes. He savaged the music, he was killing the Bartok, his throat was aching, he couldn't stop crying. His hands were meat, his fingers were cracking, he'd been at the piano for less than an hour and he couldn't bear a minute more.

He went outside to check on the ants. They were dead. The bin stank of rotten food and insect spray. He closed his eyes as if that could erase the putrid mess, started back to the house, and suddenly he was on the ground with a fierce burning to his forehead. Blood was trickling into his left eye, and Horo was nuzzling against him whimpering. He had walked into a tree, a tree that had been in the same position forever. Was he going mad? He swiped the blood with his arm, his head was throbbing. In the past he would have worked off the pain at the piano; he didn't dare try now. He went inside, past the music room to his bedroom. He pulled the curtains against the day, settled Horo on the bed and stretched out next to him. Music and George had formed him. If he could remember how, if he could piece it all together then perhaps it would return – not George, he meant the music. But in truth he wanted both.

He opens his eyes then closes them again. Anything to sleep a little longer. He counts slowly by sevens back from five hundred; at three hundred and ninety-five he gives up. He is awake, and no amount of wishful thinking will put him back to sleep. He glances at the clock, only two hours have passed. His head is aching, George is gone, his music has deserted him. Of course he can still play old and familiar pieces and no one would be any the wiser. But he knows he is done for: with no spine to learn new work he's beached high and dry. And without George to save him, he is terrified. What now to do with his life? How to fill the music-free days? If only there were a list of things to do when your usual occupation has abandoned you.

His gaze traverses the familiar room. The photos, the stuffed hawk, the model he made of the Melbourne Cemetery. He lingers on the over-sized picture of Sean on the wall above his desk, wonders if his brother can help, knows in an instant he can't. And then to the desk itself, with its clutter and the computer untouched for days. The computer with its infinite entertainments ... And an idea begins to form. He rouses himself and leaves the bed, his thoughts crystallising as he crosses the room. He clicks on the screen, is tentative as he enters the web; there are lists and plenty of them, even a special term for them – listmania – and covering topics stunningly arcane.

He begins with a list of phobias, he has done this before and knows he won't be disappointed. It seems that people can develop a fear of anything, and that makes him feel better. Apeirophobia: fear of infinity; defecaloesiphobia: fear of painful bowel movements (who would confess to such a thing?); hippopotomonstrosesquippedaliophobia: fear of long words – he laughs aloud, he hasn't laughed in such a long time; panophobia: fear of everything – if he's not careful he'll be heading that way himself; scriptophobia: fear of writing in public. There is no listing for fear of playing the piano, but the word is obvious: pianofortephobia. There's an 'add your comments' option on the webpage. He hesitates a moment then posts his contribution. He checks the list again; there's only one phobia relating to music: 'melophobia' meaning fear of music. He returns to the comments page. Why not? the worst that can happen is his suggestions are ignored. He adds 'musicophobia' – fear of music, which he thinks more descriptive than 'melophobia'; 'syncopatophobia' – fear of rhythm; 'allegrophobia' – fear of fast music; 'lentophobia' – fear of slow music; 'violophobia' – fear of stringed instruments; 'maestrophobia' – fear of conductors, he's rather proud of that one and decides to quit on a strong note. He bookmarks the site and then does a search of lists. Top site is a domain called ask.mnemosyne, but it is haphazard in design and far too broad in its reach. The second-ranked site is much more focused, and humorous too. Who would think to compile 'top 10 controversies surrounding cattle' or '10 people who did not board the Titanic'?

Music is one of the major categories on this site. He selects it and there heading the list is 'top 10 underrated Disney songs'. Further down the page is '10 famous musicians with hearing damage'. Most of the names – Neil Young? Phil Collins? will.i.am? – are unknown to him, but there at number one is Beethoven. There must be other classical musicians with hearing losses (he's often wondered about his own hearing, bombarded with sound since before he could walk); he makes a note to research this and continues on. The music lists – there are nearly two hundred – are heavily biased towards popular music, and the classical lists that are included are obvious ones like top ten classical pieces, ten interesting stories behind classical compositions, great composers who died young. There are huge gaps – pianists, prodigies, mistakes and collapses; and again he makes a note before moving to other categories. He finds lists of animal-like qualities: erinaceous (of or like hedgehogs), phocine (seal-like) and of course the more common feline, canine and bovine; there are lists of battles, others of battleships. The site is packed with lists but several of his own interests are missing. There's nothing whatsoever about cemeteries.

Using a combination of Google earth and keyword searches he sets about determining how many cemeteries there are in Australia, how many in New Zealand, in Luxembourg, in Norway. And different methods of burial. And the number of people who died on a particular day. And where they died. And how old they were. He compiles several cemetery lists, and two death statistics lists and submits them. And because he can do it without research, he posts a top ten classical piano pieces using only the left hand.

He needs to go to the toilet, he has needed to go for hours but has been too engrossed. On his return he grabs a packet of chips from the kitchen. Back at the desk he applies himself to alphabets of the world, is experimenting with a unique way of grouping them when he receives an email from the host of the site. *Great lists. Posting them up now. Keep 'em coming.* The host, Listman, suggests that if he plans to be a regular contributor he should select a username and sign up properly.

And so he does. Almost immediately he receives another email from Listman. *Welcome to the team. We've several Australian contributors* – Ausliszt *was a giveaway* – *must be something in the air down there.*

It is dawn when finally he leaves the computer. He's still in his pyjamas, he hasn't showered for close on two days, the graze on his forehead is aching but he feels better than at any other time since George died. He has sat in one spot for twelve hours, the work has been rewarding and orderly, he is better, more efficient, at compiling lists at the end of the session than at the beginning, and he'll never run out of material. It isn't music but it has occupied him and will continue to occupy him until his music returns.

And there's the crucial change. After a few hours of rewarding work he believes his music has not deserted him permanently. It will return. In the meantime he has a new job, the only job aside from pianist he's ever had. It, or rather his list persona, *Ausliszt*, will keep him going until his music returns.

2.

Sean woke early. He rolled on his side, propped himself on an elbow and gazed at Tom.

Tom was lying on his back, quietly asleep; his hair, thick, wavy and reddish, was smoothed back despite the hours in bed. He was greying at the temples and around the ears, but his forehead was still unlined, and the skin of his cheeks was fine and smooth – 'Like a pubescent boy who's been spared acne,' Sean used to joke, expecting that one day the skin would coarsen and the rosy flush would fade. But at fifty, with only the help of a mass-market moisturiser, Tom's skin was peachy. This, Sean was thinking, was the face of an untroubled man.

It occurred to Sean, gazing at his partner of nearly twenty years that sex, interesting lusty sex, was the first casualty of a gay partnership, almost as if your legitimacy as a couple was incompatible with sexual excitement. But the fact was he still found Tom sexy – he was fortunate that some gym-slicked twenty-year-old hadn't snapped him up – yet it was at least a month since they'd last had sex, and these days theirs was mostly we'd-better-do-it-otherwise-we-might-turn-into-one-of-those-sexless-couples-we-despise sex. Was it lack of time? Lack of effort? Lack of imagination? Tom was an attractive man by any measure, lying there in a take-me-I'm-yours position, just the sheet covering him, the bulging crotch. Sean feels his own arousal, just like in the old days, and – why not? – lowers himself to the bed and slips beneath the sheets, glides down the side of the long body, isn't touching, not yet, mustn't wake him, saliva pools in readiness – and suddenly an excruciating pain explodes in his right hip, rips into the small of his back, and shoots down his right leg. He doesn't move, can't move, feels faint. Breathe, he tells himself, breathe into the joint that, according to the doctor, is wearing thin from carrying too much weight. Breathe, he tells himself again, and the pain contracts into a burning ball, the lightning rod begins to subside. A couple more minutes and he crawls up the bed to his pillow. He's covered in sweat; he's limp, all of him is limp.

No one would snap him up.

He was a mess. His right hip was giving up the ghost, his left was likely to follow, his liver was tender, his neck was sagging into his chest, his chest was sagging into breasts; soon people would be mistaking him for Tom's dad.

He had turned into someone he abhorred. And while Tom had not yet given up on him, all it would take was a slender bloke with a nicely honed aesthetic sense, an Adonis with domestic flair who maintained a relationship by being present rather than skipping the country for months at a time, a man who'd left past baggage, like brothers and stepfathers, in the past where it belonged.

The pain in his hip had disappeared but not the memory of it; Sean moved gingerly as he left the bed. Time to make some changes. Firstly, a diet. He would cut down on alcohol, eliminate snacks and junk food, prune meals back to main course only. He had kept up his gym membership, a waste of money given his last work-out had been months ago, but he'd phone the gym and book an appointment with a personal trainer, and he'd do it today. That would take care of the body. Next: the boyfriend. Tom's favourite meal was breakfast in bed. Sean decided to put his relationship ahead of his diet and set about preparing his signature Perico – scrambled eggs with fried onions, tomatoes and peppers – served on a slab of sourdough toast. He set the tray with cloth napkins and a flower picked from the neighbour's garden, made a large pot of coffee and took breakfast up to bed.

Tom was propped against his pillows reading the latest *Homme*. He removed his glasses and put the magazine aside. 'What a treat.' His smile morphed into an expression of mock doubt. 'Are we celebrating something? Have I forgotten an anniversary? A birthday?' This from the date-keeper in their relationship.

Sean shook his head, set out the breakfast on the bed and slipped in beside Tom.

'I'm lucky to have you,' he said.

'As I am you,' Tom replied. 'Although luck has nothing to do with it. It's your brother we should thank. If Ramsay had held on to you, you certainly wouldn't have wanted me.'

It was an observation Tom had made many times over the years. But while Ramsay had given him up long ago, Sean knew that the reverse was not true. Since Nina had forced the issue with him, he'd been questioning old behaviours and old hauntings. He had no answers yet, but the very questions were steering him in a new direction.

Some years ago, on one of the rare occasions when Sean was at Zoe and Elliot's (it was a lunch party for Nina who was in Melbourne at the time), he noticed how Elliot, the non-drinking alcoholic, was keeping everyone's glasses topped up. 'Isn't that hard for you?' Sean had asked. And Elliot explained that you can be as hamstrung by fear of alcohol as by alcohol itself. The same could be said of any addiction, including a brother you once adored, a brother who had for far too long occupied the driver's seat in his own life's wanderings.

Chapter 16. Last of the Hot Days

1.

It was hard to know how to characterise his friendship with Beth. It certainly wasn't a romance – no furies nor flashing lights, no sex nor the desire for it – yet they slept together every night. And even if she were not grieving for a husband she adored, he still didn't believe they'd be romantically involved. But neither was it a normal friendship between a man and a woman – far too comfortable and intimate for that.

'Why's it so important to define us?' Beth said. 'Just accept it. We're close and we're uncomplicated.'

'And afterwards?'

'Afterwards?'

'After I return to Zoe.'

Beth smiled. 'The very fact of your return suggests we'll have served our purpose.'

'For me, maybe, but not for you.'

They were sitting in Beth's garden. A full moon lit the broad planes of her face, her eyes were cast into dark hollows. She was wearing a sarong, her shoulders were bare, the skin was polished and warm; her hair was caught loosely on top of her head and wisps and curls fluttered about her face. She was lush, Elliot was thinking. This woman he didn't want to have sex with was beautiful and lush and sexy.

She was still smiling, the gap between her front teeth more marked in the sharp shadows. 'No need to be concerned about me,' she said. 'I always knew you were finite. A moment of reprieve.'

'When the loss was greatest?'

The smile disappeared, she looked sad and resigned. 'Perhaps. Although it's hard to know. When Scotty first died I thought I couldn't feel any worse. And when the visitors to the house thinned out I thought it couldn't be any worse. And at the four-week mark when one of his bottles of beer fell out of the fridge, and I sat in the mess not giving a toss about broken glass, I thought it couldn't get any worse. And bundling up his toothbrush and shaving gear and throwing them into the rubbish bin and then an hour later scrabbling to retrieve them and put them back where they belonged, I thought it couldn't possibly get any worse than that. And the morning at Dight Falls when I first met you, I'd passed the entire night sitting on the couch, staring at nothing, thinking nothing, being nothing other than a woman who had lost her husband, I was convinced that things were as bad as they'd ever been. But by then I'd learned that just because I can't imagine anything worse doesn't mean the worst isn't still to come.'

She shook her head slowly. 'Loss is a cunning beast. I'm sure it has a good deal more in store for me.'

Elliot went round to the back of her chair. He stroked the side of her face, felt her lean into his hand. He stood there thinking of furies – not avenging gods and goddesses, but the passions and energies that drive you, that can throttle you, too, and knock you to the ground. Alcohol, unequal love, loss – so many experiences riven by furies and all too familiar to him. He'd had his breaks, forms of oblivion, like his van life and the old benders, like that week spent alone on Kangaroo Island, but it was the furies that had dominated. Perhaps life had never been an easy fit for him.

Until now, with Beth.

When you were really besotted with someone you were driven to impress them, to add a little gloss here, shave an edge off there; but with Beth there were no contrivances, no fiddling with the fundamentals. He far preferred this relaxed, natural Elliot to the Elliot he had become with his wife.

He returned to his chair and stared into the night. A minute or two passed before he spoke. 'Did you know from the very beginning that Scott was the man for you?'

She looked at him as if he were mad. 'Love at first sight? Of course not. Why would anyone trust first impressions on which to base a lifetime's happiness?' She shook her head slowly, it was clear she found the notion absurd. 'I'll concede you might be struck by someone's appearance or their wit or the work they do, but it'd be gross stupidity to make too much of these.' And then she laughed. 'Not that this prevents me from being a glutton for Hollywood romances: *Roman Holiday, The Philadelphia Story, Some Like It Hot, Pillow Talk, Woman of the Year, Desk Set,* even *Sleepless in Seattle.*'

The names of the films flowed with such fluency Elliot guessed how Beth had passed her own sleepless nights – not that he dwelled on this, it was her response to love at first sight that intrigued him. Romance and fantasy, was that all it had been with Zoe? That first glimpse of her in Riverside Park when he'd been convinced she was the woman for him, was it nothing more than Hollywood puff? It was as if he had bottled that first sight of her, poured it into a clear and shapely crystal vessel and screwed the lid on tight. And there he could gaze on her, he could admire and love her, and every now and then he could reward himself with a sweet heady sniff.

Over the years he'd regarded his initial response as a trusted plumb line in his sinking marriage, but now Beth had thrown this constant into doubt. For she was right: love at first sight is love of a stranger; much of what he had assumed to be true about Zoe in those early days was proven to be skewed or just plain false. Zoe didn't lie to him, his reading of her had been wrong, yet he'd held on to many of those early impressions.

He did not like these thoughts, was relieved when Beth reached out and touched his arm. 'There's one thing I'd like to do before we go our separate ways,' she said.

'Tell me.' He kept his voice steady, as if her statement had been no more innocuous than a shopping list.

She wanted to go down to the coast, she said. And she could take leave from work for the next few days so she could go now. Her gaze wandered off to the middle distance, she was chewing her lower lip. 'Scotty and I both loved the ocean, and I don't want to lose it. But I'd prefer not to go by myself. Not the first time.'

Elliot couldn't imagine making such a request dry-eyed, but Beth seemed quite calm, sitting there across the table waiting for his answer. He had told her about the family beach cottage and now he asked whether she'd like to go down there.

Her head was cocked to the side, there was a question in her expression. 'It's fine by me, but what about you?'

All at once he realised how much he wanted to be at the cottage. When he chose the rented van it was because he had needed to escape, and the cottage would have been far too noisy with memories. But now he wanted his house at the coast, and, in much the same way that Beth didn't want to visit the ocean alone, he was glad to be going with her.

His van life was over. Early that afternoon he and Beth returned the vehicle to the hire company and after a quick trip to the supermarket, they set off for the coast. It was Beth's car and she drove.

'I probably would have suggested I drive even if we were in your car,' she said. 'I'm a shocking passenger.'

Elliot couldn't say what sort of passenger he was, it had been so long since anyone had driven him. Although he did ask about Scott.

Beth laughed. 'As shocking a passenger as I am, he was a far worse driver. Once his male vanity allowed him to admit it – fortunately quite early in our marriage – I always drove.'

She was a good driver, confident and deft, Elliot settled back to enjoy the ride. It was a Tuesday, and warm weather notwithstanding, the traffic was light. Beth directed him to a container of CDs. In his car, the music library had been synced with the wireless system, including an option that predicted what he might want to hear based on his past selections. He found himself enjoying the old-fashioned way of choosing music.

'Your selection is truly classic,' he said. 'My kind of music.'

The albums were Scott's. 'He never moved on from the music of his youth.'

There were Beatles, old Rolling Stones, The Animals, Creedence, Bowie, AC/DC, Blondie, Led Zeppelin. And folk too: Simon and Garfunkel, early Dylan, Leonard Cohen, Joni Mitchell.

'Music as nostalgia?' he asked. 'Is this what we have here? Transport to the lost days of youth?'

She laughed and shook her head. 'Scott definitely wasn't the nostalgic kind. Too much of the scientist for that. And besides, he always found plenty to occupy him in the present. Music for him was either pure enjoyment or a trigger for thought, for work.'

As someone who needed absolute silence when he worked, this piqued his interest.

'Scott's work was theoretical,' she continued, 'and it seemed that music – he called it the great intangible – propelled him deep into the realms of abstraction. It tickled his fancy that Jagger not getting any satisfaction and Clapton riding his orgasmic riffs were behind his best work.'

It was so different for Elliot. Music was an extension of his emotions, and goodness knows what fictions his biographies might have become if he had worked with music playing. He actually had a special Zoe playlist containing all the music he associated with their early days. A music monument it now occurred to him, and he wondered what Nina would say about that.

He slipped Joni Mitchell's *Blue* into the CD player and the pure leaping voice filled the car. He settled back and watched the passing scenery. Neither he nor Beth felt any need to talk but every now and then he glanced at her, and at the first sight of the ocean he stretched out his arm and rested it across her shoulders. She smiled, said nothing, did not shake him off. He was reminded of that old film, *Same Time Next Year*, when Alan Alda and Ellen Burstyn meet as lovers for a weekend each year. It was a liaison that concerned no one but themselves. Of course Alan and Ellen had more than twenty-five separate meetings while he and Beth had only this one. Although why did they need to put limits on it? A connection that had been a blessing and a gift to them both, why did they need to bring it to an end?

They arrived at the cottage with hours of daylight left, unpacked and made their way to the beach. There was a glassy swell and the surfers were out in force. People and dogs were walking along the sand. With Adelaide bounding in the shallows, Beth and Elliot strolled together at the water's edge.

'If only life could always be like this,' Elliot said at last.

Beth shook her head. 'No, not always. Remember – this is our moment of reprieve.'

Elliot tugged on her arm. The two of them stood facing each other in the shallows.

'I've lacked courage in my life,' he began.

She looked surprised. 'I think you've demonstrated huge strength. You gave up alcohol, you've stuck with your marriage.'

'I've lacked courage,' he said again. 'And you can stay in a marriage out of weakness. I never thought I could leave Zoe, but if you –'

She stopped him, stopped the statement he might later regret. 'We met at exactly the right moment,' she said. 'It was always finite. And soon, very soon, you'll decide your future, with or without Zoe.'

She allowed a long silence to absorb these words before continuing. 'I can't imagine ever being with someone else.

Living with them, being married to them. But if it were to happen, it won't be for a long time. For a start I'd have to loosen my grip on Scotty.' She smiled. 'And I don't want to, not yet.'

'So friends? We can be friends?'

'I'm not short on friends, and I expect you're not either. Let's just enjoy these few days as we've enjoyed the last few weeks. It'll happen soon enough that we have to return to the real world.'

His mind had always taken him away from the present, either to better versions, or in the case of dull Peoria, to places quite different, or with his biographies into other lives, or when it came to his wife to a far more promising past. But now he made the effort; he didn't want to miss a moment of this time with Beth.

And so they embarked on their one and only holiday. Meals and beach walks together, swimming together, shopping and cooking together, talking and not talking together. And during unguarded moments when his mind skidded into the future, he felt his reluctance to turn his back on this relationship. It was ideal, it was perfect.

2.

Once she realised that Elliot had not escaped to New York, Zoe had guessed where he was hiding out. He loved the beach cottage, and he loved the ocean. Born landlocked in the middle of America, Elliot was eight years old before he saw the sea; the ocean would always mean separation – escape –

from the normal run of things. And now that she was able to look clearly at these past many weeks, see them as an outsider rather than one caught in the currents, it was obvious to her why he needed to escape.

She had arranged to take the Friday off work, family exigencies, she explained to her section head, and not far from the truth. She was tempted to drive down to the cottage in Elliot's car, then decided it could appear presumptuous, that he might think she had come to bring him home. Yet her hope was exactly that: a couple of days together, during which they'd find some of their old closeness, then he'd return home with her.

When the children emerged for breakfast she told them she'd be away for the weekend. 'Your father and I need to spend some time together.'

Hayley, who looked much in need of a good night's sleep, immediately brightened. 'About bloody time,' she said. 'I was beginning to think you'd never dump that dickhead Ramsay.'

Zoe felt herself bristle; Hayley had no right to speak this way, she had no idea how it was with Ramsay. And then she realised that Hayley, her sixteen-year-old daughter, knew exactly how it was with Ramsay. Zoe stood there, shuffling under the accusing gaze of her daughter, until she could bear it no longer and turned away. Had she really believed her feelings for Ramsay were a secret? And as astonishing as it seemed to her now, she had never really considered it. Ramsay had been as much a part of her emotional life as her parents and her children, and in the same way she would not think to question her feeling for them, so, too, with Ramsay. But there was no denying it: Elliot knew all about Ramsay, and her children did as well.

Why now, when Ramsay had finally lost his appeal did she see the situation so clearly? The harm to her own family, her own stupidity, Ramsay himself. Why now, when Ramsay was perfectly happy with his Mr and Mrs Monday, happy with his *Ausliszt* tinkerings, happy again at the piano and practising for his China trip? Why now, when clearly Ramsay did not need her and had never needed her did she understand how much she had put in jeopardy? A swag of questions and all eliciting the same answer – not the old cliché that love is blind, but that fantasies and obsessions demand a full cognitive landscape; allow the smallest space and reason might creep in.

She turned to face her children. Callum and Hayley were seated at the table; they were watching her, waiting.

'I'm sorry.' Her voice was quiet and quivery. 'I'm truly sorry.' And said again more firmly. 'I'm sorry, so sorry.'

Callum grunted supportively while helping himself to more cereal, but Hayley held her mother's gaze.

'I've known since I was a kid that away from the piano Ramsay wasn't worth the time of day.' Callum went to speak but Hayley stopped him. 'Don't bother to defend him, Cal, he doesn't need you to look after him.' And turning again to her mother, 'And he never needed you.'

He never needed you.

These words from her own daughter cut far deeper than any humiliation she could produce herself. She didn't bother to protect or defend herself; when you've been a fool and everyone knows it, you forfeit your rights.

Fortunately the attacks were finished. 'Dad can be a pain sometimes,' Hayley now said, 'but he's never had eyes for anyone but you.' She walked around the bench and gave her mother a hug. 'Go make him happy. Yourself too.'

Zoe was on the road before the worst of the morning traffic, and once she entered the highway heading out of the city she had a clear run. She turned on the radio but had no patience for the puerile games up in Canberra; she switched to the classical music station, but the piece was gratingly saccharine; she shoved in a CD of opera favourites, the melodrama grated even more; then the new low-voiced Joni Mitchell, all sweetness and breathy violins but no edge. In the end she gave up and switched the sound system off.

Her brain was on fire, her heart was racing. It was nervousness, but also euphoria – like going on a first date with someone you're keen on, and strangely thrilling when it's your husband of twenty-plus years. She allowed herself to sink into the mesmerising stretch of highway, the bright sun, the blue sky, the mood unbroken even when the traffic increased at the Geelong bypass. And then she was in the country, the sun-bleached landscape, cows sheltering in the shade of trees, and the jumble of beach scrub growing thicker and thicker, and finally, around a bend and at the top of the rise, the first sight of the ocean. It was glorious, heaven on earth – Elliot's words every time they reached this point.

A few more kilometres and she pulled into a roadside lookout and parked the car. She lit a cigarette and stood leaning against the safety rail overlooking the sea. The cliffs were giant clay-coloured pleats curving back the way she had driven and forward to where she was going. The breeze off the ocean was slight, the water foamed on the rocks below then stretched smoothly blue to the horizon. Elliot said this ocean was particularly special because Antarctica lay on the other shore. She had always made a point of correcting him; Tasmania, she said, blocked its way. But despite her meanness, she had always understood that he simply was airing his fascination of Antarctica. For years he had wanted to visit there, and on a number of occasions had actually planned trips, but each time she had found an excuse not to go: the Antarctic season stretched from November to March and Ramsay usually came home for the summer. Now she would suggest they make the trip south.

She finished her cigarette and returned to the car. She followed the curves and hair-pin twists down to the little hamlet of Moggs Creek where the road dropped to sea level. Dotted near the water's edge were joggers, and small groups of people fishing from the shore. And then the last curly climb.

It's not yet ten and she expects to find Elliot on the verandah with his book and coffee, dressed in bathers ready for his walk on the beach. He'll hear her car on the gravel, he'll know immediately it is her, and so, too, will Addie, who'll run down the drive to greet her. She'll see Elliot standing on the verandah as she rounds the bend in the drive, she'll see his surprise, his pleasure too. While she parks he'll make his way down the stairs and there he'll be, opening the car door and helping her out. He'll know why she is here, that finally she has come to her senses. Although he'll also be tentative – after so many years of waiting he won't take anything for granted. She'll take his hand – his hands have always been so soft – and step forward to embrace him.

They return to the verandah together. There's coffee left in the pot, he pours her a cup and they sit close and talk. She strokes his arm, his face. He hasn't shaved for days, the bristles are long and soft. His book is turned face down on the table, it's a collection of Anne Sexton.

'Sexton knew all about love,' she says.

He smiles and nods.

'Will you read to me?'

He is still smiling. He does not pick up the book. He takes his time. He's rehearsing silently. Then from memory he recites Nikki Giovanni's 'Just a New York Poem'. She listens closely, he's marvellous to watch, his own gaze tilts to the trees beyond, his voice is pitched low for her. The poem is achingly familiar. His reading makes her cry.

'You never cry,' he says.

She changes into her beach clothes and the two of them walk together down the drive along the road to the beach path and from there onto the sand.

And now, as she drives past the beach path, she slows down just to check he's not already waiting for her. The path is empty, no one is there. A little further on she makes the right turn into their driveway.

She's careful not to run into Addie, but there's no Addie. And there's a scattering of things on the verandah table, but no Elliot. And a car is parked in her space, a car she doesn't recognise. Could she have made a mistake? Could Elliot have escaped somewhere else? Might he have lent the cottage to friends? But he never lends the cottage. Whose car is it? Whose car? Her breath pulls hard, she feels faint, how much more of a fool can she be? When suddenly it comes to her. A hire car! With his own car at home in the garage, Elliot would need to hire a car.

She parks and walks towards the house. She'll wait for him on the verandah, he won't be long, soon everything will be all right. There are two mugs and two plates on the outdoor table, and an empty coffee pot. The pot for two. Maybe

326

Elliot was hungry and decided on a second serving of toast, and he always has two cups of coffee with his breakfast. She glances again at the strange car. The rationalisations are weakening. She forces herself to walk inside the house. Here is all the clutter missing from their Melbourne home – Elliot had insisted on it, he wanted a place, he said, that was casual and relaxed, a place where he could put his feet up on the couch without her grumbling. She takes in the hotchpotch of furniture, the prints on the walls, the books, the bowl of shells, all the ornaments the children have given them for various Christmases and birthdays, and separating from the familiar jumble she sees some knitting, a stack of DVDs, a handbag. She picks up the handbag. It is not leather. She leafs through the contents: wallet, glasses case, two pens, a pencil, diary, phone, a shopping bag in a purple pouch. Her mind has stilled. Zipped away in a separate compartment are lipstick, mints, a pill box, another pen. She sifts through the DVDs, they are all Hollywood romances, old ones – *The Philadelphia Story, Roman Holiday, Charade* – and not quite so old – *Sleepless in Seattle* and *Annie Hall* – and some quite recent ones – *Crazy, Stupid, Love, The Wedding Singer, Love Actually*. Elliot likes movies with guts and edge, movies that undercut traditional narrative – Altman, Herzog, the Coen Brothers – he'd never suggest they see a Hollywood romance, never. She picks up the knitting, such fine even knitting (she can't knit, she can't sew) and sees herself – it happens in slow motion – pulling the stitches from the needle and unravelling the garment row by neat row. She replaces the knitting on the coffee table, straightens up, draws in her breath, walks past the bedroom with her eyes averted, and enters the bathroom. She finds moisturiser, deodorant, hand cream, all supermarket brands. She avoids her own face in the mirror.

At last to the bedroom. There are four pillows in two stacks leaning against the wall. The pillows carry the shapes of two backs. Two people have been sitting up in bed. On the left side, Elliot's side, are his books, on the right side there's an old Margaret Drabble she recognises from the bookshelf in the living room and an anthology of poetry called *Staying Alive*. She opens at the bookmark. It's a poem by Charles Wright called 'Clear Night'. There is a stanza that has been underlined.

I want to be bruised by God.
I want to be strung up in a strong light and singled out.
I want to be stretched, like music wrung from a dropped seed.
I want to be entered and picked clean.

And written beside the poem in a hand she does not recognise:
I JUST WANT TO FEEL <u>SOMETHING</u>.

The book and markings are confusing but not the situation.

She returns to the living room; she is still carrying her keys. She takes a last look around. She leaves the house, she has never felt so defeated. She returns to the car. She drives away quickly without looking back.

Chapter 17. Spoils of Memory

1.

On Sunday morning Elliot awoke in Beth's bed for the last time. Sounds drifted up the hall from the kitchen where she was making breakfast. He rolled over on to her pillow, breathed in her perfume and the scent of her hair. Remember this, he told himself, remember all of this. He had showered the night before knowing what the morning would bring. Now he dressed quickly, gathered his few belongings and left the room. Just beyond the doorway he hesitated, and whether to cement it more firmly in memory or just make a proper leave-taking, he turned and re-entered.

Scott's books were still stacked on his bedside cabinet. Elliot had been interested in a couple of the histories, but Beth's reluctance when he had asked to borrow the Milosz had stymied further requests. So the books remained as they had been on his first night here. But the crystal water glass had been removed to accommodate Elliot's own, and the blue striped handkerchief together with the wristwatch had disappeared into the top drawer of the cabinet. Now Elliot opened the drawer and replaced them where he had first seen them, next to the books. The photograph of Scott that had been on Beth's bedside table was lying face up on a nearby shelf. He was about to put that back in its place too, when he realised this wasn't his business, not his business at all. He left the photo where it was and put the handkerchief and watch back in the drawer.

He had no doubt that everything would be restored to order after he was gone. Beth wasn't ready to let go of Scott even if such a thing were possible; in fact, by her own account she was hanging on to him for as long as sanity would permit.

The smell of toast and coffee wafted into the room. He sat on the edge of the bed and closed his eyes. A train rumbled in the distance, a car with its radio blaring passed in the street, a dog was barking. A normal Sunday, but not normal for him, although hard to know what constituted normal any more. It had been only a few weeks, yet long enough for him to know a different life.

He would miss Beth and he would miss being here.

He gathered himself up and made his way to the kitchen. Not wanting to leave he knew it was better to go immediately, a quick goodbye before reason or unreason had a chance to trip him up. But Beth had made them a last breakfast and he did not want to upset her. He ate with neither taste nor relish and refused a second cup of coffee.

'If ever you need me,' he said at the front door, 'you know how to contact me.'

She did not return the offer, just reached up, put her hands on his shoulders and kissed him.

'I expect your wife needs you,' she said.

His voice was muffled in her hair, the words came slowly. 'I'm not sure I need her any more.'

Beth stepped back, her hands on his arms were pushing

him away. 'So, Elliot, for the first time in your long marriage you're in a position to make a choice.'

He went to touch her, then thought better of it, and without glancing back, strode to the gate. Beth watched him leave and when he turned into the street she re-entered the house. She stood in the silent still air. The smell of toast lingered, the house felt harshly empty.

Slowly she walked down the passage to the living room, to the photographs, the fossils, the small stone animals, the octopus fridge magnet Scott had given her after a trip to the Great Barrier Reef, a scarf that had hung on the back of a chair since last winter. It was not yet eight.

She made fresh coffee, and walked over to the shelf of books that held Scott's favourites, books he had read and reread over the years and annotated heavily. She had collected these from other shelves around the house in those first dull desperate days without him. Now she selected Peter Watson's *A Terrible Beauty*, a romp through modern intellectual history that Scott had loved, a book she had not read. She settled on the blue sofa, her coffee on the table, her feet tucked beneath her and Watson's big book balanced in her lap. She fanned the pages, selected one of the more heavily marked sections and began to read – not Watson, but Scott, his marginalia, his conversation with the book which was at the same time an idiosyncratic diary of his days. He had read this book several times and had made multiple annotations, each carefully dated. A reference to Turing had him reflecting both on the mystery of numbers and the date of his reading: *B's birthday*, he writes. *Turing so alone, crushed in the end. How lucky am I.* She read all his words, eager for those entries that referred to her. An hour passed in this way, before she roused herself, replaced the book on the shelf, so many of his books still to read, and prepared herself for the remainder of the day.

When Sunday morning dawned, Zoe had not been to bed. In fact, she had not slept for two nights. On Friday she had stayed up late with Callum watching movies, desperate to shift her thoughts away from the cottage and all she had witnessed there. When Callum went to bed she, too, had gone to her room, there to remain swinging between hope and despair until morning. Last night she had forced herself to go out with friends, and when she returned home, had settled in front of the TV to wait for Callum and Hayley. She must have dozed, for when she next checked it was past midnight and neither Hayley nor Callum was home. When there was still no sign of them at one, she started to worry. By half past one she was seriously anxious. Neither had left a note, and while reason said it was Saturday night and young people stayed out late on Saturday night, it did nothing to quell her anxiety. She tried their phones several times – no success – had no idea where they were, where to start looking. They had different friends, different interests, four years separated them, so she assumed they were not together, and that made her worry even more. As the night moved forward she tolled through accidents, attacks, injury and violence. By the time they arrived home she was hysterical.

'Where've you been? It's four in the morning. Where've you been?'

She saw a perplexed look pass between Hayley and Callum.

'It's four in the morning.' She was shouting. 'What happened to you?'

They assured her they were fine, nothing had happened.

'So where've you been?' She was shouting and crying as well.

Callum suggested a brandy to calm her.

Zoe lit a cigarette.

'That definitely won't help,' Hayley said.

In the end, Hayley made a pot of tea and the three of them sat together in the living room and talked. Zoe insisted they tell her what they'd been up to. They insisted they be told what she had been up to. What then ensued were shocking revelations about bands, pubs, Hayley's hopes and ambitions and Callum's new thoughts about a career in jazz – or rather shocking to Zoe, Hayley and Callum couldn't be happier with their plans. And then came hard talk about marriage, humiliating talk about Ramsay, distressed responses to Elliot's disappearance, Zoe's fears he was gone for good.

'Dad's put up with you for so long,' Hayley said. 'I can't imagine he'd toss in the towel at the very moment you've come to your senses.'

At sixteen, Hayley did not subscribe to subtlety.

The sun was shining when Hayley and Callum went to bed. Zoe lit a cigarette and went out to the garden. Six o'clock and the birds were shrieking, it was peak hour for insects too, and overnight a huge spider web had appeared between the patio's canvas awning and the wind chimes. She gave it a wide berth. The garden was mostly shaded at this hour, although in two or three places a shard of sun hit the ground in a bright white slash. Underfoot the dry leaf litter snapped and crackled.

There was something about her, something she'd known since early childhood, as if her joints were poorly sealed, and like a house put together with glue she'd collapse when things became too heated or too cool or too blustery. These days she reinforced her joints with home-made soups and visits to sick friends but now, when she had toppled over, it felt as if nothing would get her going again.

At the end of the garden stood an ancient apricot tree. About ten years ago the tree was visibly failing. Elliot had consulted a tree doctor who advised it would be best put out of its misery. When the tree loppers had finished, all that remained was a sawn-off stump rooted to the ground. But a year later a new branch had sprouted from the stump – Elliot said it was a miracle – and now the branch itself had grown into a whole new tree. This tree was lush and thriving, this tree was far tougher than she was.

Zoe turned and walked back to the house, dragged herself to the bedroom and lay down on the bed. She rolled on to Elliot's side, her head hugged by his pillow, and there she remained, convinced that sleep was out of the question. The neighbouring children were playing ball in the garden, their dogs were barking, their mother calling and then all became quiet as she passed out with exhaustion.

2.

Seven weeks after Nina's pilgrimage to Raleigh Court, Sean, too, made a visit. He drove slowly down the court and parked outside the Blake family home. His emotions were quiet, all of him was quiet as he passed through the gate and walked up the path.

A man, sixty, maybe a little older, was painting the

wooden uprights on the front verandah. He looked up as Sean approached. More guard-dog than welcoming committee, he uttered a single unencouraging 'Yes?' Both his facial expression and tone of voice would put off all but the most tenacious door-to-door salesperson, charity collector or music fan.

'I'm Sean Blake.' Sean sounded equally tough and even more proprietorial. 'Ramsay's brother.'

'He's expecting you?' The man's tone was already in retreat.

Sean walked past him to the front door, he heard music from inside the house. 'I'm his brother. No appointment necessary.' He was surprised at the condescension in his voice. It was, he suspected, a pre-emptive strike against the nervousness he expected to be feeling but wasn't.

The man shrugged and returned to his painting. Sean entered the house. The place was thrumming with music, exhilarating, discordant, acrobatic music, a type of music better appreciated if you could watch it being played. Yet rather than move directly to the music room, Sean lingered in the hallway. This was the first time since leaving for Sydney as a teenager that he'd been inside the house.

He stood in the hallway pelted by his brother's music and felt as if he had walked into a film from his childhood. There was the same ugly light overhead, the same orange and green carpet underfoot, the hall table with the life-sized alabaster birds that had belonged to his grandmother, the mirror now speckled with age in which his mother would check her lipstick before leaving the house. It was eerie and fascinating, nothing had changed. He walked into the living room – the same furniture, the same prints on the walls, the same photos on the sideboard including old shots of him as a boy, and then to the kitchen, the cream and green kitchen clock on the wall still counting out the seconds, the huge sink with old-fashioned double taps, the same chocolate-coloured lino with the brightly coloured squares, the orange laminex benches; only the fridge had moved into the current era. He stood in the middle of the room taking it all in.

Suddenly the music changed. Weightless and mystical, it might be the sound of deep space. He left the kitchen and headed towards the music room, glancing through doorways as he passed. His parents' bedroom looked as if it was occupied, perhaps Ramsay had moved in there. But no, as he passed the bedroom that used to be his and Ramsay's, it was clear that Ramsay still slept here. There was only one bed now, a double, Sean's had been replaced by a desk with a large, late-model computer perched on top. Ramsay's posters of Liszt and Horowitz still hung above the bed, and the collage of cemeteries he had compiled during his cemetery phase was still on the wall. On the opposite wall, above the desk, was a photo Sean had not seen before. It was a huge vertical shot of himself at about twelve years of age playing the violin. The boy he once was gazed down on Ramsay's desk; this boy dominated the room.

Before he could make too much of it, Sean moved on. The mystical hiatus was short-lived for as he approached the music room there was an explosion of percussive sounds, all wind and fire and truly marvellous. He stopped in the open doorway. And there he was, his brother, just a few steps away, Ramsay at the piano in a strenuous playing, Ramsay dressed only in singlet and shorts, the ripple of muscles across his shoulders clearly visible as his hands fly up and down the keyboard. Sean approaches in a wide arc so as not to startle him, and comes to stand in the curve of the piano. An old dog sniffs his legs and then leaves him alone. Ramsay's hands are bounding over the keys in a series of octaves, moving so fast that Sean's mind leaps to those old cartoons where the speeding roadrunner is reduced to a streak. Ramsay's gaze is strung to his hands, until the octaves give way to sprinting runs and then his eyes flick up at Sean, just the briefest moment, then back to the keyboard until the piece is finished.

'There's another eight movements to go,' Ramsay says, looking up.

'What is it?'

'Messiaen, *Vingt Regards sur l'Enfant-Jésus.* That was number XII. A challenging piece if you play it at the speed Messiaen wanted.'

'And some pianists don't?'

Ramsay laughs. 'Not the keyboard cheats.' He reaches across the piano and grasps Sean's hand. 'So little brother, it's great to see you. And you couldn't have come at a better time.'

Sean is immediately on his guard. What might Ramsay want? But Ramsay, it turns out, wants for nothing.

'Yes, the best time. A couple of weeks ago, I was hardly playing at all.' He speaks in a rush, he speaks as if he and Sean were the brothers they once were. 'I'd lost the plot – like that time when I was a kid. But everything's fixed now. I've got Mrs and Mr Monday,' he shakes his head, 'no, I must remember, I've got Vera and her husband Matt to look after me. And an agent, Zoe lined me up with an agent. Three people to do what George did by himself, but it seems to be working.' Suddenly he looks worried. 'It did sound all right? The music? Messiaen was very religious, of course. But I'm hoping to produce what he wanted in my own way.'

Sean puts a hand on his brother's shoulder and smiles. 'It sounded brilliant, Rams. You're playing better than ever.'

Ramsay's face relaxes. 'Do you want to hear more? Can't play the whole lot – it takes a couple of hours. But I could continue from the thirteenth movement.' He passes the music to Sean. 'Do you want to follow?'

Sean pulls up a chair, leafs through to the thirteenth movement. With hands poised above the keyboard, Ramsay turns to him, he's smiling. 'Ready?' he asks in a hushed voice. His eyes are bright, this will be a fabulous ride.

His hands hit the keys, and with the first notes Sean is seized by the music, his whole body primed for excitement. He follows the score but at the same time he watches Ramsay: the music is marvellous, the pianist is extraordinary. The heavens could open, the mountains could tremble, waves could flood the land, winds could rattle the foundations of time, and Ramsay would still play on. Nothing can stop him. He pauses between movements, but the current is palpable, a force, a magnetism that holds him in the music.

Tom often quotes the well-known dictum that life is not a rehearsal. He's right. Perhaps you hang on to the past even if it's painful because it means you don't have to be responsible for the future. Resentment, envy, jealousy, all these occupy a lot of space, no room to think, no opportunity to evaluate or reconsider. It's easier to cling to a lost past than throw yourself on life's uncertain winds.

'Grow up, little brother,' Ramsay said to him when the bond between him and George was forming. 'Grow up, little brother,' he said.

It's time he did.

As for Ramsay, beyond the music nothing else matters. The satellites orbit around him, some fade, others sharpen, but Ramsay plays on.

Finally the magnificent piece is finished. Ramsay hovers over the keyboard in the silence, two, three seconds pass, and then he sits back and turns to his brother.

'This is what I do, Sean,' he flings out his hands in apology. 'This is what I do.'

3.

It was blazing hot by the time Nina left the flat. She crossed to the shaded side of the street and a few minutes later entered the Botanic Gardens. She was early, early enough for a slow circuit of the park.

It was cooler here among the trees, and she strolled along, stopping now and then to study some of the more exotic plants. Off to one side in full sun was a huge bed of succulents. She hesitated and then with her hand acting as a sunshade walked across the lawn to the garden. The succulents were thriving here, unlike the poor frozen specimens Daniel kept in London. If their meeting today was untroubled, she could bring him back here and show him these fabulous curiosities that might have come from outer space for all they resembled his cactus collection.

She returned to the path and ambled on. Birds had sought cover from the heat and on the lake the ducks and coots had withdrawn to the shelter of the reeds. People, on the other hand, seemed unconcerned: there were many large groups picnicking in full sun on the lawns. And over near the lake there was a wedding. She stopped to watch. It was an international affair; the bride was fair, the groom was black – from one of the African countries judging by the clothes of the guests. The two attendants, one white the other black, wore flowing gowns of a brilliant multi-coloured zigzag material. A quintessential TIF gathering, she found herself thinking, and with that illogical spontaneity that strikes every now and then she actually found herself looking for TIF committee members in the crowd.

She and Daniel had married outdoors, a small wedding in Shirley Ryman's back garden. Just before the ceremony it had started to drizzle. They made their vows under umbrellas; their faces were wet with rain for their first married kiss. They didn't care, kissing and dancing in the rain, and they couldn't have been happier. What a contrast with today. She was about to meet him in another garden. She was eager as she was then, and nervous, not with excitement as she was the day they married, but a bleary morass of resentment, hope, anger, anticipation and uncertainty.

She had suggested they meet on the oak lawn – for the shade, the numerous park benches, and for her, the solid familiarity of a favourite place when everything else was on quicksand. But she didn't want to be the first to arrive, so she made her way back to the main path and circled around to approach the oak lawn from the north.

There was some sort of game going on here, she heard it before she saw it, a rendition of 'Waltzing Matilda' buoyed by a raucous accompaniment of pipes and percussion. As she came through the trees she saw a grassy slope packed with picnickers, and snaking through the crowd, led by a tall man in a kaftan playing a recorder, was a line of children with cymbals and drums and clackers and whistles singing at the top of their voices. This Pied Piper was skipping through the crowd, gathering toddlers to teens in his wake. The sun was beating down, but neither the man nor the children seemed bothered. They tripped along, skirting rugs and sunshades, down the slope to the gully below. Firstly the Pied Piper disappeared into the bush, and one by one the children followed. The music grew fainter, the last of the children disappeared. Nina wanted to run down the slope. Where are you taking them? Where are you taking the children? And then, moments later, the Pied Piper emerged from the gully via a different path. Her heart was racing. Fear for the children? Or fear for herself transferred to the children? Whatever the reason, her response unnerved her. The children were happy, their parents were happy, everyone was having fun, no cause for concern. She took a few slow calming breaths as she made her way down the slope, past the family groups and on to the oak lawn.

She saw Daniel immediately. He was about fifty metres away, perched on the edge of a park bench facing the main path. She watched him stand and check his wristwatch, saw him step on to the path and look first one way then the other, watched as he ran a hand through his hair. Then he shoved both hands into his pockets and turned around. This was an anxious man.

They had met on three occasions since that first time, each carefully crafted to be relaxed and casual. The first had been at the National Gallery, the second a quick meal with Sean and Tom at a noisy Vietnamese restaurant, the third had been at the cinema, a new Australian film described as 'quirky', as so many Australian films were, that prompted no discussion whatsoever. They'd had a quick drink afterwards and then, finding herself on the edge of tears, she had dashed away. Today was the first time since their drink at the rooftop bar that there'd be opportunity to talk. Of course he would be anxious; so was she.

He walked towards her, took her hand briefly and they returned to the park bench together. The air was puffed up with heat, there was a scent of wood and dried grass. The sound of the Pied Piper and his young followers drifted in and out. Daniel again took her hand but this time he held it, and while she might wish she had the strength to pull away, she did not try to find it. But she must be careful, she reminded herself, as she felt a prickling of tears. How easy it would be to slip back into old patterns, just take up your customary positions as if the past fifteen months had not happened. But they did happen. *They did happen.* Daniel might think everything was on the road back to normal, but as much as she might want it to be, it was not. She withdrew her hand and shifted along the bench.

'I try to remember the details of that last evening together,' Daniel began. 'The evening I left,' as if she required any elaboration. 'But I can't. And the same goes for the whole time I was apart from you. I simply can't remember.'

How fortunate for you, she was thinking. Perhaps she should provide her own experiential museum and guide Daniel through the emotional deserts and swamps of the hundreds of days of her life after he took up with Sally. A small derisory snort escaped her, but loud enough for him to twist around and look her in the face. 'I've tried to remember, I really have,' he said, 'but it's all a blur.'

'That's fortunate for you.' She kept her tone matter-of-fact, her gaze directed ahead.

'I wonder whether it's a form of post-traumatic stress,' he said.

This was too much. Nina rose from the bench and stood in front of him.

'Let me get this straight, Daniel. You dump me with a ten-minute explanation. In the year you spend with your new girlfriend you don't contact me, not a single inquiry to see how I'm managing. And now you tell me *you* are suffering post-traumatic stress.' She cocked her head to the side, and with her face and voice dripping with sarcasm, added, 'Next you'll be asking me to feel sorry for you.'

His gaze was pitched to the dusty grass, he shuffled around on the seat – probably trying to work out how to obliterate his stupid, thoughtless poor-me statement. And it occurred to her that perhaps too much had happened, too much hurt, too much damage, for their tattered marriage to recover.

'I didn't put that very well, did I?' he said finally.

'It's not just the way you put it, it was the sentiment you expressed.'

'Do you want me to feel sorry for *you*?'

He sounded hopeful, and why not, she thought. A few apologies and a little regret would provide such an easy solution for him.

'No Daniel, keep your apologies to yourself. I don't want them. But I'd like to think you understood what you did. And I'd like to know you wouldn't do it again. But that's unlikely given you say you have no memory.'

'But you do.' He spoke slowly, each word uttered with care. 'You have memory. I'll take anything you want to dish out. Anything.'

She turned and walked away from him. With memory in her court, and only her court, she could do whatever she liked. And for a moment she felt the power of it – not that she believed him for a moment, not this man with the best memory of anyone she had ever known. She walked a little further before twisting around and observing him from a distance. She would like to see him as shrunken, but she didn't, and sinister, but she didn't, as a fool with a limping brain, but she didn't. As for his being a man without memory, Daniel had always valued his capacity to remember. That he should so disarm himself weighed in more significantly than a kilogram of sorrys. Do with me what you will, he seemed to be saying, *but please, do it with me.*

There had been a particular oak planted in this area of the gardens in the 1880s by an important man's wife, a huge tree with long, low, almost horizontal branches each as thick as the trunk of a medium-sized tree. She couldn't remember the name of the famous man, nor the type of oak, but the tree was now gone and the grass had grown over where it used to be. So many things – ancient trees, books, memories, monuments – give the impression they'll endure. But they don't. And a marriage? You want it to be solid, you want it to be secure. But it lumbers into the future on the back of its past; a past of castles, a past of straw.

Daniel was sitting on the bench watching her. She walked slowly towards him; he stood as she approached. What he had done was, and would forever remain, unforgivable. But that didn't change who he was. She stretched out her hand, felt his still-familiar closeness. The trees shuffled in the heat, the Pied Piper led the children in a merry dance, the voices of strangers rose and fell, and she and Daniel made their way home.